# THE JACARANDA YEARS

Kristin Williamson was born in Melbourne, where she gained an honours degree in history, worked as a fringe actor, taught drama in high schools, and lectured at Melbourne State College.

She moved to Sydney in 1979, where she became a feature writer for the *National Times* and a columnist for the *Times on Sunday*.

She is the author of *The Last Bastion*, a political history of WWII, *Princess Kate*, a novel for young adults which was made into a telemovie and the bestselling novel, *Tanglewood*.

Kristin Williamson lives with her husband in Sydney. They have five children.

*Also by Kristin Williamson*

The Last Bastion
Princess Kate
Tanglewood

# *the jacaranda years*

KRISTIN WILLIAMSON

McPHEE GRIBBLE PUBLISHERS

McPhee Gribble Publishers
Penguin Books Australia Ltd
487 Maroondah Highway, PO Box 257
Ringwood, Victoria 3134, Australia
Penguin Books Ltd
Harmondsworth, Middlesex, England
Viking Penguin, A Division of Penguin Books USA Inc.
375 Hudson Street, New York, New York 10014, USA
Penguin Books Canada Limited
10 Alcorn Avenue, Toronto, Ontario, Canada M4V 3B2
Penguin Books (N.Z.) Ltd
182-190 Wairau Road, Auckland 10, New Zealand

First published by McPhee Gribble, 1995

1 3 5 7 9 10 8 6 4 2



Typeset in 11.5/13.5 Bembo by Post Typesetters
Made and printed in Australia by Australian Print Group



Produced by McPhee Gribble
487 Maroondah Highway, Ringwood, Victoria 3134, Australia
A division of Penguin Books Australia Ltd

National Library of Australia
Cataloguing-in-Publication data:

Williamson, Kristin, 1940- .
The jacaranda years.
ISBN 0 86914 325 5.
I. Title.
A823.3

For Hope

## ACKNOWLEDGEMENTS

A number of people offered encouragement, made suggestions or gave constructive criticism during the writing of this novel. I thank Mark Aarons, Glenda Adams, Robyn de Crespigny, Hazel Douglas, Robert Domm, Christopher Gordon, Jill Hickson, Jackie Huggins, John Pilger, Debbie Rose, Millie Tamwoy and the Injinoo Aboriginal and Torres Strait Islander Community, Sue Walsh and especially Alison Summers. I also thank my editor, Bryony Cosgrove.

# CHAPTER ONE

There are few more agreeable times of the day than the late afternoon, when one has completed the chores and is about to embark on an evening in the company of good friends. So why, Meg asked herself, do I feel so miserable?

Mostly, Meg was buoyant, enthusiastic and positive. (Exhaustingly so, her employees complained.) She was a good-looking woman of forty-seven; tall, fair and athletic with features that were frank and firm. Her eyes were a lively blue. She carried herself almost regally and preferred to dress plainly, which bothered those well-meaning friends who thought she could look beautiful if she'd only make the effort. As a child she had wished to be a boy and had dressed accordingly; the habit of not adorning herself with jewellery or makeup had remained.

People meeting Meg for the first time sometimes thought of her as looking 'superior', which provoked envy or dislike. (This had always rather puzzled her.) She had a certain look of feeling fortunate and exceptional; a determined, hard working and compassionate person who did not tolerate fools unless they were also dear friends.

Meg had married and had a child only recently, having been rather too engrossed in her career to notice how quickly the years were passing. Now, to her surprise, she felt a new and delightful contentment.

On this blustery Friday afternoon in late May, 1993, her young son Nicholas was asleep. She and her husband Peter would be taking him out to dinner with friends that evening. It would be relaxing, thoroughly enjoyable, so it was perverse to feel suddenly so melancholy.

Meg's low-spirited state was like a hump that had attached itself to her back. But now that she had acknowledged the hump, she would have to deal with the causes.

First, her newspaper. It was a success. Avidly read by left-leaning liberals and young radicals and appreciated by intelligent middle-brows as well, it had almost doubled its circulation since Meg had started it a year and a half ago. But it was losing money because it came out weekly instead of monthly. For some time she had been refusing to accept this fact, and now, after a day spent poring over the accounts, she knew what she must do. Increase the advertising and change the paper to a monthly.

The second reason for her depression was winter. The shadows from the giant Moreton Bay fig tree had grown so long they shaded the house. The office she used at weekends became cold and dark at this time of year, and Meg was the kind of person who craved sunlight regardless of the season. Very well. She would put a skylight in the roof, and if that was not enough, she'd have bright spotlights installed to imitate the sun. She would *not* give in to depression because of something as simple as a lack of light.

The final reason for her sadness was the hardest to deal

with. At this time of year her friend Virginia usually came to stay. She had been depending on Virginia to lift her spirits and now she wasn't coming.

Virginia was an artist: erratic, impulsive, unreliable. It was to be expected that she might break a promise to come to Sydney, particularly in winter, as it would mean leaving the tropical jungle in the far north where she lived. Virginia had broken promises before. But this time Meg had been quite certain she would come. This time Meg needed her.

To ease her disappointment she had come out into the air to clear her head with something mindless. Gardening. Other people, Meg knew, did not think gardening mindless. They planned it carefully. Her friend Sally organised her gardening days ahead, with equipment laid out in rows – fertiliser, rakes, clippers, sprays, buckets, plastic bags, gloves and seedlings. Meg tended to do her gardening in bursts, enthusiastically planting a mass of bulbs out of season, then wondering why they didn't bloom. This afternoon she distractedly raked autumn leaves into piles and wondered whether she might set fire to them just so she could smell the comforting aroma of burning leaves that reminded her of her childhood in the country.

She leaned on the rake and sniffed. A cold breeze blew off the water, and as she stretched to see the 'harbour glimpses' that the real estate agent had promised when she bought the sandstone cottage, she saw that Snails Bay was flecked with little green waves and the sailboats were pulling at their moorings, chains clanking, like frightened horses in the wind.

Virginia was an infuriating friend. Sally would be disappointed, too. Virginia had sworn to them both that she would come and visit, so they had made special preparations. Now these would have to be cancelled. Virginia had not been apologetic. She'd simply said she would come down to Sydney later. How much later? She wasn't sure. Why hadn't she got in touch earlier? Because she was frantically busy building her new art gallery in the rainforest. It was going to be wonderful! Meg and Sally would have to come up for the grand opening. In fact she was *insisting* that they come. Typical, thought Meg crossly. The gallery was a dream. It would probably never eventuate.

Meg, Virginia and Sally had been friends since they were eighteen and had hitchhiked north to Townsville during the university vacation. They'd camped out, turned cartwheels on deserted moonlit beaches, pretending to be circus girls, and had promised each other they would meet once a year in some wild and beautiful place where they could, perhaps, build a hut. This would be their 'retreat from the world', where they'd gather their strength, re-pledge their ideals and 'allow no husbands, children or lovers'. It had been a naive pact, youthful and idealistic. But they had stuck to it, after a fashion, for almost thirty years.

Once a year they would ring each other from interstate or overseas to check the possibility of meeting, not in the 'hut', which had never eventuated, but at Meg's beach house, 'Tanglewood', which was isolated enough to be a suitable substitute. It was built up on stilts and had a gum tree growing through the verandah which creaked and bashed against the house in high winds.

Often a meeting was out of the question because one of them couldn't make it: 'Well, how could you possibly come, Sally, with another new baby? With a job in New York, Meg? With an exhibition about to open in Brisbane, Virginia?' They would reassure each other in spite of their disappointment.

Sometimes the disappointment would cause them to think unpleasant thoughts of the one who couldn't make it, after which they would feel ashamed. (Hasn't Sally heard of birth control? Aren't Australian newspapers good enough for Meg any more? Isn't Virginia game to try an exhibition in Sydney after three successful ones in Brisbane?)

When they did manage to meet for a couple of days at Tanglewood they talked till the small hours, drinking wine by the fire amongst the tall trees with the sound of surf crashing far below. Sometimes, if they disapproved of a partner, a career move, a political opinion, or even a selfish motive, they argued. They were truthful and cared enough about each other to argue vehemently at times, to shed tears of happiness at each other's triumphs (Sally was inclined to do this more than the other two; she had always been sentimental) and try to prevent each other from making mistakes.

Well, thought Meg, as she bashed at the leaves with her rake, Virginia is making a big mistake now.

As well as the two or three days in isolation at Tanglewood, Meg and Sally had made elaborate preparations for Virginia's stay in Sydney. She had recently confided in them that she felt so isolated up there in the rainforest that sometimes she forgot how to talk and made bird noises instead. Sally and Meg had laughed but been concerned. They had organised a dinner party with all Virginia's old friends and had cancelled work and appointments so they could, between them, spend at least a week with her. Sally had bought tickets to *Tosca*, Virginia's favourite opera, and although she couldn't afford it Meg had ordered a dozen bottles of a particular vintage wine because Virginia loved it.

Now, as Meg jabbed the rake roughly into the pile of leaves, she had to admit that the real reason she felt depressed about the absence of Virginia was not the cancellation of these preparations, but the fact that at least once a year they needed to unburden themselves to each other, to talk freely and to howl with laughter. Also, Virginia had a talent for detecting thoughts buried so deep you didn't know you had them until you'd spent a day or two with her. She was like a lightning conductor, transforming woolly ideas into well-defined flashes of brilliance. Yes, Meg needed her.

She sighed. She had also been looking forward to discussing her financial problems with her friend. Sometimes Virginia surprised her by having quite clever solutions. She had managed to raise a lot of money for this art gallery in the rainforest, whether it was ever built or not. And now she wasn't coming.

When the phone rang, Meg dropped the rake and marched inside. 'I suppose this is her saying she's coming after all,' she said grumpily to the dog.

But the voice was unfamiliar. 'Hello, Mother,' it said.

'I think you have the wrong number,' Meg replied. 'This is 810 9570.'

'Yes, I know.' The voice was that of a confident young English woman. 'May I speak to Meg McIntyre, please?'

'Speaking,' said Meg rather tersely. She was not in the mood for practical jokes.

'My name is Claudia Broderick. I'm here on a short trip from London. I thought I might call on you.'

Meg sighed inwardly. Another tourist friend of a friend who'd been given her address in the hope of some free accommodation, she thought uncharitably. The upper-class English were the worst. They thought they were doing you some sort of favour by lobbing on your doorstep completely uninvited.

'Are you a friend of Mark Ogilvie?' Meg asked, naming a young English journalist who'd insisted on taking her phone number during a flight to Hong Kong recently.

'No.' There was a long pause.

'I'm sorry,' said Meg. 'Should I remember meeting you?'

'May 30th, 1969. You met me then. It was my birthday.'

Meg went cold. She saw that her hand on the receiver was shaking. She took a breath but could not speak.

'Bede's Hospital, London, on a warm day in spring?' The voice sounded glib, far too light-hearted. 'Look, I don't want to bother you. I thought you'd be pleased.'

'I, I . . . yes, I'm pleased,' Meg almost whispered.

'Sorry. It must be quite a shock to hear from me but you did leave your address and phone number with the adoption agency. They told me you kept updating it every time you moved. For twenty-four years. In case I ever wanted to get in touch.' The voice had changed and now seemed sincere.

'Yes. I did that,' Meg said softly.

'I came to Sydney partly because I wanted to meet you,' Claudia said. 'Well, that was the only reason really. I suppose I should have written first. The adoption agency said they were sending you a note about my visit. You didn't get it?'

'No,' said Meg. 'No, I didn't.' She was in shock. She must do better than this. 'But I'm very happy that you came. I would like to meet you.' She paused and then asked anxiously, 'Are you all right?'

'Yes, quite all right, thank you,' said Claudia without hesitation. 'I'm at the Intercontinental. Can you pick me up?'

'Ah . . . when?'

'Now, if you like. I'm terribly excited. It's not every day you get to meet your mother after a quarter of a century!' She laughed. 'I believe you're the editor of some frightfully left-wing newspaper. I think that's thrilling. I've got heaps to tell you about *my* life.'

This is bizarre, thought Meg. She sounds like a debutante. How can I explain that I can't pick her up at the Intercontinental because my other child is asleep and I'm in my gardening clothes and the battered heap I drive is at the service station with a flat battery again? How can I tell her that the husband who doesn't know she exists, and who is only nine years older than she is, wants me to come to dinner at a pub because his friends are playing in a band called The Pensive Wombats tonight?

'Claudia, I'd love to see you as soon as possible but right now is difficult. What about tomorrow morning?'

'Oh.' Claudia sounded deeply disappointed. 'Okay then. I expect I should have written . . .'

'No, no. It's fine,' Meg gabbled reassuringly. 'I'm excited too. I want to hear everything about you. Everything. I'm . . . *delighted* you're here!'

'What time tomorrow morning then?'

'Early. Shall we have breakfast together?'

'Okay. Nine o'clock at the Intercontinental. I'm in room 1024. Just come up.'

'Great. I'll be there. At nine.'

'Okay. Bye then, Mother. Bye.'

She sounded like a little girl all of a sudden. Meg felt tears pricking her eyelids. 'Mother.' She leapt in the air and shrieked, 'Yo!' The old retriever gave an alarmed short bark and then lay down, staring up at her with an expression of concern. She patted his head and sat down beside him to think.

She'd asked Claudia nothing. Was anyone with her? Did she have a job? Was she married? What did she look like? Was she happy? Who were her adoptive parents? Was she an impostor perhaps? Was this all some cruel hoax? But Bede's Hospital and the warm spring day and the fact that she knew about the address being updated year after year in the hope that one day . . .

When Peter came home about twenty minutes later he found Meg still sitting on the floor beside the dog, rocking back and forth and smiling, with tears making clean little rivers on her earth-stained cheeks.

'Come here,' she said gently. 'I've got a story to tell you.' She was suddenly afraid. Why had she never told him? He'd been present at the birth of the child he believed was her first; her only child. She sensed he would feel differently about them both now.

When Meg had first met Peter Seburg he was a photographer at the newspaper on which she was a feature writer. She had thought him overanxious. He was a Norwegian who had come to live in Australia at the age of fourteen and now, aged thirty-three, he still had a lean boyish appearance but had become more confident and developed a wry sense of humour. Peter was blond, with eyebrows so pale they were almost invisible. Recently he had grown a beard which had surprised them both by sprouting forth bright chestnut which gave him a rakish, Viking-like appearance. He loved his wife and young son deeply and had even decided to give up his career as an international newspaper photographer to go freelance so he could spend more time at home with them.

Peter had checked on his sleeping son, lit the fire and now he and Meg sat side by side on the floor staring into it. But still she did not speak.

At last she began slowly. 'Remember I told you once that when I finished my degree at Melbourne University I put my plans to become a barrister on hold?'

'So that you could join the protest movement. Yes, I remember. 1968, wasn't it?'

Meg nodded. 'I helped to protect draft resistors from being arrested and organised protest marches against the Vietnam War.'

'I know. I saw the newspaper pictures of you.'

She looked at him, surprised. 'Did you? Where?'

'In the *Nation* files. Before you even bothered to talk to me, I knew who you were. I was researching you for months.'

He was joking, trying to hide his concern for her. 'How do you start a conversation with someone who flings herself in front of police horses?'

Meg looked away, distracted. 'I would have talked to you. I just didn't know you.'

He nodded and waited. 'Go on with the story, my love.'

'A month after that demonstration you saw splashed all over the papers I went to Washington at the invitation of a student group to learn more about organising protests.' Meg stared into the fire, remembering. 'It was a heady time, 1968, a year of great political upheaval. In April the civil rights leader, Martin Luther King had been killed. In June Robert Kennedy was assassinated. Americans reacted with disbelief. Student and academic power was becoming a new force. Potent. We believed it would change presidential politics and it did! It was exciting.' She sighed, gave a small shrug. 'We didn't want to be left out of it just because we were on the other side of the world. We wanted to be part of it. So I went to the States, planned to learn all I could about US left-liberalism and then travel on to Europe. The Soviet tanks had just invaded Prague and students had tried to stop them with guns, sticks, even their bare hands.'

'I would've hated all that.'

'You would have found it exhilarating,' Meg assured him. 'Anyway, in August of that year, I was staying with my Aunt Ellen, an Australian doctor who'd moved from Sydney to work at a hospital just outside Washington. During a dinner party at her house one evening, I met a professor of politics. He was regarded as a leading liberal thinker. I was impressed by him. But then he said that he was beginning to change his mind about things. He talked about 'deradicalisation', telling us that students were confused and made errors. How could they possibly understand the cause of society's ills and hope to set them right? I argued with him. Passionately.'

Peter grinned. 'Did you win?'

Meg shook her head. 'Not really. He made me furious but I re-examined my ideas. Then, as sometimes happens when people's opinions clash so violently, we found ourselves attracted to each other, and a short time afterwards, we had a brief affair.'

There was a pause. 'Did Aunt Ellen approve?'

'Aunt Ellen knew nothing about it. She had promised to look after me. I was her favourite niece, so it was a shock when I announced four months later, when the affair was over, that I was accidentally pregnant to this married man and needed an abortion. Aunt Ellen didn't want me to have it.'

'Why not?' Peter asked indignantly. 'She was a doctor.' He looked at Meg with new concern.

'She was a Catholic doctor and my mother's sister. The child would have been a close relative. The father was a good friend. She said that a termination at four months would be difficult medically, but not impossible.'

'Why didn't you tell your aunt about it earlier?'

'I simply didn't believe I was pregnant! Perhaps I didn't want to. I thought my periods had stopped because I had been travelling. That had happened to me before. And I was so busy with the peace movement, I didn't have time to think about it.' Meg looked at him. 'Pathetic reasons, aren't they? The real reason I didn't have an abortion was because it was a mortal sin.'

'But you weren't brought up a Catholic! You told me you went to a Presbyterian school.'

'My father was a Scot and Presbyterian. He won the argument about my schooling. But my mother and aunt were Catholics. I respected their beliefs and knew that if my mother ever found out I'd had an abortion she would never be able to forgive me,' Meg sighed. 'It seems incredible to me now but at the time I just didn't think having a child adopted was such a big deal.'

Peter stared at her. Why had she never told him about such an important event as this?

'You didn't ever consider keeping the baby?' His tone was more sympathetic towards the child than Meg, she thought in mild surprise.

'No! I had my whole life ahead of me and the last thing I wanted right then was a baby. The shame of being an unmarried mother didn't bother me, but I had more important things to do. Organising protest marches, liberating political prisoners, being a radical student leader.' Meg's tone was ironic.

'Well, you did all that.'

'I did,' she said quietly.

'Did you tell the professor you were pregnant?'

'Heavens, no! For all his liberalism he was a conservative man. A devoted husband and father.' Meg gave a lopsided grin. 'His family would have been shattered. Anyway, the affair was well and truly over by then.'

She poked a log back onto the fire.

'Well, tell me the rest,' he said.

'I became very active in the peace movement in Washington. It was exciting. At the end of that year Nixon won the election by promising to end the war and seek détente with the Soviet Union . . .'

'About the baby!' Peter interrupted almost angrily. 'Not about bloody politics.'

'But that's what obsessed me. Don't you see? I didn't think much about the baby at all. I just knew that when the time came I'd have it and get it adopted by a nice loving couple who were desperate for one. Aunt Ellen assured me there were thousands of them out there. And then I'd go home to Australia and get on with my career.'

'Pretty naive, weren't you?'

'Yes, I was.' She looked at him curiously. Was he blaming her? She continued quietly. 'When I was about six months pregnant and finding it difficult to hide, Aunt Ellen took me off to Italy. She thought it would be safe there because nobody knew us. She'd arranged for me to give birth in London where she knew some of the doctors at Bede's Hospital. She said it would all be very straightforward. But in the meantime we went to Italy.'

'Where did you stay?' His voice was dull, as if he was asking the question merely to give himself time to understand why she had kept all this a secret.

'In a village up in the hills outside Florence, called Settigano,' said Meg. 'We rented a stone farmhouse. It was very cold. It was supposed to be spring but it rained all the time. I went for long walks by myself up and down the steep tracks through the olive groves.'

'Where was Aunt Ellen?'

'Oh, she'd catch the bus down to Firenze and go to a concert or dine with friends. She was taking Italian lessons and she'd met some people. I didn't feel like going out. I was probably dreadful company.' She nuzzled his shoulder. 'If you'd been there you could have cheered me up.'

He stroked her arm. 'I would have made you more miserable. At nine I was a terror and I only spoke Norwegian.'

'Ah yes . . .' She nuzzled closer, urging him to understand.

'What did your parents think you were doing in Italy?'

'Having a nice holiday with Aunt Ellen. My mother was delighted. She kept writing and asking for photos of us together. We could only send her ones of our heads and shoulders. I was swelling up everywhere.'

'Did you tell anyone in Australia about all this? What about Sally and Virginia? You tell them everything.'

'Not this,' Meg said firmly. 'I thought, it's my life, my problem, my solution. Soon it will be over and I'll be back to normal. I didn't want to burden anyone else with it.'

'So you went to London for the birth?'

'Yes. I was huge. I felt so clumsy. Aunt Ellen had borrowed a friend's flat in Knightsbridge. It smelt of leaking gas and damp carpet, but it wasn't far from the Serpentine and Kensington Gardens. I used to walk there every day, wrapped in my aunt's long black cape, to look at the statue of Peter Pan and feed the ducks. Each day I'd look to see if the poor frozen daffodils had managed to burst into bud yet. There were masses of them clumped in those acres of damp green grass.'

'You were still sad?'

'No, by then I was impatient. The last weeks dragged horribly. I thought it would never be over. I waited and waited. It was very cold. After my walk each day I would read or just sleep. Once Aunt Ellen persuaded me to come with her to a concert at the Albert Hall but I was so uncomfortable sitting still that we had to leave before the interval.'

'Poor Meg.'

'Poor Aunt Ellen. She'd paid a lot for the tickets.'

'And she was with you for the birth?'

'That was the really awful thing. She wasn't,' Meg said. 'Because I was such a drag to be with I persuaded her to accept an invitation to stay with a friend in Bath for the weekend. I wasn't due to give birth for another three weeks. But on Friday afternoon, just after I'd waved her off in the taxi to Paddington station, my waters broke and it all started happening.'

Peter looked shocked when Meg started to laugh.

'It was really quite bizarre. The phone rang in the middle of it all and it was my mother from Australia. She said, "Darling, how are you?" and it took all my strength not to blurt out, "Help, Mum! My waters just broke and I'm here all alone. Tell me what to do!" Instead I had to listen to her chattering on about the family and which animals on our farm had mated, while liquid streamed down my legs. As soon as I could get off the phone I called a mini cab and got myself to the hospital.'

'A mini cab? Why not an ambulance?'

'I felt okay.' Meg shrugged. 'The driver was a West Indian. Very cheerful. He played some Harry Belafonte and made me sing along to take my mind off things. "Daylight come and I wanna go home,"' Meg sang. 'Quite appropriate as it turned out.'

'Why? What happened?'

Meg sighed. 'After I was examined I was put into a room alone. It was the size of a cupboard. I was lying on a trolley in a hospital gown with no other covering. It was freezing. There were no windows. It was like being in a coffin.'

'Were you in pain?'

'The pain hadn't started. Before it did I had hours alone to think. Up to that point I'd just been denying the whole thing. But here it was, the birth was imminent. I had no control over my body. Then the pain started. I had no concept of what it would be like. I didn't want to be a mother. I started screaming. To be on your own in that sort of pain . . . I was crying out, but the door was shut tight and nobody came. I had nightmares for years afterwards. First I called gently, "Is anybody there?" There was no sound in the corridors. No footsteps. Nothing.'

'What time was it?'

'Two, three, four o'clock in the morning. Finally I just

cracked and started screaming and screaming. I was hysterical by the time someone came. Had lost all control. It's the only time in my life that has ever happened. The last thing I remember was being pushed at incredible speed along a hospital corridor under bright lights. I must have been anaesthetised after that because I don't remember anything at all.'

'What a horrible experience,' Peter said softly.

'I cried a lot the next day, with guilt. I was ashamed I'd lost control and ashamed of being an unwed mother. I thought I deserved to die.'

'Meg, I can't imagine you like that.' Peter held her close.

'Can't you?' Meg gave a weak grin. 'It was probably hormonal. But it was while I was in this mood that the social worker started pressing me to see the baby. She said I might want to change my mind about the adoption. She was a strong-minded woman, but I resisted. It took a lot of courage. I knew what would happen. How could anyone give up a baby, the real thing? At this point it was still unbelievable to me. I hadn't seen it. I knew it was a girl and healthy. That was all I wanted to know. End of story.'

'Did you ever see her?'

'For two days I had to keep saying no. Then the social worker would leave and I'd cry, thinking I was a wicked person, but I knew what the consequences would be. If I left the hospital with that baby it would be the end of the professional life that I wanted so badly.'

'So you didn't ever see her?'

'No. Before I left the hospital and signed the adoption papers, the social worker sat by my bed and told me that the adoptive parents were both university graduates, they both loved books and ideas, enjoyed brisk walks in the woods and had been camping a few times.' Meg laughed. 'I'd said I would like the parents to be reasonably well educated, to like books and ideas and enjoy the outdoors.'

'Sounds as if she'd had them tailor made.'

'She said there had been a lot of competition for my baby. Forty couples.' Meg smiled sadly. 'On the fourth day I left the hospital and immediately felt a terrific relief. My life was going to start again. I wanted to leave London as soon as possible. I remember still feeling very fat and I had to take tablets to stop my milk. I'd expected my stomach to go *ffft!* back to normal. So I started doing vigorous exercises; 5BX. Recommended by the army.'

'You had no other reactions to giving up the baby? You didn't ever feel the sudden urge to steal one out of a passing pram?' Peter asked seriously.

'No. It was an unwanted pregnancy. I adjusted very quickly. But I decided I would leave my address with the adoption agency and whenever it changed I would let them know. Then I put the whole thing behind me. My life went on. I never told my parents or friends. I forgot about it.'

'You didn't even think of her at birthdays or Christmas?'

Meg wriggled uncomfortably. She closed her eyes. 'How did you know that?'

'I've been living with you for quite a while,' he said affectionately.

She sighed. 'On her third birthday I wrote to the adoption agency saying I'd changed my address and asked for a photo of her. I said that I'd never want to interfere with her life or her adoptive parents' lives, but would they be willing to send a small photo?'

'And did they?'

Meg shook her head. 'I got a letter back saying, "Now, now dear." Very patronising. "We can't possibly do that. When you signed those papers you signed her away. Just get on with your life and don't look backwards." So, I thought, they're right. I hadn't been exactly plagued with the need to see what she looked like.' Meg's self-assurance slipped away and she looked wistful. 'But it did seem that a photograph was a reasonable request at the time. It wasn't as if I was going to run off to England and find one three year old amongst all those millions.'

Peter went to wake Nicholas and together they brought the mail in. There was a letter marked Bede's Hospital, London. 'Better late than never,' he said wryly as he handed it to her.

Nicholas had run into the garden to play with Bill, the dog.

She read it quickly and then aloud, 'Your daughter has been here to see us. She is now twenty-four and wishes to make contact with you. We would urge you to think about this carefully. She has had psychological problems and although she has had counselling over several years she is still . . .' Meg broke off angrily. 'What a cheek! To try and stop me seeing her after all these years. To pretend that she's . . .' She turned to Peter, shaking with emotion. 'She's come all this way to see me. How dare they imply that she's crazy!' Meg flung the letter to the floor.

Peter put his arm around her. 'Hey, I'm sure she's fine,' he said gently. 'I think it's wonderful you've found each other after all this time.' But he looked down at her anxiously. He had never seen her so disturbed.

# CHAPTER TWO

Meg took a taxi to the Intercontinental next morning. She felt detached and calm as the car swept over Darling Harbour and into the city. It was a cool day, full of winter sunshine. Saturday morning shoppers strolled with bulging bags past her cab at the traffic lights, looking young and carefree. She watched a tall blonde girl in her early twenties laugh as she leaned against her boyfriend, waiting to cross the street. I expect she'll look like that, thought Meg. How strange to have a child who is already a woman.

The Intercontinental, once the historic Treasury Building, was one of the best hotels in Sydney. Meg had been there several times to interview visiting politicians, artists and industrialists. She liked the hotel – admired the way its modern architecture blended with the mellow sandstone of a century ago.

If she were a visiting celebrity she would choose to stay here, she thought idly. Claudia must have good taste as well as money.

On her way up to the tenth floor, however, Meg's protective shell of detachment fell away. Her heart started beating so loudly that she clamped one hand over it to stop people in the lift overhearing. This girl has every right to be furious with me. I abandoned her and she's become disturbed as a result. Meg leaned against the wall, breathing deeply to stop herself from fainting. But when the doors opened she walked out quite normally and followed the corridor to room 1024.

She knocked firmly. No-one answered. She looked at her watch. Exactly nine. She knocked twice more before the door was flung wide and a diminutive young woman wearing a traditional Japanese kimono stared up at her. She looked like a porcelain doll.

'I'm sorry,' Meg said. 'I've knocked at the wrong door.'

'Hello, Mother,' said the superior English voice. Claudia smiled and held out both hands. She had long dark hair, pale skin, brown eyes and was astonishingly pretty. Meg thought, there's not a trace of me. The girl reached up and hugged her. Meg hugged her back. She felt soft, like a child, and smelled of some wonderful perfume, fruity, like watermelon. They each brushed away tears, and then, seeing that they had been similarly affected, laughed with relief. Claudia said politely, 'Please come in. I've ordered coffee and croissants. And heaps of fresh fruit salad. I do hope you like it.'

Meg stumbled into the room and sat on the chair she was offered. Claudia busied herself pouring coffee. 'Milk? Sugar?' She handed Meg a large plate of fruit as well and moved her chair so that she had a perfect view of the harbour. She's fussing so frantically to hide her feelings, Meg thought. I must help to restore the balance by being calm.

'What is that perfume you're wearing?' she asked.

Claudia looked pleased. 'Calvin Klein's Eternity.'

'It's wonderful. Smells like watermelon.'

Claudia laughed. 'I'm glad you like it.'

Meg stared out at the Opera House, its hooded sails like a flock of French nuns, and at a speedboat leaving a graceful trail of white that curved like lace beneath the Harbour Bridge. Then she looked back at Claudia. This lovely young woman is my daughter, she thought, feeling strangely distant.

'It probably was quite a shock my ringing you like that. I'm sorry. I'd planned to wait until the adoption agency had contacted you and you'd agreed to see me. They didn't actually give me your phone number. I stole it.' Claudia gave Meg a mischievous look.

'Did you?' Meg laughed in surprise.

'Yes, I'm like that.' She smiled and looked pleased with herself. Meg waited, but she offered no further explanation.

'I'm so glad you're here, Claudia. You must start at the beginning. Tell me all about yourself.' Meg hoped she didn't sound like an interviewer. Why had it been so hard to call her by her name? Because she was afraid to admit Claudia was real? Or was she just avoiding being intimate?

She looked at Claudia expectantly. Odd that she felt some affection for her now that she'd discovered she was a petty thief. Was she perhaps a bit of a radical, as Meg had been?

'My adoptive parents don't know I'm here. They're petrified of you. They think you'll steal me away, kidnap my affections.'

'But you're a woman, not a child,' said Meg sensibly. 'Surely you can make up your own mind. You have a perfect right to see me, providing I agree. Don't they realise that?'

'Exactly!' Claudia sprang out of her chair and knelt on the floor at Meg's feet. 'I knew you'd understand! You're so . . . logical. I'm sick to death of being surrounded by emotional cripples!'

Meg drew back, surprised by the vehemence.

'What do you mean?'

Claudia sat back on the carpet and hugged her knees. 'They think I'm the one with emotional problems. I'm sure the adoption agency mentioned that,' she said, watching Meg closely.

'They mentioned you'd had some counselling.'

'Well, it's not me who needs psychotherapy. It's my adoptive parents, Jane and Michael. Christ! Wouldn't you have problems if you had parents who controlled your every movement?' Claudia leapt up and stood by the window, angrily tapping the glass.

Meg waited.

'Tell me about them,' she said quietly. 'Jane and Michael.'

Claudia turned to face her. The anger had drained away leaving her looking miserable, like a lost child. 'Until I was six and went to school I wasn't allowed to cut up my own food or dress myself. If I tried to do anything at all – do up a button or tie a shoelace, I was told it was too difficult. They raised me like a handicapped child and by the time I started school, a year later than everyone else, I thought I was one.'

'But that's dreadful.' Meg looked shocked. 'Why did they do that?'

'To keep me to themselves, absolutely dependent. To them I was just a possession. Their precious little jewel. Before I went to school I had never played with another child. Can you imagine that? I would stand at the window looking down into the garden in the middle of the square below our house and stare at children playing ball. I *longed* to join them. But my parents forbade it. I might have been injured, or learned some bad words.'

'But didn't your parents have friends with children you could play with? Or relatives?'

Claudia shook her head. 'Their friends were all old. And they had almost no relatives so there weren't any cousins.'

'You must have been very lonely,' said Meg sympathetically. 'What about later? Surely they relaxed and allowed friends as you grew older.'

'The best thing they did for me in my whole life was send me to boarding school,' said Claudia triumphantly. 'I insisted on that when I was ten.'

Meg's thoughts flew to Nicholas and how devastated she would feel if he asked to go to boarding school at ten. 'Didn't they miss you terribly?'

'Oh, yes. They missed me all right. They'd arrive all tearful on parents' day with presents and bribes of trips abroad in the holidays. Fortunately I managed to spend most of my holidays with friends from school.'

'They didn't mind?'

'Oh yes, they minded! But what else could I do? We didn't get on. Not from the time I was six and realised that other children weren't mollycoddled like I was. And their parents weren't cretins like mine.'

'Cretins? But I was told they were both university graduates . . .'

Claudia laughed harshly. 'And so they were. But still cretins. Cruel ones. They were very strict in spite of the love they professed to have for me. I'd be sent to my room for the slightest thing. Spilling some milk or telling a joke they thought was in bad taste. I was high-spirited and bright, you see, and they were dull. They tried to stifle me but I fought back. I was so *bored* with them.' Claudia gulped and hung her head. 'I can't tell you how wonderful it is to have found my real mother,' she said softly. When she looked up there were tears in her eyes. Meg held out both hands to her and Claudia came and sat at her feet.

'You know I always had a feeling they weren't my real parents. For years I pretended I was an orphan. When I told them about this . . . I was about twelve by then . . . they were both quite upset. But they *still* didn't let on I was adopted. Imagine! I had to find out years later. Quite recently in fact.'

'Who told you?'

'They did. I forced them. I mean, everyone noticed that I was temperamentally quite different from them and looked nothing like them. They're both grey and obese. My mother actually dyed her hair black for a few years to make herself look a bit like me. Pathetic, isn't it?' Claudia shrugged. 'I hate them. It's as simple as that. I hate them both and have done for about eighteen years.'

Meg was horrified. 'But that's awful,' she said. 'Do they know you feel like this?'

Claudia paused. 'They're pretty thick, but yes, I think they know. I mean, I've given them plenty of hints.' She laughed harshly again and Meg found the sound chilling.

'What sort of hints?'

'Oh, things like stealing their credit cards and totting up a few thousand pounds here and there. Crashing their cars. Ruining their dinner parties. Screaming at them in front of their prissy friends. Abandoning them and running away to Australia to find you.' She paused to see how Meg was taking this. 'But all that is nothing compared with my new job.'

'They don't approve of your job?'

'No. And you mightn't either.'

'What is it?'

'I'm a hostess. In Tokyo. A sort of geisha girl. I make businessmen spend their money in bars. It's very lucrative.'

'Really?' said Meg, stiffly. She had imagined Claudia might be a fashion model or a socialite with a private income, an interest in the arts and her own flat in Chelsea. 'How long have you been working in Tokyo?'

'Three months. It's a hoot. I really like it.'

'What exactly do you do?'

Claudia giggled. 'I see that you're not entirely liberated, Mother. Do I detect a whiff of disapproval?'

'Not at all.' Meg struggled to sound uncensorious and not flinch at being called 'Mother'.

'I get paid over two thousand dollars a week to chat with, dance with and pour drinks for some of the wealthiest men in Japan. They like beautiful women to maintain a steady flow of drinks and flattery. And Western women are much more prestigious than Japanese. I've become a status symbol.'

'Do you speak Japanese?'

'Heavens, no. My speaking English is much better for a client's image. The other businessmen he wants to impress will assume he speaks English, too.'

'And does he?'

'Of course not. I pretend I understand him absolutely. I giggle a lot at the jokes he tries to make and sit on his knee and whisper in his ear.'

'Ah.' Meg was reminded of a bar in Manila where she had once spent an uncomfortable evening with a man she loved who had sat a bar girl on his knee and soon afterwards paid for her to accompany them back to their hotel. Meg had broken off her relationship with him that night.

'You never feel pressured to do more than just sit on their knees?'

'Asian women who work in bars are assumed to be prostitutes, but white hostesses are treated with respect,' said Claudia nonchalantly. 'Japanese men find it thrilling just to be waited on by a Western woman. I'm a symbol of my client's standing in the world.' She pranced about in the lovely kimono, serving Meg coffee in the coquettish manner she apparently reserved for her clients. Meg grinned in spite of her disapproval. She could imagine this young woman wreaking havoc with men.

'Do the businessmen ever fall in love with you?'

'But of course. It's an occupational hazard.' Claudia was only half joking. 'The old ones get maudlin drunk and weep and offer you priceless gifts. They say all they want is for you to massage them once a day. They bribe you with family heirlooms: this kimono is late eighteenth-century Okinawan, made with bingata dye. It should be in a museum.' She displayed one graceful sleeve. 'The middle-aged ones are sleazier. They offer you apartments. Then they get drunk and beg you to let them suck your nipples or nuzzle their heads between your legs. The young ones who speak English think it's cute to insult you in front of their friends. They'll say, "You smell!" or, "You're fat!" and then burst out laughing. They're infantile. They ask questions about the colour of your pubic hair and tell each other endless jokes about penises. They're obsessed with the size. Japanese men are smaller but harder. Apparently.'

'Apparently?' Meg could not help inquiring.

'My girlfriend, Selina, who's a blonde and much in demand, has slept with a few of them.'

Meg nodded and looked uncomfortable.

'Look, you don't have to worry about me. I'm not a prostitute. I plan to have a little fun, fleece the natives and leave quite unscathed.'

Meg felt slightly sick. 'You're going back to Tokyo when you leave here?'

Claudia gave her most beguiling smile. 'Unless my mother invites me to stay with her.'

'You might not find my lifestyle exciting enough,' Meg said carefully. 'But of course I'd like you to meet my family and have a holiday with us.'

Claudia stared at Meg, eyes wide like a child's. 'Do I have brothers and sisters?'

'A brother, aged four. Nicholas,' Meg said, unable to disguise her pride.

'Is he like me?'

Meg smiled and shook her head. 'Not much. He's blond, noisy and robust. He doesn't have your delicacy, your . . . aesthetic beauty.'

'Do you think I'm beautiful?' Claudia asked bluntly. 'Because I don't.'

'Of course you are. Very beautiful.'

'I think I look like a crow. A witch,' she said harshly. 'Men don't find me attractive.'

Meg laughed out loud. 'I find that very hard to believe.'

'It's true,' she said matter-of-factly. 'They think I'm . . . mousey.'

'What do you mean?'

'Sexually. I'm not . . . passionate.'

'Perhaps you haven't met anyone you're really attracted to yet,' Meg said carefully.

I must be careful not to give advice until it's asked for, she warned herself. She was surprised that she seemed to have fallen so easily into the role of confidante. She had imagined her daughter would resist intimacy with her.

'Did that happen to you?' Claudia asked in her forthright manner. 'That you weren't sexually aroused until you fell in love?'

Meg combed her memory. 'I did fall in love with the first man I slept with, yes. But I don't remember whether I felt sexually aroused before I fell in love or after. It was a long time ago.'

'How old were you?'

'Nineteen.'

'Five years younger than me. There's something wrong

with me, I know it.' She looked bothered. 'Who was he, your first lover?'

'An artist named Taz. He used to play the balalaika and sing songs to me.' Meg blushed, to her surprise.

'So he wasn't my father,' Claudia said. 'Did you fall in love with my father, too, or was he just for sex?'

Meg drew a sharp breath. Claudia was staring at her.

'I fell in love with him, too. For a short time.'

Claudia shrugged. 'He didn't sing songs to you I take it.'

'No.' Meg smiled. The girl's hostility was palpable. 'He was intelligent, friendly, attractive. He was admired by a lot of people.'

'Was he famous?'

'Not famous. Well known, within a certain circle.'

Claudia turned on her suddenly. 'Was he crazy? I'd rather know.'

Meg laughed. 'Of course not.'

She sighed with relief. 'Then I don't understand why you didn't keep me. You loved him, he was intelligent, attractive, sane. Why in hell did you have me adopted?'

'He was married, Claudia. He knew nothing about you.'

'You mean, he doesn't know I exist?' she asked incredulously. 'Not even now?'

'No. He doesn't.'

Claudia stalked about the room, agitated. 'My own father doesn't know I exist. I could meet him in the street or at a party. I could have an affair with him and neither of us would know we were related. It's like Oedipus and Jocasta!' she wailed.

'Oh don't be so dramatic,' Meg said crossly. 'You're not likely to meet him. He lives in Washington.' She gasped at her own stupidity.

Claudia settled back in her chair and smiled at Meg with satisfaction. 'Well at least I know where to start looking. Thank you, Mother, for losing your cool and letting that slip.'

Meg's face flushed and she put a hand up to her cheek, stroking the heat back down one side of her neck. 'He was happily married. There were children. The affair was over before I discovered I was pregnant. It would be foolish to go in search of him now, Claudia.'

'I'd like to meet him, and the other children. I've been an only child as well as a miserable one. I'd adore to have a heap of brothers and sisters. What a lot of options in life I have all of a sudden.' She gave Meg a sweet smile, but Meg no longer found it beguiling.

'Oh Mother, I've hurt you. I'm sorry. *Mea culpa.*' She was suddenly out of her chair and nestling her head in Meg's lap. 'Of course I won't go and upset his precious family. The coward.' She grinned up at Meg. 'For an ardent feminist you're very considerate of male feelings, I must say.' She gave a little shrug. 'Why should I want to bother with a smug, self-centred father who dotes on nothing but his own little brood when I've got you?' Her hair in Meg's lap smelt so fragrant that Meg felt a strong urge to stroke it. Suddenly, Claudia lifted her head and said, 'Look, I'm sorry if I came on a bit strong before. I know I'm abrasive. But I've been hurt so much.' She looked like an innocent child. 'I want you to know all about me. All. I want to hide nothing from you. Okay? If you take me into your family for a while I want you to have no illusions.'

Meg felt a rush of mixed emotions – gratitude, shame, happiness, relief and apprehension. For twenty-four years she had hidden the fact of this daughter from everyone, even her husband. Now she was being given the chance to make amends.

'Thank you, Claudia,' she said humbly.

'Well, what's she like?' asked Peter, as he opened the door with Nicholas on his shoulders.

'Amazing,' said Meg with a wan smile. She kissed them both.

'Mummy, I saw amazing monsters in the museum, didn't we, Dad? Dinosaurs!'

'Really? Tell me!' Meg settled down with Nicholas on her knee. 'And the best one, the Tyrannosaurus rex, the hugest one of all weighs . . . oh, I forget what it weighs. Daddy, will we look it up?'

'We will, Nicko, but not just now. When you wake up from your nap.'

'Promise?'

'Promise.' Meg took Nicholas by the hand and they disappeared down the hallway, Meg turning to signal Peter, who was dying to hear about Claudia, that she'd be back in a few minutes to tell him.

'What does she look like?'

'Gorgeous. Like a fashion model.'

'Tall? Fair? Like you?'

'Nothing like me. Like a Japanese doll. Petite. With ivory skin and jet black hair. I was bowled over.'

'Great. What about her personality?'

Meg hesitated, then said decisively, 'There's absolutely nothing wrong with her.'

Peter smiled. 'No need to be defensive with me, my love.'

'The parents are the problem. Appallingly over-protective. Dull. Authoritarian. It's a wonder she's grown up normal at all. Oh Peter, I'm just so glad she decided to find me! I think you'll like her a lot. She's lively, optimistic, funny and quite rebellious in a way.' Meg's face was glowing.

Peter hugged her. 'Of course I'll like her. Is she coming to visit?'

'Well, I know I should have discussed this with you first, but I've invited her to stay. She wants to.'

Peter raised his eyebrows. 'Fine. For long?'

'A month or so. We could give her the sunroom. It's the nicest. She's dying to meet you and Nick. She's had such a lonely childhood. This will be like having a real family at last.'

'What do her parents think about her running off to find you?'

Meg shrugged. 'She hasn't told them. She doesn't get on with them at all, though apparently she lived at home in a flat they had built for her, until a few months ago.'

Peter looked dubious. 'You don't think you should contact them? At least let them know where she is?' he suggested.

'Perhaps. They might be worried.' But she did not seem concerned. 'Oh Pete, isn't it amazing? She'll be here in a few hours!' She hugged him, then withdrew, looking serious. 'There is something you should know.' She told him about Claudia's job in Tokyo.

'Why did she tell you all this?'

'She wants me to have no illusions about her.'

'You don't think she could just be trying to make a big impression on you? After all, she's come from a conservative background and you're a radical investigative journalist.'

'Making it all up you mean?' Meg eyed him steadily. 'I don't think so. If she's behaved a little strangely, done some rebellious things, its because she's had a lousy childhood and I blame myself for that.' She looked at him appealingly. 'You don't really mind about her staying, do you?'

Peter hesitated, torn between telling her the truth and what she wanted to hear. He had never seen her so distracted and so vulnerable. 'Can't wait to meet her!' He grinned and squeezed Meg round the shoulders. 'What relation will I be to her? Wicked stepfather?'

Meg nodded vaguely and looked thoughtful. 'The odd thing is that after the initial excitement and shedding a few tears on meeting her I feel nothing much at all. Guilt, I suppose. Yes, definitely guilt. I want to make up for abandoning her. Welcome her into this family for as long as she wants to stay. I'll do anything I can to help her. But love and affection I don't feel.' She looked at Peter searchingly. 'Isn't it awful? It's like she has nothing to do with me. She's alien.'

'It's too early for you to feel such closeness. Don't worry,' he said, 'it'll come.'

'But she's demanding. And clever. She wants it now. I feel that I'm going to disappoint her. Pete, it's strange, but she frightens me a little. All she needs is love and reassurance from me and she'll be fine. But I'm not sure I can give as much as she requires.'

'Of course you can, Meg. I've never seen you like this, full of self-doubt.' He hugged her. 'Don't let the spoilt brat get to you.'

'Does she sound like a spoilt brat to you?'

'Definitely.'

Meg looked into the distance. 'You know how I get 'melancholy' sometimes? Depressed about nothing – Virginia deciding not to come and stay, the shadows in the garden?'

He nodded. 'You've been like that this week.'

'I know. I get it every year around the end of May, that seeping sadness. I've never understood why until now. It's the memory of her birth and the loss of her.'

'Why didn't you ever tell me about it, love?'

'I honestly don't know.'

That evening, before Claudia arrived at their house for dinner, Meg agonised about whether or not to phone Bede's Hospital in London. 'Six in the evening here is nine in the morning there, right? That's northern summer time,' she muttered. 'Yes, the social workers should be well and truly on duty by now. But should I contact them and risk hearing something I don't like?'

'You'll drive yourself mad if you don't ring. Go on. As you're always advising me, "Just do it!"' said Peter cheerfully. He was marinating Tasmanian trout in fresh ginger, lemon juice and teriyaki sauce. 'If she's been living in Japan she must like fish.'

'She'll *love* your fish,' said Meg.

'She'll notice it's not quite Intercontinental fare.'

'Far superior to the Intercontinental.'

'Oh shut up. You'd tell me anything to keep me in the kitchen.' Peter grinned. He was a much better cook than Meg, who had lived on take-away food before they met.

When Meg came back into the kitchen after making the call, she put both arms around Peter from behind and kissed him on the neck. He was chopping basil and nuts for the pesto potatoes. 'So, is she crazy or not?' he murmured, while returning the kiss.

'You won't believe this,' Meg said. 'I just spoke to the very same social worker who advised me not to have Claudia adopted. She's still there, after twenty-four years!'

'The British believe in continuity.'

'She must be about sixty by now. She sounded really kind.' Meg shook her head. 'And I thought she was such a dragon.'

'Was she surprised to hear from you?'

'Not really. She wrote me that letter. I didn't even look at the signature, I was so outraged. Miss Marjorie Trent.'

'So, can you talk to the parents?' He dried his hands on a tea towel and poured vodka and tonic into a glass.

'Miss Trent said the parents were holidaying in Switzerland. Apparently they're both "in poor health". But she thought they would like to talk to me. She's leaving them a message to contact me.'

Peter handed her the drink. 'Have this. You look wrung out and Claudia hasn't even got here yet.'

Meg took the glass and sipped it gratefully.

'Claudia wasn't lying. Her childhood was difficult. The parents couldn't handle her. Too "wilful", according to Miss Trent. They were apparently quite relieved when she asked to go to boarding school. She was expelled from the first one. Too "rigid" for her. The second one was co-educational and rather lax. Somewhere in Oxford. The seniors had a bar and freedom to come and go as they pleased. Miss Trent was disapproving.'

'A bar? We didn't have student bars, even in progressive Norway!'

'In spite of the bar, Claudia did well in her A-levels and was offered a place at Oxford, but she refused to go. Her parents were "heart broken".'

'What do these parents do, apart from behave ineffectually?'

'The father's a country doctor; GP, like my dad. And the mother was a librarian but gave it up to look after Claudia. They sound pretty normal.'

'They didn't over-protect her?'

'Miss Trent says not. They were bewildered by her rejection of them. Even as a small child she raged at them until she got exactly what she wanted. Miss Trent was called in to offer advice. From the age of twelve Claudia went to a psychiatrist to see why she was prone to temper tantrums. Since she finished with therapy two years ago she's had convictions for drink-driving, theft and abusing officers of the law.'

'Great!' said Peter in dismay. 'Do we really want her here for an extended holiday? What sort of an influence will she have on Nick?' He changed to a falsetto English voice. 'Come on Nicky, let big sister drive you to the park. We'll steal a few tricycles, scream at a policeman and then I'll crash your mummy's car.'

'Peter, I have to give this a go. Okay?' She looked serious. 'I'm sorry.'

'Okay.' He sighed and went back to the cooking to hide his expression of strong doubt. 'Maybe I should take Nick over to Sally's place tomorrow and leave you two to get properly acquainted.'

Sally and Peter sat on the verandah at Hunters Hill overlooking the wide Parramatta River that flowed out into the harbour and beyond that to the sea.

'This is one of the loveliest houses in Sydney,' Peter said. 'You must be sad to be leaving.'

'I am. Oh, I am.' Sally stared out into the vast, tangled garden. 'Though I don't tell many people, Peter. Only you, Virginia and Meg.' Then she said decisively, 'I think we have to be positive about all this.'

Peter looked at her. As was her manner, she had changed the subject abruptly. 'About Claudia? Yes, so do I,' he said.

'It's a wonderful thing to have happened to Meg. A daughter! Turning up after all these years to claim her. Meg must look on this as a gift. A splendid gift. Not feel guilty about having left her as a baby. The pain of that must have been awful. Just awful. But now they've found each other they shouldn't blame anyone, but just *enjoy* being together. And you, Peter, are so generous, you'll make this new daughter feel welcome, I know.'

Meg is right, thought Peter. Beneath that practical surface, Sally is wildly romantic.

She was small and pretty, with curly brown hair and a pert smile like the picture of Miss Muffet in the book of nursery rhymes he read to Nick. But there was something determined in that smile and her hands were often clenched as if she was unconsciously controlling herself. Since she had separated from her husband, the imaginative, impractical side of Sally's nature had begun to surface. Her once immaculate house was often a mess. She smiled vaguely as if she was thinking of the new children's novel she was writing, not of organising the household.

Still, she could pull herself back into line at a few moments' notice. Decades of having to control a large family and work a full-time teaching job at the same time had made these skills hard to forget.

'And you thought Claudia was really not too bad when you met her? Not disturbed, I mean, as the letter from the hospital implied?' Sally continued, reassuring herself.

'She seemed okay,' Peter said. 'She was shrewd, looked about a lot. I think she was surprised that Meg didn't live a more affluent life. She called our house "a cottage".'

Sally laughed. 'Did she just. Well, it is. But a lovely one. And you? You're perceptive, Peter. Did you like her?'

'I felt . . . to be honest, no. I didn't like her. She seemed predatory. Probably a heart-breaker. Not my type at all. Meg is vulnerable to her and she likes that.'

Sally felt mildly disconcerted. Peter was usually so generous about other people. Was he a little jealous perhaps?

'How did she get on with Nicholas?' Sally had a theory that people who got along well with children and dogs could not have too much wrong with them.

'She was terribly keen to meet him but once that was over she seemed to lose interest. He was quite hurt. He'd brought out all his prized possessions – dinosaur drawings, caterpillar collection, favourite old teddy bears. She made no effort at all to talk to him. She just wanted Meg to herself and Nick was opposition. That's partly why I brought him over here today.'

'Good idea. We can't have poor Nick getting hurt feelings. I've got a batch of cakes in the oven. He can slosh them all over with sticky icing when he's tired of playing in the cubby.'

They both looked across to the little stone cubby-house from which Nick's contented humming was heard as he banged a toy hammer on the roof he was 'fixing'.

'He's playing the handyman, Peter. Imitating you,' Sally smiled. 'He's lucky to have such a role model.'

Sally gazed nostalgically at the cubby-house in which all of her boys had played when they were small. It was shaped like a miniature Gothic church with a steep roof and a belltower.

'Who built that cubby?' Peter asked.

'I did!' Sally laughed. 'That's why it's got such crazy bulges. I'd just been reading *The Hunchback of Notre Dame*. I *felt* like the hunchback by the time I'd crawled in and out a thousand times, patching up the gaps between the bluestone.'

'And you made the swing? And the bridge across the creek? And the fish ponds?'

'It was fun! The boys all helped. The ponds leaked at first and the fish used to lie on the bottom gasping. And the bridge is still crooked as you'll notice, but it was . . . I don't know . . . a challenge to see if we could create such things. The boys were very proud of their handiwork.' She shrugged and he knew she was thinking how sad it would be to leave it all.

'About this party that Meg wants to throw for Claudia. Do you think she'd like to have it here? It could be our farewell to the house as well as Claudia's welcome to Meg's family. What do you think?' Sally asked enthusiastically.

'I think it's a very generous offer.'

'I'll ask her then, shall I? I don't want to interfere with her plans.' Sally smiled out across the garden, already imagining tables covered in food, fairy lights in the trees, a band playing. She loved giving parties. She'd organised Meg's wedding, her sons' dance parties, and had recently cooked a dinner for eighty people to raise funds for Refugee Week.

'Virginia will be here in a few weeks. Why don't we wait for her?' Sally had a way of suggesting things she had already decided to do that was so enticing you couldn't argue with her. Come to think of it, they all three did that, Sally, Meg and Virginia. Was it some trick they'd thought up thirty years ago when they were girls, Peter wondered?

'Yes, let's wait for Virginia,' he said.

Sally beamed. 'I'm so glad you think that's a good idea.' She put an arm around his shoulder. 'And don't worry about

Claudia. Meg's probably right. All she needs is a bit of love and attention and she'll improve. Anyway, she won't be here for long.' She gave him a meaningful look and he imagined she knew what was troubling him.

# CHAPTER THREE

'There are so many Asians in Sydney,' said Claudia. 'It's one of the first things I noticed. You'll have race riots like we do in Britain if you keep allowing them in, you know.'

Meg was walking with Claudia along the boulevard at Circular Quay towards the Museum of Contemporary Art, which was one of her favourite walks. She looked around anxiously to see if the Chinese busker playing a violin solo nearby had overheard. Claudia's clearly articulated, arrogant English voice was hard not to hear.

'We have surprisingly little racial conflict here,' Meg said defensively. 'It's one of the things we're proud of. Although recently there have been a few violent crimes involving rival Vietnamese gangs in the outer-western suburbs.'

'Riiight,' drawled Claudia knowingly. 'It's only a matter of time then.'

'Not at all.' Meg felt herself growing hot with indignation. 'Out there in Cabramatta there's a strong communal spirit. There are a number of Vietnamese on the local council. It's one of the fastest growing communities in New South Wales. Naturally, there will be some growth in criminal activity.'

I sound like a lecturer in sociology, thought Meg. Why does Claudia constantly bring out the moralist in me?

Claudia shrugged. 'Well it does seem a shame that such a beautiful city as Sydney should risk becoming overrun by foreigners. Particularly coloured ones.'

'Claudia, *you're* a foreigner. So am I. A lot of the people you see in this part of Sydney are tourists, whether they're Asian or European. All Australians, except the Aborigines, have come here as immigrants. I'm a Scot. You're half Scot, half . . .'

Claudia smiled. Every time she managed to rile Meg she learned something she wanted to know. 'Half what? What was my father before he migrated to Washington?'

'He told me his people were Cockney shirt makers and that they were Jewish.'

'Shit! I don't want to be a bloody Jew.'

'Well you are. Half of you. And a quarter Catholic and a quarter Presbyterian.' Meg laughed. 'It might stop you making racist remarks.'

As they walked on around the green waters of the harbour, Meg linked her arm through Claudia's and jolted it teasingly to stop her sulking. 'You're right. It is a beautiful city. I was going to take you to see "Mao Goes Pop".' She waved an arm at a huge banner flapping over the entrance to the Museum of Contemporary Art, 'but as you don't like anything Asian and it's too nice a day to be indoors, I'll take you to Doyle's instead for some grilled John Dory.'

'What's that? Fish?'

'The best in Sydney.'

'I'm getting rather tired of fish.'

'Well, what about some pasta or Peking duck? The Imperial Peking, just over there, has wonderful duck.'

'Pasta's fine.'

Meg laughed and shook her head in disbelief. 'Your prejudices will destroy your palate, Claudia.'

As they sat at an outdoor table close enough to the harbour to smell the salt air and watch ferries gliding by, with plates of spaghetti and a bottle of Frascati in front of them, Meg felt almost relaxed beside her daughter. When a couple of young men in suits looked at Claudia admiringly, Meg found herself staring back at them with an expression of pride and possessiveness.

'Now, tell me all about your early life. I've heard about the school years, but where did you live as a very young child?' she asked enthusiastically.

'In Knightsbridge, in a large house overlooking Enismore Gardens.'

'Really?' said Meg. 'I stayed in a flat not far from there just before you were born. I used to walk in Kensington Gardens. Did you go there, too?'

'Of course. My nanny walked me there in the pram practically from the day I was born.'

Meg felt a stab of disapproval. If the childless Jane and Michael had wanted Claudia so much, how could they bear to hand her over to a nanny practically from the day she was born? Still, that was the way the affluent English believed children should be brought up.

'Did you like your nanny?'

'I don't remember the first one. She only stayed a year. There was a string of nannies. They changed every few months when I was older. I was a problem child, you see,' said Claudia matter-of-factly.

Meg laughed. 'Were you aware of being a problem?'

'Of course. My parents discussed it interminably. I used to listen in.'

'What did you do apart from throw tantrums?'

'Refuse to eat. I'd vomit if they forced me.'

'Why?'

Claudia shrugged. 'I honestly don't remember. It just became a habit after a while. I quite enjoyed watching them all getting into a tizz, parents and nannies bringing me more and more tempting tit-bits, bribing me to try just a mouthful of this, a taste of that.'

'You enjoyed the attention?'

'Of course.'

'Didn't you get hungry?'

'I had food in reserve. Chocolate bars, fruit, even tubs of icecream I'd steal from the fridge. The nanny was usually blamed for taking it. Oh, don't look so shocked. It was only a game.'

'How old were you when you did all this?'

'Aged three to six,' said Claudia, as if she had recited this information many times before.

'I can't imagine why your parents put up with it.'

'I told you they were morons.' Claudia laughed. 'It's a relief to be with you, my real mother.'

Meg was not sure she felt the same. But Claudia looked so vulnerable when she said this that she felt ashamed. Meg hesitated before saying carefully, 'Look, I don't want you to think of Jane and Michael as wicked and me as the fairy godmother. I'd have made dreadful mistakes in your upbringing. All parents do. But I want to say this to you, Claudia. I think the system of adoption is a cruel one.'

'I agree with you!' said Claudia with feeling.

'I don't say this with any self-pity, but I would support any legislation that allows adopted children to maintain some contact with their real parents over the years. If I had been able to see a photograph of you at three, if we had been able to write to each other while you were growing up, it would have been easier for both of us, and for your adoptive parents, I feel sure. What do you think?'

'Jane and Michael would have been far too terrified to allow that,' Claudia said grimly. 'I feel angry with you for abandoning me to such feeble people. My life has been ruined because I didn't have strong, intelligent parents to guide me. Look, I know I'm a manipulative bitch!' she said loudly. Other diners turned to stare. 'But if you hadn't dumped me, left me to strangers so that you could get on with own precious career, I might have amounted to something!' Claudia stood up. Tears streamed down her face. People were staring angrily at Meg. The two young men in suits seemed poised to rescue Claudia.

'Claudia, sit down at once and stop behaving like a spoilt child,' said Meg, through clenched teeth. Her voice shook with emotion.

To Meg's surprise, Claudia sat down. She handed her a handkerchief and a glass of water. Claudia dried her tears and gulped the water down.

Through her tears she said, 'Do you know, that is the first time in my whole life that I've been called a spoilt child?'

'I'm sorry,' said Meg.

'Don't be,' Claudia replied. She smiled at Meg gratefully.

'Look, Claudia. I'd love you to stay with us – Peter, Nicky and me. I'd like to introduce you to my friends, to let you feel part of my life, if it's not too late. I did abandon you. I'm sorry. I'll try to make things up to you. Will you let me do that?'

'Yes,' said Claudia very softly. 'I'd like that.'

'Thank you,' said Meg humbly. She thought she might cry herself. 'Is there anything you'd particularly like to do while you're here?' she said brightly, pulling herself together. 'Go to the opera, see the outback, visit the Barrier Reef?'

Claudia looked up at Meg with her soulful, dark eyes and said, 'I didn't come here to be a tourist, Mother. I came to see you.'

Meg still flinched every time she was called Mother. Nicholas called her Mummy or Meg. It would be tactless to suggest that Claudia call her Meg. She seemed determined to say Mother. Accepting the title was the least she could do. She smiled ruefully.

'That's fine with me.'

After a pause Claudia said, 'There is one thing you could help me with if you really wanted to.'

'Yes?' said Meg willingly.

'My career.'

'Ah.'

'I've always wanted to be a journalist. Uncanny, isn't it? I must have inherited that from you. Could you get me a job do you think?'

'A job?' Meg looked surprised. 'But you've had no training. You'd have to do a degree in Media Studies. That takes three years and it's hard to get into. About as difficult as Law. Still, if you really wanted to do it I could certainly . . .'

'I don't want to spend three years in some dull institution. You're the editor of a newspaper. Can't you employ me?'

Meg smiled in disbelief. 'It doesn't work that way, Claudia. I could give you some work experience but you wouldn't be paid. I have a small staff and they work extraordinarily long hours for low wages.'

'Why?'

'Because they believe in the need for an independent newspaper with an alternative point of view. Some of my contributors – well-known journalists, artists and cartoonists – work for nothing. My production specialist, who's a whiz on layout, is a student journalist who works for me three days a week for a pittance. You could certainly come and see how it all works and find out if you're really interested, but I'm afraid that paying high salaries isn't one of our priorities.'

'You mean all those people are being exploited?'

Meg laughed. 'To an extent. And so am I. I earn less than the production student. And I work longer hours. Most of the editing is done at home on weekends or late at night.'

'Well why on earth do you do it? You're an award-winning journalist. You could work for a proper newspaper and earn a decent salary like you used to.'

'I could indeed. But then I'd have to write on subjects my editor chose for me which I might find useless or compromising. And even if I was allowed to write on issues I felt passionate about, the copy could be censored so as not to upset the powerful individuals or situations I was investigating. Mainstream journalism can be very frustrating.'

'Well, I wouldn't mind it. Don't you get free overseas trips, airfares, hotel accommodation and introductions to famous people?'

'Sometimes. But very rarely if you work on my paper.'

'Well, forget about yours. Will you help me get a job in mainstream journalism?' Claudia asked unabashedly.

Meg stood up, put her hand affectionately on Claudia's shoulder and said, 'I'm touched that you want to be a journalist. Come on, we'll walk to the ferry and I'll tell you what I know about it.'

Christ, thought Meg, as she waited for Claudia to come back from the Ladies room, she has no sense of ethics whatsoever. Or am I just out of touch with the way ambitious young women work these days?

Clattering up the outside metal stairs of the warehouse to her newspaper office on the edge of the city next morning, Meg heard police sirens and a simultaneous scream from inside. Claudia grabbed her mother's arm in fright. Meg grinned. Through the grimy window she could see who the scream was coming from. 'Finn, the production specialist. He gets a little edgy on deadline day. Come in. I'll introduce you.'

Meg pushed open the heavy door and was greeted by the din of the office. Claudia frowned in concentration, trying to take in all the different activities at once. There were journalists tapping fast at word processors or feeding paper into fax machines, artists at tilted desks who seemed to be discarding drawings faster than they created them, the red-faced Finn at his terminal, waving his arms, shouting instructions and gulping coffee all at once and some other people talking urgently into phones.

Meg escorted Claudia from desk to desk, introducing her and sorting out problems as she went.

Finn approached, looking grim. 'Meg, I can't do the layout if the copy is as late as this.'

She nodded sympathetically. 'What are you waiting on?'

'Unemployment for page one, ocean outfalls and water purification for page seven, plans for the third runway, Bond and Elliott . . . you name it!'

Meg followed him back to his desk, sat down beside him at the screen and started flicking through the pages. In a few minutes she was up again and moving from desk to desk, asking each journalist what the problem was with their late articles. Sometimes she scribbled notes on paper, sometimes sat in front of the screen and took over. There was a lot of laughter and good humour, Claudia noticed, in spite of the general air of panic about the paper coming out.

'We desperately need more ads,' Meg confided when she and Claudia finally sat down with cups of coffee at her large desk at one end of the room. 'That's what's killing us. We need a full-time staff member doing nothing else.'

'Well, can't you get one?'

'We'd have to pay a full salary and we can't afford it.'

Claudia shrugged. 'What sort of ads?'

'Local restaurants, shops, real estate.'

'I know nothing about advertising, otherwise I could have a go at it,' Claudia offered without much enthusiasm.

'No. You concentrate on the journalism, my love, if that is what interests you.'

Claudia looked uncertain. 'It certainly seems *chaotic* in here.'

'It is. Two things are killing us,' Meg corrected herself. 'Lack of advertising and the workload.'

'What are you going to do about it?'

Meg sighed. 'I'll have to employ someone to do the ads and in order to pay that salary I'll have to do some more freelance journalism.'

'But you're already doing heaps. What other papers will you write for?'

'Decent overseas papers that pay well. The *Independent* and the *Guardian* in London, the *New Statesman*, the *Los Angeles Times*. They all take my stuff.'

'What sort of stuff? About East Timor?'

'Yes,' Meg gave her a curious look. 'Are you interested in East Timor?'

Claudia looked about the room, distracted. 'I've read a few articles on the human rights struggle.'

'I've got a whole file on it if you'd like to read more,' Meg offered enthusiastically.

'Thanks. I might do that later,' Claudia said vaguely. She seemed ill at ease in the bustling office. 'Isn't it *frantic*? I don't know how anyone could concentrate long enough to write one paragraph in here, let alone an entire article.'

Meg laughed. 'That's why I do a lot of my pieces at home.'

Meg had gone to Tanglewood to prepare it for Claudia's arrival. She wanted her to see the house at its best and, as she hadn't managed to get there for a month, she imagined it might look neglected. There would be possum dirt and fallen bark all over the verandah, cobwebs and dead mice in corners, and not enough dry wood for the fires. She had never felt so particular before. Whenever she went there with Virginia and Sally they all cleaned up together, or if they were tired, left things as they were.

Peter was driving Nicholas and Claudia up from Sydney the following afternoon and they would all stay the weekend together. Meg felt grateful to Peter. He had been remarkably tolerant since Claudia had come to stay – both of Claudia's demands and of Meg's changing moods. If Claudia said she could only drink low-fat milk for breakfast, he would drive to the nearest shop and buy some, joking that it would do them all good. When Meg was tense and absent-minded he appeared not to notice or covered for her tactfully. She had been like that ever since her daughter moved in. Meg knew she was neglecting her job, Nicholas, Peter, even the dog. To compensate she'd brought some work and her laptop computer with her to Tanglewood, which she didn't often do. She'd also taken the dog in her car because Claudia had said she didn't like travelling with big dogs who had bad breath.

Meg had not mentioned to Peter the fact that when Claudia had checked out of the Intercontinental a week ago she had no money to pay the bill and her credit card had mysteriously been lost. Meg had paid the account and said that Claudia could repay her when she was able.

Oh well, thought Meg, as she settled herself by the blazing open fire at Tanglewood, sipping a glass of red wine and listening to Jane Rutter playing Chopin's nocturnes and preludes for flute. What does it matter? I have a job I enjoy, a family I adore, friends, this wild little house on the cliff, the cottage in the city, and now I've found the daughter I thought I'd never ever see. The one regret I had in life has gone. I am an incredibly fortunate woman.

She was enjoying the peace of being alone for a night. She missed the solitude she had become accustomed to before Nicholas and Peter came into her life. Before she had a family, she used to come here to Tanglewood at weekends with only the possums, birds and brush turkeys for company, and been perfectly content. She would read, walk, think and plan her newspaper articles as she swam or lay on the sand listening to the waves crashing in. It was blissful, after being in close contact with so many demanding people during the week.

Peter understood her need to sometimes be alone and tolerated it. But would her daughter understand?

Claudia had already spent several mornings at her newspaper office in Surry Hills. Meg had also arranged with a friend who lectured in journalism at the University of Technology to allow her to sit in on some classes and talk to students to see if Journalism was what she really wanted to do. Claudia, after some initial objections, had agreed. She was meeting some students tomorrow morning before coming up to Tanglewood. Meg felt anxious about the outcome. If the meeting went well Claudia might decide to stay in Sydney and do a course. If it didn't, she might abandon the whole idea of journalism and go back to her hostess job in Tokyo.

'Oh, she'll be all right, won't she Bill?' she said to the dog. 'I do feel better now I've reassured her parents that I haven't kidnapped her. We wouldn't dream of it, would we? I don't think we could cope.' The dog whined in sympathy. 'Though I must admit, I'm getting very attached to her. I don't feel fond of her exactly, just contentedly responsible for her.'

Meg stroked the dog's head and drank her wine. What had her parents meant when they had said, 'She harbours resentment for you?' They had sounded quite pleasant except for that warning. Must feel threatened by me, as Claudia said they were, Meg thought.

The night before, she had spoken to both parents by phone from Lucerne for almost half an hour. 'Harbours resentment', she repeated aloud and the dog looked at her questioningly. Was this their way of telling her to watch it, or Claudia might damage her as she'd damaged them?

Michael had told her he'd been ill with a chronic chest condition since his retirement a few months ago, so they had rented the apartment in Lucerne where the air was good for him. They planned to stay there as long as possible. Jane explained that she had stress-related hypertension. They did not say that either of these illnesses were anything to do with their difficult daughter, but it was implied. Meg had felt sorry for them. They did not seem to have had much joy from being Claudia's adoptive parents.

They were not wealthy, Michael had explained rather glumly, but they'd spent a great deal of money on Claudia. She had been educated at private schools, given special tuition in everything from ballet to horse riding, and when she showed no interest in going to university, had done a variety of short courses ranging from modelling to origami. Unfortunately, she had not yet found what she was looking for. At this he had sighed deeply. Yes, he knew about the job in Japan and was not very happy about it. He admired her desire to be independent, of course, but thought there were more wholesome ways of gaining that freedom.

After five minutes of stiltedly polite conversation about how nice it must be for Claudia to have met Meg after all these years, and how kind it was of Meg to invite her to stay for a short holiday, Jane admitted that Claudia had borrowed their credit cards and recently crashed their new sedan, and had sometimes embarrassed them in front of dinner guests. But this was perhaps because she was a 'wilful young lady' (a nervous giggle here) who sometimes found their company 'dull'. Jane had been sure she would grow out of such high spirits and 'settle down' eventually. She said Claudia could be warm and affectionate as well as headstrong, and hoped, a little tearfully, that she would not stay away from her parents too long.

Meg sighed. She felt sorry for Jane and Michael. Did they know how much they were despised?

'They were utterly depressing, Bill,' she told the dog, who whimpered in sympathy. 'Sad. Very sad. They should have given her a good belting before she was six.' Meg chuckled, then shuddered. Would she have done that? Probably not. Had she ever smacked Nick? She didn't think so. She sighed again, then said cheerfully, 'Do you think Claudia will like Tanglewood, Bill? She'd bloody well better. Come and I'll give you a plate of Pal.'

The retriever drooled in anticipation.

'You'll have to stop dribbling, you know, if you want Claudia to like you.'

He closed his mouth politely.

'Sally really did teach you to understand humans, didn't she, crazy old dog?' She patted him fondly.

Next morning Meg woke early feeling full of energy. There was a mist across the gum trees but she could tell that the sun would shine later. She cleaned the house thoroughly, even shaking the ancient Persian rugs over the balcony, and prepared the ingredients for her famous frittata, an Italian-style savoury tart that was one of the few things she could bake. She made a salad, gathered kindling to start the fire, put bottlebrush, wattle and wild heather in pottery jugs, and then whistled to the dog to go for a walk.

When they reached the cliff overlooking the sea there was mist so thick across Lion Island that at first Meg thought it must be smoke from a bushfire. It nestled like a fleece on the ocean between the headlands. As she watched, the thick white mass moved ever so slightly and then began to lift.

'Did you see the whales?' called an excited girl on the rocks up behind her.

'No! Where?'

'Straight out between Lion Island and those rocks. There are two, a mother and baby. We've been here for hours watching.'

Meg strained to see and sure enough, a long dark-grey back surfaced, not rounded like the pictures she had seen of whales, but straight, like a rock ledge. It had nostrilly knobs, like a dinosaur. It looked prehistoric. Suddenly, a short white spurt of water blasted out of it.

'It's blowing!' yelled the girl to her companion. They were both about fourteen.

'Look! Here comes the baby. Wow! She's teaching it to dive before they go south to the Antarctic.'

'How do you know they're going south?' asked Meg.

'That's what they said on the radio. They've got a 'whale watch'. The whales have been moving along the northern beaches of Sydney all week but we never thought they'd get this far, to our little beach.'

Meg and the girls watched as the baby surfaced, rolled over like it's mother and then tumbled back into the deep.

'Amazing!' said Meg.

'Aren't they beautiful! You can't stop looking.'

Dark fins flashed out of the water, then long straight bodies. They would disappear for whole minutes and then burst up out of the sea again. People were arriving on the cliff above with binoculars and cameras.

'It's a good beach to come to. I'd bring my baby here if I were a whale,' said the first girl.

'So would I,' said Meg.

They laughed together.

As she walked back towards Tanglewood, Meg wondered if she'd ever have such relaxed conversations with her own daughter as she'd just had with these two young strangers.

She was fifty metres from the house when she saw Peter's car turn up into the steep driveway. Bother, she thought. They're at least an hour early. She had wanted to have lunch almost ready and the delicious smells of her baking frittata wafting down the hill to greet them. She hurried on. They had parked the car, were unloading bags and did not see her as she scrambled up the slope behind them. She stopped short to take in the happy domestic scene before she could interrupt it. Peter was helping Nick on with his small backpack. He looked up at his father with an affectionate grin and asked a question that Meg could not hear. Peter answered. Nick looked reassured and began to lead the way up the stone steps through the bush to the house. Peter followed, carrying most of the remaining bags, and Claudia picked up a light basket of fruit and flowers which she balanced playfully on her head. As Peter did not notice this, she called to him to look. He turned around and she wiggled her hips provocatively. 'La cocaracha, la cocaracha!' she sang, imitating Carmen Miranda. He threw back his head and laughed. A bunch of bananas fell out of her basket and he dropped the bags he was carrying to come quickly back down the steps and retrieve it. He placed it gently back in her basket-hat and stood looking down at her. She held his absorbed gaze in what seemed a long, familiar silence. Meg had been about to reveal herself by applauding the Carmen Miranda dance, but now she felt confused and excluded. She kept very quiet. Peter turned and retraced his steps up the hill with Claudia plodding behind him. After a few minutes Meg followed.

Meg and Claudia had been walking together through the national park. Now they sat side by side on a grey rock looking out at nothing but vast sky and water. Far below them the Hawkesbury River was dotted with tiny white sailboats, becalmed in the stillness. The only sound was the drone of a light plane that passed overhead like an insect and then was gone. They watched a speedboat the size of a bath toy leaving a white trail like a spider's web. To the left crouched an ancient, craggy island like a young prehistoric animal, joined to its mother mainland by a long low strip of land. Perched on top of the crag was a lighthouse like a thimble.

'It's so underpopulated, isn't it?' said Claudia, sounding puzzled. 'If this was England we'd have rows of deckchairs and umbrellas on those tiny white deserted beaches. This bush would be cleared away and there'd be hotels and restaurants running all the way down the cliffs to that sea. At the water's edge there'd be piers with bands playing, donkey rides and bingo halls.'

'How appalling!' Meg laughed.

'Why? This is a waste of good land.'

'Not at all. The national park is for everyone.'

'Then where are all the people?' Claudia flung her arms wide.

'Hiking along the tracks.'

'But we've been walking almost an hour and we haven't met a soul! It's extraordinary.'

'We've just got a bit more space than England. Didn't you ever go hiking in the Lake District?'

'Yes,' Claudia shrugged. 'I went to Windermere. But that was civilised, with tea-shops and souvenir places, not wilderness like this, with poisonous snakes and spiders.'

'Oh shut up,' grinned Meg. 'I think you're getting to quite enjoy the Aussie bush.'

'I like the tucker. That damper Peter cooked last night in the ashes of the fire was wonderful. Even the billy tea was okay.'

'See?' Meg patted her hand. 'That's your Oz blood coming through.' Then she threw back her head and laughed.

'What is it?'

'That was showing off. We *never* have damper and billy tea as a rule. We have French bread from the deli and coffee from Nicaragua.'

'You said it was what *all* Australians ate in the bush.'

'It is! The same as *all* the English in pubs drink tepid beer and eat only cold pork pies.'

Claudia smiled, and putting one hand inside the shirt Meg had lent her, pulled out a tattered envelope. 'I've got something to show you,' she said. She handed the envelope to Meg.

'For me?'

'To look at. Not to keep,' Claudia said seriously. Meg opened the envelope and found a newspaper photograph of herself, clipped from an old copy of the *Guardian*. She unfolded the whole page and saw that the photograph was at the top of an article she had written about the massacre in Dili back in November, 1991.

'How did you know who I was?' she asked Claudia. 'This is a year and a half old.'

'I've known who you are for that long.'

'Really? Then why didn't you contact me earlier?'

'I wasn't ready. I wanted to be well. And worthy of you. I was afraid you might reject me.'

'Oh, Claudia,' Meg said gently. 'I'd never have rejected you.'

'You might have, if you'd seen me before I finished therapy. I was a disaster. Paranoid, anti-social, not nice to be around. I know I'm not perfect now but I'm so much better than I was about two years ago.'

'So you contacted the adoption agency then?'

'Yes. They said they'd have to write to you and ask your permission for me to make contact. They did tell me your name and that you were Australian and a few months later I saw this article by an Australian journalist with the same name! You looked a bit young to be my mother, but when I took the article to the social worker at Bedes, she confirmed that it was you. I wasn't sure I could handle making contact with a famous mother who might not want to know me. The social worker assured me that you wouldn't have kept updating your address if you didn't want to know about me. But she said I had to face the fact that once you'd taken a good look you might just dump me again. Of course that's not the way she put it. She was far more tactful, but I knew what she meant.'

'Oh, Claudia,' said Meg sadly. 'I'm so sorry you had to go through all that.'

'That's why I wanted you to know all the worst things about me as soon as we met. I thought, "I'll give her the chance to send me away." Remember how I told you about the hostess job and the way I treated my parents that first morning? I knew that the agency would already have told you about the convictions.' Claudia paused for breath. 'Well, you know all those things and you haven't sent me away yet. So I thought I could safely show you the picture and the article.'

'And you've been carrying this around for a year and a half, waiting to be worthy of me? God!'

'Well, read it. You do sound like a heroine . . .'

'I'm no such thing,' Meg told her quietly.

'I read up all the stuff I could find on East Timor just so as

I'd know what to say to you when we met. And you've only ever mentioned it once.'

Meg didn't know whether to laugh or cry. 'And I was trying to be so careful not to talk too much about my work because I thought you'd be bored. Or think me too earnest.'

'Oh no! I admire what you do. I wish I could be as brave. I want to be a journalist but I've left it so late. The students I met yesterday were so young and they knew so much. I'm twenty-four and I know nothing.'

'Claudia, you're intelligent. If you want to, you can learn all that stuff quickly.'

'Will you teach me? Will you help?'

'Of course. But you'll have to study as well. Go back to school. Do you feel you could do that?'

'If you think I'm capable of it, I could do anything!'

Meg laughed. She remembered Virginia at eighteen telling her and Sally, 'Anyone can do anything if they really want to. I believe that. Do you?' And when they'd looked doubtful and said they could try, Virginia had been angry and said, 'No! That's not enough. Unless we believe it, we'll fail.'

Claudia reminded her a lot of Virginia.

'Well,' demanded Claudia. 'Do you think I'm capable of becoming a top-level journalist, or not?'

'Claudia, how can I possibly . . .' Meg watched her daughter's face collapse like a disappointed child's. 'Yes! I think you could. You've got brains, determination, you're forthright, fond of words. Once you learn the skills you *could* be a successful journalist,' she said with as much conviction as she could muster.

'Thank you. Oh thank you!' And to Meg's surprise Claudia burst into tears, hugged her and then waltzed her round and round on the flat grey rock at the edge of the precipice that fell away hundreds of feet to the quiet waters of the river.

# CHAPTER FOUR

Sally was waiting to have dinner with her estranged husband, Richard, at Merrony's at Circular Quay.

She missed not being able to afford places like this now that she no longer lived with Richard and he, sensing this, always invited her to the restaurants that had been her favourites. He did not mean to tempt her into taking him back by reminding her of what she was missing out on, she felt sure. He was just being generous.

She sat in the window looking out at the silver trains surging by so close you could see the newspaper headlines people were reading and at the harbour full of ferries churning home and the city skyscrapers all lit up. She gazed at all that vitality and density of life that made up the inner city she loved and wondered whether he did perhaps hope to tempt her.

The last time they'd dined together at Merrony's he had talked about buying a high-rise apartment nearby, overlooking the harbour and in walking distance from the Opera House. She had felt a surge of excitement. It was what they had always wanted. The suburbs were for the children, they had said, but when they grew up and it was just the two of them . . . She had simply forgotten for a few seconds that they were estranged and that the apartment would not be for her as well. She had betrayed herself. Her face had lit up and she'd laughed out loud with sheer pleasure. And then she'd had to pretend that the happiness was for him, his plan for himself. 'You'll be able to jog in the Botanical Gardens,' she had said, to show that she was well aware that she was almost no longer his wife, that the divorce was underway and soon their separation would be legal. But he had caught her look of shock. He had tactfully put his head down to concentrate on his dinner. She blushed now at the memory of it.

She enjoyed sitting alone waiting in this restaurant, sipping mineral water and watching the efficient young waiting staff, male and female, in their crisp white aprons swirling across the parquet floor, balancing three or four steaming plates up their arms.

As a student she had worked as a waitress at a boarding house in Lorne during every vacation. The uniforms were dowdy; long black dresses, shapeless aprons and starched white caps which inevitably drooped with the heat from the kitchen after she'd run in and out of it a dozen times. Balancing a heavy tray, she would kick the swing door from the dining room open with one foot and the blast of hot air from the vast ovens would hit her like a furnace. Being only a part-time student waitress and not a full-time professional, she had been allotted the tables furthest from the kitchen, which meant that by the time she placed her orders for roast beef or lamb with the cooks, they had run out of both and only stewed fish was left. She remembered the humiliation of having to tell her guests this news and racing back to the kitchen, hoping to goodness she was in time to at least get the pudding they'd asked for. Usually the edible ones, steamed queen pudding and jellied fruit, were already gone and only prunes with lumpy custard was left. She had hated returning to tell them this. She had felt like buying tins of Ardmona peaches out of her wages and offering those instead. She liked her guests. They were mostly families of sheep farmers from the Western District or wheat farmers from the Mallee. They were polite, appreciative, rather shy people who had worked hard all year and deserved their two weeks holiday by the sea, surfing badly, playing tennis and croquet. They deserved to get more than their third choice on the menu, too. Once, full of indignation, Sally had confronted the head chef, asking why it was not possible to cook more beef and lamb and less fish, which no-one seemed to like. He looked at her through the steam from a vat of boiled potatoes he was mashing with a metal object, his bald red head dripping sweat into the mush. Sally felt the waves of his intense dislike. 'Get outta here why doncha,' he muttered with a sneer. 'Get back ta ya university and don't try ta tell me how ta run my fuckin' kitchen!' His voice had risen in pitch to a scream. Then he'd hurled the metal object, coated in mashed potato, at her head. Sally had ducked and the object had lodged, like some fluffy missile, between two blackened frying pans dangling from hooks behind her. Sally had fled back to her guests bearing more platters of the hated fish. She was in no position to argue with this chef. He had been known to throw knives. He could sack her whenever he chose. She needed the money to live on and pay her university fees and he knew it.

How would the waiters at Merrony's have dealt with an alcoholic head chef like the one at that guesthouse? Sally sipped her mineral water and smiled.

She was enjoying this time collecting her thoughts. Today had been exhausting. As well as her teaching at the Intensive English Centre, she had been trying to organise submissions to protest against the Refugee Review Tribunal's decision to send two of her students back to East Timor.

José and Lola, a brother and sister, were aged sixteen and seventeen. Some years earlier, their parents had been killed by the Indonesian military because of their association with

Fretilin, the independence movement. José, the boy, had joined Loriku, the youth organisation of Fretilin, and his name was on a list of people the Indonesians were questioning. Lola, his older sister, had witnessed a massacre in the Santa Cruz cemetery two years ago and had left school because she was so afraid of being arrested. Many of her friends already had been. An aunt in Australia had sent money so that the children were able to bribe officials and get travel documents. Now, in Sydney, they were being well cared for by this aunt, and planning to enrol in a local high school as soon as they left the Intensive English Centre. But a few weeks ago their application for refugee status had been unexpectedly refused and they were told they would have to return to East Timor. Sally had no doubt that if they went their lives would be in danger.

She had been working back late all this week, sending urgent faxes to people in respected positions in the community and asking them to assist in reversing the Tribunal's decision. There were only a few days left now before the hearing. There had been a positive response from most people, which was a relief. But she still felt outraged by the situation. How *could* they say that José and Lola, who had already been detained, interrogated and beaten by the Indonesians and who had even dared to take part in demonstrations against them since they'd arrived in Australia, 'would not suffer persecution' back in East Timor?

Meg, of course, had been one of the first people 'in a respected position' to protest about the Tribunal's decision. As a journalist, Meg had spent a lot of time over the years either trying to get into East Timor or trying to get safely out. Sally was well aware of the frustrations reporters felt at the restrictions faced by the country since the Indonesian invasion in 1975. Sally wondered now about Meg, who might be working late in her office as she still did some nights, and felt slightly guilty about her own relaxing night she was about to have in an expensive restaurant with Richard.

Not many of her friends would approve of her eating out with a husband who had behaved as Richard had, but Meg wouldn't mind. She'd say it was a bit weak of Sally, but then it wasn't surprising – she was always compassionate to underdogs.

What would Virginia say? Virginia, who was strong and always did what she wanted. She would advise Sally to be careful. Eat with him occasionally and talk if that's what you want, but don't become involved with him again. Never. She would be adamant about that.

The thought of Virginia made Sally irritable again in spite of her good intentions. Such certainty! Such determination to do what *she* wanted. She was going ahead with the art gallery in the rainforest, building it in the most beautiful spot on the eighty hectares of land that her grandparents had left her. She was going to call it Ananda, meaning bliss, and invite well-known painters, potters and sculptors to live and work there in exchange for a few of their artworks. There would be regular exhibitions and collectors from all over the country would flock to the rainforest to buy them. How impractical! What if no-one came? Virginia would lose all the money she'd borrowed to build the beautiful Arthouse. She'd have to sell the property, which she'd worked fifteen years to transform from a cane farm into a garden full of waterfalls, forest pools and even a lake. The old canecutter's houses she'd renovated for the artists to live in would all be lost, too. So much work! A few of the artists had helped but most of the physical work Virginia had done herself. She barely had time for her own painting. Sally admired her but worried about her, too. Virginia was so determined to realise her dream of building this gallery that she borrowed money at random, had even considered allowing some shonky property developers to invest in it, until Meg and Sally had persuaded her not to.

Virginia had told Sally on the phone that her gallery was a work of art. Ephemeral, she had said. A lot of different artists had helped to build it. Some of them had created stained-glass windows, others built the spiral staircase or made wooden tiles for the curved roof that looked like a pagoda. Sally and Meg *must* come for the opening. Sally had said the airfare was too expensive, but perhaps, yes perhaps she would come. In fact she would love to. Then why didn't she just splash out and spend the money? Why couldn't she be more like Virginia? As a young girl she had been spontaneous and full of optimism but life had dealt her a few blows and taught her to be cautious. Was this why she resented Virginia who had never been curbed and still lived for pleasure?

Sally found it hard to accept invitations that were purely for pleasure. So why did she keep on accepting Richard's invitations to dinner, she asked herself? Surely it wasn't just because she enjoyed good food and wine. No, it was something more subtle. She was extricating herself gradually. Or was she waiting to see whether the great change in character that he'd promised would transpire? Perhaps she was waiting to see when he'd fall in love with someone else so she could let him go with a clear conscience. She felt a vague responsibility for him still.

A year after he had run off and left her for another woman, he had returned full of remorse and begged her to take him back. By then Sally had been through the dreadful grief and loss of self-esteem that comes with being rejected by the one you love and had come out the other side feeling rather better. She had decided that the failure of their marriage was not entirely her fault and she shouldn't feel suicidal about it.

It seemed odd, now, that she could have felt so devastated by Richard's leaving her. The marriage had lasted twenty-four years, but once he left she had wanted to be entirely alone with her grief. Meg had let her stay at Tanglewood and Virginia had stayed with her boys in Sydney. Sometimes, during the weeks alone, she had thought of flinging herself off a high rock into the sea. But that would have been too easy. At night she had dreamed of exacting revenge and was alarmed at the violence she'd felt. In the daytime she'd tried to analyse her useless life and work out what to do next. It was at this time that Meg had suggested a therapist.

For a year Sally had visited the therapist twice a week. At first she had resented going, fought against it, threatened after each session to finish up next week. But Meg had calmly persuaded her to continue.

The therapist had revealed to Sally the reasons why she had sunk into such deep depression after Richard left and helped her to work through it. She had always thought of herself as strong and independent, so it was painful to admit that being left by both parents in her adolescent years had affected her profoundly. The terror she felt at the thought of Richard also leaving her would not have been so great, her therapist had said, if she'd had a secure and loving childhood.

When Sally was fourteen, her father, whom she loved and admired, left Sally and her mother, remarried, had a son, and did not see Sally again until she visited him just before he died. By then he was too weak to understand that she no longer hated him for abandoning her, so she had carried the guilt and sadness of this with her.

Sally had spent her teens trying to cope with a mother who was clinically depressed and had threatened suicide many times before she managed to do it. Sally's therapist said that subconsciously she blamed herself for the death. She believed she had not been good enough to make her mother want to stay alive. And this was why Sally herself had sometimes felt suicidal. This was her most shameful secret. She had hated herself for having such thoughts. But since she'd had the therapy, she hadn't had them any more.

Her therapist had said it was not surprising that Sally, in her adult life, had a strong desire to please the people she loved. She was terrified they would leave her. If they behaved irrationally, she'd pretend not to notice and behave extra cheerfully. Her friends saw her as a very positive person. She would overlook her husband's outbursts and put up with any small cruelties he might inflict. She had simply repressed the knowledge of his affairs because it was too painful.

'Why didn't you tell Richard that if he ever had another affair you would leave him?' the therapist had asked her once and she had found the question startling. So logical. But she had never even thought of doing that.

What she had faced gradually was that if she had been able to say such a thing to Richard and mean it, they might still be together.

Just as she had completed her therapy and had even begun to enjoy her independence, Richard had miserably reappeared, promising to change into the sort of husband who'd be worthy of her. Sally had found this touching and had felt great compassion for him but she had told him that she did not want him back. He had been shocked and found her new self-confidence hard to accept. The dinners, she told herself, were a civilised form of weaning him away from her.

She hoped he would meet someone soon. There had been 'dates', though rather unsuitable ones, she thought. For a man who was such a good companion, mildly distinguished and wholly presentable, his tastes in women were odd. He seemed to favour either very good-looking, self-centred, rather silly girls or highly neurotic, near-alcoholic, exhibitionist and self-destructive older women. One of these was an actress named Priscilla Martin.

In her youth, Priscilla had acted in plays by Terence Rattigan and Noel Coward (*Nude With a Violin* was her favourite) and had sung the lead in *Salad Days* and *My Fair Lady*. She had performed with the local theatres of every regional city in Australia. When she grew older she had toured the backblocks, from Bourke to Bega. She was a trouper, a character. She had almost been a star. But now she was tired and a little bitter.

Sally had met her by accident when she called by Richard's flat at Bondi Beach to return a book he had lent her. He had rung her one morning to ask for it back and she had agreed to drop it in on her way to watch their son Steven play basketball. She had asked Richard if he'd like to come and watch the game with her. Steven had made it to the Firsts which was quite an achievement, she explained casually, not exactly wanting to make Richard feel guilty for never having been to watch his son, just to make him mildly uncomfortable. He had been vague about accepting her invitation, saying he was pretty tied up, and when she arrived at the flat she saw why.

On the tiny balcony overlooking the surf and draped in nothing but a piece of batik sat Priscilla. She was a large woman and the material was not quite adequate. It was tied sarong-like in a knot between her breasts and rode up unevenly above her knees. Her feet were bare, her long red hair blowing in the breeze and although it was only ten in the morning she seemed completely drunk.

They had been eating breakfast – strawberries, passionfruit, honeydew melon and champagne. Sally was embarrassed. But Richard, dressed neatly in shorts, shirt and sandals, seemed quite relaxed when he introduced them. 'Priscilla lives a few doors down. She brought me some fruit from her amazing garden.'

Sally nodded, smiled, deposited the book amongst the fruit peel and tried to get out the door quickly. But Priscilla had no intention of letting her escape. She was curious. 'Try this melon, Sally. You simply must.' She hacked a slice off and thrust it at Sally on the point of a dangerous-looking knife. Sally took it, although she wasn't keen on melon. 'And have some champagne. The melon goes *marvellously* with fizz.' She poured a small amount into her own empty glass, tossed it backwards into the sea, laughed wildly and refilled the glass, presenting it to Sally with a flourish. 'There. All clean. Not that I have any germies. It would be a brave germ that tangled with me!' She laughed raucously. And Richard, to Sally's astonishment, joined in. His laughter was quieter, as if he were watching a performance from which he was slightly detached but still warmly appreciative. Was it possible he found this voluptuous, abandoned creature attractive? Priscilla was certainly sensual. Sexy, even. Sally felt enraged. Priscilla threw back her head of falsely red, frizzle-curled hair and laughed so hard Sally thought she would choke. And Richard sat mildly beside her looking entertained.

As she drove off over the hills to the sedate suburb of Waverley, to the safety of a game with rules and adolescent energy spent leaping about for a purpose, the rage evaporated and Sally felt profound relief. She gave a short laugh.

She had been disturbed by Richard's odd behaviour, alarmed by the feverish, fast-talking, over-painted Priscilla in his pristine white flat with its monastic wooden furniture, tasteful rugs and carefully selected paintings (selected by both of them, as a matter of fact; he had asked her to come to the gallery and advise him). She had felt pleased knowing that she had contributed some of her taste to Richard's home. It made her feel content to think of him living there, sailing in his solitary ship at the northern end of Bondi Beach. And now he'd been invaded by a siren, with naked flesh and snake-like hair, bringing her offerings of sickly fruits to tempt him to transform the innocent vessel into a love nest. Sally felt revulsion and indignation which she knew was utterly pathetic. Back came the anger so suddenly she could have howled.

Yes, there was ambivalence surrounding her feelings for Richard.

Priscilla decided she did not like Richard's wife. One shouldn't jump to conclusions after only one meeting, of course. But she had heard enough about Sally from Richard to put her off for life. She was 'a fine person', he said. He admired her. She'd brought up four sons practically on her own and had a career at the same time. She'd always been supportive of Richard, proud of his achievements and loyal to him in spite of his affairs and now, thought Priscilla, even after she'd dumped him, she still dutifully returned his books as soon as he asked for them! She didn't hurl them through the window, smashing glass and vases of flowers. She didn't yell down the phone, 'Come and get them your bloody self!' She returned them pleasantly and made polite conversation with her husband's would-be lover. She was a saint. Sickening.

Sally, Priscilla decided, was one of those women who always made you feel uneasy. She had felt gross sitting on the balcony in only her sarong in front of Sally. Yet a few moments before, she'd felt like a goddess. Sally was judgemental, in spite of her impeccable manners. She'd made Priscilla feel gauche and graceless. So she had *become* gauche and graceless. Sally was a bore. She'd probably never given Richard a decent fuck in his whole married life. Yet he continued to love her, he said, and still hoped to persuade her to take him back. He was deluded, poor darling, and needed rescuing. He was a good-looking man, distinguished in his medical profession and financially quite well-off. A very good catch indeed. What he needed was a few months away from Australia and that beloved wife and family, travelling the Greek islands with Priscilla as his guide. Then, if things were working out between them, she would take him on to Bali, to the village beneath the volcano where she owned a cottage by the lake. She would teach him to swim out into the middle of this bottomless lake that the local people said was haunted. She would take him by boat across to the island on the other side where the locals wouldn't go because their ancestors' skulls were whitening on the hillside and spirits roamed freely. She would take him along the black sandy pathway from her cottage to bathe in the healing warm springs for which the village was famous. Afterwards her servant would grill small silver fish from the lake and serve them with large green beans and red rice. They would sit side by side on batik cushions looking down at the mysterious lake, drinking gin and tonics with ice that the servant would have smashed from a block with the mallet. Richard would think it was heaven. 'You have been my salvation, Priscilla,' he would say.

'Guess who I saw today?' Peter asked Meg as they carried in heavy bags of fruit and vegetables from the market. 'With a glamorous older woman?' He put his load down to open their front door.

'Older and more glamorous than me?'

'Most definitely.'

Meg thought. 'Richard!'

'How did you know?'

'Sally told me that he's seeing some raunchy old siren with flaming red hair.'

'That's a bit rough. I thought she looked quite attractive.'

Meg snorted. 'Her name's Priscilla Mason. She's an actress. I met her once at a party. She told a very funny story. I liked her. But then she drank so much she became abusive. Not just to me. To everyone there. It was pretty ugly. The host put her in a taxi and sent her home but she apparently abused the driver so badly that he dropped her at the police station and she spent the night in the lock-up.'

'Poor thing. Why didn't the host drive her home himself?'

'Because he didn't appreciate being called a pillow-biting, wimpy little cock-sucker with fairies' taste in decor, flossy balls and no culinary skills whatsoever.'

Peter threw back his head and laughed. 'And what did she say about you?'

Meg pushed the door open with her shoulder and

staggered in carrying the bags. 'Think I'm going to let you hear that?' She grinned. 'Poor Richard.'

'Maybe she's cut down on her drinking,' said Peter thoughtfully.

Now it was Meg's turn to laugh. 'You know, Peter, what is absolutely infuriating about you?' He shook his head innocently. 'You think of something nice to say about everyone.'

'Yeah, well,' said Peter in a heavy Norwegian accent, 'Hitler was not such a bad guy and Attila the Hun, I always thought, was pretty much maligned . . .'

Claudia was out seeing a movie on El Salvador with a young man she had met at a lecture on political journalism. They were joining friends for a Thai meal in Glebe afterwards so Meg, Peter and Nick were alone for the evening.

To celebrate this rare time of intimacy they ate dinner by the fire, balancing bowls on their laps and laughing a lot about nothing in particular. Afterwards, while Nicholas was playing in the bath and Peter and Meg were sitting back to back by the fire, Peter said, 'Maybe you're right. That actress, Priscilla, might be bad news for Richard. But why shouldn't he go out with her? He has to start looking around. He'll never leave Sally in peace if he doesn't get a chance to find someone else.'

'So Sally and I should just shut up about his bad taste in women?' Meg smiled.

'Yes, I think so.'

'We should just let him make some terrible mistake? Go off with an alcoholic or a bimbo who'll fleece him of his cash and then dump him like the last one did?'

'Come on, Meg. He's not that stupid.'

'Okay, okay.' Meg shrugged. 'I haven't said a word to him and it isn't as if Sally would say anything to dissuade him from going out with whoever he wants. She's got far too much pride for that.'

'No, but she can look hurt, and that's worse.'

'Or a little bit shocked at his behaviour. She does that to her sons and they shape up pretty smartly. Sally is a tyrant in her own subtle way,' said Meg with approval.

'And you're her accomplice.'

'Thanks,' said Meg.

There was a loud splashing from the bathroom. 'Coming, Nick,' Meg called and dashed off to attend to him. As she soaped his smooth young back her thoughts drifted far away.

'That's good, Mummy. Do it harder,' Nick giggled, but she let the flannel drop into the water, staring into space.

'Mummy!'

She turned to him apologetically. 'Sorry, Nicko. Daydreaming. Now your hair. Ready?' There were squeals.

She rubbed him dry by the fire, smelling his wet, glossy head and his warm, clean limbs. She had almost left having a child until too late. Her life had been so full of work that she had kept on postponing the most important thing of all until, at forty-three, finding herself accidentally pregnant to a man she no longer loved, she'd decided to go ahead and have the child anyway. And then, just before Nick's birth, she had met Peter.

She smiled absent-mindedly, remembering the way he had been shy with her at first and how she had been too embarrassed to mention that she was pregnant and he had noticed but pretended not to. 'We were so coy about you,' she said to Nick, who repeated the unfamiliar word, trying it out. 'Coy, coy. What's a coy boy?' Meg made a face, dropping her gaze and fluttering her eyelids to show him and he laughed, delighted by her silly expression. 'Do coy boy again!'

Despite the fact that Peter was fifteen years younger than Meg, they had fallen in love and he had been with her ever since, although they had not married until Nick was three years old. Now, a year later, they felt like a family.

Meg had been surprised at the way she had changed. The committed career woman, the journalist who was used to leaping on a plane with a few hours notice and heading off to war zones, whose bags were permanently packed, who thought the adrenalin rush of danger and the fierce competition to get the story before anyone else was normal, had discovered the delights of family life. A simple meal by the fire, shopping at Paddy's Market on weekends, gardening, taking Nick to the park for a swing, rubbing him dry by the fire like this – all the activities she would once have expected to bore her cross-eyed – were now the things she looked forward to.

And Claudia, she was relieved to admit, who had at first been so disruptive to the small family, was now tolerating their contentment and beginning to feel part of it. Meg and Peter had tried hard to include her in everything they thought she might enjoy but looked forward to the rare times, like tonight, when she took herself off to do something with people her own age.

'I'll make pancakes and we'll eat them with our fingers by the fire, shall we?' said Peter, coming in. Nick nodded enthusiastically. 'Can I have banana in mine?'

Peter, who had also enjoyed the challenge of covering international events but who had yearned for some time to live a less hectic life, had watched Meg's transformation with relief. He had not been sure when they met if she would ever slow down and become even mildly domesticated. But the birth of Nicholas had changed her. Peter still believed he did most of the housework although he enjoyed being in charge of these things. Now that he'd renovated the garage in the garden and transformed it into a studio he worked increasingly from home. And having the waters of the harbour lapping against the low sandstone garden wall he had begun to indulge in his childhood fascination with boats. He'd told Meg stories of the days he'd spent as a teenager racing tiny sailboats off the coast of Oslo. This was what he said he missed most since leaving Norway. Now, at weekends, he often went next door to the boatyard where ocean-going yachts and luxury launches were renovated, to lend a hand with some sanding or help haul a boat into dry dock. The boatyard owners were looking out for a second-hand boat for Peter, something classy, made of wood, not fibreglass. He was doing a photo essay on the craftsmen in the boatyard and the little bay that was their workshop. Meg was pleased to see him so absorbed and promised to learn to sail when he bought his old boat.

She was also trying to be less of a workaholic. Her newspaper was in the process of being changed from a weekly to a monthly and she had begun to delegate tasks she once would never have entrusted to anyone but herself. Nick and Peter had humanised her, she said. She loved them dearly.

Nick's biological father, who had a wife and family of his own, had shown almost no interest in him. Peter was the man he called Daddy and whose surname he had chosen. Meg had offered hers but Nick had politely declined. And McIntyre-Seburg was too hard to say, he'd decided. Nick Seburg was the name the four-year-old preferred.

As Meg started to help him into his pyjamas Nick suddenly pulled away and said, 'Wait! Before I put them on I'll do a dance. It's a wild boy's dance. Watch me, Daddy! Watch, Mum!'

'Okay. Just for a minute or you'll catch cold,' Meg said. She and Peter sat back on the floor and waited. The 'wild boy' was something new.

Nick crouched low and hummed a strange dirge-like note. Then, using the striped towel as a cloak, he leaped up and swished it menacingly at unseen enemies. Was he a Zulu warrior? The chanting became a chatter. A monkey-man? He danced rhythmically, lifting his feet high in a primitive stomp. There was some taunting of the enemy with an imaginary spear, and much eye-rolling. Perhaps they'd watched a documentary at nursery school. After a few minutes the dance finished abruptly. Nick slumped on his back across a large cushion, naked except for the towel that he used to mop his brow with.

Meg and Peter clapped loudly and Nick, enjoying the applause, just lay there with his eyes staring straight ahead and his limbs collapsed at odd angles as if he were in a trance.

As Meg looked down at him a strange thing happened. He slowly transformed from a golden-skinned child with hair like pale silk to a dark boy with black hair. The towel flung across one side of his face became a scarf with which he had tried to stop the blood that poured from his head and the cushion he lay back on, eyes staring straight ahead, was a gravestone. He was still a child of four but he was Timorese and had just been shot during a demonstration at the Santa Cruz cemetery.

'What's the matter?' Peter was holding her arm and staring hard at Meg.

She shook herself out of the trance. The Timorese child had gone and Nick stood looking up at her anxiously. 'You wouldn't answer us, Mum.'

# CHAPTER FIVE

Meg had not expected to witness a massacre. Three months before her marriage to Peter in January, 1992, she had been in Dili, the capital of East Timor. Her thoughts, as she boarded the plane from Darwin to travel the hour and a quarter across the Timor Sea to her destination, were still on her wedding plans. The party was to be held in their own garden by the water. Guests had been invited, trestle tables and white linen cloths borrowed, food promised by friends who could cook and music promised by friends who could play. It was to have been a modest wedding but the guest list was growing rather long.

Meg was wondering whether it mattered that there were now seventy guests instead of forty, and had just decided it would be worse to hurt the feelings of thirty friends than to give them a little less to eat and drink. She looked out of the plane window at the rugged mountains covered in dense forest and reprimanded herself for being so self-indulgent. Hidden in that isolated jungle were the 'bandits', the 'chicken thieves', the 'disturbers of the peace', as the Indonesian military called them: thousands of Timorese guerilla fighters and their families.

Some of them had been living there since 1975. Many were civilians who'd fled with the Fretilin forces to the mountains after the Indonesian invasion. Others were a new generation of educated young people who had recently escaped from the towns. Their struggle for independence and freedom was brave but their lives were bitterly hard.

Officially, Meg was on her way to cover a 'goodwill' visit from the Portuguese, who had once ruled East Timor. But in fact she was going there to find out how the resistance was faring and to report it in her newspaper. She had agreed to do radio interviews and to write some articles for foreign newspapers as well.

Meg had been to Dili twice before. The first time was in March, 1975, a few months before the Indonesian invasion, after which the borders were closed and two hundred thousand people had allegedly died as a result of war, famine and disease. In October, 1989, taking advantage of what appeared to be a new era of openness and pretending that she was there to cover the visit of Pope John Paul, she had returned to East Timor. What she really hoped for was an interview with the leader of the East Timorese Resistance, Xanana Gusmao, who had gone into hiding with the guerrillas and hadn't been interviewed since 1975. Although she had come close to finding him, the military had become suspicious of her and she'd felt that she must abandon her attempt in order to protect Gusmao.

For the next two years Meg had tried without success to get a visa to go back and report on the situation in East Timor but journalists, particularly Australians who had criticised the proposed Timor Gap Treaty, in which Australia and Indonesia planned to divide the profits of East Timor's rich oil and natural gas reserves in the Timor Sea, were not welcome.

By September, 1991, however, the situation had changed. Military cooperation between Indonesia and Australia had resumed and the Australian Broadcasting Commission, which had been banned for ten years for reporting unfavourably on East Timor, had been allowed to base a correspondent in Indonesia.

East Timor was to be visited by an important delegation from Portugal and the Indonesians were anxious to create the impression that in the country they had invaded, the resistance was unpopular and the people were now 'integrated', better educated than they had been under Portuguese colonial rule, economically secure and happier. Meg applied to enter the country on a tourist visa and, to her surprise, was accepted.

Peter had wanted to go with her. 'I could protect you and get some good pictures at the same time,' he'd offered ruefully.

'That's a contradiction.' Meg had laughed. 'I'd rather you were here protecting Nicholas and trying to cut down the guest list for our wedding,' she'd said firmly. Reluctantly he had agreed to stay behind.

Meg thought nostalgically of Peter at home in their cottage by the harbour, playing ball with Nicholas and Bill, the old golden retriever that Sally had lent them because he was devoted to young children and hers were growing up. Smiling as she thought of Peter nurturing the garden to make things bloom for their forthcoming wedding, Meg had arrived in East Timor alone.

She had taken an ancient taxi through the steamy streets of Dili and checked into the Hotel Turismo. This was where journalists, the military, well-to-do tourists and visiting dignitaries stayed. It was a relic from the days of Portuguese colonial rule and had starched white tablecloths, gracious curved arches and a courtyard covered in flowering bougainvillea. Recently it had also been the setting for protests, arrests and bloody beatings.

A small advance team from the United Nations was being allowed into Dili to finalise arrangements for the Portuguese visit in the first week of October and Meg had managed to coincide with them. They would probably be staying here, at the Hotel Turismo. She would meet them and perhaps be able to exchange information. The advance team would be more likely than the official delegation to see whether students and dissidents were still being persecuted.

Meg had imagined she might see some skirmishes but she had not been not prepared to see killing.

As she wandered the streets of Dili she noticed that a mass of red and white Indonesian flags were being distributed by soldiers.

But calling on her old friend the Bishop, who lived a few doors from the Hotel Turismo, she learned that the East Timorese people were secretly preparing their own flags to wave at the Portuguese delegation. Even though a lot of agitators had already been arrested and hidden from sight, there would be an ugly confrontation between the military and those who believed in 'Independence or Death', the Bishop predicted. He said he had heard that just outside the town bulldozers were working at night to dig massive pits.

'What on earth for?' Meg had asked, although she thought she knew.

'While the delegation is here the military will pretend to tolerate those who demonstrate and wave banners for freedom, but once they leave, the crackdown will come.' He shrugged sadly. 'By then you and other journalists will have left us so the world will never know how many lie in the burial pits.'

'It's probably just a bluff. A plan to intimidate the demonstrators. Burial pits?' Meg had shaken her head in disbelief. But next day she'd hired a battered taxi on the pretence of sightseeing and travelled twenty kilometres to the village of Tibar. She discovered that what the Bishop had told her was true.

A few days later, on October 27, the people of Dili learned that the Portuguese visit had been cancelled.

The security forces, suddenly released from their role of benign peacekeepers, went in search of action. They'd discovered a group of high school students whom they'd accused of being dissidents. The students had run away and taken refuge in the grounds of a church but they'd been quickly surrounded. In terror for their lives, some had begun tolling the church bells while others knelt and prayed. Meg, exploring the streets of Dili in her role as a tourist, had heard these bells and noticed that they sounded urgent. Shortly afterwards she'd found out that the soldiers had disregarded the sanctity of the Church of St Antonio de Motael and had shot one student dead and arrested dozens more.

Dili had been very quiet for a few days after this. Meg had felt a strong urge to stay on to see what might happen next. The signs were ominous – the death of the student, the arrests, the stories of detainment, rape and torture that she'd heard from ordinary people who gathered for safety at the Bishop's house. Almost every family has someone who has suffered or disappeared.

Perhaps she stayed on because she wanted to see that the horror of the burial pits, which she had discreetly photographed, was a lie. Every day she expected to be visited by the Indonesian police and told that now the Portuguese visit was cancelled she must leave. But days passed and she was approached by no-one. She pretended to be enjoying her life as a tourist, visiting the few places of interest: the port, the museum and the church. She took pictures with her tiny Instamatic camera, even sketched a little, but never carried either notebook or tape recorder.

Meg kept in close touch with the Bishop, visiting him for afternoon tea in the dark-walled parlour with its high bookshelves and ornate wooden furniture. The drapes were heavy and deep red, blocking out the light and keeping visitors safe from prying eyes. It had been a grand room once but now was shabby, the carpet threadbare and the cushions worn. The Bishop served tea from fine china cups, a little cracked, and made his own biscuits which were hard and very sweet. At these quaint formal teas she would often meet students who spoke Tetum, the Timorese language, in defiance of the Indonesians who had banned all languages but Bahasa. They told her there were now seven burial pits on the outskirts of Dili.

At six o'clock on the morning of November 12, she went with some of these students to the memorial mass for the boy who had been shot in the grounds of the church. She walked with the procession of hundreds that gradually increased to thousands, through the streets of Dili and on to the Santa Cruz cemetery. There were school children, old women in traditional dress, people of all ages waving banners in Portuguese and English. She felt safe amongst them, playing the role of a tourist swept along by the festive spirit. As they passed the Governor's office the chants of 'Viva Independencia!' and 'Viva Xanana!' were deafening.

Later she heard that somewhere in the crowd an army major had torn a banner from a Timorese and had been stabbed in retaliation. Soldiers had then stabbed two teenage girls. But Meg had seen nothing of this. She had been caught up in the euphoria of the chanting.

The huge crowd of mourners was led through the high white stone gates of the cemetery by young girls carrying armfuls of flowers. A student with a megaphone relayed the prayers to those who could not get inside. Meg photographed all of this. When the ceremony was over people started moving off, walking back along the dusty road towards the town.

But suddenly they were blocked by soldiers. They arrived in truckloads, wearing camouflage gear and carrying automatic weapons. Hundreds more wearing dark green uniforms came jogging from the direction in which the procession had come.

The mourners stood in silence, waiting. They seemed stunned. Then some of them began rushing back into the cemetery. The soldiers started firing.

Meg had not managed to get inside so she was able to run out of the direct line of fire and throw herself down behind some large stones at the side of the road opposite the gates. She watched in disbelief as the automatic firing felled people as they ran in all directions. Bullets bounced off gravestones and made holes in the walls that surrounded the cemetery. People lay bleeding or staggered about screaming, blood pouring from their wounds but still trying to support each other – young girls, old people, children of four and five. The gunfire continued sporadically for half an hour. Then she saw soldiers move in and begin kicking those who were not wounded and batter them with rifle butts. The screams were replaced by moans and prayers.

Later, three army trucks appeared and were loaded with

the bodies. She photographed this quickly. Then a water-truck arrived and soldiers washed away the blood.

Although security forces had blocked off the whole area, and helicopters were whirling low above, Meg managed to convince the soldiers on duty she was a tourist who simply wanted to get back to her hotel. She said she had got caught up in the procession by accident. They let her go but took away her camera.

Back at the Hotel Turismo, still in a state of shock, she had talked in hushed tones to a British photographer who had been inside the cemetery and said he was lucky to be alive. His camera had been smashed and he had been badly beaten, but before this had happened, he'd managed to bury some rolls of film amongst the gravestones. He was hoping to get back there and retrieve them. He, like Meg, was determined to get out of Dili as fast as possible and report the atrocities in the world press. He said that his friend, a cinematographer who been outside the cemetery, had managed to get some footage, and he would see that Meg got a copy, provided they all managed to get out alive.

That evening, Jakarta issued a press statement saying nine people had died in Dili. But a few days later, when the handful of western journalists who had been visiting Dili on tourist visas returned to their countries, a different story appeared on TV screens, radios and in newspapers around the world.

In spite of her photographs, Meg was never able to prove that the burial pits had been used but she wondered where the three trucks outside the Santa Cruz cemetery, loaded with what must have been hundreds of bodies, had taken them.

'Please don't go back there!' Peter said.

He lay in bed beside Meg but he did not look at her. It was later on the same evening that she had seen the vision of Nicholas, her fair-haired son, transformed into a Timorese child, stretched across a headstone, trying to mop up his blood with a scarf.

Meg stared at Peter. In the past he'd been tolerant of her need to go to dangerous places but lately he had changed.

'You've got a child, not to mention a husband, who is terrified every time you go off to some godforsaken war zone for the betterment of mankind,' he said angrily. 'I can understand why you did it in the past, when you were young and unencumbered but now . . . Is it fair, do you think?'

'No, it isn't fair,' Meg said calmly. 'But it's what I do. It's my job.'

'Bullshit! Your job is journalism. You're an editor now. There must be some mad young thing on your paper who'd do the hero stuff as well as you if you'd just offer them the chance.'

Peter wasn't usually so aggressive. Was he jealous, Meg wondered? Did he resent the fact that she hadn't lost her nerve over the years? Or was she really expecting too much of him?

'You're right, it *isn't* fair,' she said. 'I do expect you just to take over when I go; look after Nicholas, Claudia, the dog, the house, friends, the bills . . .'

'And do my job?'

'And do your job.' She sighed. 'I'm selfish.'

He nodded grimly. 'And when you come home you're different.'

She gave him a questioning look.

'Cut off. Closed. Nobody home.'

'Am I? You've never said that before.'

'Well, you are.' He looked hurt. 'Nicholas can't get through to you either. He says you go weird. Tonight was awful.'

'I'm sorry,' she said.

She had occasionally confided in other journalists who'd worked in countries ravaged by war and famine and they had agreed that they couldn't share the horrors they had seen. Meg found that ghastly images flashed up before her when she was most relaxed; when happiest, like this evening.

What could she do but cut off for a moment?

'It's seeing death. You think you've hardened yourself to it. But it haunts you when you least expect it.' Meg put her arm around Peter and hugged him close.

Meg woke up at three the next morning and stared at the ceiling. She listened to the waves lapping against the jetty as the tide came in and to the clunk, clink of sailboats rocking on their moorings in the little bay just beyond the back gate. She heard the fruit bats in the old Moreton Bay fig tree in their garden screech and whirl. She thought of her son asleep in his red tubular steel bunk next door wearing his banana pyjamas, with the old golden retriever asleep on the rug below him. She thought of Claudia, her new-found daughter, and she looked across at Peter asleep beside her and felt that she had never been as happy in her whole life. How could she risk losing any of this? It was madness to keep on going away. It was selfish. Peter was right.

But then she thought of Xanana Gusmao, who had been captured last November, placed in isolation and prevented from presenting his defence plea which the judge had dismissed as 'irrelevant'. At his trial, to which no foreign journalists were permitted, he was sentenced to twenty years in an Indonesian prison. Recently he had been reported saying that he accepted East Timor as being part of Indonesia. He had allegedly encouraged his followers, still hiding in the bush, to surrender and do the same. This so-called confession was a sham, she felt sure. The trial had been a farce. If there was any earthly way a journalist could get inside East Timor and report the truth of what was happening, she wanted to do it.

'You really think you should go?' said Sally. 'With your record as a journalist, it's most unlikely the Indonesian Government will give you a visa.'

'I'm not even going to apply for one,' said Meg. 'I have another idea.' Sally waited but she said nothing more. Apparently she did not intend to.

Meg was driving Sally to the Leichardt pool. Sally had said she admired Meg's self-discipline in swimming every morning before she started work and now Meg had persuaded her to come, too. Sally was not sure she would enjoy this, particularly as it was nearly winter and the pool, although heated, was open to the elements.

'How long will you be gone?' Sally asked as they drove past the mental asylum that had recently become a Writers' Centre.

'Two weeks or less. No time at all. It'll be quite safe. I won't be on my own.'

'Is Peter going, too?'

'Meg laughed. 'He'd love to, but no. Someone has to mind Nick. And Claudia.'

'What will Claudia do while you're not there to entertain her? She could come to work with me!' Sally suggested enthusiastically.

'No, Sal. Teaching Vietnamese and Cambodian kids English for half the week and helping them find jobs and places to live isn't really her scene. Claudia is not exactly the nurturing type.'

Sally shrugged. 'It could be exciting for her, finding out about our ethnic communities. I could introduce her to some friends at Cabramatta. There's a fascinating community of mixed races out there. If she wants to be a journalist, surely she'd find that interesting.'

Meg looked doubtful. 'She's not quite as keen on being a journalist as she was.'

'Really? That's a shame. You've worked so hard at getting her into courses and helping her with ideas for her first article. What happened?'

'I think she discovered it was quite hard work!' Meg laughed. 'Never mind. She's still mildly interested. But drifting more towards fashion now, she says.'

Sally pulled a face. 'Well, I expect she must do what she wants. You've certainly taken her out to a lot of stimulating places: galleries, law courts, parliament, concerts, lectures, picnics, lunches with foul-mouthed, funny journalists. I heard she was quite a hit at Kinsela's.'

Meg gave a hoot of laughter. 'Poor Nathan and Paul! They were so good to take her there and introduce her to their friends. I gather they got a bit more than they bargained for.'

'No, no. They said they had a ball. Once they got past the "door bitch". My sons don't often go to such exclusive night spots, they told me. Probably a lie. But Claudia encouraged them to stay and dance till dawn!'

Meg smiled. 'I like her energy. She'll have a go at anything.

Except sporting activities. She refuses to play ball with Nick and she wouldn't dream of coming swimming.'

Meg parked the car and they walked fast, bracing themselves against the wind, down the slope to the pool.

Sally shivered. 'How warm is this water?'

'Twenty-seven degrees. Once you're in, it's fine. Like a tepid bath. You don't notice once you start swimming.'

Unlike Meg, Sally was not a strong swimmer. She looked at the serious rubber-capped heads in goggles ploughing up and down the pool, two or three to a lane, and her heart sank. Thick steam rose from the water in great white clouds and evaporated into the cold blue sky.

'I brought you some goggles,' Meg said, handing her a green pair. Meg snapped hers on over her cap. Being tall and athletic she was not in the least intimidated by the professionals in the pool.

'I've never had much success with goggles,' Sally said. 'They tend to leak and then I panic. I don't really need them anyway. I only do breast-stroke.'

Meg laughed. 'Really?'

'Yes, I'm like those funny Europeans.'

'Didn't you ever learn to do the crawl? At school?'

'I tried. But I was always terrified of putting my head under water, so I never got the breathing right.'

'I thought all Australian kids were forced to overcome that fear.'

'Not me. I was so ashamed I couldn't do it that when I was about fourteen I got myself a holiday job so I could pay for swimming lessons from a proper coach, but he just made me do lap after lap with a kicking board for the first two lessons so I decided not to waste any more of my hard-earned cash.'

'Poor Sal.' Meg's parents had paid for her swimming coaching from the time she was six. She knew Sally's background had been different. 'Try these goggles anyway. They don't leak and you'll get further on each stroke if your put your face under occasionally.'

Meg dived in and streaked off down the 'fast' centre lane and Sally walked down the steps of the lane nearest the edge of the pool, which she supposed was used for geriatrics doing aqua aerobics. She pulled on the goggles and dipped her face in the water to prove that they leaked. They didn't. She took a deep breath and struck out, holding her head high above water. It was pleasant swimming along looking around at the streamlined bodies surging past and being enveloped by the steam as it rose towards the gum trees that were backlit by a watery sun. She watched large silver planes passing overhead on their way home from Bangkok and New York and Tokyo. Sally estimated that one plane crossed the pool every two minutes. After a few laps, finding she was not as exhausted as she thought she might be, Sally swam a few strokes with her face under water to test Meg's theory that this would make her go faster. It did seem easier and because she could see well through the goggles she didn't feel panicky. How odd, she thought. All I've needed all these years was a decent pair of goggles.

She noticed that a man in a Coca-cola cap and thick red goggles in the lane beside her was also doing breast-stroke, submerging himself out of sight with every powerful stroke. As they were parallel she decided to pace herself against him. She forced herself along, half choking with the effort but determined to be as fast he was. At the end of the lap she clung to the railing gasping for breath but grinning triumphantly to herself because she had kept up. The man swung himself out of the water. He was at least eighty years old.

'Did you know that our mother's having swimming lessons?'

'What! At her age?' said Toby, who was thirteen. 'But she can swim. I've seen her.'

'Only breast-stroke,' said Steven. 'And a bit of backstroke, but she nearly drowns herself. You know how she looks. Embarrassing.'

'I know.' Toby put his homework to one side and said seriously, 'I thought people of that age were, you know, too old to learn new skills.'

'Not swimming, stupid. Only things like working computers and pre-programming the video.'

'Ah,' said Toby.

Steven and Toby, Sally's youngest sons, continued to share a bedroom even though their two older brothers had recently left home and there was now a room available each. They needed each other's company, Toby felt, because the house had become suddenly quiet and rather lonely. It wasn't just the absence of his older brothers but the other kids, too. He missed them. The house had to be sold. He knew that. It was too expensive for just his mother to keep. Still, he wondered sometimes why his father, who was well-off, had insisted on having his share of the house right now when it had been such a marvellous communal house full of kids who really needed it.

Steven, who was sixteen, liked the peace now that nearly everyone had gone. He needed it to study. Next year he had to pass the Higher School Certificate. He hadn't ever really enjoyed the chaos that had reigned after their father left home. Before that everything had been neat and ordered. Rigid, perhaps. But he hadn't minded. Lists of chores stuck on the fridge door. Meals served exactly on time. Homework timetables and sports practice days taped to the desks in each boy's bedroom. (It had been his mother who organised all this, not his father, but after he left she had changed.) Big noisy family meals with friends and relatives were held only at weekends. During the week the house had run like a well-oiled machine and Steven had loved it.

Then had come the eruption. His father had walked out with two suitcases one night without even saying goodbye. A few months later his mother, who'd pretended she was fine after he left, had taken herself off to Meg's beach house to have a minor nervous breakdown. They'd been minded by their mother's mad artist friend, Virginia. Actually, Steven had to admit after a week of getting used to her, he quite liked Virginia. She made them all laugh and she cooked things they'd never eaten before like rabbit stew with prunes and chilli pasta. She had taught them all to cook and to shop once a week at the fish market in Pyrmont which was more fun than the local supermarket as well as being cheaper, so they'd had a bit of money left over to spend on whatever they liked. Of course they'd all had to iron their own school shirts which had been a drag but she'd taught them to paint and sketch and carve things out of wood and she'd let them do their homework round the fire in the kitchen. Dogs had been allowed to sleep on beds and friends were able to stay whenever they liked. She'd taught the older boys how to drive her car and dance the Lambada. They'd neglected their sport and their school work had suffered quite a lot. But when their mother came back she seemed to approve of the changes, so things had never really got back to normal.

And then the orphans had arrived. His mother had always been compassionate towards lost or wounded birds and animals. But this was more serious. These were kids and they'd actually moved in. Four of them in the space of a few weeks. Her own sons had been obliged to share bedrooms. Steven had resented this. His three brothers, who were inclined after initial doubts to accept their mother's madcap schemes, had thought of it as an adventure or as their duty because they were a middle-class white Australian family who'd never had to experience anything like the horrors that these Vietnamese and Cambodian boat kids had suffered.

And so they had all lived together for nearly two years, four natural kids and four foster ones.

There had been good times, of course. They had all learned things about each other's cultures and families. Once they'd got to know each other they had laughed a lot and shared the chores, cooking up bizarre mixtures and teasing each other about their peculiar eating and washing habits. Nathan, his older brother who wanted to become an actor, had done brilliant imitations of everyone. But they'd felt loyal to each other and protective. Paul, the eldest, had learned some Vietnamese from Lanh, who was the only girl, and he had taught her to play the violin and then they had fallen in love. That had been okay. They had all approved of Lanh. She looked about twelve and so innocent but she was nineteen and pretty strong-minded. Once someone had painted slogans in red paint right across the high sandstone fence at the front of their house, 'Go home, slants,' and, 'Australians who shelter dog-eaters should be strung up.'

Steven and Paul had been so angry they had wanted to go out and find the offenders and beat them up. But Lanh had told them not to. 'We must just remove the graffiti as quickly as possible so as not to shame them,' she had said in her serious way. 'It is ignorance that makes people do such a thing and we should feel sorry for them.'

Another time, Vinh, Lanh's younger brother, who'd been brought up in refugee camps where he'd learned a few bad habits, had stolen their mother's only valuable jewellery, a diamond engagement ring and a long pearl necklace, and had then run away. Nathan and Paul had gone after him, found him sleeping out in the back streets of Darlinghurst and had managed to buy both pieces back from the jeweller he'd sold them to, even though they'd had to pay much more than Vinh had sold them for. He had returned to the house a few nights later with the money he owed them and Paul and Nathan had not asked how he came by it. Sally had never discovered the loss of her jewellery and had believed Vinh when he told her that he had been spending a few days away with relatives in Cabramatta.

Well, now things were different. Vinh was studying Tourism at the Bankstown Institute, while he ran his own business cleaning houses. He was renting a flat with his cousin and he owned a car. In five years he'd be an important entrepreneur, Steven predicted. He could just imagine Vinh driving a Mercedes with personalised number plates.

The Cambodian boys, Long Mau and Son Cao, whose mother had died and whose father had been tortured in a re-education camp, had just finished school and they both had jobs: Long Mau as assistant to the chef in a Cambodian restaurant in Newtown and Son Cao in a bookshop in the city. They were sharing a house in Darlinghurst with some friends and visited their father regularly, even though he didn't always recognise them.

Lanh and Paul had been 'an item' for over two years now and had finally moved out to live together in a tiny flat above a Chinese herbalist's shop in the Haymarket, just near the Sydney Institute of Technology where Paul was studying Communications and Lanh was doing Accounting. Paul had also become involved in planning a new television current affairs show produced by young people. Steven suspected it was going to have a heavy emphasis on politically correct topics like racism, sexism, drugs, the Australian Republic and homosexuality. He thought it was a waste that Paul had not used his brain to get into Law at Sydney University, after which he would at least have had the chance of earning a decent living. Law was what Steven aimed to do.

Nathan, who was eighteen, had auditioned for NIDA, the National Institute of Dramatic Art, and narrowly failed to get in. He had been told he had a lot of talent as an actor but was too young and should spend a few years gaining experience before auditioning again. This had depressed him greatly. How could he get experience without any training? He'd started working as a kitchen-hand in the same Cambodian restaurant as Long Mau. He was saving frantically for an airfare to New York, where he said he'd go and clean dunnies if he had to while he learned to be a method actor with Lee Strasburg. He rented a dilapidated room not far from the Actors' Centre in Surry Hills so that he could take classes while he saved for New York. Steven thought it was a fantasy. He was afraid Nathan might drift into drugs if he didn't get into NIDA next year.

Steven was a worrier about his family. He worried about Paul and Lanh marrying. They were too young and although he didn't want to seem racist, Vietnamese rarely married Australians. How would Paul cope with her uncles and cousins in Cabramatta, who were so possessive? Lanh was fine; he liked her a lot, but she was so dependent on Paul and so determined to marry him. Paul would never get to see the world or have fun with friends once he was married.

Steven was concerned that Nathan was too intense. He smoked continuously. Unless he had some success in acting soon he'd become self-destructive, get into bad company, sacrifice his talent.

Steven worried about Toby, his youngest brother, because he was naive and too trusting, and he worried about his mother having to leave the house in Hunters Hill that they'd all grown up in. She'd said she didn't mind. It was time to go. They didn't need all that much space now it was just the three of them. But for the past fifteen years he'd watched her scraping wallpaper, sanding floors and painting ceilings, restoring the place lovingly for her family. She'd created the wild, wonderful garden they'd all played in, too. She was lying. She did mind leaving. But she wasn't going to make a fuss. She'd already given the dog away to Meg who had a garden. Steven knew his mother would hate living in some tiny terrace with bars on the windows in the inner city.

Steven worried about his mother and his father, too. He still couldn't understand why they'd split up. They didn't hate each other. They had dinner together about once a month, for God's sake. When they talked on the phone they laughed like old lovers, which was what they were, he supposed glumly. When his father occasionally dropped by he was as shy and awkward as some new boyfriend. It was sickening.

Steven had been angry when they broke up. It wasn't just the inconvenience, the insecurity. It was the hurt. He had been in love with their love for each other. Did that sound crazy? And when it died a bit of him did, too.

As his father had been, Steven was competitive and good at his schoolwork. He'd chosen to stay on at St. Mark's, a private school, when his brothers had opted to change to a high school two years ago to help the family budget (and for ideological reasons in Paul's case; he was sickeningly correct about such things).

What would his schoolfriends think when he moved out of the comfortable big house in Hunters Hill to some hovel in Redfern?

Steven worried that he was not good-looking enough to ever get the kind of girl he wanted. His older brothers were spunks, charmers who'd never had any bother. But the lucky gene pool had evidently dried up by the time he came along. Not that he was ugly. Just tall and skinny, clumsy and covered in acne. It made him want to puke every time he looked in the mirror. His mother was always telling him it was temporary, 'the gangling stage'. She took him to the doctor who prescribed pills and expensive creams for his skin. How come his brothers had never needed such treatment?

The kind of girl he dreamed of having was Claudia. Hopeless. She pitied him so she didn't bother flirting with him like she did with Paul and Nathan. Claudia flirted with just about everyone. Paul and Nathan didn't take it seriously. Steven fantasised that he was the spunk of the family and his brothers were the 'uncoes': *Claudia came out of the bathroom draped in nothing but a white towel. There was steam rising from her. Steven held out his hand. She smiled and the towel fell to the floor . . .*

This fantasy made him feel less depressed about life.

# CHAPTER SIX

Sally sat at one end of the large old kitchen table and surveyed her four sons eating breakfast. It was a Sunday morning and they had agreed to meet at home to plan the forthcoming party which was to be both a farewell to the house and a welcome to Meg's new daughter.

'You're an intelligent lot but you all treat each other like idiots,' Sally observed with affection.

'Yes, you're right. We feel more comfortable with fellow idiots,' said Nathan, who was dark, slim, playful and had a wonderfully expressive face. His eyelashes were the longest Sally had ever seen on a young man. When he was a child, people had remarked that he was far too beautiful for a boy.

'I suppose you're aware that some people think we're peculiar because we seem to enjoy each other's company more than the company of anyone outside the family,' said Paul. At twenty-one he was the eldest and the most responsible. He was tall and fair, with fine hair that he had grown to shoulder length since leaving home; the right image for a lead singer and guitarist in a popular university band. Whenever he visited home Paul paid Sally the courtesy of tying his long hair back, which she found touching.

'Did Lanh think we were peculiar?' asked Toby perceptively. Although he was thirteen he still looked like a child. Slower to mature than his brothers, he was wide-eyed, sensitive, generous and had a lot of friends.

'Yes, but she doesn't any more,' Paul said.

'I know she did at first. She was hurt by us,' Toby looked apologetic.

'Well, of course she was,' Paul replied. 'We were bloody rude, making all those stupid family in-jokes that no-one but us could understand.'

'I know,' said Steven, 'but they were fun.' Steven's hands and feet had suddenly grown too big, his sixteen-year-old body too long and thin. His pale brown hair flopped messily across one side of his face and, in spite of the potions he plastered all over his face every night, his acne was spreading. He was intense, moody and highly intelligent.

'You can get to understand them if you listen for a while,' said Toby. 'Lanh understands them now. I've heard her make jokes like that herself.'

'Sometimes,' Paul agreed. 'Not often. Pass me the jam, Tobus.'

'Elephant or rhino?'

'Rhino, thanks. No bunyip left?'

'Sorry, I ate the last bit,' said Steven, showing him the empty jar of lime marmalade.'

'Anyone need an umbrella?' Nathan enquired from the kitchen bench.

'Yes please, I'm all sticky,' said Sally, waving her honey-covered fingers at him.

'I'll have one thanks, Nathus,' said Toby.

'You, too, Steffus? Umbrellas for everyone coming up. Eyes shut?' Nathan brought a packet of paper napkins to the table and as each member of his family obediently closed their eyes he unfolded napkins and placed them on their heads. 'Open eyes,' he instructed, and they did so very seriously, then took the napkins off their heads and wiped their hands, parodying a childhood habit.

'Now where did that custom come from?' Sally asked. 'Why did we start calling napkins umbrellas and putting them on our heads?'

'And closing our eyes? No idea,' said Paul. 'No wonder Lanh thought we were weird.'

'I remember where the Steffus, Nathus, Tobus, Paullus came from,' said Steven. 'Nathan was mad on Asterix comics.'

'Oh yes,' said Sally, remembering. 'He was only about seven. They were about Gauls being invaded by Romans who were all called things like Tacticus and Octopsis and Caractupiss.'

'They were great comics!' said Nathan. 'The Gauls were uncouth hunters who ate wild boar and the Romans were the snivelling, cultivated oppressors.'

'Why did they all speak Danish?' asked Toby innocently.

'Tobus, you moron, because the comics were in Danish!' said Steven.

'Why?'

'Because we were in Denmark. They were Danish bloody comics!'

'He was only two. He can't remember,' said Paul. 'We lived there for a whole winter. It was freezing. We had to, because Dad was guest professor at the university. You nearly died of frostbite because we pushed you through the snow in an open Aussie pusher instead of a frost-proof Danish pram. The Danes used to look at us as if we were being cruel to animals.'

'How did Nathan understand the comics if they were in Danish?' Toby persisted.

'Becoss I vent to Danish skol unt learnt Danish!' said Nathan, in the lilting storytelling voice of Danny Kaye reciting *The Little Mermaid*. 'In ze effenings I vould read to you, the stupit baby, the literature of Denmark, Asterix comics, vich you obviously remember vith great affection.'

'Boys, boys,' said Sally. 'We really should get on with planning this thing.'

'Ya, Mutter. Vot iss it ve shoud be plannink?' said Toby, who admired Nathan enough to imitate him almost perfectly. 'De stupit baby iss asking you a sensible kvestion.'

'Lordy!' said Sally, laughing. 'How did you all get to be so mad?'

'It's all your fault, Ma. You used to make up these crazy games to amuse us when Dad was away. It cheered us all up,' said Steven.

Paul nodded. 'You did. And then we all got into the spirit of things and added our own bits of madness. When Dad came home he didn't know what we were talking about.'

'Really? We shouldn't have made him feel excluded,' said Sally thoughtfully. 'Did we do that?'

'I don't think so,' Nathan said. 'He was usually too busy to care anyway. No, I don't mean that in a nasty way,' he reassured Steven who had been about to protest. 'I think he just thought we were playing slightly bizarre games that he didn't particularly want to be part of because he had more important things to do.'

'We included him in the umbrella game,' Toby remembered. 'He didn't mind that.'

'No, he didn't. But he couldn't stand us calling the strawberry jam rhino and the apricot jam elephant,' Paul grinned. 'Once, I was with him in the deli and he couldn't remember the proper name for lime marmalade and all of a sudden he went red and blurted out, "Bunyip!"'

They all fell about laughing.

'Poor Dad,' said Sally. 'He would've been mortified. Now I have to ask you all, quite seriously. Should we invite Dad to this party or not?'

They were silent.

'Yes,' said Toby. 'This was his house, too. I think he'd like to say goodbye to it.'

'But he's the one who wants to sell it!' Steven protested.

'It doesn't make economic sense to keep a house this size for three people to live in,' Paul said.

Nathan shrugged. 'I could move back home.'

Sally looked at him quickly. 'Do you want to? Or are you just trying to be helpful?'

Nathan grinned. 'A bit of both.'

'Even with four, it would still be extravagant to keep it. Particularly as Dad needs to buy a flat for himself,' Paul said.

The others looked at him curiously. He had always been the one most critical of his father.

'Why should we all have to move out just because Dad decides to piss off?' Steven asked belligerently.

'We could invite Vinh and Long Mau and Son Cao to come back,' Toby suggested eagerly. 'Nathan wants to come and you and Lanh could come back too, Paul. It was great when we were all here together.'

'No,' Nathan said. 'Mum's right. I was just trying to be helpful. It wouldn't work. They're too old to be foster children any more. We're all settled in new places.'

'But you said you'd come back!' Toby protested.

'I did, and sometimes I get lonely and wish I could. But I'm nineteen and it's time I started learning to live on my own,' Nathan said. 'How'm I going to cope in New York if I'm only used to being in a nice, happy family? The soap powder runs out and I yell "Ma! I got no soap to wash me undies".'

Toby grinned. 'You come home to do your washing, anyway.'

'Yeah, well, I've still got a lot to learn, haven't I? It's tough out there Tobus, but it's time to go,' said Nathan melodramatically. 'Paul's right. Dad needs a place to live. Families do break up. Family houses have to be sold. It's sad but it happens. So . . . do we invite Dad to the break-up party?' He surveyed his brothers like a benevolent ringmaster. 'I say yes.'

'So do I,' said Paul.

'Steven?' Nathan asked.

'If he comes I wouldn't want to talk to him,' Steven said morosely.

The others exchanged looks.

'Since he's been back from the States, and that's well over a year ago, do you know how many times he's come to see me? Exactly five.'

'Maybe you're not very friendly to him,' Nathan suggested.

'Why in hell should I be? He's the one who broke the family up! He's the one who left us and went off with a bimbo for a whole bloody year. Then, when she dumps him, he comes back and expects us to give him a big welcome. What a nerve! I don't blame Mum for refusing to take him back and I can't understand how you guys are so damn nice to him after what he did. He's a fucking loser!'

After a pause Sally said quietly, 'We were all hurt by what happened, Steve. But we were lucky. We had each other. And we had good friends who helped us to get over it.' She looked at him sympathetically. 'You haven't quite recovered. And I haven't either. I still feel sad. But I have other things now that I didn't have before.'

'What other things?'

'More independence, a growing career as a writer, even a bit of pride. And I think you have things that you didn't have before, too.'

'Me?'

'Yes. You have more confidence, more determination. Look what you've achieved in the past two years.'

'Achieved? What have I achieved?' he said dismissively.

'You won the under-sixteen tennis competition!' said Toby.

'And a scholarship that covers all tuition fees at St. Mark's. None of us ever did that,' said Paul.

'And you got into the Firsts basketball team. That was my dream,' said Nathan. 'But I only ever made it to the Fourths.'

Sally nodded. 'You used to say you could never do any of those things because you weren't good enough.'

'Okay, but what's that got to do with Dad?' Steven asked.

'I think you did those things to prove to yourself that you *were* good enough,' Sally said. 'Even though you were feeling miserable without Dad, you pushed yourself to prove that you could do just as well without him.'

'I could do *better* without him. I don't need him,' Steven said bitterly. 'None of us do.'

'Steve, the best thing you've achieved as far as I'm concerned, is that you've become a nicer person. Once you were a bit self-centred. But since Dad left you've been . . . kinder – to me, to your brothers, to the kids we invited to live here. When people are sad you comfort them because you've experienced real sadness yourself.'

'So, am I supposed to thank Dad for teaching me to understand sadness?' said Steven darkly.

'No, I don't think so. But perhaps you should try to forgive him.'

'Why should I?'

'Because you're a generous person, Steve, and because he's more lonely than we are right now.'

There was silence. Steven sat with his head bent. He'll burst into tears in a moment, thought Sally. Or let forth a stream of abuse about his father. But he only lifted his head up, looked around at them all and said quietly, 'Okay. Invite the old bugger.'

The others grinned.

'Good on ya, Steffus,' Nathan said.

Later, as Paul drove Nathan home in his battered Volkswagen to his bare little room, he said, 'Do you really wish you could move back home?'

'Oh sure.'

'Well, why don't you? Just until the house is sold. Mum would be glad of the company. Steve's a bit hard to live with at the moment and Toby's never home he's got so many friends to visit.'

'It would be easier for me at home. And cheaper. And I do miss them all. But I've made new friends, Paul. You know how it is.'

Paul shrugged. 'Anyone you couldn't invite home?'

'Maybe.'

'Who? Actors? Disreputable overly-dramatic people like yourself?' Paul laughed. 'Mum would love them!'

'I don't think so. Anyway, they're not all actors. Some of them are Vinh and his friends.'

Paul gave his brother a sharp look. 'I thought you'd stopped seeing him since he moved back to Cabramatta.'

'He drops by once in a while.'

'Is he still selling drugs?'

'Making up to seven hundred dollars a day on the streets.' Nathan gave his charming, false Jack Nicholson smile.

'Jesus, Nathan, have some sense. Keep away from Vinh.'

'Come on man, he was our brother. Tobus wants us to invite him back to live with us. One day he'll probably be your brother-in-law.'

'If he's not dead first.' Paul looked grimly straight ahead. 'What happened to that course Mum helped get him into? Tourism, wasn't it? I thought he was doing that at night and running his own cleaning business in the daytime.'

'Too slow for Vinh. You know Vinh. He's driving a brand new Toyota Celica now. Renting a unit with some other members of the gang.'

'Gang?' said Paul in disbelief. 'He's not running round with those street kids with flick-knives who fight the Lebanese?'

'No, no, nothing like that. Vinh's in the 5T gang,' said Nathan with mock pride. 'That's like making it to the Firsts basketball team at St Mark's.'

Paul gave him a withering look.

'Sorry, bad joke.' Nathan said. 'He's Lanh's brother and you're right, we should be worried.'

'What's this 5T gang?'

'Members have to be experienced in the 5Ts. Remember your Vietnamese? *Tinh* means love and sex, *tien* means money, *tu* means jail, *toi* means criminal charge and the other *tu* means death of a close friend or gang member. When you've had a bit of all five you get tattooed with a T above the nipple.'

'You're making this up.'

'I'm not. Except for the nipple bit. The T can be on the upper arm if you're squeamish.'

'God, you're callous. If Mum knew about this . . . When was Vinh in jail, anyway? Lanh didn't know about that.'

'He asked me not to tell her. Last month. It was only for a night. Then we got bail.'

'We? Who's we?'

'Myself and a few of his friends. The conviction wasn't for drugs, you understand. Vinh's not stupid enough to get caught for selling heroin.'

'Nathan, you're talking about him as if he's some kind of hero. He's a pissy little gangster and a drug dealer and Mum gave him the chance to be something much better. I'm really appalled that you think he's so great. What's happening to you?'

'Growing up, I guess.'

'Bullshit! You're growing smaller and stupider.'

'Better than being blind and holy.'

Paul screeched the car to the side of the road and pulled up. 'Look, you can walk if you like.'

'Sure,' said Nathan. He started to gather his backpack and coat from the back seat.

'You're an idiot! You know that? You think it's cute to hang out with drug dealers?'

'No. Some of them are arseholes. But a few of them are ordinary guys who didn't have nice middle class lives like us. They arrived here on boats without parents and have been living on the streets ever since,' said Nathan passionately. 'They look after each other, Paul. Like Mum looked after us and Vinh and Lanh and Long Mau and Son Cau.'

Paul was listening. Nathan paused, then continued, talking fast and with pent-up anger, 'There's one gang called Trai Lu Lac. Know what that means? "Young men with no family or home". There's about fifty guys in that gang. They share units, look after each other when they're sick. Sure they fight if they're tackled by another gang. Wouldn't you? But they don't want to be gangsters forever. It's short term. They can earn good money on the streets. They support each other. Like family. They're a subculture. People like you should be making documentaries about them, or writing essays on the phenomena for a degree in Sociology or Criminology at university.'

'God, you're a cynical little bastard,' Paul hurled Nathan's backpack and coat back into the car. 'Get in. I'll drive you home.'

'Thank you, brother,' Nathan smiled.

Sally was feeling optimistic the morning after having breakfast with her four sons. It was rare to see them all together. Other people might find them eccentric, even obnoxious, but to her they were a delight. She missed not having Paul and Nathan still at home.

When they'd separately announced within a few months of each other that they wanted to move out, she'd repressed the urge to cry out, 'Please don't!' and bribe them to stay.

When Paul had said he needed time alone with Lanh to work out their relationship and that it was difficult to do this in a communal household like theirs, she had looked at him calmly and said yes, it might be wise to start to live an independent life. She had tried to be enthusiastic. A one-bedroom flat above a herbalist's shop in Chinatown within walking distance of the university sounded just the thing. Noisy perhaps, and not very clean, but certainly private. The cockroaches in the cupboards could always be tackled and the muggers who might lurk in the narrow streets after dark would surely realise that attacking a local of limited means was both unethical and unprofitable. Such hopeful thoughts wafted through Sally's mind as she struggled to accept her eldest son's plans. Yes, it would be stimulating living in Chinatown, she told him. Exciting. An adventure.

But with Nathan it had been harder. He was younger, had no partner to share the shock of living out of home. And he had a desperation to succeed that Paul did not have. It would be hard enough, at nineteen, to prove to the world that you were capable of becoming a fine actor, without having to do it alone.

She must not deny the selfish element either. She would miss the confidences she and Nathan exchanged, his generosity, his energy and the way he made her almost cry with laughter. She would feel bereft without him! But she had steeled herself not to show this, even offering to help him find a room to rent. He had looked mildly surprised at this. She had cheerfully agreed that it was better to be out there on your own finding out about the world. Although she hated his decision, she supported it.

However, both Nathan and Paul did come and visit. On the pretence of borrowing things – hammers, saws, ironing boards, buckets, even recipes, they came back regularly to check on her. Was she going grey with grief? Were Steven and Toby too demanding? Did she need a good laugh? And each time they came they seemed more appreciative of what she had done for them when they lived at home. It was rather touching, Sally thought.

She was bemused and pleased to notice that Nathan and Paul still believed when a major event like a family party was to be planned, the older sons should do it. They had done it very competently, she thought, despite the initial problem of whether or not to invite Richard.

Now she had accepted the fact that the house must be sold she was looking forward to her new life. It would be simpler. She would find a little terrace house in the inner city big enough for three with a sunny courtyard for the pot-plants. It would be close to shops and a park and public transport. She could walk to galleries and theatres and catch the bus to work. Perhaps she would not need a car at all. If she sold it they could afford holidays. She had always wanted to go hiking in the wilderness. Would the boys come to Cradle Mountain with her? Probably they'd prefer a holiday up north, diving amongst the tropical fish on the Barrier Reef. If her new children's book sold as well as the last one she might be able to afford both!

She was modest about her writing, regarding it as a part-time occupation. Teaching was her real job. Her first book, an adventure story for ten-year-olds, had been bought mainly by family and friends. But her second book, a grimly imaginative story of exploited young circus performers of mixed race, set in the future and aimed at twelve to fourteen-year-olds, had caused quite a stir. In this book Sally had quietly rebelled against the idea that young adult fiction for girls should be cheerful and nurturing, whereas boys could read books about rage and depression. Some school libraries had rejected it for presenting 'dark' characters. But she had received a mass of letters from individual girls demanding a sequel. This had delighted her.

Sally was now referred to by others, as she had not dared to refer to herself, as a writer. Twice she had been invited to writers' festivals and she now had a contract for two more books. Her writing career was beginning to take off. Thinking of this, she sighed with satisfaction.

In her small terrace house she knew she could work harder. Now that there was only herself, Steven and Toby to support she would need less money. She could cut her teaching down to three days a week and write all the rest of the time in her little room that would look out over rooftops. Without a large house and garden to look after she would finish it in no time.

There would be new friends to make in the inner city, younger, less prosperous people than those in Hunters Hill. Perhaps she could be helpful. She imagined giving young mothers with too much to carry rides home from Paddy's market, possibly collecting their children from school when they were too busy. No, no, she must stop thinking like that. She had just decided to sell the car and get on with her writing.

These thoughts floated idly through Sally's head as she sat at the garden table opening her mail. Today was her writing day and she could relax at lunchtime with a cup of coffee and a sandwich, a luxury she looked forward to after the hectic week of teaching.

Most of the letters were bills which she put aside for later. There was a postcard from an old friend who was escorting her architecture students through Italy: *Over-stimulated by our whistlestop tour of Roma, Firenze, Milano and Venezia, at night they dance and drink until dawn in the rooms next to mine. I've threatened to fail the lot of them if they don't shut up and let me sleep. I am too old for all this! I miss you. Annelise.*

Sally smiled. Annelise had once been rather wild herself. How fortunate I am to have such delightfully forgetful friends.

There was a bulging packet of letters from a Year Eight class at a country high school, readdressed by her publisher. They must have been set an assignment on her circus book. She enjoyed getting these and read each one, searching for signs of coercion from the teacher, but mostly the letters seemed spontaneous. One girl wrote that her book was 'unreal' and, perhaps contradicting herself, 'what really happens'.

There was also a brief note from Virginia. Sally instantly recognised the distinctive, dramatically deep purple ink.

*Dearest S,*

*My Ananda Arthouse is almost finished! 'Tis magic. A tower in the rainforest. The opening date is July 10. There will be rare works of art, fireworks, sublime music and dancing under the stars. You must come! You will ride in a steam train through the canefields at sunset, sipping champagne. Be there! You promised nearly thirty years ago you would. So do it!*

*Much love, V.*

Underneath was a vibrant pen and ink sketch of a pagoda in a jungle with fireworks exploding in the background. Sally laughed and went to phone Meg.

'Did you get your invitation?'

'I did. More like a royal command.'

'We did promise to be there you know.'

'What! When we were eighteen?' Meg snorted.

'Yes, I remember it clearly. It was bright moonlight and the three of us had been cartwheeling on the beach. She said that one day she'd build a magic place in the forest. For artists to perform. There would be fire-eaters, lions and dancing bears . . .'

They laughed.

'Look, why don't we go?' Meg said. 'You deserve a break and now the paper's coming out monthly I could take a few days off. Claudia's decided to accept your boys' invitation to go skiing that week.'

'Of course! I'd forgotten. Nathan and Paul have been skiing at Perisher for years so they know everyone. They've organised a bunk for her at the lodge where they stay. It isn't luxury accommodation but the snow is good and she'll meet lots of young people. Nathan and Paul will look after her.'

'I'm sure they will. They've been marvellous to her already.'

'She does ski, doesn't she?'

'Oh yes. It's about the only sport she's good at. She was a schoolgirl champion in Switzerland, so she told me. Though you can never be absolutely sure with Claudia,' Meg said ruefully.

'How has it all been going with her lately? Peter told me that she wasn't speaking to him any more because she'd demanded he take some modelling shots of her for a possible job and he'd refused.'

'Yes, he did. He doesn't like doing fashion photography, I know, but it was a bit mean.'

'So Claudia and Peter are still clashing?'

Meg sighed. 'He thinks she's destructive and she wants his attention as well as mine. It's so silly. And such a pity. They seemed to be getting on so well at the start. He was marvellously patient with her. She *is* difficult sometimes. But now he seems to have had enough. I'm sure all she needs is love and attention. She was treated like an emotional cripple when she was young and sometimes, when I look at her, I see that same handicapped child. She's sweet most of the time, but occasionally she'll burst out in a fit of rage. Like she did when Peter refused to take those photos.' Meg sounded sad. 'Anyway, I believe she's asked your Steven to take them now and he's agreed. Do you mind?'

Sally laughed. 'Not at all. Steven thinks she's gorgeous. And he's quite a good photographer. He won a prize at school last year. His subject matter up till now has been limited to sports teams and unusual rock formations. So this should provide quite a challenge.'

Meg laughed. 'Claudia will flatter him outrageously. Better warn him not to take it seriously.'

'I will.' Sally sounded mildly apprehensive.

'Don't worry. I'll have a word to Claudia about it. She actually quite likes it when I give her motherly advice.'

Sally felt doubtful about this but decided to be positive. 'So the trip up north is a definite possibility for us. My boys will look after Claudia and you can leave without guilt.'

'Exactly.'

'Okay then. Let's go!'

# CHAPTER SEVEN

The air smelt sweet like molasses as the little steam train passed through a tunnel of sugar cane, dappled green and made of long, whispering leaves. Safe and peaceful, thought Sally, as she sat in the open carriage, like being an ant in a pea pod. But soon they were on the other side and the train's whistle screeched and ah! – there were the mountains, stark, deep purple and shrouded in dramatic mist. Smoke billowed in the distance. Patches of flame were licking at the edge of a black ploughed cane field. The train, moving slowly, was carrying passengers from the city to the rainforest. They were drinking champagne and laughing a lot, because although they were looking forward to this evening they were a little nervous about being so far from shopping malls and hotel foyers. Most of them were tourists. The Americans and Japanese had dressed boldly in designer junglewear: coloured khaki with the odd splash of leopard skin. Ready for adventure. One man wore a safari suit and a straw pith helmet with Raffles Hotel emblazoned on the side. But the remaining passengers – media personalities, local councillors, people in the hotel and travel industries and social 'identities' from Cairns had dressed like party-goers. They wore pointy-toed shoes, silver jackets and had hair coiffed so splendidly they might have been going to an opera or a ball.

Sally and Meg knew none of these official guests although they exchanged smiles and nods as travellers do when they are thrown together in odd circumstances. The two friends felt oddly privileged, the only people on the train to know just how long this little journey had been planned.

Sally looked hard at Meg to see how she had aged. She was still slim with shoulder length hair the colour of wheat. If it turned grey the change would hardly be noticeable. Unfair, thought Sally. Her own hair, which was dark brown, had needed to be touched up to hide the grey for years now. Sometimes Sally neglected it on purpose, challenging the colour to make her feel different. Wiser, perhaps. Once, when she had permitted the grey to show, a schoolgirl had insisted on giving up her seat for Sally on the bus and she had felt indignant. She did not wish to look old, just dignified. When she was really old, she thought, sixty-five or seventy, she would let the hair flow like a white mane behind her. She would become sagacious, a crone. Young people would follow her about to hear her stories. So she daydreamed as the little train jolted its way through the cane.

Did Meg think about growing old, she wondered?

The skin on Meg's face was firm and gleamed golden brown in the late afternoon light. But there was a loosening at the neck, Sally noticed, and creases around her eyes. Sally knew she has these, too. Laugh lines, her sons called them when they were feeling generous and crow's feet when they were not.

Meg gazed out at the fields and seemed to smile. With confidence, thought Sally. She was always confident, even when she was eighteen, but then it was a driven, forced kind of confidence. Now there was containment. Serenity.

'Do I seem serene to you?' she asked Meg out of the blue.

'Absolutely. Like a Buddha,' Meg replied unhesitantly. Then she laughed. 'Compared with what you used to be.'

Sally felt reassured. 'Are we typical middle-aged women, do you think?'

'If we were we wouldn't be taking part in all this madness.' They looked back along the train at the serious tourists and excited socialites who were shrieking with laughter because they were not at all sure this excursion was wise. Sally was not sure either.

A gallery on the edge of the rainforest? Who would tramp along dank tracks to buy a painting in the wilderness? Which artists would agree to live in such a remote place? Would anyone come to the concerts that are supposed to raise money to keep the project going? If it failed there would be debts to pay. Virginia had borrowed from banks, fortunately, not property developers. Meg and Sally had added a little of their own money to help complete her Arthouse. Perhaps this was foolish. But they could not resist indulging her fantasy. Virginia's enthusiasm is contagious. She has always been good-looking but when she is fired up about something she really wants to do, she looks radiantly beautiful. Friends and bank managers don't stand a chance.

Virginia Arezzo is an artist. She has grand passions, not moderate ones like normal people. Over the decades she has embarrassed, infuriated and delighted Sally and Meg. They have been both proud and exasperated to be her closest friends.

'Where is she?' Meg asked Sally. 'I would have thought she'd be here on the train to reassure us.'

'She can't be. She's waiting at the Arthouse to receive the distinguished guests.'

'More distinguished than we are?' Meg pretended to be indignant. 'Who are they?'

'Politicians, merchant bankers, curators of galleries, art critics, people with power and money.'

Meg shook her head in admiration.

'She'll need them,' Sally said.

Virginia had delegated the task of train hostess to Marina Riley, one of her Aboriginal students. Marina popped the cork on another champagne bottle and a few of the guests shrieked. Then one of them pointed, asking anxiously, 'Is that a bushfire?'

'Nuh, they're burning the tops,' said Marina, elegantly dressed in a short skirt of white satin, high heels and earrings that shimmered. She knew that as the public relations person she should be poised but she was far too excited. She sprang up onto a seat, almost knocking a glass from the pith helmet man's hand, and pointed. 'Look! That's Brush Turkey Creek. We're nearly there!'

Now the flames were closer. Three cane farmers in broad-brimmed hats stood staring as the train passed by. The passengers waved tipsily. One of the farmers grinned very slowly, showing white teeth and waved back. The others looked away.

Sally and Meg exchanged glances. 'They could burn us all to a crisp if they wanted to,' said Meg.

Sally stared back at the three solitary figures and shrugged. 'I know she invited them.'

A few minutes later the train stopped. A number of passengers stood up expectantly. 'Are we here?' Hoots of laughter.

'No, we're still in the canefield.' They craned their necks to see what was happening up ahead. 'What's the hold-up?'

Smoke was billowing close to the train and the crackle of flames was menacing. A few passengers began to cough. Others held handkerchiefs over their faces. 'My God, it's hot!' one man said. His face had turned bright pink. 'What seems to be the problem?'

'Something blocking the train line,' Marina said, frowning. Then, remembering her responsibilities, she turned to beam at the bothered man. 'Not to worry. They're fixing it. More champagne?'

'How long will they take?' The man was breathing heavily and perspiration poured in sticky streams down either side of his face.

'Hang on a jiff. I'll go and see.' Marina handed the opened

bottle of champagne to Sally with unspoken instructions to keep the passengers happy, leapt lithely down into the cane and bounded off towards the front of the train.

'I'll go, too,' said Meg quietly, and following Marina, disappeared into the sea of green.

'Watch out for taipans!' yelled a tipsy social columnist from the *Cairns Post*. 'Wouldn't catch me wading through that spiky stuff.'

Steam from the engine and smoke from the fire made it hard at first to see what was lying stretched across the track. When it cleared Marina reacted with revulsion. 'Bloody bastards,' she muttered.

'Who would do that?' Meg asked, bewildered. 'Tie a dead cassowary to the railway track?'

The engine driver was struggling to untie the bird's long neck from one side of the track while his assistant untied its feet from the other.

'Neighbours, that's who.' Marina was angry. 'Redneck farmers who don't want artists, especially Aboriginal ones, anywhere near their property.'

'But why that poor bird?'

'Because it's rare and protected. Sacred to our people.' Marina turned away from the gruesome sight. 'The cassowary is my totem,' she added gravely. 'So it's a bit like killing my brother. To warn me not to get too confident just because I've got white friends.'

'That's outrageous,' Meg said grimly.

'Yeah.'

'How many of the artists working at Ananda are Aboriginal?'

'Sometimes there might be eight or ten of us. Sometimes only three. But me, I'm always there. See, I'm not just a student but the resident public relations officer.' Marina grinned cheekily. 'Wearing satin and pearls, driving posh cars, chatting to the politicians. Drives those racist farmers crazy!' She laughed. 'Come on. We better get back before our friendly neighbours choke the guests with cane smoke.'

The gallery gleamed like honey in the late afternoon sun. It was tall, like an oriental pagoda, and made of warm wood. Surrounded by lush, tangled forest and set in a natural amphitheatre, its reflection in the lake was like a shimmering temple. The scene was like a stage set for some extraordinary drama.

'She's done it,' said Meg. 'I must admit I never thought she would.'

Sally shook her head in admiration.

They could see Virginia in the distance, in a long blue gown, smiling and shaking hands with important guests. After a few minutes she appeared beside them.

'Well?' The calm, gracious look she'd put on for the dignitaries had vanished. Her eyes were sparkling. She danced on the spot. 'What do you think?'

'It's a triumph,' Meg told her.

'Stunning. Much more beautiful than I imagined,' said Sally. 'And you don't look so bad yourself.'

'Don't look too hard at my fingernails.' Virginia screwed up her face in a parody of excitement. 'You came! You both came. You weren't sure it would happen but you still flew all this way and . . . here we are, ya buggers!' She gave them each a hug, a rough one, the kind she would give in the old days when she wasn't sure they believed in her schemes.

'I apologise,' Meg said seriously, 'for being such a doomsayer all these years.'

'You were right about one thing. I'd have been wiped out if I'd borrowed from those crooked property developers.' Virginia lowered her voice. 'A couple of them are here; I think they'd quite like to be sponsors.'

Sally looked panicky. 'Don't!'

Virginia laughed. 'Of course I won't.' She grabbed Sally by the arm. 'Come and meet the Minister. He's lovely and I think he wants to buy a painting. I want him to get a good one but his wife . . . ' she whispered, 'has no taste.'

When the sun went down the fireworks began. There was a crack, the streak of a brilliant shooting star reflected in the lake and soon the whole sky was full of fizzy, technicolour explosions.

'Look,' said Meg, straining to read her program in the dark. 'We're even going to have an aria from *Tosca*.'

When all was still again and the sky was dark a troupe of Aboriginal dancers emerged from the shadows. Surrounding the guests, they moved stealthily with painted faces and limbs, chanting eerily, then aggressively stamping to the drone of the didgeridoo. Suddenly they leapt onto the stage and, lit by a spotlight, began to dance. They imitated a cassowary, then transformed themselves into kangaroos. They became storks stepping delicately through the mangrove swamps. They enacted the story of a good man fighting the force of evil spirits. Next they rubbed sticks together, the lights on stage were dimmed and the dance continued by flickering firelight. Smoke billowed forth representing evil. The dance became frenzied. Gradually evil was forced away and the embers burnt low until at the end one of the dancers stamped out the fire with a bare foot. There was applause.

'Magic,' Sally whispered to Meg.

'Dreamtime meets the tourists,' Meg whispered back.

'Sceptic!'

The Minister for the Arts made a speech saying this was 'another first' for Queensland and pledging just a little more money 'to help things along'. A ribbon was cut and a plaque unveiled. Artists from all over the country applauded. And then the diva, all in white, sang her aria.

Afterwards Meg and Sally drifted through the crowd eavesdropping on patrons from the smart cities in the south making admiring comments. 'The beauty of this place,' said a pale, distinguished-looking man in a white linen suit. 'So remote. But it's worth the eight hour journey from Melbourne just to experience it.'

One Sydney gallery owner, well known for his cynicism, said dreamily, 'Ananda means bliss? Well, yes, I can see why she chose that name.'

'Is it true that some of the Aboriginal painters who work here have been invited to show their work in Düsseldorf next year?' asked a young art critic, eagerly. 'Or perhaps it was Art Cologne?'

'Düsseldorf. I've heard the same rumour,' said the white linen suit.

'I wonder if any of them are here tonight.' The critic looked around hopefully. 'I'd like to meet them. Particularly Harry Wirra and Jack Napangada.'

'*I'd* like to buy a few of their paintings before they get such outrageously high praise from the European critics that their prices go through the roof!' said the gallery owner.

The others laughed sympathetically.

Marina glided up to Meg and Sally and whispered, 'Gunna warn Uncle Jack and Uncle Harry about that lot.'

Frogs croaked, cicadas sang, geese and guineafowl screeched, fireflies gleamed like sparks in the dark and the waterfall continued to cascade invisibly over the high black rocks.

A young man in a dinner suit mounted the platform and stood still in front of the microphone.

'Is that Guy?' Meg asked Sally. 'I haven't seen him for years. It looks like Guy but . . .'

'Healthier? You're right. He's been here for three months, helping Virginia dig trenches, build fences, paint the ablution blocks . . .'

'Really? He left an expensive apartment in New York to do that?'

'He sold the apartment. Where else do you think Virginia got the money to complete the gallery?'

'Sold his graduation present?' Meg grinned. 'His father must be furious.'

Virginia's son Guy had lived most of his life in New York with his father, who was wealthy, remarried and disapproved of Virginia. For the past twenty years Virginia had spent everything she'd earned either on airfares to see Guy or on building her Arthouse.

Guy cleared his throat ready to speak. He said he had just spent one of the toughest periods of his life trying to keep pace with his mother. There was laughter. He spoke self-deprecatingly of his physical fitness compared with hers and the audience laughed some more. There was obvious affection for them both. Guy said it was Virginia's passion that had created this extraordinary place. Even though he had not lived with her since he was a small child, he said, he loved and admired her greatly.

Virginia, looking proud of her son and touched by his introduction, took the microphone and invited the guests to come into the gallery. 'You will be our very first visitors. The artists and I are delighted to have you,' she said sincerely. 'Feel free to roam about, look at the paintings and introduce yourselves to the artists. We've prepared a little feast for you. And some strange cocktails which we'll pass around, made of lychees, mango, white rum, Cointreau and zapote. Don't be alarmed. They're delicious.'

The guests laughed and applauded.

'Remember, everything you see, not only the paintings, was created here at Ananda. The fruit in the cocktails, the crabs, the quails' eggs, goose-liver pâté and sun-dried tomatoes, even the trout and kumquat,' she said proudly. 'We're a self-sufficient community. Please come in and enjoy yourselves!'

They crowded in. People who could afford it, and even some who couldn't, rushed to buy the paintings that had been donated by the artists. Soon there were very few paintings left without little red stickers. Sally and Meg raised their eyebrows at each other across the crowded foyer. The Aboriginal artists, who had stood shyly apart at first, were now mingling with the guests, and the dancers, who had removed their white makeup and changed into jeans and T-shirts, joined the crowd moving up the spiral staircase to gaze at the paintings.

There was a wide selection. Marina, acting as a guide to Meg and Sally, pointed out the work by local Aboriginal artists – everything from traditional images of wild birds, pigs, dingoes and flying foxes stencilled like rock art figures, to intricately worked compositions of oil and wax crayon, as well as large canvases covered in washes and a powdery pigment that looked like earth and natural rock.

'I love this one; it's called *Listening Earth*. Feels like heat, blood, heart, bones, everything that lies just under your footprints.'

'Who painted it? I can't make out the signature,' Sally asked.

'Aunty Ruby. A friend of my mum's. She lives down in Cairns but she's been a resident here for a couple of months. Been to the Townsville College of TAFE, too. She's not well known like Uncle Harry and Uncle Jack. But I reckon she soon will be. Uh huh, talk of the devils . . . '

Virginia, flanked by two tall men, approached Meg and Sally. 'May I present Jack Napangada and Harry Wirra, who will soon be world famous, so shake their hands while you can get near them,' she said proudly. The men looked embarrassed but pleased.

'She talks a fair bit of rubbish for a smart woman, wouldn't you say Jack?'

'I would. But she gets a kick out of flattering older men like yourself, Harry. Now why she'd want to butter me up is another question altogether.' Jack winked at Sally and Meg.

Meg laughed and congratulated both of them on their work. Sally asked about the show in Düsseldorf, but they both shook their heads. 'I'll believe that when it happens,' said Harry with a slow smile.

'Are these artists really all your uncles and aunties?' Sally asked Marina.

'Nah!' Marina laughed. 'They're no relation. Just the way we feel about each other. Got hundreds of cousins, grandmas, uncles. Just a Murri custom.'

'I like it,' Sally said.

'What about your paintings, Marina? Are any of yours here?' asked Meg.

'Up the back, with the beginners,' she replied with a grin. 'Come on. I'll show you.'

Marina's paintings were vibrant, naive works, mostly acrylics, of what seemed to be her daily life. There was a large, joyful painting of a group of Aborigines swimming in a waterhole in the rainforest, with one pale white woman. 'Virginia, in case you didn't know,' she explained. 'She's in this one, too.' Here

Virginia was the focus of a large group of very dark people who did not look as friendly as those frolicking in the waterhole. The landscape was beautiful but harsh – red earth dotted with anthills and a blinding blue sky. 'That's Cape York, where I come from. That's my family.'

'They don't look too pleased to see Virginia,' Meg observed.

Marina shrugged. 'They've never met her. How would they know?'

'I love the swimming-hole painting. Is it for sale?' Sally asked.

'Sure. I'll let you have it cheap,' she said cheerfully and led the way back to the main gallery to get a red sticker.

'Sally! Hey Sally!' A smiling young man was calling to her from the other side of the gallery. He hurried through the crowd to meet her and they stood side by side, beaming at each other.

'Thought it was you. What on earth are you doing up here so far from civilisation?' he asked.

'I might ask the same of you.'

'I'm here to promote a book we've just published on Aboriginal artists, some of whom are here.' He waved an arm at random.

Marina appeared with the painting and Sally handed over her cheque. 'Virginia says to let you take it now because you'll be leaving before the exhibition's over.'

'Oh thanks, Marina. That's great,' Sally said.

'What! Buying a painting?' the handsome young man exclaimed. 'Not one of Jack Napangada's is it? You must've made more out of that circus book than I thought.'

Sally laughed. 'Meg McIntyre and Marina Riley. This is Timothy Grey who is a publicist for Seagull and helped me sell my last book so well that I can afford to buy paintings. Marina is the artist by the way, not her Uncle Jack, but it won't be long before she's just as famous.'

'I'm very impressed,' said Timothy appraising both the painting and Marina.

Marina flashed Timothy a brilliant smile and tossed her

head so that her earrings glittered dangerously. 'I'm a publicist, too. I can smell bullshit a mile off.'

Timothy affected a deeply wounded expression. 'Miss Riley, I *never* flatter.'

Marina threw back her head and laughed. 'Well, nice to meet you, Tim,' she said and sauntered off.

'Timothy,' he whispered after she had gone, and then to Sally, 'What a babe!'

'I wouldn't let her hear you say that,' Sally warned.

He clasped her hand. 'I know, I know. Radical feminist, lesbian artist, black sister but *never* babe. Ah, what a misery to be a red-blooded male heterosexual in the nineties! See! I've done it again.' He looked down at their clasped hands in mock horror. 'I've touched a female artist. I'll be accused of sexual harassment.'

Sally put an arm around him and he dropped his head to her shoulder, pretending to be inconsolable. 'I'll testify to your innocence, Timothy.'

His head flew up. 'Who wants to be innocent? I want to be hugely guilty but not right here in public.'

Sally humoured him by playing the helpless victim for a minute, leaning against him in a swoon.

'Seriously,' said Timothy quietly in her ear. 'When can I see you back in Sydney?'

Sally looked flustered.

'May I call you?

'If you like.'

'Thank you,' he said sincerely.' I'll do that.' Then he said a polite farewell to Meg and disappeared into the crowd.

'Well,' said Meg shrewdly. 'That was interesting.'

Sally blushed. 'He's just playing games. Very charming. But pretends all the time.'

'*Some* of it looked real.'

'Oh Meg, don't be ridiculous!'

'Do you like him?'

'I hardly know him. He looked after me for a week when my book came out.'

Meg looked blank. 'Looked after you?'

'You know,' Sally said impatiently, 'escorted me to all the interviews and readings, hired the taxis to radio stations, held my hand before I had to stand up and read to five hundred brawling school kids . . .'

'Literally held your hand?'

'Yes! Why not? It's his job to make authors feel good about themselves so as they don't make bloody fools of themselves in public and ruin the book sales!'

Meg laughed. 'Listen to yourself. So defensive! What on earth is wrong with a little dalliance? He's not married is he?'

Sally shook her head.

'Well then? What's the problem? He's good-looking, bright and obviously lusts after you.'

Sally shook her head quite vigorously. 'I just don't believe in that sort of thing any more. It's so . . . messy and undignified!'

Meg almost exploded with laughter. 'I never thought I'd hear you say such a thing. You! The wild, passionate romantic. Don't be so bloody . . . prim!'

Soon music started up outside. People, still holding their cocktails, began dancing under the stars. A corporate sponsor who was dancing with Marina suddenly grasped the microphone and after introducing himself confessed he had not really wanted to come tonight. 'But I'm delighted that I did. This Arthouse is a splendid idea. Your publicist, Miss Marina Riley, has just explained the scholarship system to me, and my company would like to be the first to donate six scholarships to allow young artists to work here.'

There was applause. Meg introduced Sally to some arts journalists she knew. As they moved off into the crowd she commented, 'Usually those two badmouth each other. Tonight is the first time I've ever seen them exchanging pleasantries.'

They overheard students who hoped to work at Ananda chatting enthusiastically to the famous artists they'd never had the chance to meet before. Meg and Sally watched it all and beamed.

'I'll admit it now,' said Sally. 'Like you, I didn't really think she'd do it. I thought she was a dreamer.'

'She is. But she's also utterly determined,' Meg said.

Marina, who had released the sponsor into the throng now that he had performed so generously and was refilling their glasses with champagne, said, 'Determined? That's an understatement. She refuses to take no for an answer. Never forces people. She just radiates such good vibes they change their minds! The local council was dead against her plans at first and *all* the bloody farmers. There's still a few farmers behaving like bastards, but some of the others are here tonight and they're having fun. Look!' She waved an arm at the animated crowd. 'The whingeing buggers are enjoying themselves!'

Sally laughed. 'Virginia's like a lightning rod that transforms destructive forces into positive ones,' she announced, as if she'd made a revelation.

Marina nodded vigorously. 'Half the people here were enemies before tonight: politicians against businessmen, art dealers against artists, students criticising successful painters, critics blasting experimental ones, the local council against the whole damn idea of an artists' retreat in the rainforest, especially when half of the artists are black. And now they're all together, talking and laughing and being so proud of this place, you'd think they bloody created it.'

'She'll probably tell them they *did* help create it,' Sally laughed.

'Probably,' Meg said. 'Remember when she called it Great Green Hell?'

Sally nodded. ' A failed cane farm surrounded by a forest full of poisonous snakes turns into – paradise.'

# CHAPTER EIGHT

'So, how was it up in paradise?' asked Peter when, three days later, Meg came home.

'Quite wonderful it was,' said Meg with a little mysterious smile. And Peter found himself feeling slightly jealous and excluded, as he often did when Meg came back from being with Sally and Virginia. He disliked this feeling in himself. He wondered if Meg ever noticed. But no. There she was, serene and confident as ever, smiling to herself. 'Queenly' was the way she'd been described to him by the photographers he worked with before he'd met her. That was four years ago. It had taken months to manoeuvre himself into her sight lines. She had been formidable. Now she was softer, he liked to think, since she'd married him.

'And how are you?' said Meg, looking into his eyes and taking both his hands in hers. He looks weary, she thought, sitting on the sofa and pulling him down beside her. 'Nick didn't wear you out?'

'Nick exhausted me!' he said. 'I thought I did pretty much all the housework and childminding round here already, but when you're not here it's bedlam.'

'Really? I'm surprised,' she said ruefully. She stroked his hair.

'I forgot things. Stupid little things: Nick's playlunch, his change of clothes for nursery school, to pick him up early on Friday. I forgot to put petrol in the car and we stopped dead on the freeway.'

Meg laughed sympathetically. 'God, how awful. Were you towed away?'

'No, we got pushed. Caused a dreadful traffic jam. Nick thought it was terrific.'

'What happened to him on Friday when you forgot to pick him up?' she asked anxiously.

'He was rescued by Katie's Dad. He said he forgot to pick her up early the week before.'

'Poor Nick. Was he upset?'

'No, he said he wants to go to Katie's house next Friday, too. They have chocolate biscuits and they're allowed to watch violence on TV.'

Meg laughed. 'He *is* precocious for four, isn't he? I thought his teacher was exaggerating. It's all your fault. You give him far too much attention.'

'Oh, I've missed you! Don't do it again. Don't go away and leave me,' Peter moaned. She knew he was joking but it still made Meg feel guilty about the forthcoming trip to East Timor.

'Any news from the snowfields?' she asked, to change the subject.

Peter put his head in his hands in mock despair. Then he grinned up at her. 'Claudia rang the first night to say she couldn't possibly stay in such primitive accommodation. 'But Peter, it's a *hut*!' He mimicked her upper-class English accent very well. 'There's no central heating, just a *boiler* and no kitchen staff. We have to cook our own *food*. It's appalling.'

Meg pulled a face. 'Poor Nathan and Paul. Did they have to cook for her?'

'I told them not to.'

'Oh, you shouldn't have. They wouldn't have minded. She can't cook at all.'

'Well she'll have to bloody learn. Don't over-protect her. She's a spoilt baby. Twenty-four and she can't boil an egg.'

'I know. It's awful. But if she's miserable up there . . .'

'Miserable! She's having a ball. She rang back last night to say everything's fine. Her room-mate sprained her ankle so she's doing all the cooking, the others take turns at stoking the boiler, the snow is perfect, she's met a gorgeous ski instructor who just happens to be an opera singer and owns a silk shop in Lucerne where she used to spend her holidays and she's bringing him home for the weekend.'

'Here?' Meg said in alarm.

'It's all right. I said she couldn't.'

'Oh,' Meg faltered.

'Well, we don't know him. He sounds like a prize phoney and we haven't the room.'

'I know, but she hasn't met any man she really likes since she arrived in Sydney.'

'No bloody wonder!'

'You're being a bit hard on her, aren't you?'

'Look Meg, I know you're racked with guilt about Claudia and believe that all she needs is love and attention and she'll stop being so bloody-minded, but she's trying to destroy this family. Can't you see that?'

'No, I can't. I think you're overreacting because she yelled at you over those fashion photos you refused to take. Why *did* you refuse by the way? It couldn't have been all that much of a chore to take a few photos that might have helped her get a job in modelling.'

Peter eyed her steadily. 'I refused because she wanted nude, salacious stuff and the thought of taking pictures like that made me sick.'

Meg's mouth fell open. 'But she told me . . .'

'I know what she told you. She lies, Meg. Face it. Your

beautiful daughter lies just about better than anyone I know. I'd be very surprised if it was fashion modelling she is hoping to get into with those photographs and I certainly don't want my name on that sort of filth.'

Meg sat very still. 'She asked Steven to take the photos for her when you refused. Did you know that?'

'No! Poor kid.'

'Claudia?'

'Steven! She wanted whips and dildos. Look Meg, that hospital was right. She is a little crazy.' Peter strode towards the door.

'Where are you going?'

'To ring Steven. See if he's okay.'

When he came back he was grinning.

'Well?'

'He took the photos but refused to let her pose the way she suggested. He told her he didn't want to compromise the purity of her image.'

Meg laughed. 'She believed him?'

Peter nodded earnestly. 'He meant it! He's going to enter her photo in a competition at school. About goddesses and ancient mythology. She had to be draped from head to toe in white. Apparently she enjoyed it, thanked Steven for his concern about her image and afterwards they had a really good talk about photography.'

'No bondage gear then?'

'He didn't mention any.'

Meg burst out laughing. 'Oh Peter, I do love you. You're so *serious*. She hugged him. 'Look, we've still got three days together before Claudia gets back from skiing. Don't cook tonight. Let's take Nick out for pizza. Then we'll come home early, have a big bubble bath together and go straight to bed,' she said suggestively. 'I'll give you a massage.'

'Let's have it now. The massage, not the pizza.'

Meg threw a pillow at him.

Sally was working late on her word processor, struggling with the second draft of her new novel. When the phone rang she jumped. A call this late could mean that one of her sons was in trouble. An accident. Police. She willed herself to be calm.

'Hullo.'

'You sound as if you've been meditating by a lily pond since sunrise.'

'Timothy!'

'Call me Tim. I loathe it from anyone else, but from you, I'll endure it.'

'You gave me a fright. It's almost midnight.'

'I know. I've been staring at the wall trying not to call you for hours.'

'What a lie.'

'I have! Been trying to work out something kind to say about this new brat-pack, wonder-kid novelist I've got to promote and all I can see on the wall is your beautiful face.'

Sally had been about to laugh but he sounded so serious she didn't.

'I know you're awfully busy and you've given yourself a deadline to finish the draft by tonight. I'll get off the phone in a second but first will you promise to let me come over and see you tomorrow?' He anticipated her protest and cut her off. 'Just for half an hour!' There was a pause. 'We could walk the dog.'

'The dog's gone to stay with Meg.'

'Oh,' He sounded deeply disappointed. 'Well, we could do some other useful chore together. Weed the garden?'

'You're incorrigible,' she said fondly.

'I know how precious your time is and I don't want to waste it. But I miss you, Sally. I want to see your face, your curls, your eyebrows.'

'My eyebrows?'

'Yes. I've never seen such eyebrows. They arch like fine new moons.'

Sally laughed. 'Oh shut up.'

There was silence. Then she said, 'Okay. Come tomorrow if you must.'

'In your coffee break? A whole half hour?'

'For twenty minutes.'

'Ah, now I can sleep. And dream of you. Goodnight, Ms. Moons. Until tomorrow.'

When she hung up Sally sighed. He was such an actor. Like Nathan. And he joked her into relaxing her routine. Was she too rigid? Richard, her husband, had accused her once of being a controller. But then she'd had to be, to keep the juggling balls of husband, children and career all flying through the air at once. Now that there was only career and two children to keep aloft she should be able to relax a little. But she did not want Timothy to juggle as well. Still, he was persistent. And she enjoyed his visits. He made her laugh. He flattered her and pretended to be in love. It was a game, she knew.

He told Sally he had first seen her at a publisher's cocktail party and had been drawn to her serenity but couldn't pluck up the courage to speak to her. Him! A publicist. Later, he'd connived to have her as his author so as he could get to know her. They had got along well. He had behaved like a charming nephew, Sally thought. She had been fond of him, was pleased to see him each morning of the promotional tour, had become interested in his confidences and grateful for his care. A bond had been created between them that week which was typical for author and publicist, Sally supposed.

On the last evening of their three-day country tour, staying at a motel by an artificial lake in Bateman's Bay, he had taken her to dinner. It was winter and, apart from one other couple they imagined were honeymooners, the dining room was deserted. They had laughed a lot, whispering jokes about the food, which they decided was reheated wedding reception fare, and the rooms, which were all 'bridal suites'. When he had suggested, rather shyly, that she might like to share his suite that night, she had felt it would be ungracious to refuse. Indeed, she wondered if this might not be the final task for a conscientious young publicist, in stroking the author's ego.

But he had been so ardent in his lovemaking and she had been so passionate in response that in the morning they wondered if this were not something more serious.

Still, Sally had decided on the drive back to Sydney that they should 'cool it'. There were adolescent sons at home who had been critical before of men who were over-attentive to their mother. And besides, it was most unwise to become involved with the people one worked with. As Sydney loomed closer Sally reprimanded herself for having committed such a foolish blunder. She had imagined that Timothy would feel as she did, that although their night together had been such a delight, it would be wise to resume their lives as usual, continuing to be nothing more than friends. But he had gazed at her dreamily all the way back to the city and made plans for them to be together. Sally had been touched but had not taken them seriously.

She had been surprised when he rang her half an hour after she'd reached home and begged to come over. She'd agreed, finally, and they'd made love again, just as passionately, on the floor of her study. 'This is absurd, Timothy,' she had said as they showered together, hurrying in case either of her sons should come home early from school. And he had replied that it wasn't absurd: she was a unique and beautiful woman and he wanted to be with her constantly. She had stroked his wet head and wondered.

Being strong-minded, Sally had gradually got her own way and Timothy was reduced to weekly visits of less than half an hour when they talked over coffee or walked in the park. He had, at first, not believed that she would reject him, but now he covered his loss with elaborate game-playing or pretending to be smitten by other women.

Sally wondered if she should introduce Timothy to Claudia, but feared he might get hurt rather more seriously than he pretended to be by her. She wondered why, as Meg had suggested, she could not just abandon herself and enjoy the relationship until it came to its natural end. But she was afraid of becoming emotionally involved. Meg was right. Sally had been a hopeless romantic when young, falling in love constantly and painfully. Now she was older and wiser and had learned to control her feelings. Yes. Self-control was an important factor in Sally's new life.

Sally, dashing downstairs for a bite to eat at lunchtime (she still won't take a proper lunchbreak on the days she works from home even though she's been doing it for two years. Home, unlike the school where she taught for twenty-five years, does not seem a legitimate place to have a lunch hour), hears on the radio an interview with Virginia's mother, Franca Arezzo.

Sally knows that Franca has been writing her autobiography for many years. Virginia has told her it's a hobby that amuses her mother and helps pass the time since her father died and her sisters moved with their husbands to Montreal and London, rather like weaving a tapestry that will never be finished. But now here it is, not only finished but published, and Franca, on national radio, is talking with confidence and a certain amount of passion, about fleeing from Mussolini's Italy to Australia in search of a better life and then being interned for the whole of the war. She says that although she deplored the ignorance of officials she loved the people and the landscape of her new country. She is talking about the need for Australia to declare itself a republic. 'But of course it is time to break away from Britain. We are grown up now. It is time to show our independence. Yes!' Franca laughs with enthusiasm. She sounds younger than she did when Sally first met her thirty years ago.

Sally listens to Franca, speaking in her Italian accent which is still, after fifty years, quite pronounced, and feels a surge of pride, as if this is her own mother.

She thinks of ringing Virginia in far north Queensland to see if she is listening but then she would miss part of the interview herself so she doesn't. She feels possessive of Franca. Anyway, Franca has probably asked Virginia to listen.

The interviewer, who prides himself on his sensitivity, is treating Franca like a dignitary.

'When your husband, Giacomo Arezzo, was Professor of Italian at Melbourne University, I believe you had a kind of salon in your house, where students and artists would meet regularly for meals and conversation. It was quite famous, wasn't it?'

'Famous? Oh no, I wouldn't say that. I would cook, Giacomo would talk, our daughters sometimes would recite or sing, the students would try out their Italian, people would tell jokes, eat, argue about politics, perhaps the artists would paint a mural . . .'

'Where? Where would they paint a mural?'

Sally can imagine the way Franca would shrug. 'Wherever there was space. On the garden wall. It was white. In the kitchen. On the refrigerator.'

'Really? The refrigerator.'

'Yes, yes. Why not? Fridge art was very popular in the sixties.'

'But some of those artists were famous. What happened to their paintings when the fridge had to be thrown away?'

'In those days we did not throw them away. We fixed them up again. Forty, maybe fifty times we fixed them. Once a year.' Sally chuckles. She knows Franca is lying. Having a joke at the earnest interviewer's expense.

She was one of the students who had hung around the Arezzo house when she was eighteen, full of awe. She had envied Virginia her family: their liveliness, their artistry, their beauty, their talk, their generosity and their friends.

Franca then had been overshadowed by her husband and daughters. She had seemed always to be in the background, smiling, serving delicious food, watching and applauding. Now they had all gone it was her turn to perform.

It had been Franca who came to Bethesda Hospital in East Melbourne to collect Sally and her firstborn son and drive them home to Carlton. Where was Richard? Working, probably. Yes, of course. In those days fathers were not encouraged to hang about hospitals, making a fuss. He hadn't been present at the birth either, although he'd visited every evening for a week, bringing flowers he'd stolen from the Treasury Gardens on his walk to the hospital and taking her nightgowns home to wash by hand. When she'd told him excitedly that she was going to be discharged on Thursday morning, he had asked why she couldn't wait until the weekend as he was taking a Genetics class on Thursday. She had felt hurt although she'd tried not to show it. But Franca, who happened to be visiting, had said that if Richard didn't mind she could collect Sally and the baby on Thursday morning and drive them home. Richard had said he'd be grateful, particularly as they didn't own a car.

Franca had arrived on Thursday looking excited. Her only

grandchild had been born in London and she hadn't even seen him. Sally liked the way she took charge, telling the nurses what to carry, asking the doctor for details of Sally's next visit and writing down her medication. Sally had thought that this is what it must be like to have a mother. They drove home in the big, comfortable Fiat, opened up the little terrace house, laid the baby in his new bassinet, gleefully tried out the changing table, made themselves a cup of real coffee, ate the Italian *crostini* Franca had made, and laughed together as they sat in the autumn sunshine. Sally had let herself imagine, for an hour or so, that Franca really was her mother. Franca had made Sally promise to have a nap in the afternoons, to drink plenty of milk, eat red meat and not go back to work until Paul was at least three months old. Sally had felt guilty about going back when he was only six weeks but she and Richard had needed the money.

Now, hearing Franca on the radio, Sally feels close to tears she is so proud. She must write to her. No, first she must read the book. Better still, she'll ring Franca in Melbourne and tell her how happy she was to hear her, congratulate her on finishing the book and tell her how she misses her. Would that be too presumptuous?

Sally realises that she has never even told Virginia, who was in London at the time, that Franca drove her home from hospital. Perhaps she does not want to share the experience. Virginia, after all, can have an intimate time with her mother whenever she wants to. Sally feels cross with Virginia for living at the opposite end of Australia from Franca and rarely bothering to visit her.

Virginia has no idea that Sally feels aggrieved with her. She has other things to worry about. Now that her Ananda Arthouse has opened and the euphoria has died down; now that she is no longer the centre of attention in the local newspapers and the television cameras are prowling after newer celebrities, the shadowy figures are creeping back.

Her two nearest neighbours, cane and avocado farmers

who had refused her invitation to the opening of the Arthouse, as well as the president of the local council who accepted, have all written letters of complaint through their lawyers. The farmers have claimed that the noise caused by fireworks, singing and dancing on opening night kept them awake until the early hours of the morning and had an adverse affect on their next day's work. The noise of buses and a steam train travelling close to their properties was upsetting to the animals. Animals? There were a few chooks, thinks Virginia indignantly. The neighbours threaten that if such noises ever happen again they will issue court orders to have Ananda closed down.

After these complaints, the council has reconsidered its decision to allow the Arthouse to operate. It has declared that the whole idea of commercialising farmland is undesirable and if there is any further disturbance, a restraining order will be issued.

Virginia had politely warned both neighbours and councillors that there would be some noise at the opening celebrations, to which they had shrugged and said it was a Saturday night and they often made a bit of a racket themselves on Saturdays. So these letters make her angry.

She is afraid that the concert she has planned for next month – and this will be another triumph she imagines – with an internationally famous Australian pianist having agreed to donate his services entirely free of charge to aid the artists, might have to be postponed until she's had time to placate the neighbours and the council. All this is tedious. She has spent long enough soothing their ruffled feathers, talking them out of paranoia. She has invited them to the gallery, to meet artists informally at a special little lunch she and the students cooked in front of them. There she'd explained that there wouldn't be many fundraising concerts, but those there were would be classical music, much quieter than amplified rock. The audiences would be well behaved. No drunkenness. Just the odd glass of champagne. The steam train would no longer blow its whistle if that disturbed their animals. She thanked them for their suggestions and offered them all free tickets to the forthcoming concert and they had seemed pleased. They'd admired the grand piano she had borrowed from the Conservatorium of Music in Brisbane on which the famous pianist would perform, and the cane and avocado farmer's daughter, Deidre, had been allowed to play *The Dance of the Gnomes* at the top end while Virginia improvised chords at the bottom. They had smiled and nodded and accepted Virginia's hospitality and now they were threatening to close the place down! What was behind their objections? Envy? Resentment of the artists' outstanding exhibition? Fear of the fact that they were Aboriginal and successful?

Guy had flown back to the United States to start Graduate School at Harvard so Virginia was not able to rant to him. But Marina was a comfort.

'Yeah, well. What would you expect from a pack of rednecks?'

Marina had gone to high school with some of the children of the local farmers and councillors and, even though Aborigines made up about a quarter of the school's population, she'd suffered racist jibes occasionally.

'They're an ignorant mob, Virginia. Can't stand anything different. Don't let it get to you. Pretend you didn't get the letters.'

'What?'

'That's what we'd do when migloos teased us in the playground. Pretend you can't see or hear them. Drives 'em crazy.'

Virginia smiled. 'I suppose I could try.' But she did not look convinced.

'Course, if the migloos were really bad, like hitting us and stuff, we'd get a few of our big fellas together, get some sticks, stones, bricks and have a war.' Marina laughed. 'We didn't want to fight but if they forced us, well, we usually bloody won!'

'You think I should go over to the Maloney's and hurl bricks through their windows?'

'Yeah! And shoot a few of their precious chooks.'

Virginia laughed. 'And drive the Land Cruiser up and down over those canna lilies in front of the council chamber?'

'Yeah, and blow up the bridge!'

'So the Puccis will have to swim to get to the pub!'

'And then they'll get eaten by a croc. The whole bloody family!'

This infantile game made Virginia feel better. She was grateful to Marina, who looked at her with concern, in spite of the hilarity.

But before any of these threats to neighbours and councillors could be carried out, the cyclone warnings started.

# CHAPTER NINE

There had been cyclones before. Storms they were called until they became too destructive. People up north did not panic easily. They were used to the elements wreaking havoc: torrential rains, rivers flooding, washing away livestock and vehicles. But this cyclone looked as if it could be serious. It wasn't just a storm. Until recently they were always called after women – Cyclone Tracey, Cyclone Matilda, Cyclone Dawn. It was about time they named one Cyclone Billy or a Cyclone Bruce.

Virginia thought about this as she stacked the more valuable paintings in the cellar and removed pottery from the shelves of her small house on the hill above the lake. The students and resident painters were packing up their valuables in the other two houses and they would all help to secure the gallery. Then, Virginia decided, she'd insist that everyone heed the radio warnings to evacuate. She found accommodation for them in Cairns for a night or two in a motel that belonged to some friends of hers, until the storm blew over. She still thought of it as a storm even though it was now being described, rather ominously by the media, as Cyclone Jezebel. She would stay on in her house, which was built on high ground and was more solid than the others, which were old canecutters houses she'd had shifted to Ananda on semitrailers and renovated for the artists. She'd have the Land Cruiser and plenty of food. If the phone lines and power were cut she'd still be safe. The cellar would stay dry even if the roof blew off. She didn't think for a moment that it would.

So when the wind began to howl in a new way, like an animal, with a rhythm like breathing, when it roared so loud she couldn't hear the radio although it was turned up almost to full volume, she began to wonder.

Then the radio cut out and the lights died as well. It was dark outside and in. She lit two silver candelabra and placed them at either end of the long refectory table where everyone ate dinner and held meetings. The candles threw eerie shadows on the high cathedral ceilings. She sat at one end of the table drinking a glass of wine and trying to remember the speed and diameter of the cyclone so that she could calculate how much longer it might go on, but the roar of the wind interfered with her thinking. She walked about the room feeling exhilarated, flinging her arms wide and throwing her head back. She sang a few bars from *Rigoletto*. '*La donna e mobile . . .*' She danced a few steps, humming the orchestral part.

The phone rang. It was Sally in Sydney saying that yesterday she'd heard Franca interviewed on the radio about her new book. Had Virginia heard it? No? She was sorry she hadn't rung then. She'd also heard there was a cyclone heading down the far north coast and what on earth was that noise? When Virginia explained Sally was incredulous that she hadn't evacuated with the others. 'You might be the last person to speak to me alive!' Virginia joked.

'Don't be bloody funny.' Sally sounded angry. 'You've always been fearless but this is the limit. Get down in the cellar at once. Please. I'll ring the local police and see if they can rescue you.'

Virginia laughed. 'The last person the local police would want to rescue is me!'

'I'm ringing them anyway.' Sally hung up.

The phone rang again and it was Marina. 'Virginia, are you bloody mad? I thought you'd gone ahead of us to Cairns. What are you doing? The bridge has gone. There's no way out now!' She was screaming. 'You going to swim, you bloody fool? We can't get you out! The cyclone hasn't even hit you yet!' She started to sob.

'Marina, calm down. I'm fine. I've got food. If it gets worse I'll go down in the cellar. Don't worry about the bridge. When the creek goes down I'll wade across and if the croc comes too close I'll kick him in the head.' She laughed. The phone went dead.

Virginia sighed. The bridge falling was a shock. She did not feel quite as brave as she had tried to sound. Usually she was able to use her fear, transform it into energy but she had already done that, working feverishly all afternoon locking animals away, wrapping up valuables, securing doors and windows. Now there was nothing left to do but wait.

It was so dark she couldn't see what was happening outside. She'd heard a crack as if a large tree had snapped. When a fork of lightning illuminated the sky, she'd seen waves on the lake. She was glad the quails, geese and ducks were safe inside the fowlhouse Guy had helped her build.

She drank two more glasses of wine, ate some cheese and dry biscuits, lit the lantern and went down into the cellar where she lay on a pile of cushions and soon went to sleep.

When she woke in the early morning pale light was streaming in through the open cellar and the dreadful howling wind was silent. Virginia climbed up the ladder into what had once been her living room.

It was lighter than usual because the roof at one end was not there. It had been broken off cleanly as if a giant had lifted it, like a piece of pie crust. Perhaps to make up for the theft of roof the giant had deposited a large tree inside her living room. Virginia's first dazed thought was that it took up so much space she'd have to shift the furniture out. She walked around the tree. It was a laburnum, very leafy. Its roots splayed out at one end, looking like a hairy spider covered in red earth. As the tree had fallen the roots had made a pattern on the wall that looked vaguely like a cave drawing. She cocked her head on one side to get a better view of it.

Beneath the tangled branches of the tree, her refectory table, candles and empty wine glass lay crushed. Lucky I did go down the cellar, thought Virginia. A few windows were broken, the rugs were soaking wet, some paintings had been knocked off the wall and a sofa squashed flat. Apart from that everything was as it had been.

But when Virginia walked out onto the verandah and looked down the valley towards her paradise gardens where there had been the lake full of water lilies, the art gallery like a temple and the restored artists' houses on stilts, she saw the real devastation.

Sunk in the shallow end of the lake and listing to one side was the borrowed black grand piano. Trees were strewn about like twigs. A staircase leading nowhere was propped against a giant fig. One of the houses had lost a stilt and leaned precariously over a small crater full of water, made by a ripped up tree. The other house had twisted to face the opposite direction and had no roof. Power lines hung in a tangle and there were bits of fence and roofing iron and henhouse dangling from the trees that still stood.

And the shimmering temple, the honey-coloured Arthouse that had stood at the edge of the lake now lay across it, half submerged.

'She's in shock. I saw the aerial shots of it on television. It looks like Armageddon,' Sally said to Meg. 'I said I'd go up there, help her try and patch things up, which would be pretty hopeless, I know, but at least I'd be with her.'

'What did she say?'

'No. Definitely not. She said she wants to be alone. She sounded dreadful.'

'We can't just leave her be.'

'If she says no, she means no. But I think we should keep phoning and be ready to fly up there at short notice.'

'She's got Marina. But the others aren't much support, the artists and students. They all seemed rather dependent on her.' Meg said. 'There are a few good neighbours – Bengt, that Danish fisherman and the Fiorelli family, who were friends of her grandparents.'

'Ah yes, the cane farmers who collect paintings. She might let them help.' Sally said. 'The army's been brought in to organise the clean-up. The whole area was hit but the devastation at Ananda was worse than anywhere else apparently. Did you see that shot of the pub at Gurrunga deep in water and all those farmers still drinking on the verandah hurling tinnies cheerfully at the rescue helicopters?'

Meg nodded. 'The same cretins who threatened to take Virginia to court if she dared let a concert pianist perform anywhere near their property. Will she stay now that she's lost so much?'

'I can't imagine her giving up, but this morning when I spoke to her, she sounded like a different person.'

Virginia sat on her verandah and looked across the ruined valley. The light, after the rain, had made everything look brilliant. She could not help but admire it. The tree trunks were blacker, the grass emerald green, the fallen buildings golden and even the dead geese and ducks, flung from their shattered home by the wind, looked like blindingly white petals strewn on the grass.

The grand piano, still protruding from the lake, looked surreal. Although it was on a slant, the whole keyboard was above water. She had a bizarre thought: perhaps the famous pianist could still perform. He would wade into the water lifting his coat-tails and play Chopin standing up. He was the sort of generous eccentric who might do that in a state of emergency and for a good cause. This situation was both, thought Virginia.

When the army arrived with amphibious vehicles to help salvage the wreckage they found Virginia up to her thighs in the muddy lake playing *Valse Brilliante* in A flat, Opus 34, Number 1.

The sergeant approached her timidly, but when she lifted her eyes from the keyboard she was beaming. 'Amazing!' she said, 'Hardly out of tune at all.'

Later that evening, when the piano had been hauled safely into her living room from which the tree had now been removed, a tarpaulin stretched across the roof so that she no longer looked up at the stars, Virginia played more of Chopin. The music was like water running over smooth rocks, a creek bubbling on and on, with flourishes at rockpools. Delicate as raindrops at first and then rumbling ominously, gathering strength, threatening to become dangerous before going back to being a lacy trickle of drops. She played all the watery Chopin she could remember, all the pieces she and her sisters had practised for years under their mother's tutelage, and when she had finished she felt better, as if she and the beautiful piano had somehow survived their ordeal.

That evening Franca Arezzo telephoned Virginia from her terrace house in Parkville, Melbourne. After seeing the television news Franca had waited a half hour before phoning in order to collect herself. She knew that her daughter would not welcome hysteria.

'I have just seen what that cyclone has done to your Ananda. Tesora, it is terrible. Why didn't you tell me?' She struggled to stay calm.

'Ah well, Mama, you would have worried. And the phone lines went down.'

'Of course, of course. You are all right?'

'Fine, Mama. I believe that your book's already published. Congratulations! Sally heard you on the radio.'

'My book? Si, si. The book is all done and people are buying it. Which is good. Good. But you, my darling, what will you do now? You should come down here. Stay with me. Get away from that mess.'

'I've got a bit of cleaning up to do first.' Virginia made herself sound cheerful.

'You should leave it. When such a disaster happens, leave it!' Franca's voice was rising in spite of her good intentions. 'It is too heart-breaking to start right away to clean up. Or, if you must do it, I will come up there now and help you.'

'No, Mama,' Virginia said firmly. 'Thank you, but no.'

'Tch! Always so stubborn. Then promise me that when the cleaning is done, you will take a holiday. Get away from that place. You are always working, working. For years. Go and stay with Camilla in London, or in Montreal with Giovanna. You haven't seen your sisters for so long. They have children you've never even met. Disgraziata!'

'Si, Mama.' Virginia smiled to herself. Since she was a child her mother had scolded her and then, instantly, recanted.

'Of course *they* could have brought the children to see *you*. They both are well-off and you are always in such debt because of your generosity and grand ideas. Oh, Virginia, it is so sad what has happened to you!'

'Mama, I'm fine. Really.'

'I was just remembering, the other night, when I was sorting out some old photographs, how you and your sisters would recite the piano for your father's students and how you were always, and this I should not admit . . .'

'My father's favourite.'

'Always. It was not good for your sisters to know this. I tried to hide it, of course, but your father was not so subtle. You looked like him. So fair, when your sisters were dark. Such a performer! Like him. He loved to show off.' Franca sighed deeply. 'I do miss him.'

'Si, Mama,' Virginia said. 'Me, too.'

'You know, I'm glad he didn't live to see what has happened to the beautiful farm his parents left you. He would have been heart-broken.'

This was becoming morbid. 'You're right, Mama,' Virginia said brightly. 'I do need a break from this place. As soon as the worst of the cleaning up is done I'm going north.' The suggestion surprised her. She hadn't realised this was what she would be doing. 'To stay with some people at Cape York.'

'Who? What people? I don't know who would want to live so far north as that. They would fry in the heat.'

'Aboriginal people. Marina's relatives. The land is beautiful – all red earth, white sand and blue sea. Do you want to come with me, Mama?'

'No, my darling, I do not. But you go. It is a good idea you go anywhere away from that Ananda.'

'Oh?' Virginia detected a warning in her mother's tone. Had the neighbours who had been her grandparents' friends told her something unpleasant?

'Si, the Fiorellis have telephoned me,' Franca said, anticipating her question. 'They are concerned for you. They say you have made enemies of the other neighbours who don't want entertainment. They say there is a petition to close your Arthouse down. They want you off the land. They are angry with you and some of them are violent people. Be careful, Virginia.'

'Have you seen this petition?' Virginia asked Marina, as they scrubbed mud off the verandah the next morning.

'I've seen it. They're passing it all round Gurrunga. Buying people beers in the pub to get them to sign it. They wanted me and my mum to sign. What a cheek!'

'How many signatures so far?'

Marina looked uncomfortable. 'Quite a few, I reckon.'

'Who started this . . . petition?' Virginia pronounced the word with distaste. 'Puccis or Andersons?'

'Andersons, I'd say. Mum hears all the gossip doing the counter teas.'

'The Andersons have wanted to get hold of this land since my grandparents owned it.'

'I heard that, too. And now there's all the more reason to force you out. Apparently a developer down in Cairns has made them an offer. He wants to build a big tourist theme park but he needs rainforest and a waterfall. The Andersons don't have those. You do. So you see why they're passing round the petition. They want to close down the Arthouse, buy this land and then sell the lot to the developer at a huge profit.'

'I think it's time I paid the Andersons a visit,' Virginia said grimly.

'I wouldn't do that.'

'Why not?'

'They're mad bastards. All got shotguns, even the kids. And they're pissed most of the time.'

'You think they might shoot me?' Virginia grinned. 'The people who've sat around my table eating meals I've cooked, whose kids I've taught to paint and play the piano?'

Marina shook her head. 'You don't really know them. Don't go there, Virginia. Just don't, okay?' She looked distressed.

'Marina, what is it? What's going on?'

'There are rumours about you,' she blurted out. 'Horrible, mad stuff they're passing round the pub.'

'Rumours?' Virginia widened her eyes and pretended to be shocked. 'Really? Don't keep me in suspense. What rumours?'

'That you're into black magic. Witchcraft!'

Virginia laughed out loud. 'Will they tie me to a ducking board and dunk me in Crocodile Creek seven times to see if I survive, do you think, like they did to witches in the Middle Ages? How pathetic!'

'You shouldn't joke about it. They're nasty when they're drunk. I've seen what they can do to people who . . . don't fit in. Aboriginals are used to it. We're careful around them. We expect the police to look the other way. But you . . . you just think you can get away with anything.'

'What else have they been saying at the pub?'

'That you're a whore and a deviate.'

'Wow!'

'That you grow dope and corrupt young people who come to Ananda to study art . . .'

'Whom do I corrupt?' Virginia was suddenly serious. 'You, Marina? Do they say that?'

'Yes, they say that.'

'Bastards!' she said angrily.

Virginia drove the old Toyota Land Cruiser across the creek that was still rushing and muddy up the slippery bank to the Anderson's banana, cane and avocado farm. She drove fast, in a fury.

The army had done the worst of the cleaning up but there was still a lot to do. She had been dragging debris out of the lake all afternoon, trying to calm herself. Her hands were covered in cuts and scratches.

The day after the cyclone, she recalled, she had sent presents to the Andersons of tinned and frozen food from her cellar. She had heard that both of their four-wheel drive vehicles had been crushed and imagined they might need supplies. As she drove up their track just on dusk she saw that although the garage was wrecked, the house, gardens and plantations were quite unscathed.

She parked under a big tree some distance from the house because there seemed to be a party in progress. Loud country and western music came from a speaker propped up on the back of a truck. Two or three women, having finished spreading a cloth on a trestle table in the shade, went back inside the house. The guests outside were all men. A couple of them were tending an animal of some description which was roasting on a spit. The rest were gathered round a beer keg, talking and laughing raucously.

As she strode along the driveway she recognised some of the parked cars as those of her other neighbours, the Mahoneys and Puccis. But the Fiorellis' vehicle was not there. She wondered what the Andersons were celebrating. A birthday for one of their sons? She didn't know the older boys as well as the young ones so it was unlikely they'd invite her to their party despite the fact that they were her nearest neighbours. Perhaps this was the wrong time to confront their father about the rumours. No, damn it. They were outrageous. She'd take him aside and get it over with.

When she was within a few metres of the house there was a shout and the men around the keg looked up. They stared at her in silence. She waved to them, although she didn't recognise many, and called out cheerfully, 'Hullo!'

The next few minutes were a blur. She was walking in the direction of young Deidre Anderson, who had just come from the kitchen with a tray of buttered bread and hadn't seen Virginia, when she was hit from behind and crumpled to the ground. She remembered feeling foolish. Had she been smashed by a falling tree bough? She lay there. Her head felt heavy and she was too dizzy to get up. She saw feet and boots above her and heard a male voice say, 'Bash the bitch. Give it to 'er.'

Another unfamiliar voice said, 'Go on, Les. She's tresspassin' on your property. You said you was gunna belt her. Now's ya chance!' There was some coarse laughter.

'She's only a bloody hippie. A feral.'

'And she reckons she's an artist. Druggie, more like.' Was this the voice of Brett Anderson, the eighteen-year-old son, who'd helped her mow five hectares of grass last October and told her of his secret ambition to go to Sydney and learn to play rhythm guitar?

'Lady Muck lyin' in the mud!'

'That's where she belongs.' The voice was full of hatred. One of the boots flicked her loose shirt up, exposing her black brassiere.

'Wouldn't ya high class mates from the city like to see ya now, eh? All them art dealers and stuck-up professors. All them boong-lovers. Hey, she looks like she could use a drink, Les.'

'Sorry, we're outa champagne. Have a beer, love!'

Virginia felt a splash of cold liquid pour over her face. She flinched. There was loud laughter.

'She doesn't like it much, Brett. Not what she's used ta. Only Four X.'

'Hey! Whatcha doin?' It was the voice of nine-year-old Deidre. Virginia opened her eyes and held out her hand, trying to smile. 'What's the matter with Virginia?' she asked the circle of men. 'Why's she on the ground?'

A few of them looked abashed. 'Reckon she's a bit tired,

love.' said her father. There were some chortles. 'Tripped over a root and couldn't get up.' The men exploded with laughter.

The child bent down and took Virginia's hand. 'You orright?' She scowled at the men. 'She's hurt her head. Look! There's blood.'

'Ooh yeah, so there is. Sorry, love. You help her get to her vehicle. She'll need to go home and clean herself up.'

'It could've been nastier,' Marina said. 'If Deidre hadn't showed up.'

'I know that.' Virginia sat on her bed while Marina bathed her neck and cheek with a cloth and warm water. 'They were drunk. I was stunned. Couldn't speak. It was terrifying.'

'You've probably got mild concussion. You should stay in bed.'

Virginia lay back on the pillow. 'You know what I feel? Grateful. Pathetic, isn't it? I just feel grateful that it wasn't worse.' Virginia closed her eyes.

'I told you not to bloody go over there, didn't I?' Marina scolded passionately. She was close to tears. 'They're animals! A pack of animals when they're pissed. You can sue them. I'll be your witness. Deidre, too. She knew what was going on, I bet.'

Virginia shook her head slowly. 'They wanted to intimidate me and they did. I had no idea they hated me like that. I've never felt such . . . violence. And most of those men I didn't even know.'

'They're Les's drinking mates from Gurrunga. He's probably been whingeing about you for months in the pub. To your face he wouldn't say boo, but when he gets his mates around him he's a big man. Gutless wonder. Who was it hit you?'

'I didn't see. Someone came from behind. I've only been knocked out once before, when I fell off a horse at twelve.' She shook her head. 'I can hardly believe it happened. Makes you feel humiliated. Powerless. Dirty, somehow.'

'Like being raped,' Marina said, hearing the quaver in her voice.

Virginia looked at her sharply. 'Yes. Makes you understand

what it must be like.' She continued to stare until Marina turned away. 'Did they ever . . . ?'

'No. Not me.' She sloshed the cloth into the basin of water. 'Don't want to talk about it.'

'Those men. They raped someone?'

'It happened years ago. I don't want to talk about it! Don't you ever *listen*?' She pulled away from Virginia's outstretched hand, fighting back angry tears.

The next morning Marina was gone.

Virginia drove into Gurrunga to find Marina's mother, Hannie, who worked as a chef at the local pub, but the publican said she'd taken three weeks leave to go to Cairns. She was having a holiday down there with her cousins. She'd left an address, but there wasn't a phone. She'd taken the younger kiddie with her, but he could almost swear that Marina hadn't gone.

Virginia tried everyone else Marina knew in town, mostly young Aboriginal friends. No, they hadn't seen or heard from her. Not for weeks. They thought she was out at Ananda.

She decided to drive the hundred kilometres to Cairns and find Hannie. On the way she thought about Les Anderson and his mates. She was thankful their victim had not been Marina. But who was it? One of the Aboriginal girls she'd just visited perhaps? But it happened years ago. How many years? How much had Marina witnessed? Had the rapists been caught? Punished? Her neighbour! The man she'd invited for meals, whose wife and children she was fond of. She felt revolted.

Marina was not with Hannie, who was sitting on the verandah of her cousin's bungalow with her legs propped up on a cane settee. Hannie was a dignified woman who laughed easily, but there was a sadness about her, too.

They sat in the shade under the purple bougainvillea vine, sipping strong tea. Melanie, her younger daughter of seven, appeared with a plate of Tim Tam biscuits. 'Aunty Merle said to bring you these.' She offered them to Hannie and Virginia, ate one herself, then sauntered over to the monkey bar wedged high up between two boughs of a mango tree. She scrambled up quickly and turned a series of expert somersaults, ending up hanging upside down by her knees. Virginia applauded. 'You look like a fruit bat, Melanie.'

Hannie shook her head. 'She wants to be an acrobat.'

'She's very good. Does she go to gym?'

'Police Boys' Club,' called Melanie from her upside down position. 'They let girls go there now.'

'Good for them. I bet you're better than a lot of the boys, anyway,' called Virginia.

'Yep. Better than most of them.'

'Tomboy, she is,' said Hannie proudly.

Hannie did not seem concerned about Marina's disappearance.

'Last time I heard from her was a couple of days ago. She sounded great. Said she was helping you clean the place up, scrubbing all that mud off the walls and getting everything back to normal. Seemed real cheerful.' Hannie looked searchingly at Virginia. 'Didn't have a fight with anyone did she? Marina can be a bit touchy. Goes off in a huff about almost nothing sometimes.'

Hannie was a perceptive woman of about her own age and for a few seconds Virginia was tempted to confide in her. But Marina might not want that. 'No, nothing like that,' she said breezily. Virginia felt guilty about having burdened this overworked woman with the disappearance of the daughter who was supposed to be in her care. 'She's probably back at Ananda right now. Probably went to see some friends in Gurrunga. I had to come down to Cairns to collect a parcel from the airport. Thought she might be here and I could offer her a lift home,' she lied unconvincingly.

Hannie smiled. 'Look, I wouldn't worry about Marina. I used to worry, when she was fourteen and wild. But now, what a change! She loves the job out there and she reckons you're the best art teacher in Australia. She was telling that to young Melanie when she came home the other week. I'm just so grateful she's got a life and a career that she enjoys. I'd like to thank you for that.' She nodded emphatically and held out both hands to clasp Virginia's.

'I'm lucky to have her.' Virginia hugged the other woman, feeling humbled. She made her farewells and promised to let Hannie know if Marina didn't turn up.

On the drive back to Ananda she thought about Hannie's gratitude and the hard life she had led. Hannie was from Cape York. Marina had been born up there. Her father was an Islander who'd gone back to live on Badu Island when Marina was a baby and never returned. When Marina was four Hannie had re-married and moved across to Broome. Her new husband who worked as a pearl diver, had found Hannie a job as ship's cook. Being at sea for weeks at a time they did not see how they could cope with Marina. Families often shared children around so the decision that Marina should stay at Cape York in the Injarli community with her mother's sister Tilly was not considered odd. Marina had told Virginia that her early childhood was wonderful, growing up with her cousins, swimming together on deserted beaches and going to an Aboriginal school. She had hardly ever seen white people until she was twelve.

By then Hannie's second marriage had collapsed and she'd moved to Cairns where she had found a job cleaning at a motel. There was no high school in the Injarli community and Hannie had wanted Marina to come down south to live with her so she could go to high school in Cairns. Marina had been excited by the prospect of living in a big town and seeing her mother again. They shared a caravan out the back of the Pacific Palms Motel, near the bottle shop. But Marina had missed her life with the Injarli people more than she expected. As soon as she finished high school she planned to go right back up north. She'd almost been expelled for 'disruptive behaviour' in her early teens, she'd once told Virginia. But when, in her final year, she visited Ananda on a school excursion and met Virginia, she decided to become an art student there. Hannie had applied for the job of assistant chef at the Gurrunga pub, a few miles away from Ananda, to be close to Marina. Virginia had invited her and young Melanie, who was then only three, to live at Ananda too, until they'd saved enough to buy their own house. It had been hard for Hannie, working full-time with two children, but she'd usually managed to find jobs where she could be close to them. For a while, after she left Ananda, she'd worked as housekeeper for the Fiorellis, Virginia's closest neighbours, and Melanie had moved there with her. Melanie was much lighter in colour than either Hannie or Marina and neither of them ever mentioned who her father was, so Virginia had not asked.

Now, as she drives home past the lush cane farms, she wonders.

That night Marina phoned Virginia. 'Where are you?'

'Guess!' There was a burst of laughter.

'Gurrunga?'

'Cape York!'

'What? How did you . . . ?'

'Plane. I had some money saved. I needed to get right away.'

'Are you okay?'

'Yep. Fine. No worries. Spending time with my people. With myself . . .'

'With yourself? Great! I was really worried. Why on earth didn't you leave a note?'

'Because I didn't bloody feel like it!'

There was silence. Virginia felt her heart begin to pound, an ache in the back of her throat. But she only said calmly, 'What upset you? Was it Les Anderson and his mates?' 'They're nothing. I said I didn't want to talk about it.' Marina sounded hard and dismissive. 'I just need to spend time with myself. Where I grew up. This land up here, it's my sanity. I miss it. You should come up and see it.'

'Should I? Do you want me to?' Virginia asked her carefully.

'I told you I did. Months ago I invited you but you were too busy getting ready for the grand opening.' Virginia heard the disapproval in her voice. 'Ah, look, I'm not blaming you. I'm just as bad. All I thought about was my job, my big responsibility as a public relations person, charming the politicians, the businessmen, even the bloody neighbours . . .'

'I'm sorry. I didn't know about Les Anderson . . .'

'Look, just shut up about him will you!' she said passionately. 'Ignorant bloody migloo! What do you know about us Murris? How would you know what it's like to be a single black mother?'

There was a shocked silence. Who was she talking about? Virginia sensed it was better not to ask. She said quietly, 'I know what it's like to be a single white mother.'

'Huh! There's no comparison. None. You were a rich white artist living in London.'

'I was poor, Marina. I've told you all about it.'

'Well I'm telling you there's no comparison. What would you know?' she said belligerently.

There was silence. 'Marina, please tell me what happened with Les Anderson . . .'

'It's not your bloody business. Look, I've got to go . . .'

'Wait! Don't hang up. I'll come to Cape York. Okay? I'd love to. Just tell me where you are and I'll come up there.'

'Yeah? Well, good. Okay then. Come.' Marina's voice changed suddenly. She sounded pleased. 'You can meet Aunty Tilly and all the other relatives.'

'Can't wait to see you. Just wish you'd given me some warning before you pissed off.'

'Ah well. You know me. Unpredictable. Part of my charm.' She laughed.

'Your mum sends her love. And Melanie.'

'Yeah? I miss them.' Marina gave details of the flights and they agreed on a date for Virginia's departure in a few days time. 'Don't forget that parcel of stuff, will you. I hope it's not too heavy to load onto the plane. It's only clothes and medicine.'

'Why didn't you take it yourself?'

'I was going to but I was in a hurry. Sorry. I packed it ready and all but then I thought, shit, I'll miss the flight, so I dashed off and only took hand luggage.' There was a pause. 'I know I'm selfish. But we're a thousand kilometres from the nearest big town up here so we really need that stuff.'

'You're not coming back here, are you Marina?' Virginia said sadly.

'Look! I don't know what I'm doing. Okay?' She sounded angry again. 'I'm just a bit fucked in the head right now so don't ask me. It's peaceful up here. You can think straight. Bring your paints. The landscape'll blow your mind.' The thought seemed to calm her. 'This land is my sanity. And it won't be just a holiday for you, either. I reckon you might learn something.'

There was a pause. 'I hope so.'

# CHAPTER TEN

At Melbourne Writers' Week Sally had met up with Franca Arezzo, whose autobiographical novel had suddenly become a critical and popular success.

'Sally, now we are famous authors together, we must go out and have a drunken dinner!' Franca had suggested in her generous Italian manner. Sally had laughed and protested that the panels for childrens' writers were always scheduled early in the morning because the authors were not expected to have hangovers like adult novelists.

'So, we will have a literary lunch and have our hangovers in the afternoon,' Franca had declared, and promptly at one she had collected Sally from the Writers' Centre in her ancient Fiat, which Sally realised was the same car in which Franca had driven her home from hospital with her first baby more than twenty-one years ago. 'It is so difficult to find parts for cars these days. Why? I don't know. The car works perfectly, except for the lost bits. It was ten years old when I bought it, so now it must be more than thirty. It communicates with me in the dialect of Napoli although it was made in Turino.' Franca sighed. 'Of course it is old but we understand each other.'

Franca herself must be in her late seventies, Sally realised. She was dressed elegantly, in a cream linen suit, with an Italian straw hat and walked with the help of a cane stick. She drove the car carefully into an underground carpark, 'Ah, I hate these bunkers. How does one find the way out?' Sally and Franca emerged, blinking, into the daylight and climbed some wide steps through a maze of new office buildings towards Southgate. Suddenly a gust of wind hit them hard and Franca's arm shot out to catch her hat. From beneath its beautiful brim two pieces of thin white paper rose into the air and gradually unfurled. Sally stared. 'Toilet paper, Franca? Your elegant hat kept on with toilet paper?'

Franca looked embarrassed. 'Ah! Who would have known if not for the wind?' They watched the familiar strips of paper rise and rise, floating over the stark office blocks, into the grey sky and away towards Port Phillip Bay. Then they began to laugh helplessly. 'I hope I'm a writer as original and unconventional as you one day, Franca,' Sally said fondly.

'You are already original, Sally. And eccentricity like mine will come with old age.'

Franca had booked a table at Blake's, by the Yarra. They sat together in the window looking out at the crowds of people promenading. 'Only once a year at festival time does this sedate old city come to life. Then it throws off its dignity, eats and drinks in the street, taps its feet to the jazz bands on the footpath and expects to be entertained,' Franca pronounced. 'Look at that. Street theatre!'

A young bride, veil flying, was running full pelt past the restaurant hotly pursued by a groom who was pleading with her to forgive him. She turned briefly, gave him the finger and ran on across an arched bridge. He picked up the white satin shoe she had lost and followed, looking stricken. On the bridge she allowed herself to be caught, listened to the groom who was now on bended knees, appeared to forgive him and embraced him passionately. The watching crowd applauded. The couple, encouraged, continued their embrace on the ground, rolling over and over until they reached the water's edge. The crowd gasped. Some cried, 'Watch out!' The loving couple did not hear. At the last instant before falling into the murky waters of the Yarra the bride and groom sprang to their feet and bowed graciously. The audience clapped wildly.

Franca and Sally laughed. They sipped their wine and Franca said, 'Just like Virginia's wedding. Such a pair of performers. Always fighting with each other and then passionately making up. So exhausting to watch.' She nodded at the street actors. 'Just like them.'

'So you weren't sorry when the marriage ended?'

'Not at all. Except that Virginia has never wanted to marry again. I feel concerned for her up there alone in that jungle. Not accepting anyone's help. You are her friend, Sally. What do you think?'

'I think she's amazing. Full of energy and spirit in spite of getting almost wiped out by the cyclone. I do think though . . .'

'Yes? What do you think?' Franca sounded almost impatient.

'That she's changing somehow.'

'Changing? How?'

'I'm not sure. Becoming more introverted, perhaps. I find it hard to feel close to her lately. And so does Meg. Perhaps it's just that we live in cities and she doesn't. It could be as simple as that.'

'And that's the only change?' Franca seemed unsatisfied.

'You think there's more?'

'Yes, I do. But I may be quite wrong. I hope so.'

Although Virginia had told no-one but Marina about her visit to the Andersons, it seemed that the news had spread and the neighbours were showing signs of remorse.

'You should do a deal with those Andersons before you leave, Virginia,' Mrs Fiorelli had advised her. 'You withdraw the accusations of violence against them if they withdraw the petition to close your place down.'

They sat together on the verandah of Virginia's house in two rocking chairs that had belonged to her grandparents. Nina Fiorelli was ten years younger than Virginia's grandparents would have been if they'd still been alive, but she had been one of their closest friends. She must be over eighty now, but was still remarkably sound in mind and body. She put this down to hard work and a large family.

'Of course you should get an apology. And compensation too. You should get that,' the old lady advised. 'But knowing what brutes those Andersons are, I wouldn't bet on it.'

'They've apologised already. As far as they're capable of,' Virginia said. 'Les Anderson sent his wife over here with a sponge cake yesterday and a message to say one of his mates was celebrating getting a divorce and they'd all been a bit "under the influence" when I arrived. Mrs Anderson explained that Ted, the mate, had been a bit down on women lately and I happened to look like his wife. That's why he hit me. She said Les and Ted were already hard at work rebuilding my bridge so she hoped there were no hard feelings.'

'Do you believe that? He hit you because you reminded him of his wife?' said Mrs Fiorelli in outrage. 'I've seen her. She weighs ninety kilos and she looks like a bull.'

'He probably just wanted to hit *any* woman. As Marina said, he'd just heard Les complaining about me in the pub, saying I was uppity and giving him a hard time and then I happened to come along. Bingo!'

'That would be right,' said her neighbour bitterly. 'Well, he picked the wrong woman this time. Sue the bastard!'

Virginia looked at her sharply. It wasn't like Mrs Fiorelli to use such strong language. 'No, I'll talk to him first.' She smiled. 'You'll be pleased to know that Les Anderson's already withdrawn his petition. He actually sent me the grubby sheet of paper on which all the protesters names were listed. He'd written "Cancelled" across it like a dud cheque and then ripped it in half. He sent the torn list over with his wife as well as the cake.'

Mrs Fiorelli snorted in disgust.

'There is something I'd like to ask you about Les Anderson,' Virginia said. 'Marina was quite upset about what happened to me at his place. It reminded her of something else. Something much worse that happened many years ago. She didn't want to talk about it. Do you have any idea what it was?'

Nina turned to look out across the lake. She had known Virginia since she was a child and had always been frank with her. But she looked uncomfortable now.

'I thought you knew. It was in the papers.'

'What was?'

'The rape. Though it was never called a rape.'

'How long ago?'

'About eight years. It was a nasty business.' Nina Fiorelli shook her head.

'Who was involved? What happened?'

'They called it a sexual assault. Rape was never proved. Les Anderson and some mates got very drunk down in Cairns one night. Celebrating something or other. Winning at the races? I can't remember. Anyway they found an Aboriginal woman asleep in a caravan behind the pub and, allegedly, sexually assaulted her.'

'Who? Who was the woman?' Virginia asked urgently.

Marina would have been thirteen. Living with her mother in the caravan near the bottle shop out the back of the Pacific Palms Motel in Cairns.

'She wasn't named.'

'Why not?'

'She didn't press charges. The case never went to court. The story is that Les paid money to have it hushed up.'

'Paid money to the woman?'

'No, to the police.'

Virginia stared hard at her neighbour. 'Do you know who that woman was, Mrs Fiorelli?'

'I do. But it wouldn't be fair to her to say.'

'It wasn't Marina, was it?' Virginia demanded desperately.

Mrs Fiorelli shook her head. 'I won't say any more.'

'It was her mother, Hannie, wasn't it. And Marina knows! Was she there? Just tell me that much. Did she see?'

'No, no. She was staying with the cousins because Hannie was working late,' the old woman blurted out, and then looked ashamed of herself.

Virginia nodded grimly. 'But she found out soon enough. Melanie? Fathered by a pack of . . . Jesus! Why weren't they ever brought to trial?'

'No witnesses. No proof. Just the word of one single black woman against three respectable white farmers.'

'It's outrageous!'

'So it is. But don't let on you know. She's a very proud woman and she wouldn't thank you for your sympathy.'

'Who else knows about this?'

'Not many people. It was all hushed up. No fuss. Hannie's relatives, the cousins down in Cairns know. They took her and Marina in after the baby was born.'

'And the relatives in Cape York, do they know?'

'I wouldn't know about that. But I don't think Hannie and Marina would burden them with any sad stories unless they had to.'

Sad stories? Was that all it was? Virginia thought of the gratitude with which Hannie had told her how Marina was enjoying her life at Ananda. She felt outraged on Hannie's behalf and on Marina's. No wonder Marina sometimes disappeared after an unexplained burst of anger.

'But Hannie works at the pub where Les and his mates drink! How can she stand to see them?'

'She doesn't look. She doesn't have to. Hannie is the chef. She works in the kitchen, not the bar.'

Virginia shook her head. 'It must make her sick to be anywhere near them.'

'It's a good job and Hannie's a dignified woman. She looks right through scum like Les Anderson and his mates. She withholds her bitterness but I know she feels pain underneath. When she was working for me I tried to talk to her about it once but she couldn't bear to.'

'Could she still press charges?'

'It's not impossible. But she won't. There's Melanie to consider.'

'Of course.'

There was dancing the night of Virginia's farewell: South American, Aboriginal and seventies rock and roll. Joe Cocker in his cracked, pure English accent of 1972 sang 'Delta Lady', one of Virginia's favourites, and the artists and students, one by one, took their turn to dance with her along the verandah, narrowly avoiding colliding with the rocking chairs on which they had sat to listen to her lectures and to argue with her about Picasso and Miro.

As she danced the artists crooned the chorus, swaying and forming a circle around her, doing a mock backing number.

'I'd like to steal that Cocker record from you. It's unique,' Guy had told her just before he left for New York. 'Can't get it on CD, not anywhere in the States.'

'You musn't! Your father and I used to dance to it in our tiny flat in Chelsea just before you were born. It was the only record we owned,' Virginia had said. It wasn't often she spoke with affection of his father, so Guy had left it with her.

Her farewell had been a happy one. There had been a feast before the dancing, prepared by the students and the Fiorellis. Bengt, the Danish fisherman, had brought live mud crabs. There had been platters of pasta, crab and mangoes from the few trees that had not been destroyed. The Fiorellis had brought wine and several other neighbours had contributed vegetables and home-made pies.

She was leaving Ananda in the hands of the artists who'd opted to stay on and paint. Harry and Jack were working hard to prepare for their exhibition in Düsseldorf, and the students who were learning from them had offered to keep the grass mown. Builders were gradually repairing structural damage but no geese, ducks or bantams had yet been bought to replace the dead ones. The winds had died completely, the sun shone and the newly planted seedlings in the vegetable garden were already starting to shoot.

The twenty-seater plane flies low along the sea. The water is pale aqua in colour, with dark patches of coral underneath. There are atolls shaped like swimming pools: oblong, triangular, curved, oval – a fleet of shallow pools following each other across the sea. Some are like opals cut open, revealing black veins. Others are pale green like birds' eggs, brownish to white at the edges and then deep blue as they blend into the sea. Small white clouds make shadows like ink blots on the water far below.

The waves, at the edge of the islands look frozen, not crashing and pounding as they must be, but as still as a painting. Islands snake off into the distance forming a dragon, a fan, a prancing sheep.

The plane is full of people in shorts and bush hats, islanders going home. An old, grey-haired man talks to a younger one who is huge and very dark with long curly hair. He clutches a box with a plastic wading pool inside, a present for his children. The other passengers read the *Cairns Post* and doze behind their sunglasses.

The dragon below has five humps and its mouth is wide open. It looks more like a serpent now. You can see how mythology began, Virginia thinks. There are two islands flat as plates, like giant footprints, stranded in the sea.

Now there is land below and white sand dunes patterned by the winds, mountains of sand, rippling down to the sea.

Virginia dozes and dreams of being threatened by large heads that float above her like islands. They are male islands. They sneer. Their pink mouths open and shut like sea anemones. She cannot hear what they are saying because their voices are loud and distorted. If she could hear, she would be able to reason with them, tell them that she is no enemy. A friend. Neighbour. There is no need for violence. But they are moving closer. Roaring in their terrifying, incoherent voices. She wakes in a panic. The air-blower above her head has been turned on full and is blasting her left eardrum.

When Les Anderson and his drinking mate, Ted Murphy came to call on Virginia the morning she left they had been sober. Almost unrecognisable from the night of the party, they had been apologetic. They were surly about it, certainly, because they had no choice. They'd been told by some of the neighbours who hadn't been there but had heard about the ugly incident, that they could be in strife with the law.

Although she did not feel it, Virginia had behaved calmly. She had asked with genuine curiosity whether Les hated her. He had denied this, looking foolish, but admitted to some resentment. The reasons were not clear, even to him. Her heart was pounding with anger, but she probed him gently and discovered that misogyny was at the heart of it. Les said he did not resent women who were safely married and spoken for, but he implied that those who tried to be independent and pushy, who had schemes and property and power were dangerous. The only way to subdue them was with violence. And Aboriginal women who were independent and not married? How did he feel about them? She had asked the question pleasantly, as if quite innocent and only idly curious. But his reaction was instant. His eyes narrowed and he took a step towards her, his body threatening, but she stood her ground. 'I know all about the "incident" that happened years ago, Les. And it makes me sick to the stomach. I'm not proud of living next door to a man like you.'

# CHAPTER ELEVEN

At Bamaga airport, a tin shed surrounded by red earth and some giant anthills, Virginia was met by Marina's Uncle Dusty. He was tall, dignified and did not appear to like talking much. His hair was grey, his bushman's clothes neat. Part Aboriginal, part Murray Islander he was an elder of the Injarli community.

Dusty loaded Virginia's small bag, and the bulky parcel Marina had packed and a box of fruit into the four-wheel drive van with Pindaroo Wilderness Lodge written on it. 'No more passengers to collect. We can get goin' I reckon,' he said.

As the Toyota jolted over pot-holed roads and through patches of rainforest, Virginia asked about Marina. She had expected her to be at the airport and felt disappointed, but tried not to show it. 'Marina paints well. Have you seen any of her work?'

Dusty shook his head.

'Hannie's bought her own house in Gurrunga, a nice old wooden place with a verandah and a big garden. She sent a box of mangoes. And young Melanie's seven, doing really well at school and wants to be an acrobat.' Dusty nodded but kept silent. 'Hannie said to tell you that they miss you all,' she continued, encouraging him to say something, but as he still did not respond, she asked, 'How many people are there in the Injarli community?'

'Lotta people there now. Four, maybe five hundred. Five different tribes. People comin' from all over. We been settled there since 1900.'

'Marina tells me the community is entirely self-supporting and you're taking charge of your traditional lands.'

'That's right,' Uncle Dusty did not elaborate.

'She said you own about eighty thousand hectares and you've just bought the Pindaroo Wilderness Lodge from an airline company for over two million,' Virginia said. 'That's fantastic.'

Uncle Dusty nodded and looked worried. 'Lotta money to pay back. We had to get a big loan.'

'Well, I think it's marvellous that you did. And the Lodge is running well?'

'Only been going a few months. Seems okay.' Dusty stared out at the bush. 'You'll see for yourself. That's where you'll be staying.'

'Oh?' Virginia hadn't realised she'd be amongst the white tourists. She had hoped to be staying with the Injarli people, thirty kilometres away. Dusty saw that she was disappointed.

'More comforts at the Lodge. Swimming pool. Hot showers. Three meals a day. We even got a fax machine,' he chuckled. 'Much better for you there.'

'But when will I see Marina and her relatives, Aunty Tilly, Uncle Bill and all the cousins?'

Dusty grinned. 'Relatives? They all around. Can't miss 'em. Tilly, she works in the kitchen, Bill takes the guests fishin'. Most of the older cousins work as waiters or in the office, the kids come and swim in the pool at weekends and I'm the driver.'

Virginia laughed. 'Well that's a relief!'

'Only white people on the staff are the manager and the naturalist,' Dusty continued. 'Angus, the manager, he's overseas, tryin' to get customers. We're not doin' too bad. We been on TV. Some tourist program. But we need the Americans and the Japanese, Angus reckons. They the ones with all the cash.'

'Right.' Virginia smiled. The reticent Uncle Dusty was becoming eloquent on the subject of business management.

'How will the Americans and the Japanese cope with taipans and death adders, do you think? And the crocodile-infested surf? And dengue fever?' she asked mischievously.

Dusty considered the question impassively. 'I reckon we just tell 'em to watch out.'

When they arrived at the Lodge after travelling through dense rainforest, hot grasslands dotted with tall red anthills and mangrove wetlands, it was like an oasis. Having seen no other human being on their rugged two hour drive from the airport it was a relief to hear voices. Behind the high wooden sign saying, 'Pindaroo Wilderness Lodge', Virginia caught sight of the promised swimming pool set amongst paperbark trees. Dusty gave her a quizzical look and she laughed, admitting he had been right; she would enjoy a few comforts.

'Only a few hundred metres to the tip of Cape York out there,' he pointed towards a beach. 'Northern-most tip of Australia. Only a hundred and twenty kilometres to New Guinea if you get fed up here with us.' He grinned. 'Take one of them Pindaroo motor dinghies, you be there in a few days. Catch a few barramundi on the way.'

'And what about the crocs? How far out do they swim?'

'Been seen two hundred kilometres out to sea,' said Dusty seriously. 'Reckon they'd be followin' all the way.'

Virginia shuddered. 'I think I'll stay with you lot.'

At the little open-air office, with its posters showing local fish, birds and smiling Injarli children, Virginia signed herself in and waited with her dusty bag and boxes until she was ushered across under the trees to a table beside the pool by a shy young girl who introduced herself as Linda.

'You hot? I'll get you a drink.'

She brought a tall glass of orange juice with ice, mint and lemon floating in it. Virginia was grateful. The temperature was in the high thirties.

'Is Marina about?' she asked Linda.

'Marina? No. In a minute I show you to your place,' Linda whispered. Then she smiled and went silently away.

Uncle Dusty had disappeared. The other guests were nowhere to be seen. As it was early afternoon Virginia supposed they must all be out fishing, hiking or birdwatching. She felt rather alone. She wandered into the open-air dining room to look at the sepia photographs of early white settlers – women in high-collared lacy blouses with long-suffering expressions and wiry men in wide-brimmed hats, rifles slung across one shoulder. Local Aboriginal paintings covered the rest of the walls. There was no sound except the wind in the trees and the cheeping of birds.

Suddenly, from behind a curtain at the back of the dining room, she heard peals of cheeky laughter and two black children with halos of fuzzy hair looked out. Then a large, dignified woman came forward, grasped her by the hand and said softly, 'I am Aunty Tilly.'

Tilly was the woman who had been the greatest influence on Marina in her early years. It was Tilly who had brought her up since she was four. There was a resemblance to Hannie. They had the same strength, gentleness and sad, resigned expressions.

'So tell me, how is my Marina getting on down south?' asked Tilly in her soft, deep voice, smiling with expectation.

'You should be proud of her. She's doing very well.'

'I hear that she wants to be an artist and that you've been teaching her.'

'I have. And she is very promising. But she has a full-time

job apart from painting. She's in charge of publicity at the Arthouse. Did a public relations course down in Cairns. Did she tell you?' Virginia fumbled in her bag to find the photos of Marina in her glamorous short white dress and high heels on the night of Ananda's grand opening.

Tilly examined them, nodding gravely and handling them with great care. 'She's grown up beautiful. Looks like she knows where she's going, too. That makes me happy.'

Virginia looked puzzled. 'But you've seen her. She's here.'

'Marina?' Tilly shook her head slowly. 'She has not been here for many years.'

Virginia laughed in disbelief. 'But she phoned me from here a few days ago! We talked for half an hour. She said she was expecting me today.'

'She phoned to tell us you were coming and to meet you. But Marina has not been here since she was twelve.'

'What!' Virginia shook her head. 'Am I going crazy? Where is she then?'

Aunty Tilly shrugged. 'She didn't say where she was calling from. I thought she was with you. She asked us to look after you because you were tired and needed a rest. You are welcome to stay here as long as you like.'

'Well, thank you. Yes.' Virginia looked bewildered. Was this some pathetic prank of Marina's? She certainly had a wacky sense of humour. Perhaps she'd turn up in a day or two. Perhaps not. It wasn't very bloody funny. Virginia had work to do back home. She couldn't sit around here like a tourist, waiting for someone who might not bother to turn up.

Tilly finished looking at the photographs of Marina and handed them carefully back to Virginia.

'No, keep them. They're for you.'

Tilly seemed moved and nodded her thanks.

Virginia realised she'd been behaving rather badly for a guest. 'I'm sorry. I'm just a bit surprised, that's all. I'm sure she said she was ringing from Cape York. She wouldn't be at the Injarli community, would she?'

'No. I came from there this morning.'

'Could she be staying somewhere else up here?'

'No. She would have told us if she was coming. We'd all want to welcome her. All of us.' Tilly nodded emphatically.

'Ah.' Virginia shrugged. 'I must have misunderstood . . .'

She made an effort to be pleasant. 'Marina told me a lot about her childhood up here with you. She says it was a marvellous time.'

Tilly nodded. 'I missed her when she left,' she said simply.

'She said that without your letters that first year away, she would have given up trying to fit in down south.'

'Yes, but her mother needed her.'

Resentful thoughts were racing through Virginia's mind. The wretched girl had conned her into lugging a huge package of medicine and clothing up here to her relatives because she couldn't be bothered bringing it herself. She pretended Virginia needed a rest but really she was making a convenience of her. She was playing power games. What had she said before she left? You never listen. Running away was an attention-getting device. All that stuff about needing to go far away, the land being her sanity, was bullshit! What was really the matter with Marina?

As Virginia sat drinking coffee with Tilly in front of a forest of fan palms that first afternoon, she willed herself to calm down. Marina would not thank her for making a bad impression on her relatives. She was probably so nervous about what they'd think of her, she'd decided to stay away for a bit, leaving them to get to know each other. She would turn up when she was ready. Virginia had even told her mother that she was going to Cape York for a break as soon as the worst of the cleaning up was done. And now it was done. Marina knew she'd like the landscape and hoped she'd get on alright with her relatives as well. After all, it was Marina who'd organised Virginia's flight, arranged for Uncle Dusty to meet her at the airport and Aunty Tilly to welcome her at the Lodge. She'd only lied that she was already here so Virginia would come immediately. It was quite true: Virginia did need a rest, did need to get away from Ananda. Marina had been considering her, not using her, and she was, as she'd often admitted, unpredictable. 'Part of my charm'. Yes, she would turn up in a day or two. Virginia would wait. Get to know her relatives so she wouldn't be just an 'ignorant bloody migloo'. Relax. Walk. Paint. And listen to the stories Marina said they all told.

In the background a small black child splashed by himself at the shallow end of the pool and sometimes called to Tilly, who would wave at him to let him know she was watching.

'Tilly, how did you come to be part of the Injarli community?' Virginia asked. And Tilly began her story, which was Hannie's and Marina's too.

'I was the daughter of Jamu Tagwan and Grace Solomon, both Badu Islanders,' she said. 'The Aborigines worked for my grandfather. That's how we got together, Aborigines and Islanders, and why we're still together now at Injarli. Six companies he ran, starting in 1936, fishing for *bêche-de-mer*, trochus and pearl shell. We grew with them and we know their lives.'

'Marina said your father was one of the first councillors at Injarli.'

'He was councillor, teacher and mayor. Like a dad to everybody. My mother taught the ladies to cook and garden. People came together from all places – east, from here, down the Gulf, west. Injarli means meeting place. Sitting down.'

Virginia smiled. Such a simple name. Perhaps, if she'd called her Arthouse 'meeting place' instead of 'bliss', it wouldn't have met with disaster.

'We were the first Aboriginal community to be self-supporting,' Tilly said proudly. 'My grandfather, Atlas Tagwan, used to get the boys from Injarli, when they went out on the boats, to take a shilling out of their pay each week and put it in the bank. They put it in the fund for the community. They did that till the 1970s. Then a white man who used to play football with our boys, a friend from the courthouse, he says, "You got a lot of money." We didn't know that. So we bought a store. We started being self-sufficient. We told the government, "We don't want handouts." Some of the old people were unhappy about that. So they still gave them the pension. Now they've all died. TB or leprosy.'

Tilly drew smoke deep into her lungs.

'I heard it was you who helped in buying back this place from the airline company.'

'No, it was Jack Bourke, he pushed it. He's a politician. In 1986 I met the manager of this Lodge, Angus Grey, at Injarli. Me and my husband were staying on a boat. My husband's a white man.'

Virginia looked surprised. She had not known. Marina had not mentioned it.

'I asked Jack and Angus to dinner on our boat. Angus was talking. "I'm going over to Europe. I'm finished with the Lodge. The Injarli will have to get it back," he said.

'"How?" I said.

'"Fight through the government."

'I looked at him. "Good idea," I said.

'So we did fight through the government, with Jack Bourke doing the negotiating. I helped organise. We had rallies, got our money out of the bank. Then we got a loan and we had this place.' Tilly's eyes gleamed with triumph. 'When the airlines owned it we were not allowed to come in here. There was always a sign saying "Full", even if it wasn't. Now we had all our mates in here. When the other people from Injarli first arrived to work here and saw all the Aboriginal kids swimming in the pool their faces would go funny. I'd say, "You not happy? I can tell by your face." They took a while to get used to us being in charge here.'

'Your husband helped, too?'

'No, I left him a few years back. He started smoking grass, drinking rum and getting crazy. He'd hit me and once he threw me out of the boat into the water. I said, "That's enough for me." '

Virginia looked sympathetic and wondered whether Marina had known this crazed husband. Guessing her concern Tilly said, 'Marina never liked her Uncle Greg even when she was a little thing. She wrote to me when I left him; said it was the best decision I ever made.' She grinned.

'So now you're assistant chef here?'

'That's right.' Tilly gave a secretive smile. 'But what I'd like to do is be a guide. Talk to people about nature and that, show them the caves where our people did drawings in the old days. Get out of the kitchen.'

'You should do that,' Virginia said enthusiastically. 'Much better than a white person trying to explain about your food and plants, myths and customs.'

'I think so. I've been reading about the history, too. I want to change it, tell it from an Aboriginal point of view.'

'That's a great idea, Tilly! You know, it's probably no coincidence, but your sister Hannie told me once that what she'd really like to do is get a job as a native guide with some tourist company in Cairns. Did you know that?'

'No, she didn't tell me that. I reckon it'd be harder down in Cairns. Tourists just want to go snorkelling and to discos and that. They not so interested in native customs.'

'You're right. Hannie hasn't had one job offer. But being a native guide could work up here. When could you start?'

'Well, I gotta be patient. We already got a naturalist here. Ben.'

'I heard.' The fact that he was white was tactfully not mentioned.

Tilly nodded. 'He does a good job. But soon as he leaves, in maybe a year, I'll be ready to take over.' She smiled, looking pleased and confident.

'You can manage a four-wheel drive full of tourists over those rough roads while you talk?' asked Virginia in admiration.

'No, no! Uncle Dusty will drive and I'll just do the talkin'.' Tilly laughed, as if the idea of her driving was preposterous. 'I never drive now. Not now.' She suddenly looked deeply sad.

'I heard about your daughter, Tilly. I'm so sorry,' Virginia said gently.

'I was driving, you see. She was asleep in the back. She'd been working late and I came to pick her up. Some drunks smashed into the back of us.' Tilly shook her head. 'They'd been to a party at the football club.'

Tilly smoked silently. After a minute she said, 'Anyway I got my daughter's three children with me now.' She nodded towards the pool. 'The little one, he's here at the Lodge, but the big ones are back at Injarli.'

'It must be hard working full-time and looking after three children,' Virginia said sympathetically.

'No! They look after me!' said Tilly cheerfully. 'And if it gets too much, I can always send them to live with Hannie down near you.'

'You could,' said Virginia thoughtfully. The casual way Aboriginal people exchanged children still bothered her slightly.

The small boy had left the pool and came shyly to sit on Tilly's lap. He looked curiously at Virginia under long dark lashes. He was a beautiful child, aged about four and looked more Aboriginal than Islander. She imagined Marina sitting on Tilly's lap at the age of four.

'Do you ever go back to Badu Island?'

'We used to go for Christmas when we were kids. But we didn't like it over there. We didn't speak the language any more.'

'And here, what language do you speak?'

'Creole.'

Virginia had heard this language, an indigenous pidgin, at the Jackey Jackey airport at Bamaga.

'Do any Islanders still speak their original languages?'

'Not many. My father did. When the missionaries came from the London Missionary Society way back in 1871, they didn't like us speaking our own language.'

'Or worshipping your own gods or telling your own stories or living in your own kinds of houses, by the sound of it,' Virginia said indignantly. She wanted to ask why Tilly's people had put up with the missionaries, allowing their customs and symbols to be destroyed. She waited to see if Tilly would volunteer an explanation but she just gazed with dignity into the distance, inhaling smoke.

After a minute Tilly shrugged. 'The missionaries did some good things as well. Showed us how to stand up to the white bosses, taught us about money, how to save. They stopped the men fighting, too. Changed them from crazy warriors into very smart businessmen.' She threw back her head and gave a deep, husky laugh.

Virginia smiled. Marina had been right. She would learn things up here.

# CHAPTER TWELVE

Virginia was disillusioned with people. She wanted to sit on the rocks alone and watch the ocean.

That night she lay in bed in her hut listening to the trees all around making the sound of waves. Through the wooden slats of the wall, moonlight shone like sun through sails. Bamboo creaked like masts. The hut seemed to shake and roll like a ship. Outside she could see the outline of palm trees bending against the wind.

She had wanted to come to a remote part of the world to get back in touch with something she had lost. She felt exhausted by the battle she had fought over the past years to launch Ananda Arthouse – the wrangling with local councils, the constant reassuring of bank managers and suspicious farmers. It had, of course, been worth the effort. The Arthouse opening had been a success. But then, so soon after the success, had come the violence. First the cyclone, then the rumours and finally the personal attack. Virginia had been more hurt by this last thing than the rest.

It was not the first time in her life she had fled. Both times before she'd been escaping from relationships. She'd run away from her husband, Lewis Baines, and then from the artist she'd lived with for five years, Heinrich Scherner. Was she running away from yet another angry man? Was this to be the pattern of her life?

Of course not, she told herself. She wasn't afraid of Les Anderson. She'd confronted him. She'd been shaking with rage, not fear. Well, perhaps it was a little of both, she admitted. But it was true, she did not want to live next door to him any more. Was that why she'd run away? Would she find what she needed here at the northern-most point of Australia?

Marina had believed she would. Virginia felt excited by Marina. Possessive of her, too. She loved her spirit, her humour, her litheness and her cheeky grin. She loved Marina's beautiful flowing, unrestrained voice when she was telling a story to her relatives, using her whole body. Missing her was like an ache. She had pursued her to this remote place without realising why. Was she in love with Marina?

Sometimes Marina told Virginia she wanted to be with her forever and at other times, like now, she hurt her by behaving like a confused child. She had told Virginia how she loved her strength and courage and the way she looked and walked and laughed. Marina had been imitating her for years, she said. Hadn't Virginia noticed? She'd said how 'right' it felt to be with her.

Virginia had tried to be patient, to let her take time to know what she felt. But it hurt to be abandoned here at the very tip of Australia.

'Virginia! You awake?' The voice at the door was soft but persistent. The wind had dropped. Sun streamed through the wooden slats. A gecko was croaking somewhere up above her head. 'I brought you some breakfast,' said Linda. 'Can I come in?'

'Yes. Oh thanks! The door's not locked.'

The girl's dark head appeared, smiling shyly. She carried a tray of bacon and eggs, toast and tea. 'Breakfast was nearly over. I thought you might get hungry if you missed it.'

'Oh, you're wonderful! What's the time?'

'Ten o' clock,' Linda giggled. 'Aunty Tilly said you was real tired.'

'Ten! It can't be. I never sleep later than six-thirty at home.'

'Well, here's different,' Linda said. 'Aunty Tilly said when she's finished in the kitchen this afternoon she'll come over and see you.'

Virginia went for a walk on the beach. The tide was low. There was no sign of human habitation at all except for one dinghy, belonging to the Lodge, tied to a mangrove tree that grew in the middle of sand that stretched away like a desert. The roots of the tree reared up like some giant insect, dwarfing the boat, which lay on its side like a joke, so far it was from the sea. But in a few hours this boat, still tied to the tree, would be floating.

Climbing a rocky headland, Virginia followed a narrow path along the top of the cliff. She kept a sharp watch out for snakes. Brown snakes and rock pythons were easy to see and were mostly timid. It was the taipans and death adders, well hidden and aggressive, that were dangerous.

Below, the sea was green, a glimmering bay rimmed with blinding white sand. Pudegha, the bay was called. It had been the fishing and hunting ground of Aborigines for fifty thousand years and looked no different now than it had for generations. There were still crayfish and mud crabs, oysters and barramundi to be fished here. The bay was lined with wongai trees loaded with red plum-like fruits and there were brush turkey eggs, snakes and goannas to hunt on the land. Virginia had been told to look out for the two rock mounds on the headland that used to give the Aborigines warning of canoes approaching from the island of Muralag before the Europeans came.

She clambered down to the beach and sat there resting. There was a mound of ashes nearby. Tilly had told her that Aboriginal people still made fires on this beach and cooked fish and damper in the ashes, just as they'd done for thousands of years. She'd also said that in 1979 the Bush Pilots Airways had obtained a lease of five square miles which included the tip of Cape York and this beautiful beach, such an important part of Aboriginal history. It had taken the people thirteen years to get back control of their land.

Virginia was hot. It would be blissful to dive into those waves, she thought. Then she remembered the salt-water crocodiles. She would have to be content with walking on wet sand.

'That old croc lives down the end of the beach, he can travel fifty, maybe sixty kilometres an hour when he's chasin' ya,' Dusty had warned her before she set off.

'He won't chase me if I keep away from his end of the beach, though, will he?' Virginia had asked in mild alarm.

'Not today maybe. Not tomorrow or the next day even. He's just waitin' and watchin' ya. But on the fourth time you come walkin' along the same place, that's when he chases ya.'

'Ah.' Virginia sighed with mock relief. 'I'm quite safe then.'

'That's right,' Dusty said gravely.

He had told her that his totem was the crocodile which meant he had a close link with the sea. She wondered if this was why he waited with such patience and apparent lack of interest while she asked a mass of questions and only replied to the few that interested him.

Last night after dinner Dusty had opened up a little and told Virginia the story of how the Islanders had won a victory against the white bosses by using a combination of humour and passive resistance. In 1935, when he was fifteen and had just started on the 'company boats', a pearling fleet of luggers owned by the Murray Island people, the Islanders had gone on strike. They had wanted to be paid in cash rather than being given credit in government stores. The Queensland Government, which abided by the Aboriginal Protection Act, had threatened to confiscate the boats and transfer them to other islands.

'"That's okay. You do that and we won't go pearling or

fishing no more. We'll live from our gardening," we told their boss. He got real mad then, hit the chief council man and told him he was sacked. Their boss left then. He sent in police from another island to keep us under control. We didn't like that too much. We threatened to kill him if he ever came back to Murray Island. So they sent another man, the second boss. He calls a meeting with us to talk about the company boats but we won't talk. We sit very quiet for a long time in there. Then all of a sudden one man, he jumps right through the window and goes runnin' away. Then the next man jumps and the next. Pretty soon there's no one left in the meeting with the second boss. All gone out through the window.' Dusty laughed. 'The second boss, he treats us a lot better after that.'

'What happened to the first boss?' Virginia had asked.

'He was sacked because of the way he treated us. After that we had no more "yes men" on Murray Island.'

'And just a few years ago you had the Murray Island Land Case that has become the famous Mabo.'

'That's right. It all started on Murray Island. Hands off my land in the name of Mabo!' Dusty grinned. 'Now we got the legal right to say who comes onto our land to fish, mine or develop tourist places.'

'What do you think, Dusty? Will the Mabo idea work for Aboriginal communities in other places?'

'Couldn't say. It works for Murray Island people. They the ones that thought of it.' He had looked away, not wanting to discuss it further. The crocodile had descended underwater.

Virginia had been walking along hard wet sand for almost an hour at Pudagha. Not a creature in sight. She felt her strength gradually returning. Solitude was what she needed. She did not even miss Marina as keenly as she had at first. Was this partly why she'd tricked Virginia into coming here alone?

By day she would walk and think and in the evenings she would listen to the stories of the traditional people and perhaps, she hoped, learn some wisdom from the elders.

Tilly, although she was an Islander, not Aboriginal, was an

elder of the Injarli tribe, and that evening after dinner she told Virginia she believed in spirits. Virginia was not surprised but she asked for an example.

'When the airlines owned this Lodge and the white boys and girls used to stay here, there was always sickness. The guests got fever and vomiting. Or something would bite them and they'd have to be rushed to hospital and get a drip on them. Then they don't want to come back. Some days, if they went for a walk, a wild boar would run at them, or a bull would come out of the scrub. Now we got the place back, there's no curse on the land. So there's no sickness, no dangerous animals, no bad storms or cyclones.'

'The cyclone that hit my place, Tilly – could I have done anything to stop it?'

'Maybe. If you and the others that live nearby had got together and made a ceremony of cleansing, it might not have hit you so bad.'

Virginia nodded thoughtfully.

She made a decision. 'Tilly, you came from Badu Island. Do you know who Marina's father was?'

Tilly stared at her. 'Marina's father's not from Badu. He's a Murray Islander.'

'Oh. I didn't know that.'

'You know Marina's father. Know him well!' Tilly threw back her head and laughed.

'I know him?' She looked astonished.

'You talk to him all day, listen about the crocodile . . .'

'Uncle Dusty!'

'That's the one. Only one he talks to is you. Likes a quiet life, Uncle Dusty. Shy fella. And you've got him telling stories . . .' Tilly broke off in mirth. 'Hannie was a talker. Didn't want a shy bloke round the place. So Uncle Dusty goes off home to Murray Island. And in a few years, when Hannie's gone off to Broome with that other fella, Riley, who talks his head off, Uncle Dusty he creeps back. Nice and quiet here then. Till you come, that is!' Tilly laughed and Virginia joined in.

'Poor Uncle Dusty. I had no idea.' They mopped their eyes.

When they recovered, Tilly confided, 'Sad thing is Marina's

never really met her father. I reckon they'd get on real well.'

'So do I.'

The next day Uncle Dusty disappeared.

'Did I scare him off?' Virginia asked Tilly anxiously.

'You might have.' Tilly was teasing. 'More likely he's taken the plane to T.I.'

'T.I.?'

'Thursday Island. There's a political meeting up there he wants to go to. And there's someone he wants to meet.'

Every morning Virginia rose early and clambered over the rocks or through bush to walk miles along deserted beaches. She began to notice reptiles she hadn't seen before, primitive creatures derived from the Gondwanan times – a jewel skink of spectacular colours, with a coppery brown head and a body striped black, brown and white. Behind a boulder one late afternoon she discovered a ring-tailed gecko, patterned in velvety fawn and white with eyes that bulged like a frog's. In the bay one morning she caught a glimpse of marine turtles mating. But she avoided the estuaries and mangrove swamps where crocodiles might be lurking. Once she was terrified to see a mangrove monitor a metre long sunning itself on a log by the beach. With its speckled skin, narrow snout and beady eyes it looked just like a crocodile. When it shot out a long forked blue tongue Virginia sighed with relief.

Sometimes, on her solitary walks, she would look up and see a black kite with a forked tail, flying overhead. As soon as bushfires start, Tilly had told her, these kites come in big flocks to snatch up injured animals.

Once, walking through a patch of rainforest, she had seen a yellow-billed kingfisher, really a New Guinea species and quite rare, according to Ben, the naturalist.

Virginia began carrying a pad and coloured crayons to sketch unusual birds and creatures and would later ask Ben or Tilly to identify them.

She discovered pale yellow honeyeaters, a metallic starling with a bright red eye and a magnificent male riflebird, which is supposed to be promiscuous. Her favourite was the great bowerbird which builds a complete avenue of sticks like a grand entrance hall to entice the female into his nest.

Perhaps, thought Virginia after some days of observing nothing but birds, I will turn into a dotty old ornithologist.

But at night she'd go out with a searchlight to discover other creatures. At first with Ben and a small group of guests she looked for bandicoots, possums and wild piglets. Later, alone, she discovered rarer things – sugar-gliders, spotted cuscuses, quolls and a spectacled flying fox.

Sometimes she took Tilly's youngest grandson, Solomon, on short nature walks. He was fascinated by butterflies and together they made a net to catch some. Once they caught a male birdwing while it was feeding on yellow blossoms. It was coloured rich green, gold and black. They only kept it for a day because Solomon thought its mother might be lonely, which Virginia found quite touching. Solomon, with his dark curls, reminded her a little of her son Guy at that age. She remembered rolling madly out of control down a steep grassy slope with Guy, punting an old boat down the river and collecting blackberries in a billy. But this had been in Sussex, England. With Solomon at Cape York, she tracked goannas through the ochre sands, stalked butterflies in the rainforest and ate plummy red fruit from the wongai trees.

She and Solomon became fond of each other. When she sat under a tree with her sketchbook, he would imitate her, holding the small sketchbook she'd given him at exactly the same angle and frowning in concentration as she did.

Tilly, emerging from the kitchen one afternoon, seeing them playing together in the swimming pool, said, 'I see I am losing my grandchild. Now sometimes he calls you Grandma.'

Virginia laughed. 'Grandma?' she said indignantly. 'Do you Solomon?' Then she remembered that Tilly was only fifty-one, two years older than she was.

Virginia leapt out of the pool and heaved the wriggling Solomon after her. She rubbed him dry with her towel. 'So, you call me Grandma, eh, you rascal!'

'That's all right. I don't mind,' Tilly reassured. 'At Injarli he got lots of grandmas, cousins, uncles. We all like family there. Solomon, he likes you to be part of that family.'

Solomon nodded gravely. 'I like you to come to Injarli. See my sisters. Be my grandma. Live with us.'

'That's a very big compliment, white person being invited to Injarli community,' Tilly said.

'Thank you Solomon. I accept,' said Virginia humbly.

Sally, who was slightly younger than Virginia, had been saying for some time that she was looking forward to having grandchildren. What a thought!

She must write and tell Sally that she'd beaten her to it. She had just been adopted by one.

Virginia had been living at Injarli for three days when early one morning there was a commotion. She was standing on the river bank at her easel painting the white sand, red earth and blinding blue water when she heard a truck drive in. Then the yelling started. There was laughter, screaming, yelpings of delight. She turned towards the mayhem crossly. The painting was going well and she did not want to be interrupted. She squinted her eyes against the glare to see who it was that had just arrived and was being welcomed so exuberantly. There, in the middle of the crowd, beaming and waving, was Marina.

'So why did you hide from me?' Virginia asked her later that morning as they sat together on the quiet river bank.

'I was nervous.'

'That your family might not like me?'

Marina nodded. 'It wouldn't have been your fault. It's a different culture, that's all.'

'So you left me here to make my own mistakes.'

'That's right.' Marina grinned.

'Thanks a lot.'

'Anyway, Aunty Tilly thinks you're okay. And my cousins and most of the uncles. So you did all right, I reckon.'

'Where were you all those weeks?'

'Didn't Aunty Tilly tell you?'

Virginia shook her head, looking mildly hurt.

'Well, she didn't know where I was either till a few days ago.' Marina let sand run through her bare toes. 'I was in T.I. with my Dad.'

'Uncle Dusty?'

'That's the one. I went there looking for him because I heard he went there for meetings sometimes and I'd never met him, see? But he wasn't around. So I waited. I knew you'd be alright up here with Aunty Tilly.'

'Learning wisdom from the Murris so's I'm not such a bloody ignorant migloo?' Virginia smiled. 'And how was it? When you met him?'

'Good.' There was a pause. 'Real good.' Marina beamed with pride. 'He's an elder. Did you know? Fancy me having an elder for a dad.'

'Your mother didn't tell you?'

Marina shrugged. 'She never talked about him. Maybe she felt sorry that she ever left this place.'

'And you? Are you sorry you left?'

'When I was a kid up here, there was nothing better than this river,' she said, gazing dreamily out across the water. 'We didn't have toys. We'd run around in the bush with a tyre, a stick, a bottle. But we had a spiritual life. And a lot of love. But now I want more.' She grinned. 'Must be greedy. I'm an indigenous person with ambition.' She laughed. 'You've done that to me! Been my inspiration. I want to come back to Ananda and learn to be a better artist.' She hugged Virginia, then held her at a distance and looked at her searchingly. 'If that's still okay.'

Virginia stared and after a pause she said seriously, 'It is. I think it is okay,' Then she laughed with relief and happiness. 'I wasn't sure before I came up here just what I felt. But I've had a lot of time to think and now I know. I love you very much, Marina.'

'I love you, too. I have done for about three bloody years.'

Next morning they rose early and Marina took Virginia along the creamy sand, past the sighing she-oaks under a sky still tinged with pink and gold to the giant milkwood tree.

'Uncle Dusty told me to look at this. His grandfather planted it sixty years ago.' There was morning dew on the leaves and a mist around the rising sun.

They sat with their backs against the tree trunk and said nothing for a while. They were deeply content.

'What will Uncle Dusty think about having no grandchild to plant another milkwood tree?' Virginia asked quietly.

Marina leaned her head on Virginia's shoulder. 'He won't like it. I can tell you that. But he won't be as bad as some of those political black brothers I met with him in T.I. They'll see our partnership as a form of genocide.' She shrugged. 'Anyway, I wouldn't want to bring a child into the world, even if I wasn't with you. I've seen too much abuse in families, from the time I was small.'

'Aunty Tilly's husband, Greg?'

'How did you know about Greg?' Marina turned to her in surprise.

'Aunty Tilly told me he was violent and that you'd never liked him. That's all.'

'I was four when he started. Used to sit me on his knee. Sick. I can't even talk about it . . . makes me want to puke.' She stripped papery bark from the tree and hurled it into the bush.

'Did Aunty Tilly know?'

Marina shook her head. 'He made me promise not to tell and when you're four you think grown-ups are gods so you do what they say.'

'How long did this go on?'

'Years. On my ninth birthday he told Aunty Tilly he was taking me deep-sea fishing on his boat for a treat. I said I'd only go if I could take the other cousins with me but he refused. I sharpened the knife we used for chopping bait and when he tried to get me down I slashed him on the shoulder. He told Aunty Tilly he'd cut himself on the anchor and he never tried anything again. I still hate the sight of boats.'

Virginia shook her head. 'You were a brave little kid.'

'No, just desperate,' Marina said matter-of-factly. 'What about you? Didn't men ever have a go at you when you were young?'

Virginia looked thoughtful. 'In a way, I suppose, I had a go at them. When I was ten a friend of my father's used to give me a ride home from piano lessons at the university every Friday. He was a professor, like my father. Of Fine Arts, I think. Later he became vice-chancellor. He was a distinguished-looking man, with flowing silver hair and rather expensive tweed trousers. He smelt of aftershave and Gauloises cigarettes. He told me that he had a strange affliction that only a small girl's hands could relieve. He said he had caught a rare disease in the tropics during the war and he needed to be massaged between the legs of his trousers.'

Marina's eyes widened. 'And you believed him?' She struggled to control her laughter.

'I did as a matter of fact. For quite some time. Or I pretended I did. I used to quite enjoy the power I had over him. He was so desperate to be "massaged".'

'Outside the trousers?'

'Of course.'

'Did he ever touch you?'

'Never. He was always a gentlemen. He used to thank me profusely afterwards. I felt like Florence Nightingale.'

They laughed and laughed.

'What about you? You've had boyfriends?' Virginia asked.

'But I've never slept with any. My cousin, who's the only girl I've told I'm gay, said, "You're not trying." But I just don't like the thought of it.' She shuddered. 'It doesn't attract me.'

'What will the family say when you tell them about us, Marina?' Virginia asked her seriously.

There was a pause. 'It's not so bad for an Aboriginal woman to admit she's gay these days. Once, there was a taboo. You could get kicked out of your community.' She looked thoughtful. 'Some black sisters will warn me of the conflicts there'll be because you're white and our cultures are so different. Some of my aunties will say, "At least you won't get abused by a man like we were." A few girl cousins will say I'm filthy. And the aunties will watch me carefully when I nurse my nieces . . .'

'No. Really?'

'You bet. Better watch it yourself, Virginia,' Marina said cheekily. 'People are pretty damn scared of lesbians.'

'And Hannie? What will your mother say?' she asked anxiously.

'I think she'll say, "I don't like you being gay and I'm sad because I'll have no grandchildren from you, but I love you because you're my daughter and you've chosen a beautiful partner, even though she's a bloody migloo."'

Virginia laughed.

# CHAPTER THIRTEEN

Sally's forty-ninth birthday, and the end of an era. August 28th, 1993. Fifteen years in one mellow sandstone house overlooking water. Fifteen years since she, with Richard and the children, had gathered their courage, left behind lifelong friends and moved from Melbourne to Sydney. Did the guests concern themselves with such portentous events? No, they were coming here to enjoy a party.

Guests were invited for eight. Some were already on their way. Those who had to come from Cabramatta, or even further away, from Patapong, the beach village on the Central Coast where they'd met the family on holidays, were worried about the long drive home. Those who hadn't been to the Hunters

Hill house before and were unaware that a lavish amount of food was always supplied, were wondering whether they should eat a sandwich before starting off.

Officially this was a party to farewell the house. A break-up party, it had been called. Did this mean there would perhaps be things to break? Old pianos, family portraits of relatives no longer favoured, ancient sofas with springs sticking out? Those who did not know the family intimately but who'd heard they were unusual wondered about the nature of this break-up party.

Virginia did not wonder. She had arrived from the far north a few days before. Cape York had given her energy and a sense of calm, she said. Sally thought she looked wonderful. After a few weeks alone at Cape York, she told Sally, she'd been joined by Marina and they'd travelled across to the Northern Territory together. Then she'd returned to her cyclone-ripped land and thrown herself into the task of restoring the buildings, trees and gardens. She had worked hard for a month and when she'd exhausted herself as the artists and neighbours who'd helped, she had done what she'd promised to do, come south to see Sally and Meg.

She'd arrived at Sally's place three days before the party to help get things ready. She and Sally had spent the first two days laughing a lot in the garden, shopping for food, and arguing, advising and listening to each other while Sally cooked. Now, on the eve of the party, they were putting the finishing touches to Sally's feast.

'You know, in spite of the fact that it's already been sold, this house of yours is still a haven,' Virginia said. 'I feel very safe in it. You've created an atmosphere of peace. I hope whoever bought it appreciates that,' she remarked as she and Sally rubbed garlic around the salad bowls and washed the soft lettuces, chopped sun-dried tomatoes into slivers and lightly fried pine nuts to sprinkle on top.

Sally did not want to discuss the new owner, a rather obnoxious young property developer who had talked loudly of his plans to cover her polished wooden floors with wall-to-wall carpets, block up her marble fireplaces and install central heating. She said thoughtfully, 'I can imagine a large family still living here in a hundred years time. But perhaps by then they'll be part of a museum, living relics for tourists to gape at. They'll go on with their daily tasks of making the salad while they're videoed by Koreans and Chinese.'

'Yes, they'll be the wealthy tourists of the future.' Virginia hurled avocado peel into the rubbish bin. 'I wonder what the Chinese of the twenty-first century will make of bourgeois Australian family life.'

'I imagine the typical Australian family of the future will look much more Asian than it does now,' said Sally. 'And perhaps more Aboriginal, too. What do you reckon about this proposed Mabo legislation? I think it's one of the gutsiest decisions our PM has made.'

'So do I. It's about time we approved Aboriginal land rights. Yet look at the outcry! Hysterical people on talkback radio convinced that they're going to lose their backyards, mining magnates calling the High Court decision on Mabo naive adventurism, politicians marching out of meetings refusing to accept that decision.'

'How dare they!' Sally slapped the wet lettuce wrapped in a tea towel against the bench. 'But look, it's still not clear what Aboriginal people really want. The people you met at Cape York, what did they think about Mabo?'

'Well, Eddie Koiki Mabo is a folk hero up there, as you can imagine. He was the first one to oppose the sale of land to Torres Strait Islanders or anyone else. Because they had worked the land for generations they had a right to it, he said. You must have read about the famous Murray Island Land Case?'

Sally nodded. 'He won in a High Court action, didn't he?'

'Yes. And that made the Injarli people, the ones who were born on Murray Island, determined to win back the land and fishing grounds that they'd lost in the 1980s. So of course they support Mabo.'

'Of course,' said Sally. 'But will the Mabo idea transfer successfully to other parts of the country? If Aborigines can't prove an affinity with the land and miners want to use it, what then?'

'Well, in the Northern Territory where Marina and I have just been, there are mining companies everywhere: Jabiru, Palm

Valley, nine of them altogether. So far there's been no Aboriginal veto on any of them. It might come, of course,' Virginia said. 'But at present the Aborigines negotiate very successfully. No problems, according to my friend on the Northern Land Council. Naturally, Aborigines want to be involved in the negotiating process and if they feel excluded they'll go back to court. The days are over when whites can just bulldoze Aboriginal rights.'

Sally grinned. 'You've become very passionate about this, haven't you?'

'Boring you, am I?' Virginia flashed her a dark look and for a second Sally was afraid, as she had been thirty years before, when Virginia had suddenly seemed to despise her for lacking courage and conviction.

'Oh shut up, that's not what I meant and you know it,' Sally said with affection. 'I'm full of admiration.'

And instantly Virginia's anger disappeared.

Sally had noticed Virginia's mercurial mood changes lately. She supposed they were a result of the cruel loss of her Arthouse.

It could never be rebuilt the same way. Many of the artists who had helped to build it slowly over the years had left Ananda now, Virginia had explained. Perhaps, some time in the future, when there was money and inspiration, other artists would build a different gallery. Perhaps they would not. The small amount of money Sally and Meg had invested in the building had been lost. Did Virginia feel guilty about this? Not at all.

Sally had found Virginia's way of looking at the value of property odd. She could not understand it. It was naive. If Virginia had bothered to insure her building she and the other artists could have started rebuilding immediately.

Why would they want to, Virginia had asked? And then she'd said, only half laughing, 'Anyway, all property is theft.'

Sally had sighed. It was useless to reason with her in this mood. Virginia had sounded increasingly strange since the cyclone, as if she was reassessing everything – property ownership, ambition, even her friends. When Sally had offered again and again to fly up there and help her, or just be there as a comfort, Virginia had said she wanted no-one. Marina was there, she'd told Sally, and Sally had felt a pang of jealousy. Marina was a child, not a friend of thirty-odd years. How could she possibly comfort?

'Why didn't you bring Marina down to Sydney with you this time?' she asked Virginia now. 'She would've enjoyed the party. And she could have met Claudia.'

Virginia raised her eyebrows. 'I'm not sure how well she and Claudia would get on.'

Sally laughed. 'They're both very frank. They might have found things in common.'

'Claudia's a racist and a snob. Marina would have loathed her.'

Sally looked up in surprise at the vehemence of this remark. 'Oh come on, Claudia's not that bad. But I agree, it would have been embarrassing if the daughters had disliked each other.'

Virginia gave Sally a bemused stare.

'We've all been very lucky so far. None of our children have really clashed,' Sally continued innocently.

Virginia laughed. 'Marina didn't come because she has rather a lot to do at Ananda at the moment. She's started painting with real energy,' she said, busying herself at the sink. She felt the colour rising in her face and Sally's perceptive stare. Was this the moment to tell her friend about the woman she was in love with? But what if Sally was shocked? What if the relationship with Marina didn't last? Virginia's heart was pounding high up near her throat.

'Are you okay? You've gone all pink.'

'Yes, fine.'

'Here, have a glass of iced water.' Sally poured one from a jug in the fridge and looked at her friend with concern. 'It's not the dreaded menopause?'

'Shit! I hope not. I'm not even fifty yet.'

Sally smiled. 'Mine came at forty-three. Remember? It's not so bad.'

'Well, you've always been precocious, Sally. I'm not expecting any interruptions to my sex life for years and years yet.' Virginia declared.

'It doesn't have to make a jot of difference to your sex life!' Sally protested. 'If anything, it makes you freer.'

'Oh yeah?' Virginia laughed. But the moment had passed. She had no intention of telling Sally anything now. Instead she began prattling about the trip she and Marina had made to the Northern Territory. 'It inspired us to get more Aboriginal culture into Ananda and let Aboriginal people take responsibility for it.'

'Really? I hear there's some tourist operation run by Aborigines in Katherine. Does it work?'

'Certainly does!' Virginia perched herself on a high stool and leaned enthusiastically forward, resting her elbows on the kitchen bench. 'The Jawoyn tribe claimed some land that used to be a cattle station so as they could develop Aboriginal business ventures. Along came a mining company. They made a settlement. The Jawoyn gave up the right to claim native title and in return they now have part of the Katherine Gorge. The mining company provides the tribe with scholarships, cleaning jobs, that sort of thing. When I was up there, four out of the twelve guides employed on the Katherine Gorge tour were Aboriginal. One was even a woman! She drove the boat as well as explained how the Gorge was sixteen hundred million years old. She showed us where the crocodiles nested and how the melaleuca tree, whose roots hold the river bank together, was also used for building shelters, making blankets and paintbrushes for the Jawoyn tribe. Tourists love it when an Aborigine explains the rock paintings and sacred myths,' Virginia said passionately. Her eyes were shining. 'They tell their stories as if they're letting you into a secret. And you can see how they love the land.'

'So why aren't all the guides Aboriginal?'

'Because they're shy. A lot of them find it uncomfortable to talk in public. They're not pushy like us. And they're certainly not greedy, no matter what the mining magnates say.' Virginia remembered what she was supposed to be doing, tasted the salad dressing and then added more lemon juice.

So why are things working well in the Northern Territory and not elsewhere?' Sally asked.

Virginia took a deep breath. 'Mainly because of Whitlam's

national code on Aboriginal land introduced there back in 1983. Mabo would probably never have taken a decade to resolve if the other states had adopted that code,' she said adamantly.

Sally stopped what she was doing and gave her a searching look.

'What?' asked Virginia. 'What are you thinking?'

'What are you up to? I know you've always been interested in Aboriginal land rights and culture and so on, but lately you've become . . . obsessed. You've been tearing around the country doing nothing but find out how different communities live, manage tourism, fight for their rights. What's going on?'

Virginia turned away and looked out the window. Sally waited. Suddenly she swung around, flushed with excitement. 'I'm handing back part of my land to the Aborigines.'

'What?' said Sally, dumbfounded. 'Who?' she asked foolishly.

'They're a local group. Descendants of the Mundu Barangai people who used to live near the gorge in Gurrunga.'

Sally stared. 'You know them?'

'Some of them. They live just outside the town in a settlement that used to be a mission. But they don't own the land.'

'You're giving away your Ananda? Your beautiful land in the rainforest?'

'Part of it. I don't need it all. There's eighty hectares.'

'But you're broke. In debt. Shouldn't you sell the land you don't need to pay the debts?'

'Sell it to a developer who'd put up ghastly crocodile parks, marinas and apartments? No thanks, I'd rather give it to someone who'll leave it as it is.'

'Well, I think that's a great idea,' said Sally doubtfully. She felt relieved that she and Meg had no money invested in Virginia's land. 'If you can afford it.'

'I can't afford it. But I'm going to do it,' said Virginia with that touch of spirited defiance that brought back to Sally a flood of embarrassing memories. Like Virginia at twenty, inviting famous artists to exhibit at the tiny gallery she managed in a back alley near the university and offering to pay their interstate travel and accommodation expenses, then, when they'd all accepted, rushing out to beg the airlines for free tickets, hotels for discounts and restaurants for cheap meals.

Part of Virginia's motivation for this sudden generosity was, of course, philanthropic, but part of it was also to shock, thought Sally. Very well.

'I'm shocked,' she said, and then laughed. 'I read that a man in Cape Town gave his land back to the original inhabitants the other day. The neighbours thought he'd gone mad.'

'Mine think I went mad years ago. But don't worry. I'm not totally irresponsible. I'm paying back the bank loan before I give anything away.'

'How?'

'We actually made money on the sale of all those paintings at the opening of the Arthouse, you know.'

'Congratulations!' said Sally with relief. 'And what will these Mundu Barangai people do with your land?'

'Well, a lot of them are artists who've been working at Ananda for years anyway and the others are . . . I'd say, unorthodox entrepreneurs. They'll want to create something like what the Injarli people have done, I imagine, maybe run a wilderness lodge. They say they'd like to take white tourists on fishing trips to the gorge and walks through the rainforest to find bush tucker and traditional medicines.'

'Do any of them know about that sort of thing any more?'

'A few of them do. Hannie, Marina's mother, is an expert, even though she wasn't born here. She's been trying to get a job as a native guide with the big white tourist companies for years. But they don't want to know about it. They're only interested in trips to the outer reef on giant catamarans.'

'So Ananda will become a native tourist centre?'

Virginia laughed. 'No! The people will live there and do what they like. Some of the community leaders, people I've already talked to, will organise mini-bus trips to the rainforest and Cape Tribulation and the mangrove swamps, but instead of just having picnics they'll learn about plants, birds and animals, be taken to where all the battlefields were, the burial grounds, the sacred sites. People like Hannie know all the old myths and customs, the foods of the forest, even some of the songs.'

'They won't have to perform corroborees for the tourists?'

'Not unless they want to. And then the dance would be more likely to be about how their Toyota got bogged in the creek than about the way some hunter speared a kangaroo.' Virginia laughed. 'The Injarli people danced on the beach for some tourists while I was there and they had rather strange-looking aluminium boats on their heads with little registration numbers on them and bits of wire sticking out representing the spray.'

'What on earth did the tourists think?'

'Well, they didn't complain. The clever ones probably worked out that this was the modern Injarli way of letting you know that powerboats go much faster than dinghies. Quite as legitimate a story to dance to as any of those about spearing kangaroos.'

'So these people will entertain the tourists but only in the ways they want to?' Sally asked.

'Precisely,' Virginia said. 'They'll behave like themselves. If some feel shy and don't want to talk, that's okay.'

Sally breathed a sigh of mixed admiration and apprehension. 'Will all this be legal?'

'Absolutely.'

'And where will you live?'

'In my house. I'll keep that. And go back there to paint once in a while. But mostly I'll leave the place to them.'

'What about the artists?'

'Those who want to can stay on. There's plenty of room. It will be a mixed community, but the Aborigines will own most of it. And they'll manage it.'

'What does Marina think of all this?'

'She's delighted, of course. Thinks it's the start of . . . Don't ask me any more. It's too early. But it's definitely happening. Don't tell anyone. It's still . . . a sensitive issue.'

'I bet. And a brave act. How will your neighbours feel about this?'

'They'll be furious,' Virginia smiled.

Meg dressed in a rush for Sally's party. She was used to dressing fast, applying the minimum of makeup and slinging into a handbag precisely what she would need. Years of being a journalist had taught her this habit. She wondered if, at the age of seventy, she would still automatically be hurling into a handbag a notebook, tape-recorder, pens, extra batteries, cosmetics, wallet and keys. Perhaps by then she would also need thick eyeglasses, pills and a fold-up walking stick. What a ridiculous thought. Her own mother was almost eighty and she used none of these things.

Claudia had commented on the way Meg prepared to go out to dinner or the theatre like someone racing to catch the last plane out of purgatory. Claudia had also criticised Meg's habit of announcing her full name in a very brusque manner whenever she answered the phone. 'It's unnerving to personal callers. And you never talk long on the phone. You don't chat,' Claudia added. 'You just deliver the message and get off the line fast as if you're expecting a much more important call.'

'Oh,' said Meg, reprimanded. 'I'm sorry. I suppose it's because in my job I often *am* expecting a more important call. At least, a call that's not personal.'

'Exactly,' said Claudia. 'Did you hear what you just implied? Personal calls are not as important to you as calls to do with your career.'

'Oh, nonsense!' said Meg. 'Of course they are. I just don't want personal calls when I'm working, that's all.'

'But sometimes, when you work from home, personal calls come through and the callers can sense you don't want to talk to them. And it isn't only phone calls. If Peter or Nick or I try to talk to you when you're thinking about work, you're completely cut off. I think you should watch it, Mother.'

Thinking of all this, Meg sighed deeply. She was unnerved by having her behaviour monitored. It was as if she was a recently discovered and prized specimen that needed to be studied, recorded and corrected if its development was displeasing. At first she'd been touched by Claudia's close attention. But now that the attention had become critical, and those apparently harmed by Meg's poor performance included her husband and son, she resisted it.

'Will I be publicly introduced at this party?' Claudia now asked her as she stood in the doorway, watching Meg brush her hair with vigorous, quick strokes.

Meg laughed. 'On a platform? Like a guest speaker? No, I don't think so. You already know a lot of people who'll be there. I'll take you around and introduce you to anyone else you'd like to meet. Sally's parties are pretty informal.'

'But I thought the party was being given partly to welcome me, for you to acknowledge that I am your daughter.' Claudia looked petulant.

'Well, it is and I will. But not by standing up in front of the crowd and making a speech.'

'So you're not as proud of me as you pretend?'

'Oh Claudia, I am deeply proud of you. You know that. But you wouldn't enjoy it if I made a formal declaration. Stood on a box and pointed you out like an exhibit.'

'How do you know I wouldn't? You always assume you know exactly what I would or wouldn't enjoy.'

'Well, I don't care whether you'd enjoy it or not. I think it would be tasteless and I'm not going to do it.'

Meg gave Claudia a quick kiss to show that she refused to continue this foolish debate, then beamed at her, thrust the hairbrush into her bag and dashed out of the room.

'Arrogant bitch,' she thought she heard Claudia say as she raced down the hall, but she couldn't be sure.

'And who'll be there?' asked Peter as he drove them all out across the Iron Cove bridge, over the water past bobbing boats towards Hunters Hill.

'At least a hundred close friends and relations I should think,' said Meg. 'I should really have bought more tarts from Darling's Treat.'

'We've got eight large ones! Strawberry, pecan pie, pear, apple, apricot . . .'

'Have we got citron?' Nicholas asked eagerly.

'Yes.'

'Good, I *love* citron,' he confided to Claudia who sat in the back seat beside him.

'Do you know what citron means?' she asked him critically.

'No. What? It tastes like awful old sour lemons but I still like it.'

'That's what citron means.' Claudia looked out the window, dismissing him.

'Awful old sour lemons?' asked Nicholas in astonishment.

'Lemon,' she said emphatically, as if he were a moron.

'Oh.' He looked chastened.

Oh no, thought Meg, she's doing it to him as well.

'Who'll be there that I haven't yet met?' asked Claudia. 'Anyone my age, or will they all be ancient?'

'Like Meg, you mean?' Peter smiled at Meg affectionately.

Normally, when he made cracks like that she would just laugh, but tonight, because of Claudia's criticism, she was feeling vulnerable.

'No, some of them will be almost as young and unspoilt as you and Peter,' she said sweetly.

Claudia gave her harsh laugh and said conspiratorially, 'Well Peter, you and I will have to gather a few of the spunkier youngsters together and see if we can't find a nightclub as soon as the olds stagger off to bed. What do you say?'

'No thanks. Nightclubs bore me cross-eyed.' Peter shot a concerned look at Meg.

'Ooh Peter, what a party pooper,' Claudia crooned.

'Don't worry, Claudia,' said Meg evenly. 'I'm sure you'll find someone to pick up.'

What is happening to me? she thought in alarm. I'm behaving like a bitch to my own daughter.

'I hardly think so,' said Claudia airily. 'They'll all be dead bores if they're friends of yours – workaholics who believe in *causes*, dull people with no dress sense who are without exception as old as Methuselah. Wait! I'm wrong. There will be some exceptions,' she announced with mock relief. 'Nathan and Paul will be there! Now Nathan is cute but I suspect he's gay or addicted to something, and Paul with those long blond dreadlocks is quite a spunk but he's practically married to that scheming little Chinese person. What's her name?'

'Lanh. And she's Vietnamese,' said Peter tightly.

'What an appalling waste! There's absolutely no-one else of vaguely my vintage and I'm going to be bored to sobs . . .'

'Shut up!' Meg exploded. 'Stop the car, Peter. Turn around and we'll take Claudia home. I've never heard such arrogant, racist crap in my life. If that's what you think of my friends, Claudia, then I don't want you at the party. I'm ashamed of you!'

Nick stared with wide, disbelieving eyes at his mother's red face. Peter pulled the car over. There was silence.

'Sorry. Sorry, Mother,' said Claudia, sounding contrite. '*Mea culpa*. Sorry, all.'

Meg had no idea whether she meant it but after a short, tense silence she signalled to Peter to drive on.

'What's *mea culpa*?' Nick asked very timidly.

'My fault, darling. My terrible, awful, dreadful fault,' Claudia told him sweetly.

Meg felt wretched. Recently she had been having moments of feeling quite furious with Claudia. Things had certainly changed since the day on the cliff above the Hawkesbury when Claudia had clung to her and wept with gratitude about Meg's offer to help her become a journalist. After a few weeks of being allowed to sit in on lectures and join discussions with the students in the most highly regarded media course in Sydney, Claudia had declared that journalism was both boring and too difficult. She did not like the students she had met in the course. Although at first they had seemed stimulating, after a while they had revealed themselves to be work-obsessed, unfashionable and very dull company. Perhaps she, at twenty-four, was just too sophisticated to go back to studying in any institution, she concluded. Still, she had become interested in fashion design while she had been there. She had met some students studying in the design school who had shown her around their building and demonstrated the way computers could be used to design anything from a chair to a ball gown. She had found it comparatively easy to work the computers and had come home declaring that these days computers could do anything. She said she felt she had a flair for fashion and she might possibly enrol in a design course in the new year.

Meg, who had persuaded friends and associates that Claudia was so passionate about becoming a journalist that they had allowed her the special privilege of access to a course for which she had not yet qualified, felt humiliated. Claudia, it seemed, was a dilettante.

Claudia was irritated when Meg did not make the same strenuous efforts to help her gain access to the course in fashion design.

'You're a snob, Mother. No doubt about it. Fashion is frippery to you. Not worthy to be put on the same plane as investigative journalism. Weren't you ever interested in fashion, not even in the swinging sixties?' she had asked with a touch of sarcasm.

Meg, remembering herself in flared jeans and psychedelic shirt with hair much longer and messier than it was now, said, 'Certainly, I'll show you some old photos if you like.'

But Claudia wasn't interested.

'So you really don't have any contacts in the design school? I thought you knew everyone in this city.'

Meg had shaken her head. 'Sorry.' There was no point in continuing along those lines.

The night after Meg's refusal to try and pull strings to get Claudia into the design school there had been a blood-curdling scream in the middle of the night. Meg and Peter had sat bolt upright in bed, their hearts racing. 'She's being attacked,' Meg cried out. Peter grabbed a baseball bat from the cupboard and Meg had the poker from the fireplace in their room and they both raced silently down the passage to Claudia's room. The light was on. The door was open. There was whimpering. The attacker might still be there. They flattened themselves against the wall, preparing to burst in. Peter crashed into the room first. Claudia was sitting up in bed rubbing her thigh. 'A creature. It bit me,' she sobbed pitifully.

'What creature?' Peter darted about the room looking for a mad dog, a snake, a poisonous spider.

'Show me,' said Meg, taking Claudia's hand away from the place she was rubbing.

'Nooah! It's too painful,' she wailed. 'I think it was one of those flying creatures.'

'A mosquito?' said Peter.

'Yes, it stung me and now I could die of malaria!' The wailing became louder.

'Sssh! You'll wake Nick.' Meg was laughing. 'Claudia, Australian mosquitoes are absolutely harmless. Let me see.'

Claudia shook her head and rocked back and forth, wailing.

Meg sat on the bed and put an arm round her shoulders.

'I'll get the calamine lotion. That'll fix it,' Peter said. He rolled his eyes at Meg and went off to the bathroom.

'What's that? An antidote? Will it kill the poison?'

'There's no poison, my love. It's a soothing lotion that'll take the heat out of the bite. Tomorrow you won't even know where it is.'

'But it's all red. Look!' Claudia lifted her short white silk nightgown and revealed the bite high up on her thigh. Peter came in with the lotion at that instant and looked discreetly away. He handed the bottle to Meg.

'Let me dab some of this on it for you,' Meg said.

'Nooah! It hurts too much.' The wailing began again and now there was another wail from Nick in the bedroom next door.

'I'll go,' said Peter, eager to escape.

'No, stay. Please,' sobbed Claudia. She looked appealingly up at Peter.

Nick's wails increased. He sounded frightened. Meg dashed out of the room. She returned a minute later with Nick on her hip and stood in the doorway. Peter was gently daubing the pink mosquito bite with white lotion and explaining to Claudia that malaria-carrying mosquitoes were only found in the tropics.

Later that night in bed, she and Peter had laughed about Claudia's hysteria and Meg had forgotten that she had, for a moment, been upset by the sight of her husband rubbing lotion on her daughter's pretty thigh.

Now, on the way to the party, Claudia had tried again to upset her and succeeded rather well. Meg leaned back in her seat, breathed deeply and tried to make herself feel calm. Tonight she wanted a little fun and to enjoy the company of her two oldest friends.

# CHAPTER FOURTEEN

Sally has finished making salads and all the other things she has baked and marinated over the past few days. She has arranged pheasant and fish, pork, pies and terrines on platters garnished with fresh herbs, flowers and berries from her garden and now she sits alone, with a glass of champagne, on the old rope swing tied to the giant magnolia tree.

It is magic to be alone in your garden, she thinks, after having prepared a feast for guests you are fond of. It is dark and the trees glimmer with tiny white lights looped through their branches like fireflies. The garden smells of iceberg roses. Camellia bushes have dropped their bright pink and pale pink petals to make carpets on the grass. The sad three-noted cry of the brain-fever bird drifts down from the highest branches above her swing. Inside she can hear the band tuning up. But outside there is only the creak of the rope as she gently swings and the lament of the bird that must soon migrate.

From the upstairs balcony Nathan Mathieson watches his mother swinging dreamily and smokes a cigarette. He waves the smoke away into the trees so it will not waft down and make her look up and discover him. He wants to watch her unobserved. She looks, he thinks, like a little girl, as she leans her head against the rope. Only three years ago he used to leave his diary lying about, hoping that she would read it. On one page he had written, 'No-one in this whole damn world will ever understand me and no-one in it loves me except my mother.' She had read it and been touched as he'd intended. Had he meant it? Or had he just wanted her sympathy and attention? He had got it, anyway. When he announced, shortly afterwards, that he wanted to become an actor, she had been strongly supportive. His father had thought it a foolish aberration and tried hard to dissuade him. At the time he had been hurt by this. But now what did it matter what his father thought? He was quite fond of his father and did not blame him for his lack of understanding but he no longer felt the need to gain his approval. It was his mother who made him feel alternately guilty and full of pride.

He was afraid for her now. What he had become involved in would distress her. He was frightened of himself, of the necessity for daring.

Downstairs, the tall cedar double doors between the dining and living rooms had been opened up to make space to dance, and Paul's band was setting up. He played lead guitar and shared the vocals. Lanh, his girlfriend, who once had played the violin in a classical trio with Paul, had decided that managing this band was better than playing in it, and since she had taken over the business side of things they'd been booked for quite a few gigs. Now she busied herself checking amplifiers and leads while Paul laughed and chatted with his group, most of them university students like himself. Paul was pleased with his new independent life. His course was going well and his relationship with Lanh was more stable now they lived in their own place. She often snapped at him these days, like a real wife, he thought with affection. She resented the time he spent with his friends playing music or working on the proposed television program. He tried to involve her in these things for some of the time, but he liked a bit of time alone with his friends. Lanh could sometimes be suffocating, which he did not like to admit because he loved her dearly.

Steven and Toby were stringing red, yellow and blue balloons down the hallway, looping them through the banisters and up onto the landing. It looked festive and not very sophisticated, like a children's party, but it was their contribution and the little kids would like them. 'Nick asked if we'd be having any dinosaur balloons,' said Toby with a grin. 'He said one of his friends had them at his birthday party.'

'God, the things kids expect these days,' said Steven in disgust.

Sally has come inside to find Meg and Virginia leaning against the fireplace laughing. Their heads are thrown back and they look relaxed, abandoned.

'You didn't tell me you'd arrived,' says Sally to Meg, accusingly.

Virginia laughs louder. 'How dare you slip in without permission?' she tells Meg.

Sally wrinkles her nose at them, acknowledging that she does have a tendency to try and control things, but this is her party so why not? She goes across to the sideboard and pours herself a glass of champagne and one for each of them.

'We have waiters tonight,' she says with mock grandeur. 'But they must be busy stacking bottles in the bath.'

This reference to the parties of their youth makes Meg and Virginia laugh some more but Sally says, 'I'm serious. That's what they're doing.'

'She's serious,' says Virginia.

Claudia comes into the room to see what they are

laughing at. Sally embraces her and Virginia pours her a glass of champagne.

'Claudia, you look beautiful!' says Sally in admiration.

Claudia smiles her thanks and sits down to observe them. She thinks them odd. They are so lacking in self-consciousness when they are together, even her mother, who knows that Claudia disapproves of her. They are well-educated women and yet they are not at all well groomed. They do not appear to care about this, indeed they don't appear to care what anyone thinks of them.

Virginia, for example, laughs too loudly and is overweight. She could still look attractive if she wanted. Her eyes are an extraordinary deep green, she has perfect teeth and a stunning smile but her cheeks have grown puffy. Her nose is still impressive – patrician and straight. But her hair is too long and beginning to go grey. Why doesn't she tint it? Her clothes are bizarre. She likes flowing dresses made in India, capes woven in Africa and chunky Moroccan jewellery. One day she will appear in a full gypsy skirt with dangling earrings like a fortune teller and the next in formal black coat-tails with black tights and a white vest like the conductor of an orchestra. Why doesn't she find a style that will enhance her good features and hide the fact that her hips are too wide?

Sally is petite and quite pretty but she dresses like a child, in whatever she happens to find appealing in the dress-up box of her wardrobe. She has no sense of fashion. Her clothes are remnants from the sixties and seventies, embroidered cheesecloth blouses, waistcoats, baggy velvet trousers, fringed shawls with little mirrors sewn onto them. Sometimes she will put on a jaunty black beret, a cape and lace-up boots that look almost fashionable, but this is accidental, not intended. She has attractive brown curls which flop about loosely but like Virginia, she is in need of a decent haircut. Her makeup is embarrassingly dated. She still puts green on her eyelids.

And as for Meg, she is far too cautious. Sensible, well-cut designer suits that never date for the office. Almost no makeup and jewellery. Jeans, sneakers and loose shirts for weekends. She dresses in monochrome as if a splash of colour might betray the fact that she has a wild streak in her personality beneath the unruffled surface. Although she is middle-aged, she is tall, slim and a natural blonde. She could be striking, but for some reason she does not wish to be noticed.

As Claudia ponders a method of dragging her mother and her two best friends into the 1990s the door bell rings and the guests start arriving.

By half-past ten Sally's buffet feast has been largely demolished and oyster shells with cigarette butts in them lie on the mantelpiece beside empty wine glasses. Duck bones wrapped in paper napkins nestle, forgotten, under chairs.

Sally, moving from group to group, escaping occasionally to the stairs to look down on her party, sees that people are mixing rather well, the Vietnamese talking to the Australians, the young to the old, the employed to the unemployed, the feminists to the mildly macho and her estranged husband to his most resentful son. Sally looks away from this last pair. She does not want Steven to catch her staring. She is grateful to him for making the effort to be civil to Richard. They are leaning together, heads down, not making eye contact and Richard is doing most of the talking. She hopes he is not foolish enough to be delivering a lecture.

There is Peter introducing Claudia to an admiring circle of Vietnamese boys. She graciously allows her hand to be shaken by each one. There is something of Meg in Claudia after all, Sally notices. That 'queenly' quality.

Now Sally moves down again into the throng, joining some groups, overhearing others. Meg is arguing with Justice Fenning, an old friend of Richard's, about a young reporter on her newspaper who has refused to reveal the identity of her sources to the Independent Commission Against Corruption.

'She'll be found guilty of contempt and could face two years in prison if she continues on this ideological crusade,' says the Judge condescendingly. 'As editor, shouldn't you be offering her some advice?'

'What advice? Persuading her to abandon the journalists'

code of ethics?' Meg is angry. 'She is a competent professional, doing her job, providing sensitive information which the public has a right to know and for this she's about to get a criminal conviction. It's ludicrous! Have you ever thought, Malcolm, that perhaps it is the law that needs overhauling? Journalists need a shield against prosecutions of the kind Jenny Douglas is facing.'

'What, some legal privilege to help protect the free media?' he scoffs.

'Exactly!'

'Hi,' Claudia glides up, clasps Meg's hand and gives Justice Fenning a melting look.

Because Meg is too furious to speak, Sally intervenes. 'Malcolm, this is Meg's daughter, Claudia Broderick. She's here on a short visit from London.' Sally then ushers Meg away and leaves the judge to Claudia.

'I expect she'll be all right with old Malcolm,' says Sally. 'Though he has just been left by his third wife and is probably on the prowl,' she adds doubtfully.

'If Claudia's at all interested she'll stalk him first. She's quite a hunter. I hope she reduces him to a quivering heap,' says Meg.

They grin at each other.

'And makes him offer her an apartment,' says Sally.

'Without even so much as a massage in exchange.'

'She'll insist on one overlooking the harbour.'

'And we'll all go and visit,' says Meg.

Sally laughs and then says seriously, 'Is Claudia still planning to go back to that job in Tokyo?'

'If she doesn't get accepted into the fashion course she's set her heart on next year.'

'How difficult is it to get in?'

'Quite difficult. She's working on building up a portfolio of designs. She has good ideas. I've set her up in that small sunny room out the back with a brand new drawing table. And my old computer, which she says is pretty useless,' Meg laughs. 'She doesn't approve of second-rate equipment. But she seems happy working out there. Peter's good company for her when I'm away at the office. He's been marvellously tolerant. I couldn't have coped with her alone.'

'She's a bit of a hypochondriac, I hear,' Sally smiles. 'Peter told me about the mosquito bite.'

Meg groans. 'She's a drama queen. Best to ignore it. Though I must say she gave us a hell of a fright.'

Sally looks thoughtful. 'You're still planning to go off to East Timor in a few weeks?'

'Certainly, though I haven't a hope of getting in as a journalist.' Meg lowers her voice. 'I have a plan that is a bit bizarre. I'll tell you about later if you promise not to breathe a word.'

'Does it involve James Parker?' Sally asks anxiously.

'It does,' Meg looks excited.

'You're meeting him there,' Sally whispers. 'You're going in disguised as a travel agent and he's pretending to be a bird watcher.'

'Shut up!' hisses Meg and gives Sally a look that makes her realise she isn't too far from the truth.

Sally shakes her head as if she can't believe such madness and walks off to attend to a group of guests who are getting increasingly raucous.

James Parker is one of Meg's oldest friends, an Australian journalist who, for thirty years, has been covering wars from Vietnam to El Salvador, from the Gulf to Cambodia. His writing and documentary films about parts of Asia that have been exploited or neglected by the West have made him a controversial figure. He has won many international awards.

A few years ago Meg had encouraged James to leave London and edit a new independent newspaper in Sydney, but although he'd been enthusiastic about the paper, it had been Meg who'd eventually taken on the job and James, still racing around the world from one danger zone to the next, who'd encouraged her. Meg had often wondered if he'd always intended her to take the editor's job at the *Australian Independent*, and had felt grateful to him for convincing her she could do it. Still, she also wondered sometimes whether he would have been bored stuck in one place, and wished she was able to race off like he did.

Of course Meg feels excited at the prospect of collaborating with her old and admired friend James Parker on a piece of investigative journalism in East Timor. But, thinks Sally unhappily, for reasons both political and domestic, now is not the right time.

Sally moves across to talk to Meg's ex-editor, Mike Riordan, who looks a lot healthier since he has given up newspapers to write books. He is intelligent, perceptive and very fond of Meg, with whom he worked for eight years. Perhaps he will have some wisdom to offer. But Mike is more interested in Meg's new daughter than her proposed visit to East Timor.

'Now Sally, you've known her for thirty years. How on earth did she manage to conceal a twenty-four year old daughter from a close friend like you?'

Sally says there are some things too difficult to share even with a close friend. Mike, being a journalist and insatiably curious, finds this answer unsatisfactory. He looks at Sally hopefully. He really wants to know the story. Sally outlines the facts, leaving out Meg's emotional trauma, which Mike is smart enough to work out for himself. When she has finished, he sighs, shakes his head and says, 'Well, it must be a blessed relief to her after all these years.' He glances across at Claudia, who is talking animatedly to the ageing Judge who gazes down at her in fascination and asks wryly, 'And how is the young lady coping with her new situation? Making a favourable impression on her mother's friends by the look of it.'

'Enemies,' Sally corrects him, smiling.

Mike nods. 'I heard Meg having a run-in with His Honour earlier. She's right, of course. What's an old fascist bastard like that doing at one of your excellent gatherings, Sally?'

'He's our neighbour, an old friend of Richard's. Been a bit lonely, lately.'

'Ah. Well, once you move to Redfern you won't have a problem. He'll be far too terrified to accept your hospitality there.'

'Redfern's getting quite gentrified. I'm not sure I'll be able to afford it if the prices keep on going up,' Sally retorts. They laugh, clink glasses and Mike's eyes stray back to Claudia who is giggling and flirting outrageously.

'Not much alike, mother and daughter, are they?'

Sally admits ruefully that they are not.

People have taken a break from dancing to Paul's band and are gulping down great quantities of wine and water. They seem extraordinarily thirsty. Sally wanders over to Paul, who in his sunglasses and long unkempt hair bears a striking resemblance to the singer he is imitating, Lenny Kravitz, and asks as tactfully as possible whether in the next bracket he might play something the older people can dance to.

'Absolutely!' he turns to the band with a grin. 'We've been saving the best till last, haven't we guys? Nothing but the Eagles, the Doors and J.J. Cale from now on.' He takes the microphone and announces that it is now 'nostalgia for the seventies time' and launches into 'Life in the Fast Lane'. As he belts out the song, people of Sally's vintage take to the floor in dozens, pumping their bodies to the raunchy beat alongside the teenagers, who seem to be quite familiar with The Eagles in spite of their antiquity.

After this bracket there is applause from the dancers. 'More nostalgia!' cries the Judge, who is dancing with Claudia.

Virginia, dancing with Lanh's Uncle Ngoc, calls for Joe Cocker. Meg tells her not to embarrass the band. They don't know Cocker; he's far too old.

Paul acknowledges the applause and heckling with typical rock star humility, then announces with mock sincerity, 'The next song is dedicated to three ageing hippies who've tried all the substances, been down all those trails and despite their beads and headbands, have still emerged with hearts of gold and pure as the driven snow – the Tanglewood girls!'

The band breaks into J.J. Cale's 'Cocaine'.

Sally looks shocked. 'What does he mean? We've never taken cocaine!' she tells her partner, one of Paul's university friends.

'Really? Paul told me you all still take a snort before breakfast.'

Sally laughs and gives him a whack. 'Did he just?'

'If you want to get down, down on the ground, cocaine!' sings her oldest son in a gravelly voice, parodying her era. Meg and Virginia seem to be enjoying the joke, so Sally decides not to worry. It is a relief to see Paul, who is usually so responsible and earnest, behaving very differently.

Sally moves from group to group, passing food and refilling glasses, introducing people, overhearing snatches of gossip about Woody Allen and Mia Farrow in court over custody and child abuse allegations, the demise of Perth millionaire Alan Bond, how the 2000 Olympics will affect Sydney and impassioned discussions about the advantages of Australia becoming a republic.

The raucous group have stopped arguing about the difference in standards between Melbourne and Sydney theatre (the most vociferous defenders of Melbourne theatre are ex-Melburnians; the Sydney people do not believe their theatre needs defending so they argue quite affably, which infuriates the Melburnians).

Now they have moved on to arguing about public broadcasting. 'I don't mind the ads on SBS as much as I thought I would,' says Sally, joining in. 'They're quite classy and they don't intrude because they're placed at the beginning and end of each program.'

'Oh, but you think of something good to say about everything!' says Adele, an old friend of hers who has worked at the ABC for years. There is laughter, most of it affectionate and some slightly pitying. Naive Pollyanna. Is that how they think of her? Sally shrugs. She has had rather a lot of wine herself and she finds this idea quite amusing.

Lanh is standing on the edge of this group of high-powered middle-aged performers, looking interested but intimidated. Sally ushers her in. 'Lanh is doing research for a new half hour weekly show on SBS. Current issues that concern young people,' says Sally enthusiastically.

'Really?' Adele is interested. 'I heard about that. I hope you're representing young Australia as a multicultural society . . .'

'Well of course she is! It's SBS,' says Eric Wales, a commercial broadcaster, who looks drunk.

Adele waves at him to be quiet.

Sally watches Lanh nervously to see if she will cope.

'Young people are mostly ignored by the media unless they're in trouble,' she says politely. 'We want to show that we're not all inarticulate louts on drugs. We have a lot to say. And yes, we have an Aborigine, two Greeks, a Swede and a half-Chinese on our team as well as me.' She smiles at Eric pleasantly. 'I think it's time we stopped depending on white middle-class males to represent our point of view.'

There is silence. Sally beams.

I must go and talk to Richard; he'll imagine I'm avoiding him, she thinks conveniently and glides away.

She looks about but cannot see Richard. The waiters are gathering up abandoned plates and glasses. They are not real waiters but university friends of Paul's who have offered their services at budget rates. Sally makes a mental note to pay them more than they asked for. One of them has even discovered some prawn heads hidden behind the mantelpiece clock. He raises his eyebrows at Sally as if to question her choice of guests with such disgusting habits and she smiles her agreement. Perhaps it was one of the children playing a trick.

She joins her neighbour, Bevan White, a professor of English at Sydney University and Lanh's Uncle Ngoc, who is now doing well as a wholesaler in Cabramatta, and has just been back to Vietnam for a visit to his brother. 'Sally, you know there are Australian gum trees on the road out of Hanoi?' He nods enthusiastically. 'They take out the eucalyptus oil, sell it for many dong.'

'Great. How is your brother getting on?'

'My brother now owns a house made of brick. Before Doi Moi in 1986, there was not one brick house in his village, now there are forty, all with electricity and some with TV. In the bar in his village there is Pepsi cola and karaoke!'

'So although the capitalists lost the war, they won the peace,' says Bevan White wittily. 'Isn't it a touch capitalist for a communist to own a brick house?'

'No, no. To be rich is not against the teachings of communism,' says Ngoc. 'But all the people should be equally rich.' He smiles at Sally who nods her agreement.

'Unemployment in Vietnam is more than twelve percent now. But in Australia it is not much less. There are many Australians doing business now in Vietnam – developing oil-fields, roads, a stock exchange. In Vietnam we remember that Australia protested against the war and withdrew before America.'

'And the Americans? You Vietnamese are pragmatic people. Surely you're encouraging the Americans to do business?' Bevan White enquires.

'Not so many. If the Americans want to be friends with Vietnamese now, we will be better off and they will be better off. If they don't, we will survive.'

'Ngoc, do you ever think of going back to Vietnam to live?' asks Sally.

'No. This is my home. My wife, my children, my niece, Lanh and my nephew Vinh, we are all Australians now. I'm going to become naturalised, Sally. Didn't I tell you?'

'No, Ngoc. That's wonderful.'

'The trip back to Vietnam made me sure I was ready to be an Australian. Sally, you have been so kind to my family. Will you come to the ceremony?'

'I'd love to, Ngoc.'

'I thought I'd lost you.' Sally, finding Richard alone in the garden, looks relieved and then feels foolish to have betrayed her need to find him. He is just another guest, after all, and has his own quite separate life now. She was afraid he might have brought the raucous red-haired Priscilla who would perhaps have made loud judgemental remarks about the overgrown garden, but he has been sensitive enough to spare her that indignity.

'I was just looking at the wisteria climbing along the verandah. I remember when you planted that. Fifteen years ago. Almost as soon as we moved in.'

Sally shrugs. 'Someone else will enjoy it now.' She imagines she sounds quite pleased to be leaving and congratulates herself on being so completely unemotional.

'You'll miss it all,' he says gently.

Oh shut up, she thinks, and turns away to hide the tears pricking her eyelids.

'I was wondering if, now that the house is sold, you might like to go away for a holiday.'

'Holiday?' she repeats stupidly. 'Where?'

'A cruise really. Just a short one. On a sailing ship. Around French Polynesia.'

Sally stares at him uncomprehending. Is this a bad joke? They had planned, when they were first married and very poor, that one day they would sail around the islands in the wake of Captain Cook, diving for fish from their boat, anchoring off tropical islands with mysterious peaks that seemed to beckon, like the one called Bali Hai in the film *South Pacific*.

'It's quite luxurious. You don't have to haul up the sails or anything. They're computerised,' Richard stopped. 'Of course, we'd have separate cabins.'

'But why not take someone else?'

'Because I'd like your company. We've always wanted to go and I can afford it now and I'd like you with me.'

'What about Priscilla?'

'I don't want to take Priscilla,' said Richard. He turned to look at her and she saw that his face was gaunt and sorrowful. 'I have cancer of the liver and prostate, Sally. It's inoperable apparently. Please come.'

# CHAPTER FIFTEEN

'You're not going with him?' Virginia sat opposite Sally on the old velvet sofa, her bare feet curled underneath. The party had just finished, the last guests had left and dawn was breaking.

'Yes, I think I will.'

'But why, Sally? He's using you, playing on your sympathy, your sense of duty, dragging you back into being his wife. Don't you see what he's doing?' Virginia was scandalised.

'It isn't just duty. I want to be with him.'

'Are you sure?' asked Meg, more tolerantly. 'It's a frightening time for him but if you agree to the trip you'll feel obliged to look after him later, won't you?'

'Whether he recovers or not you'll be stuck with him for

the rest of your life. If he gets worse you'll have to nurse him. It could take years. He doesn't deserve you!' Virginia was outraged.

'It's unbelievable that he's asked you to take him back in this way. When he was well you refused him and now that he's sick he's got the nerve to try and change your mind.'

Sally knew why Virginia felt angry. This situation reminded her of what she referred to as her mother's 'martyrdom'. Franca Arezzo had been in what she believed to be a happy marriage for twenty years when she discovered that her husband, for most of that time, had kept a mistress. Hurt and furious, she had asked him to leave. Soon afterwards he had suffered a severe stroke and Franca had taken him back and nursed him at home for seven years until he died.

Sally could see that despite their different levels of tolerance, both Virginia and Meg were waiting for an explanation. 'Okay,' she said, 'I agreed to go with him partly because he genuinely needs me, and people like to be needed. Also because I do still care a lot for him and the thought of him dying distresses me. Finally, I'm going because I believe he has changed for the better.'

Virginia rolled her eyes. '*Déjà vu*.'

'Your mother said that about your father?' Meg asked.

'Exactly. Almost *exactly* the same thing. And then she exhausted herself looking after him for years and years. Look, I loved my father but he was a bastard. If he'd recovered from that stroke he'd have been off out the door after some other woman as soon as he could walk. My mother swore that he'd changed, learned a lesson. He was sorry for the hurt he'd caused; he hadn't realised how painful it would be for her. He wept tears of remorse, she told me. But I know my father. He was acting!'

'How can you be sure?'

'Oh Sally!'

'Your father was a charmer. We all admired him. He *expected* to be loved. Your mother seemed pleased he was so popular. She was innocent, unsuspecting. Isn't it possible that he kept his mistress a secret because he didn't want to hurt your mother? And when he discovered how shattered she was he felt genuinely sorry?' Sally said. 'You told me that he never saw the mistress again.'

Virginia sighed. 'He never saw her because she was banned from the house by my mother. But he wrote to her.'

'How? He was paralysed.'

'He dictated the letters.'

'Who to?'

'His favourite daughter. Who else?' said Virginia with a touch of bitterness. 'I delivered them, too.'

'Behind your mother's back?' Meg looked surprised.

'Yes. Disgusting, wasn't it?' Virginia shrugged with distaste at the memory. 'The whole thing was pretty sordid. That's why I didn't visit him as much as I should have. I couldn't bear the hypocrisy.'

Sally and Meg gave sympathetic nods.

'I feel sorry for the mistress, too.' Sally said.

'I knew you'd say that!' Virginia burst out. She shook her head in disbelief. 'I bet if Saan, his old lover from Los Angeles, walked in here now and said (here she adopted a falsely concerned American accent), "I just heard about Richard. My God, I'm so sorry. I feel devastated", you'd comfort *her*. You would!'

Sally laughed in spite of herself. 'I don't hate Saan. Though I certainly did once. Look.' She became serious. 'Richard might recover. I want him to. If I can do anything to help in that recovery, I will. That's really why I'm going on this trip. He wants me there and I'm going. It doesn't mean I'm going back to being his wife. I'm not. I'm a friend. When we get back from the cruise he goes straight into hospital for radiotherapy and I'll be there to do whatever I can. Just like I'd do for either of you.'

Meg nodded.

Virginia shook her head.

'It's more like a private yacht than a passenger ship. It has four masts and travels under sail for about seventy-five percent of the time. It's 134 metres long and it carries 140 passengers,' said Richard, who had always been fond of detail.

He had spread out a mass of colourful brochures on the long refectory table in his Bondi flat and seemed delighted that Sally was taking such an interest. She picked up a brochure with a picture of a Tahitian girl in flowers and bikini paddling an outrigger canoe through shallow opal-coloured water and read, '*Ce dépliant contient tous les renseignements utiles aux visiteurs, ainsi que des cartes de Tahiti, Moorea, Raiatea, Huahine, Bora et de plusiers autres îles et atolls.*'

'That's where the boat takes us, to all of those islands,' said Richard enthusiastically. 'We anchor offshore and go in by small boat to explore them. Then, at night we come back on board to dance and feast or just lie about on deck looking at the stars. There are no rostered activities, no dreadful competitions for the knobbliest knees or whatever. And the food on board is fantastic, apparently.'

'Will you be feeling like eating it?' Sally asked him gently.

'Oh yes! I feel absolutely fine. That's the irony of it. Not until I get back and the treatment starts will I feel anything at all. I'm going to enjoy these nine days. Race ashore, climb mountains, explore markets, go deep-sea diving, snorkel and just lie about on a palm-fringed beach relaxing. And I want you to enjoy it too, Sally.'

She laughed. In his determination to be normal he had almost forgotten about her. 'Thank you. I might not be as energetic as you, but yes, I'll certainly enjoy it.'

She pondered Richard's brave response, wondering how much of it was for her benefit and how much for his. Perhaps he would tell her, some late evening on deck, drifting on a sea of ultramarine, past islands with thatched huts and village churches with thin white spires, how he really felt.

'Is Dad really dying?' Toby stood at the door to Sally's bedroom in his pyjamas late one night and asked the question harshly, as if he had been lied to previously and now demanded the truth.

'We don't know.' Sally patted the bedcover beside her and he sat down, staring out the window. She stroked his neck. 'His cancer is advanced, he's been told. It doesn't mean the situation's hopeless. He wants to fight it and that's important. He's very determined to live.'

Toby turned to face her, looking close to tears. 'Do you think he'll live?'

'I don't know, Tobes.' Sally hugged him. 'Us wanting him to will help.'

Steven and Toby were packing. They had been invited to stay with Meg while Sally was away. They were pleased about this, as they were fond of Meg, Peter and young Nicholas, although Toby had some reservations about Claudia.

'If he wasn't dying, do you think she'd go away with him?' Toby asked his older brother.

Steven laid a pile of T-shirts on his bed and looked non-committal. 'She might.'

'Not very likely though, is it?' Toby stuffed a pair of football socks into his backpack. 'I mean, she goes to dinner with him, but that's just because they're friends. He's paying for everything. You don't take someone on a luxury holiday unless you're in love or desperate.'

'He could be both.'

'What about Priscilla, that lady he introduced us to who was making lunch at his flat?'

'She's a tart. I told him that.'

'When?' Toby looked shocked.

'At the break-up party for our house. I said I was glad he hadn't brought that tart.' Steven scowled at his brother. 'How was I to know he had cancer?'

Priscilla was in a rage. It was a low trick her friend the doctor had pulled on his estranged wife and she had fallen for it. She had a good mind to beetle out to the family mansion in Hunters Hill and spill the beans. Not that Richard was lying completely. He did have cancer, but it wasn't as bad as all that. And it certainly wasn't hopeless. What a line of bullshit! Once he got back from his second honeymoon cruising around French Polynesia he'd pop into hospital, have some chemo or radiotherapy, put on a bit of a pathetic act to his wife about the pain and nausea, and there he'd be, safely back in the bosom of his adoring family, being nursed back to perfect health and all forgiven. It made you want to puke!

And the rotting mansion, overgrown with his wife's jungle garden that he'd always loathed, had been sold. How convenient. Married women were so stupid. He'd let her go through all the hassle of selling the house, all the heart-break of leaving the place she loved and soon he would offer her a poky flat in a high-rise with a glimpse of the harbour, because that's what *he* wanted, and she'd jump at it. Yes, thought Priscilla, I might drive over there and enlighten the poor bitch. Not that I care about *her*. It's just so unfair. He was going to be mine.

Nathan, being an aspiring actor, was attending an Actors' Benevolent Fund Raiser at The Wharf. He had been invited by one of his tutors from the Actors' Centre, Grant Neville, which was fortunate, because he could not have afforded to be there otherwise. Neville was gay, but Nathan felt confident of his own heterosexuality and enjoyed the older man's wit and company. He was also quite pleased to be introduced to the prominent directors and actors that his tutor seemed to know.

A vast barn of a rehearsal room with high pylons and beams had been transformed for the evening into a Gothic dining room. Round tables had been hired, covered in white linen cloths, silver candelabra and lashings of trailing ivy and blood-red rose petals. 'Stolen from the Botanical Gardens, I fear,' hissed Neville into Nathan's ear. 'There'll be musk rose petals in the soup. You wait.' Nathan grinned.

Spotlit against the gloomy rafters high above their heads, a platform suddenly appeared. Astonishingly it held a baby grand piano. 'Ah. Performance time.' Neville leaned back with an air of expectation.

A couple in top hats and spangles appeared on the precarious performance space. The man sat down at the piano, the woman draped herself on the lid and they sang several spirited satirical songs. The audience below craned their necks and applauded. Then the woman tap-danced a few steps horribly close to the edge of the platform, the couple bowed and made way for the next act, a tightrope walker and an acrobat.

'Fantastic!' said Nathan when the daring performances had finished.

'Show-offs.' Neville closed his eyes in mock disdain. 'Ah, here comes the rose-petal soup.'

Nathan sniffed, acknowledged that it was indeed rose-petal and asked, 'How did you know about that?'

'Because my job was to steal the petals of course,' Neville replied with a poker face and was pleased when Nathan laughed. 'Ah, Priscilla. Welcome! Sit down.' Neville made introductions all around the table.

Nathan had no idea who Priscilla was but she recognised him straight away. His father had told her of the son who was determined to be an actor, and she'd seen a photo of him in the local newspaper, playing a comedy role in some co-op. She decided not to spoil things by letting the young man know of her connection with his father.

Nathan shook hands with Priscilla and looked directly into her eyes as he had been taught to do since childhood. What he saw was a large, theatrical, flamboyantly dressed woman of perhaps fifty who was, nevertheless, quite attractive.

What she saw was a remarkably handsome young man about nineteen, who looked just worldly enough to be seduced. She glanced briefly at Neville to see if he knew what she was thinking. He narrowed his eyes at her as if to say, 'Hands off. He's mine', but she pretended not to understand and launched into an anecdote about a famous Russian director who had recently visited Sydney to direct *Uncle Vanya* and been completely misunderstood by the actors, with disastrous results. Nathan found her story hilarious, as she had hoped he might. The others at the table, who had heard it before, laughed good-naturedly because she always told it well. Only Neville pursed his lips in silent contempt.

In the taxi they share on the way home, Priscilla, very drunk, snuggles into Nathan's armpit and tells him that she is more miserable than she has been for many years. Her lover, she tells him, is a distinguished man, a gentle, intelligent, sensitive man who has recently escaped an unhappy marriage he has been in for decades and has just begun an idyllic new life with her. But now he has decided to go back to his dreary little wife. 'What a shit!' sobs Priscilla, smearing mascara onto Nathan's borrowed white dinner shirt. 'What a pathetic, gutless wimp my beautiful new man turned out to be.'

Nathan, who is drunk, but not as drunk as she is, utters soothing noises and strokes her wild red hair. He is used to confidences because, despite his youth, he is the kind of man in whom women tend to confide. He attracts women in distress. When still a schoolboy, he would arrive home with a young woman who had become seasick on the ferry and was too afraid to continue the journey, or one whose car had broken down at a traffic light and who needed to phone a garage, or one who had lost her cat in the park and needed to cry for ten minutes and have a cup of tea before she continued the search with his help. His family had unfeelingly referred to these women as Nathan's lame ducks. But Nathan does not think of Priscilla as a lame duck. She is more of a magnificent firebird whose flame has been temporarily quenched by some watery old man too weak to deserve her.

'Look, I know what will make you feel better,' says Nathan and she looks up at him lustfully, but he laughs, looks embarrassed and shakes his head. He leans down and whispers something in her ear. Priscilla sits up, apparently alert and wipes the smudged mascara from her eyes. 'Have you got some?'

Nathan screws up his eyes and glances in the direction of the driver. Priscilla drunkenly puts her finger to her lips.

'Would you like to stop by at my place for a few minutes and try a little of that medicine?' he asks her quietly.

'Better idea is, you get the medicine and we take it to my place,' suggests Priscilla, peering out the window at the narrow streets of Surry Hills. 'Got a better view at my place; can see the ocean and the sunrise and magnificent cliffs. Only hovels down here. Not very inspiring. Streets full of dog shit and dope pedlars.' This last observation seems to amuse her and she bursts into peals of laughter. Nathan darts out of the cab and up the back alley to his room, returning in three minutes with his backpack.

'Oh, staying awhile are we?' Priscilla now affects a Lady

Bracknell persona. She sits very straight in the back of the taxi and attempts to look haughty.

'Only if your ladyship finds my company worthy,' Nathan replies, slipping easily into the role of Ernest.

'Worthy? I do not want worthiness, young man. I want to be hugely entertained!'

'I shall do my best Ma'am.'

'Well, was I entertaining?' It was late the next morning. They sat on a tiny balcony above the ocean drinking strong black coffee. Nathan wore a borrowed Balinese dressing-gown and Priscilla was draped inadequately in a piece of batik. She wore sunglasses and did not look at all well.

'Hugely, my darling,' she said wanly. 'You were wonderful. You cheered me up. And the 'medicine' was bloody fantastic. I'm almost fifty and I've never, in my life, snorted coke before. Isn't that amazing? I have led a sheltered life. But thanks to you, Ernest, I won't be sheltered any longer!' She flung her arms wide and then grimaced with pain, putting a hand to her head.

'Are you all right, Lady Bracknell?'

'Awwgh!' she groaned. 'I drank too much cheap plonk at that awful dinner. What a pack of egotistical swine actors are! Why we attend benefits for them, I don't know. Except that one day we'll all be in need of the Benevolent Fund. You too, Ernest.' She eyed him over the top of her sunglasses. 'Where, may I ask, did you get that cocaine?'

'A friend deals it. Sometimes he gives me a few grams. That was my nineteenth birthday present,' said Nathan with an innocent smile. 'Don't worry. I'm not an addict.'

'How very sweet. You shared your nineteenth birthday present with me. I'm touched.' Priscilla took off her sunglasses and mopped her eyes. They were red and puffy. 'You're far more generous than your father.'

Nathan straightened in his chair. 'You know my father?'

He did not particularly want his father to hear about the cocaine or about the night he had just spent with this woman older than his mother.

'Well of course I know your father, Ernest. You were *not* found in a handbag in the cloak-room at Victoria station,' she said with majestic indignation. 'You happen to be quite well bred. Even though you are not down on my list of eligible young men, although I have the same list as the dear Duchess of Bolton . . .'

'How do you know my father?' Nathan interrupted. The Oscar Wilde game had suddenly lost its appeal.

'I told you all about him in the cab on the way home. Don't you remember? Or were you too drunk? I confessed my love for him. You comforted me. You understood. You offered yourself and the magic medicine to make me feel better. You were a darling.'

Nathan was speechless.

'You *were* too drunk. You don't remember?' she asked sadly.

'I do remember. You told me about a lover but you didn't say who he was. You certainly didn't mention his name!' Nathan stood up. He was angry. 'My father is ill. He has cancer. Did you know?'

'Yes of course I know. But he isn't dying of it. He's exaggerating the seriousness of it to make your mother sorry for him. He wants her to take him back.'

'Look, I'd better go. I'm sorry.' Nathan dashed into the living room, then turned back distractedly to ask, 'What do you mean he's exaggerating? The cancer's inoperable.'

'I'd check with his doctor about that if I were you. You're a well-bred young man, Ernest, but far too gullible.'

'Will you be frank with me?' Nathan asked.

'Of course,' said Sally.

'You've spoken to his doctor?'

She nodded. 'I've been with Dad to see him twice.'

They sat side by side on a log in the garden under the frangipani tree. Its creamy petals made a carpet on the grass and Nathan shredded them one by one.

'The situation is this. He has cancer of the prostate and liver. Only five percent of people with liver cancer can be treated by surgery and he isn't one of them.'

'So how long has he got to live?'

'If he doesn't respond to chemotherapy or radiotherapy he'll probably last six months.'

'Christ! Is that all?'

'And if he does respond, he'll last longer. Two years, perhaps more.'

'But that's nothing!'

'It seems a lot to someone who's been thinking in terms of six months,' Sally said.

'But either way he's doomed.'

'Maybe not. There's a new technique that's very exciting that could beat the cancer altogether. Cryotherapy, it's called. You use liquid nitrogen to freeze the cancer cells rather than excising them. It's being pioneered right here in Sydney. Dad knows the professor who's working on it and he's very hopeful it will help.'

'But how long will he last then? Another six months?' asked Nathan hopelessly.

'Possibly. But it could be better than that. He could be cured.'

'With liquid nitrogen?' Nathan was sceptical.

'Look, when we come back from this trip Dad will start radiotherapy for both the liver and prostate cancers and if either fails, he'll immediately be operated on using the cryotherapy technique. Apparently, liquid nitrogen is injected into the tumour cells and forms an ice ball. The ice ball destroys the cancerous cells and leaves behind benign scar-like tissue.'

Nathan gave her an admiring look. 'You've been studying it thoroughly.' He remembered her researching biology assignments for him in his final year at school when he'd given up hope of passing; she'd persuaded him he could get through and he'd done it. 'What rate of success has this professor had with his ice balls? He won't be just using Dad as a guineapig, will he?'

'He's treated a hundred and fifteen patients who were given six months to live and just under half are alive two years later and a few are tumour-free. That's people with liver and bowel cancer. He's only performed one prostate operation and so far, he says, the signs are very encouraging.'

'What? The patient's not dead yet? God, it's so depressing!'

Sally sighed. 'Well it is, but it's worth a fight. Don't you think?'

'Sure. I do, yes. It makes you feel so fucking lucky to be well. And I think it's great you're sticking with Dad through all this.' He slumped forward and put his head between his hands.

'What is it, Nath? Hey. Don't be too sad.' She put her arms around him. 'I think Dad's got a very good chance of pulling through.'

'Have you met Priscilla?' Nathan turned to face her.

'Yes. Once at Dad's flat. Why?'

'What did you think of her?'

'Well, I must admit I didn't think much of her.'

'Bit of an hysteric? Like most actors?' Nathan grinned.

'You've met her, too?' Sally smiled.

'Last night at a dinner. Would you say she was . . . malicious?'

Sally looked concerned. 'What did she say to you?'

'That Dad was putting on an act for your benefit. His cancer wasn't as bad as he's making out. That he's using it to try and get back together with you.'

'His cancer *is* bad. As I've just told you. I think he's very frightened. When you're frightened and have cancer I imagine you look around for the best help you can get, both medical and emotional. Dad thinks I'll be more emotional help than Priscilla and I expect she's upset.' Sally looked angry. 'But she shouldn't be saying he's exaggerating his illness to impress me. Yes, I do think that's malicious.'

'She told me that Dad was really happy with her.'

Sally shrugged. 'Why has he left her then?'

'Because he's sick and you'll look after him better?'

Sally looked wounded. 'He's been asking me for months to have him back, Nathan. I've said no because, although I'm still very fond of him I feel better living on my own at present. I prefer to be friends.'

'Okay. So, imagine as a friend you look after him for two or more years. You give up your work, the independence you've fought for, the possibility of other men in your life, so that you can devote yourself to him. He gets better. He goes back to Priscilla. Or someone else. How do you feel then?'

'If he got better I'd be grateful no matter what. If I changed my mind and wanted him as a husband I'm sure he'd be pleased. If I didn't, he could go back to Priscilla or someone else. I wouldn't have any right to feel resentful.'

'Ah, but you *would* feel resentful! Whether you had a right to or not.'

'Would I? Is that what you think?' She looked bemused.

'Yes I do.' Nathan was adamant. 'You want to know what I think? You do still love him. You don't want Priscilla or any of those other little bimbos to have him. You know you shouldn't take him back because it's not ideologically correct when he's been such a bastard; because you're having a really good life without him and your friends Meg and Virginia will think you're pathetic and not a good feminist if you do take him back, but I think you really love him!'

'Do you just?' Sally laughed. 'You're sure you're not projecting your own wishes onto me just a bit?'

Nathan shrugged.

'Well, you could be right. You always were a smart little bugger. Very perceptive. Quite astute,' she said with affection, and then sighed. 'The truth is, I really don't know what I feel. I certainly care enough for him to want him to get better. That's the first thing to tackle. Then I'll think about the other thing.'

'Good on you, Ma. By the way,' he said gravely, 'I'd better tell you, because malicious people like to gossip and you might hear it from another source.' He looked away. 'I slept with Priscilla last night.'

Sally stared at him in disbelief.

'We were both pretty drunk and I didn't know she was Dad's ex-girlfriend. I was kind of sorry for her. Now I don't mean that to sound condescending to older women.' He held up a hand to shield himself from what she might say next. 'She was quite attractive and very funny, at least until she started crying about this lover who'd walked out on her. I didn't know it was *Dad*!' He looked appalled. 'Anyway you'll be pleased to know we didn't fall in love.'

Sally looked up at the sweet-smelling blossoms of the frangipani and drew a deep breath. Then she turned her head away and her body started to shake. Nathan saw with astonishment that she was laughing. Still looking away, she held out one hand and he took it. The laughter was contagious. They sat side by side on the log, hand in hand and shook with silent laughter.

# CHAPTER SIXTEEN

On the flight to Papaeete, Richard slept a lot.

Sally had been too excited to sleep and had started reading Vikram Seth's *A Suitable Boy*. It was a hardback of fourteen hundred pages, too heavy to hold above your head while stretched out on a lounge chair on the deck of a sailing ship and probably not quite the right thing to be reading on a south seas holiday anyway. She should have chosen a paperback by James Michener, but she had wanted to read this. She decided to get a good start on it before the serious business of relaxation began.

Burying herself in this saga of Indian political and family life would take her mind off the guilt she felt about taking ten days leave from her job and about handing over the responsibility of her two younger sons to Meg, who had quite enough to cope with already. Claudia was becoming increasingly difficult. Apparently she'd been having a series of affairs with older men, including the Judge she had met at Sally's party. She'd abandoned him after a week and become involved in quick succession with a newspaper editor, a merchant banker, a corporate lawyer and a member of State Parliament. Meg had warned her that although she had every right to enjoy herself, she should not become promiscuous. Claudia had been furious and accused Meg of being jealous and old fashioned. Sally believed it was only a matter of time before there would be a mighty blow-up between them and Claudia would leave. She felt sure that Meg would then blame herself for the failure of their relationship.

Perhaps having Toby and Steven to stay would make Claudia behave better, Sally thought. She did not think it could make the situation any worse.

Nicholas had begun wetting the bed, a sure sign of tension in the household and Peter spent an increasing amount of time at the boat builder's next door, restoring a tiny ferry he had bought cheaply and hoped to use commercially one day to take people on picnics around the harbour.

Toby and Steven thought Peter's plan to become a part-time ferry man was a great idea. They had friends who already wanted to hire him and his boat for birthday parties. It would be excellent to dance on board a ferry draped in coloured lights and balloons, they said. Peter had agreed to anchor in some quiet bay or land them on an uninhabited island. He also promised Toby and Steven free trips for their own birthdays if they helped him work on the boat at weekends. They had agreed enthusiastically to this. Yes, perhaps the plan for them to stay with Meg and Peter would work out well after all.

Before she left Sydney, Sally and the boys had begun the awful task of packing to leave Hunters Hill. They had decided to rent a place in the inner city for six months to see how they liked it before buying anything. Now Sally asked herself if she was delaying buying a house to see what would happen with Richard.

He looked pale sleeping in the seat beside her. He had eaten and drunk very little, she noticed. He seemed grateful to have her with him and talked mainly about the trip, avoiding personal subjects. She wondered if she would ever be able to tell him about Nathan and Priscilla. She supposed not. He would not find it at all funny. She smiled now, remembering. Was she perverse to find such a thing amusing? She supposed she must be. It was bizarre. And ironic. To think that she had brought up her sons to be compassionate to women in distress and one of them, in obeying her, had unwittingly slept with his father's mistress.

Why isn't she shocked, outraged, revolted by the thought of her beautiful unspoiled teenage boy sleeping with an over-painted, over-dramatic woman of nearly fifty? Perhaps because he is not, she suspects, as unspoiled as all that.

Nevertheless, thinks Sally, she is relieved that Nathan had the sense to thank Priscilla kindly for her offer to help him with his audition pieces for NIDA and decline.

If he got into the National Institute of Dramatic Art, which auditioned two thousand students a year and accepted twenty-one, it would be a miracle, but due entirely to his own efforts.

In Papaeete, Sally and Richard must spend one night at a hotel waiting for their sailing ship to arrive. The hotel is out of town, high above the sea. It is late afternoon when they book in. They sit by the pool which is a fantasy of waterfalls, fake mountains covered in vines and bright flowers and little bridges to swim under. The pool curves about like a lake; it even has a sandy beach. They watch a wedding party arrive to take photographs in this paradise. The Tahitian bride is dressed in white guipure lace, like the brides Sally used to stare at in the photographer's window in Geelong in the 1950s while she waited for the bus home from school.

The bridegroom, in a fuchsia tuxedo, has blonded his hair. The bridesmaids wear pink satin, like nighties, with artificial roses in their hair and they giggle constantly. There are pageboys in bow ties and crisp white shirts, a huge mother-in-law in a tight-fitting suit and another in a flowing mu mu that looks better, and lots of men in dinner jackets. They pose for photos in front of the fake waterfalls that cascade beside the palm trees and hibiscus, looking happy. Will Richard live to see any of his sons marry, Sally wonders?

The sun is sinking. 'We deserve some champagne!' says Sally to Richard. 'We've been very good.' He nods enthusiastically and goes off to the thatched hut that is a bar to get some. She had thought of just going to buy it herself and presenting it to him as a surprise but she doesn't want him to think she is pampering him, making the most of what is possibly his last holiday. He would be upset by that. She has to be careful.

But when she looks at his retreating back she sees how changed he is – how much older and more vulnerable. He reminds her for an instant of his father. She feels a wave of pity and affection.

The wedding party has left. Sally watches a speckled hen leading five tiny chicks along the pathway, under her table, up some stone steps, along the grass to where rainwater has made a pool. The mother shows the chicks how to peck and drink the water which they obediently do. But one chick has stopped to eat some crumbs under a table and is still at the bottom of the steps. Suddenly realising it has lost its family, it cheeps in terror. Sally is surprised at the loudness. The others ignore it. Eventually it finds its own way up the steps and scuttles along the grass to join them.

Richard must feel like that terrified chick, thinks Sally.

He comes back with a bottle of Moët & Chandon and places it triumphantly on the table in an ice bucket, daring her to say he has been too extravagant. She smiles at him and says nothing.

Far out to sea they watch three fins, black and sharp. Sharks? Dolphins? No, it is three board riders in the middle of the ocean. What must it be like to be alone like that in a vast sea, Sally wonders? The board riders are spreading out now, paddling in to shore. The sun sinks low behind clouds like a biblical painting. The paddlers move slowly through the golden light. There is a ship on the horizon, like a mirage, suspended in gold. Will our ship be like that one, she wonders? Suddenly the sun comes out from behind clouds, a golden orb. Dazzling. It rises behind the black trunk of a she-oak. And rises. Bathing them both in an aura. Oh Richard, be peaceful. Don't fight too hard, thinks Sally.

They sip their champagne and smile at the sunset.

When they board the ship at five o'clock next afternoon they are served more champagne. Richard leaves his glass untouched and Sally realises, with a wave of deep regret, that she had been thoughtless suggesting they share a celebratory bottle yesterday. Champagne would be about the worst thing for his liver. But he had drunk it to please her.

Next there is registration in the lounge.

The passengers are excited, chattering and moving from seat to porthole, balancing drinks and luggage, calling out to people they recognise, hugging and exclaiming. They remind Sally of students returning to a popular boarding school after a boring holiday with their parents. Most of the passengers are Americans. Perhaps they are a group. Perhaps they meet each other on board the luxurious *Windsprite* once a year. Millionaires slumming it on the south seas. Sally overhears different accents – English, French, Spanish, but none are Australian. The passengers seem to be mainly couples, middle-aged or older. There are a few large families – well-bred Bostonians with accents like the Kennedys and many tall sons who all look the same.

The *Windsprite*, with its graceful masts, polished teak decks and gleaming brass does not impress them at all. Nor do the Indonesian and Filipino crew, standing in line wearing white, smiling and saying intimately to each one, 'Welcome aboard'.

Suddenly there is a fanfare on the piano and a very lively woman of about thirty-five bounces into the lounge with a microphone. She is brightly painted and dressed, as the brochure has advised all passengers on board *Windsprite* to dress, with 'casual elegance'.

'Welcome to the *Windsprite* cruise, ladies and gentlemen!' She sounds American as apple pie. Sally is disappointed. What had she expected? A French-Tahitian hostess with flowers in her hair? 'I'm Trish, your hostess for the next seven days and I'll be meeting you here in the lounge every afternoon at five to tell you about our program for the next day.' Her voice is rapid, loud and artificial. A brittle wind-up doll. She rattles off information about water sports – windsurfing, waterskiing, kayaking, banana-boat rides, snorkelling, scuba diving and sailing – most taking place from the platform aft of the ship in mid-ocean. She prattles about the ships amenities: massage and beauty salon, in-cabin videos, casino, sauna, fitness room, infirmary and satellite telephone calls to anywhere in the world that can be made directly from your cabin. Onshore tomorrow there will be trips deep-sea fishing, four-wheel driving, helicopter flying, horse riding or picnicking by outrigger canoe to an island or motu. Just sign up at reception.

'And tonight, after dinner, there will be dancing under the stars to the ship's own Polaris Trio!' Trish concludes and sweeps an arm at the pianist who gives her a grand finale. 'Maruru! That means thank you,' she shouts like a cheerleader as she marches off the platform.

And most of the passengers chorus, 'Maruru!'

Sally gives Richard a look that says, 'What have we got ourselves into?' but he only smiles and shrugs.

That evening very few people dance under the stars to the Polaris Trio because the sea is extremely rough. Sally begins to feel queasy at dinner time and can eat nothing but consommé. Richard cheerfully picks away at all four courses as the waves surge against the portholes and waiters do quicksteps with trays above their heads and manage miraculously not to spill a drop. There are not many in the dining room and several people leave their tables in a hurry. The ship pitches and rolls. After dinner Richard suggests they go up on deck for some air. At the bar they meet the first mate, a Yorkshireman who is rather drunk and tells them that the captain, a Dane, enjoys a bit of rough sailing. But this is nothing. Just a bit of a swell. A few months back they had seas so high that a wave swept a fridge full of Tuborg beer off the upper deck right into the ocean. The captain had been furious because it was his personal supply.

The very thought of one man consuming a fridgeful of beer makes Sally apologise to Richard and flee to her cabin. After parting with the consommé and her seasick tablets in the wash basin, she lies palely in the cabin as big as a stateroom, hanging on to one side of her double bed to keep herself from being pitched onto the floor. The digital clock shows that it is only 8.30. Sally wonders if Priscilla, on her first night of this luxury cruise, would have succumbed to seasickness and been such useless company and supposes glumly that she wouldn't.

Next morning the seas are calm. Sally and Richard eat breakfast outside on the deck as they sail towards the island of Huahini. The sun sparkles on green water and the creamy white sails rise and fall like classical dancers. They are nosing into a secluded bay where a dozen brown children leap and splash on the beach waving a welcome.

They have booked into 'a native historical tour' of the island which sounds dull after Trish's suggestions of helicopter and horse rides, but it is what they both prefer. As they stand at the rails watching the ship tie up and waving to the children, a friendly couple from Sacramento introduce themselves and say they are on the cruise to celebrate their twenty-fifth wedding anniversary. They look expectantly at Sally and Richard to see what they are celebrating. Sally changes the subject, asking if they've been on a cruise like this before. 'No, but our friends have. We came as a group of six; there are discounts if you bring extra people.'

Ah, says Sally, understanding. She and Richard had been almost the only couple in the dining room not part of a group of six.

The historical tour is conducted by a woman of about Sally's age who is half Tahitian, half American. She has luxuriant long dark hair, wears flowers and laughs often. Madeleine tells her small group that she grew up in Santa Barbara and came to Huahini at sixteen, married a local and has been back to the States only twice since. 'My sister who still lives in Los Angeles said to me, "You can't raise children on that island. They'll grow up with bananas for brains." But my children speak three languages, French, English and Tahitian, and they are both at university in Paris now while my daughter's three kids are not doing so well – one on drugs, one in analysis and one in jail!' She laughs, though not heartlessly. 'Huahini is a paradise for children. There is no crime, no racism, endless sunshine and abundant food.'

'What about wars with other islands?' asks an older woman sceptically.

'In the last century people from Bora Bora used to come across and steal our food and women.' Madeleine laughs. 'They still do!'

'No crime at all?' asks another woman in disbelief.

'Only rape. And that is only of tourists.'

There is some uneasy laughter. This is a rather tasteless joke. But Madeleine is serious. 'Sometimes young lady tourists come on motorbikes to swim at our beaches and they think, "A deserted beach! I'll take my clothes off". And this, to the locals, is an invitation to have sex. So when a young man appears from the coconut plantation beside the beach to oblige the young woman, she screams and he is accused of rape. It is an unfortunate misunderstanding due to different customs.'

Sally and Richard nod in sympathy with this and try to hide their amusement at the disapproval of their travelling companions.

They trundle over winding unmade roads in their little bus through the sparsely populated island with its lagoons full of fish, clams and crab and lush forests, beneath which there are crops of avocado, yams, vanilla, breadfruit, watermelon, coconuts, bananas, papaya and pineapple.

'Who owns this beautiful land?' asks a Chilean man. 'The French?'

'The original inhabitants own it,' says Madeleine proudly. 'The Polynesians. It is passed down from generation to generation.

Each son or daughter who marries is given a piece of land to build a house on.'

Sally asks how the Polynesians get along with the French, who still test nuclear weapons on the island of Mururoa and Madeleine looks unhappy, telling her quietly that there is a resistance movement of twenty thousand in Tahiti led by Oscar Timaru. 'People protest peacefully about the nuclear testing and other things – the high tax on cars and TV sets, even electricity. A small car here costs thirty thousand US dollars and a TV two thousand.'

'The French still have military bases on Tahiti?' Sally asks.

'Yes, unfortunately. The people of Huahini held out four years longer than the other islands against the French Government takeover in 1945. But now we are a French protectorate. They see us as a feather in their cap.'

Once Richard might have been embarrassed at Sally's political questions and signalled her not to stir up trouble, but now he looks tolerant. Interested.

Madeleine takes her little group to Maeva village, an open-air museum of restored religious sites, once the greatest group of temples in the South Pacific and now just a platform of large paved stones. 'This is called the marae. Here, eight royal families lived side by side under the protection of the sacred mountain, Moua Tapu. The marae were built in the sixteenth century. Here, Polynesians worshipped the god Thane.'

'Is this where humans were sacrificed?' one of the Americans asks.

'Yes, occasionally. They were not killed here, but brought to the temple already dead. They were killed by a blow to the head with a stone. Human sacrifice was a punishment for crime against the king, stealing or disrespect.'

Madeleine explains that in Polynesian folklore, the two islands that form Huahini were once joined but Hiro, the mischievous god of Thieves, sliced his canoe through it, producing double islands joined by an isthmus.

Sally finds the myths fascinating and wants to know more. Richard is more interested in Huahini's anthropological history and asks about the problem of incest on this small island of fishermen and farmers where the nearest island is several days canoe ride away.

'Yes, yes,' says Madeleine, quite unembarrassed. 'Incest was a problem on the island until the Protestants came. They recognised it at once and brought teenagers across from Bora Bora to play basketball. The church groups interchanged.'

'So there was incest here until quite recently?' asks the older American woman, looking shocked.

Madeleine nods and says cheerfully, 'We are not so cautious in our sexual liaisons as Americans. We are not so possessive of each other, either. If a couple wants a child and cannot have one themselves, they will ask friends or relations to give them one. That is quite common. And if a grandmother is lonely she will be given a child to keep her company.'

After they had said goodbye to Madeleine, and the other tour group members had climbed the gangplank to escape the hot sun, Sally and Richard wandered along the waterfront street, shaded by giant acacia and almond trees. There were a few Chinese stores selling tins of food, some Polynesian boutiques with coloured *pareos* tied to the trees outside and some locally made pottery arranged on the footpath. Sally examined the pots and stroked the *pareos*. 'We must buy some presents soon,' she said.

Hardly anyone was about because it was steamy and the middle of the day. A few young men sat talking on motorbikes in the shade. There was a strong smell of frangipani and damp earth. 'A sleepy town, Fare.' Richard remarked when Sally caught up with him. 'It reminds me of Bali before the tourists wrecked it.'

'You mean twenty-two years ago?'

'Is it twenty-two years since we were there? I suppose it must be. It was before Paul was born.'

Sally nodded. They walked on in companionable silence.

'That was a great trip to Bali. Riding the scooter all over the countryside. We even went up that volcanic mountain. What was it called?' Richard asked her.

'Mount Batur.'

'That's right. It was black. The roads were black gravel. Very steep. Quite dangerous. Madness, really.'

Sally laughed. 'We should do it again,' she said before she could stop herself.

'What, ride a scooter?'

'Why not? We could hire one on Morea or Bora Bora. Go off exploring without the tour groups.'

Richard looked doubtful, then suddenly pleased. 'Okay, if you like. Though Trish might not like it. She'd rather we lined up poolside for a snorkelling lesson.' He mimicked Trish's 'organiser's prattle' rather well.

'Or a gaming session in the casino.'

'Or pareo-tying in preparation for Polynesian night.

'Did you hear that there's going to be a honeymooners' get-together in the disco tonight?' said Sally, appalled.

'I imagine even honeymooners get bored with each other,' Richard said. 'Though we didn't.'

'We didn't have enough *time* to get bored. One night at a guesthouse in Lorne.'

'It was nice, though. Seemed luxurious to us. Big verandahs. Miles of lawn. We played croquet. Why did we choose that old-fashioned place?'

'It was inexpensive. And I used to work there as a waitress.'

'Ah, yes! You wanted to see it from the pampered guests' perspective. But there was someone there who scared you. A chef, wasn't it? He was still there. He recognised you and sent us a special bottle of wine. He seemed all right to me.'

'It was terrible wine. Sparkling burgundy. He used to give it to the girls he managed to entice into his flat at the back of the kitchen. He called it a leg-opener. He hated me because I'd never go in there. That wine was an insult.'

Richard laughed. 'The bastard. Why didn't you tell me? I'd have flattened him. Well, no, I don't suppose I would have. He was pretty big, I seem to remember.'

'He was. And quite mad after a few drinks.' Sally smiled. 'He'd have carved you up with the bread knife and ruined our honeymoon.'

They stood on the deck of the *Windsprite* looking down at the children playing in the shallows, waiting for the ship to signal that it was leaving Huahini. As soon as the captain gave the command, four of the strongest boys unhooked the giant rope from the wharf and, still clinging to it, hurled themselves into the sea. Then, like a swarm of Lilliputians, the other children, who'd been waiting in the water, grabbed hold of the rope along its length, were lifted out of the water high into the air and swung from it like monkeys, retreating hand over hand as it was wound mechanically into the ship. As the engines started up, large waves were created, making the children scream with delight. Still clinging to the rope and perilously close to the ship's giant bulk, they dived off at the last minute into the waves.

Sally sighed with relief as the ship surged out to sea and the children, still waving and yelling from the water, were safely left behind. Richard shook his head. The Danish captain, standing on deck near them, merely shrugged. Evidently this daredevil ritual was performed every week without mishap.

Sally thought of Nathan, aged eight, swinging on a rope twenty feet in the air from the jacaranda tree in their garden, wearing nothing but a strip of fake fur, acting as Tarzan, full of confidence, yelling, 'Wawawaw!' just like the movies. She had watched in disbelief as he hurled himself out into the void so fearlessly and gasped when his foot caught in an overhanging branch, suspending him upside down like a bat, wailing and helpless. She had called to him not to panic but hold on, dragging a mattress out of the house to soften his fall, counting the seconds until the firemen arrived with ladders and a safety net.

'Sort of mad stunt Nathan would've enjoyed,' Richard said, smiling as he looked back towards the boys in the water.

'Mmm,' Sally said. He had been in Boston during the months of Nathan's convalescence from two broken legs.

Meg has decided to go ahead with her plans to visit East Timor in the guise of a 'tour adviser'. The plans are risky, but she thinks her trip will be worth it.

She is part of a team of five led by James Parker. If they are successful, their report from inside East Timor will be the first accurate one since the massacre in November, 1991, almost two years ago.

Parker, who plans to make a documentary film, has teamed up with a British doctor who is doing a medical survey, which means that he will be able to carry a video camera to be used in hospitals and is unlikely to be searched. They will travel separately, the doctor flying directly to Dili, and Parker flying from Bali to West Timor and then driving over the border at a place where he is unlikely to be checked. Parker will travel with his regular documentary director who will operate a small camera. Both of them will be posing as 'tour advisers' on a fact-finding expedition, with the intention of setting up tourist ventures in East Timor. Tourism is apparently being encouraged by the Indonesians. Parker and his director have researched the tourist industry thoroughly, even having fake business cards printed and carrying fake address books and other documents likely to prove that they are genuine advisers.

Meg, as the Australian representative of a fictitious company called Eastern Adventure Tours (EAT) will also pose as a tour adviser. She will follow a slightly different route, flying from Darwin to West Timor and then meeting up with the two British 'advisers', supposedly by accident, in a hotel in Kupang. They will then, apparently spontaneously, decide to share the cost of hiring a four-wheel drive vehicle and a local driver to take them over the border and on to Dili.

Meg also has a stack of business cards, with the fax number of EAT, which, if checked for authenticity, will have Peter at the other end to send suitable replies. She has other documents to substantiate her claim to be in the travel industry – brochures with the company name stamped on them, lists of clients, even a souvenir carry bag with Eastern Adventure Tours emblazoned across one side. She will carry a camera to take pictures of the beautiful scenery for the brochure she is pretending to compile that will entice tourists to visit East Timor.

'And who is the fifth member of the team?' Peter asks Meg, as he shows her how to operate the small camera he is lending her.

'A British cameraman who filmed the Santa Cruz massacre two years ago. I helped him smuggle out the footage that was screened around the world.'

'What's his name?'

'It depends. He operates under a number of aliases and has several different passports. This time, I believe, he is posing as a wildlife photographer, with a particular interest in birds. He'll try to get up into the mountains to film the Fretilin guerilla army.'

'And you wouldn't be crazy enough to go with him?'

'No, Peter, I wouldn't.' She grins. 'Not that I wouldn't love to try.'

Peter turns away to hide his resentment. 'Not much point going up there anyway. Now that their leader is locked away in a Javan prison, the guerillas have probably disbanded.'

'Not at all. There are still a lot of Gusmao's followers up there, and they've been joined by younger men and women who left Dili in fear for their lives after the Santa Cruz massacre.'

Peter shrugs. 'Well, just be bloody careful.' He zips up the camera bag.

'You don't think your camera might look a bit too expensive for a lowly 'tour adviser' to carry?' she asks him.

He shakes his head. 'Just one question,' he says, looking concerned. 'If this British cameraman or doctor happen to bump into you and the others in the main street of Dili, what then?'

'We pretend not to know them. We have absolutely no contact with them until we're safely out of the country.'

'And no contact with me either, I take it?' he asks glumly.

'No contact with anyone. I'll fax you if I can in an emergency, that's all. Don't worry, my love, I'll only be gone two weeks.'

'And you think you're going to cover the length and breadth of East Timor in that time?'

'The interviews have all been prearranged through contacts in London, Lisbon and Australia. There's a team of five of us, remember. There should be enough material for a documentary film as well as a mass of newspaper and television coverage.'

Meg can barely contain her excitement, her impatience to get started. She tries not to notice Peter's gloom.

It is September, 1993, and the Australian Prime Minister has just been to the United States where he has urged congressmen to take a 'broader view' of human rights in Indonesia so that economic interests will not be damaged. Since the Senate Foreign Relations Committee has just voted unanimously to ban US arms sales to Indonesia unless it improves its human rights record in East Timor, this warning is embarrassing.

Obviously the Prime Minister's action contradicts Australia's policy that raising human rights issues does not jeopardise trade. Meg feels this is a vital time to get inside the invaded country and report what is really happening. But respected Australian journalists, including those with valid visas, are still being refused entry to Indonesia. A few weeks ago one was marched away at Singapore airport by Indonesian immigration officials, told he was on a 'black list' in spite of his recently issued visa and detained for twelve hours like a drug trafficker before being put on a plane home. So Meg is convinced that requesting a visa as a journalist is hopeless and assuming the role of EAT consultant (she rather likes the image of an all-consuming travel agent) is her only chance. There are no restrictions on tour advisers. She has a new passport with no profession listed on it. She would be very unlucky if some immigration official from two years earlier happened to recognise her and consulted his black list of journalists. This is a risk she is willing to take.

Peter is not at all convinced and argues with her. She is surprised at his vehemence. To try and change her mind he even defends President Suharto.

'Look! Indonesia is showing signs of economic stability at last. Australia has become its sixth largest source of imports. Did you know that? Suharto is becoming *benign*. So it's only a matter of time before you'll be allowed in as a journalist, quite legally. Why not wait till then? Suharto's reducing the prison sentences of all the rebels and dissidents.'

'Sure, Xanana Gusmao now has only twenty years to serve, instead of life imprisonment,' Meg replies, unimpressed. 'I wanted to go to his trial in May but they wouldn't let me in.

Those who did attend were outraged. International jurists believe there should be a protest about the way it was conducted. Gusmao wants a referendum on Indonesian rule in East Timor and a mass of Timorese support him so he's locked away forever. He won't last twenty years in that prison.'

'You're not going to try and visit him I hope. You're not that crazy.'

'No, I'm not. But I want to go into East Timor and find out what is happening. No one *knows*. I want to interview people and report the truth. That's all.'

'Why do *you* have to go? Why not let that hot young investigative journalist on your paper have the honour? Jenny Douglas. She hasn't got children and a husband. Let her go!' he shouts.

Meg looks bewildered at this outburst. Doesn't he realise how important it is for her to go?

'Jenny's talented, sure, but . . .'

'You told me she was a young Meg McIntyre in the making. She's keen, bright, full of courage. Let her go!'

'I've got good cover. I'll be all right, Pete. Really.' She tries to reassure. This is disturbing.

'You don't want to give her the chance to compete. Perhaps show you up. You're a control freak!'

'Peter, don't be such a bastard.' Meg is angry now. 'Jenny's too young, inexperienced. I've been writing about East Timor for nearly twenty years. This is my story. Jenny doesn't even know the team.'

'Ah. The team! Led by the famous James Parker. That's another reason you have to be there. Of course. And the brilliant British photographer with no name and half a dozen passports. Who *is* this guy? Why all the secrets? Isn't it possible, just possible, that I might be equally as brilliant as this guy with six false names?' Whenever he is distressed, which is rare, Peter's Norwegian accent becomes more pronounced and he loses control of his English. Meg sees that he is miserable and suddenly realises why. She feels ashamed.

'Peter, darling, don't.' She holds him close. 'We'll work together again soon. I *love* working with you. I wish we could this time. But this job is James's idea. His plan. His team. He knows them all. And if you think there's anything romantic between James and me, then don't.' She laughs. 'We're old, old friends. He's got a clever and beautiful young girlfriend and I've got you.' She kisses him.

Peter shrugs, still hurt and angry. 'What can I say?'

'Just say you love me.'

He turns away.

She hugs him from behind and snuggles into his back. 'Toby and Steven will help you with Nick. They get on marvellously together.'

He folds his arms in front. 'And Claudia. Who'll help me with her?'

Meg sighs. 'I know. I know. I'm sorry. But it's only for two weeks, maybe less. She'll probably improve as soon as I walk out the door.'

'I'm not washing her clothes any more, I told her that. And she can do her share of the cooking like everyone else.'

Meg grins. 'You're beginning to sound like the house master.'

'I know. It's pathetic.' He turns around, grabs her and hugs her so tightly that it hurts.

'Ouch! Why don't we leave the menagerie on its own tonight and go out somewhere, like we used to. Dance? Or see a movie?' Meg's eyes widen. 'I know. Let's book a room!'

'Okay. I know a good place. There's a bar with a piano: Rick's.'

'Really? I don't know it. Is it a hotel?'

'Sort of. It's in *Casablanca*.'

Meg groans.

'I thought you were supposed to be the expert on old movies,' Peter smirks, still mildly resentful.

'Not at all. For an older woman I'm quite hopeless,' she concedes. He kisses her. 'Well, shall we go or not?'

'Yep. Let's do it. But I've got a better idea. How would you like to spend a romantic night at sea?'

Meg looks blank. 'Where?'

'On my boat, the *Empress of Snails Bay*.'

'It's not seaworthy. You told me it might sink.'

'I'll tie it to the wharf so we won't have far to swim. Come on. You like adventure. We'll listen to the waves all night and watch the sun rise over Goat Island. I'll even make you a thermos of cappuccino for the morning. We'll take our sleeping bags and some cushions . . .' He is already gathering them up.

'Pissed off, have they?' Claudia stood in the doorway, wearing shorts and a halter-neck top, one arm full of rolled up design paper, the other flicking her long hair off her neck. 'God, it's hot.'

'Want some lime juice?' Steven offered. He stared at her a second too long. She noticed this and gave a knowing smile, which caused him to blush.

'They're sleeping on the *Empress*. Testing her out,' said Toby quickly, noticing his brother's embarrassment. 'We're in charge of Nicky.'

'Bliss!' said Claudia, flopping onto the sofa.

Steven handed her the juice.

'It's all right. He's asleep. I read him three stories,' Toby told her.

'What a little saint you are,' said Claudia unpleasantly.

'No, not really. I enjoyed it,' Toby answered innocently.

Steven raised his eyebrows at Claudia behind his brother's back.

'How old are you, Steven?' She stared at him boldly.

'Seventeen next March.'

'Sixteen and a half. Almost.' She gave a mocking smile. 'Ever done drugs?'

Steven laughed and tried not to show his embarrassment. 'Maybe.'

'What kind?'

'Smoked a bit of dope.'

'Wow! Your mother would be *furious*. Does she know?'

Steven shook his head and looked awkwardly at Toby.

'What about you Tobes?' said Claudia.

'I don't smoke.'

'Thirteen and you've never even had a puff?'

'I've tried it but I didn't like it much.' Toby said, shamefacedly.

'Very innocent boys.' Claudia nodded her head like a wind-up doll. 'And to think your brother is a dealer.'

They stared at her. Steven laughed. 'Bullshit!'

'Which brother?' asked Toby.

'Nathan. He's a dealer in hard drugs. You didn't know?'

'Bullshit!' Steven said angrily.

'I can prove it to you. May I have another lime juice, Steven?' she asked him sweetly.

# CHAPTER SEVENTEEN

Nathan waits in a coffee bar in the Haymarket for Vinh and two members of his gang. They have business to discuss. The Haymarket, on the edge of Chinatown, is a logical place to meet. Lots of Asians eat here, watch movies, shop for food and clothing. Since the area has been smartened up the tourists come to photograph the high ornate gates at the entrance and the rows of long-necked red roast ducks that hang in restaurant windows, and to lift their small children onto the backs of the two stone lions that are said to be the guardians of Chinatown.

At Chinese New Year there are festivals in these narrow streets. Fireworks explode and dragons dance to the deafening sound of drums and cymbals.

Nathan is fond of Chinatown. When he was a child the family often came here for yum cha breakfasts on Sunday mornings.

Afterwards they would wander up and down the alleyways sniffing the exotic smells of Chinese herbs and spices. His mother would always buy something odd to cook with – a wok, a Chinese cabbage, some ginseng. She liked trying out unusual recipes. They'd shop for rice-paper lampshades and little cane chairs and tables so light they could carry them home under their arms. His father would say that the furniture was too flimsy, even for children. Rubbish. His mother would laugh off his protests but then, tactfully, she'd encourage the boys to select something else – a beautiful paper fish that floated in the wind, a box kite, some tiny brass bells that tinkled to hang by the baby's cot.

Nathan smiles to himself at these family memories and feels comforted. What he has to do tonight is not pleasant.

When Vinh and the two others enter the coffee bar, people do not turn to look. They are ordinary, well-dressed Vietnamese boys in their twenties. They could be students. They smile and greet Nathan relaxedly, sit down at the laminex table and order cappuccinos. They all converse quietly in English. They could be talking about a football game. Suddenly there is a change in the friendly tone and one of the Vietnamese boys stands up, scraping back his chair and flinging himself angrily away from the others. He darts out into the street and disappears. The other two Vietnamese stare accusingly at Nathan. One of them pays the bill and the three of them leave together.

Not until they are in the alley does Nathan feel afraid. Vinh has left him with these two gang members he hardly knows. They walk close on either side of him. What had he imagined? That Vinh would defend him, explain to them that he had every right to stop working for them when he thought the job was getting dangerous? That even though Nathan was not a gang member he respected their code and would never betray them, never talk to the police? Nathan knew there was no way he could reason with these two; their English was not good enough and they were desperate to protect their racket. Vinh had left because he knew the situation was ugly and he didn't want to witness what these boys might do to Nathan.

As they walked in the dark alley Nathan decided to try an old schoolboy trick that had worked for him before. Suddenly he pointed up ahead of them at the entrance to a dark warehouse and shouted as if warning them of an attacker, and in the instant they were distracted he turned on his heel and ran as fast as he could in the opposite direction. The boys were close behind him. He remembered nothing after that.

When he regained consciousness he was still in the alley, slumped over a garbage bin and bleeding from the head and shoulder. He felt nauseous. Painfully he drew a handkerchief from his jeans pocket and mopped up the worst of the blood. Then he dragged himself slowly in the direction of the flat above the Chinese herbalist's where his brother, Paul, and Vinh's sister, Lanh, were living.

Paul was alone in the flat when Nathan staggered in. He felt grateful. Lanh might have panicked – screamed at him and blamed him for being such a fool as to get involved with her brother's gang. He knew he'd been a fool. But he didn't want to hear her say it. He felt weak. He just wanted sympathy and nurture.

'Shit!' said Paul.

'Vinh's friends. Well, you warned me.' Nathan held up one hand, nodded, tried a grin, admitting his folly. 'Told them I wasn't going to deal any more.' He slumped against the wall. Paul helped him to a chair.

'What were you dealing?'

'Only coke. And only to a chosen few. Nothing else, I swear.'

'Fucking idiot.'

'Thanks.'

Paul brought him a glass of water, lit him a cigarette and examined his head. 'Nasty cut. Doesn't look deep though. Was it a knife?'

'I don't know. I passed out. My shoulder's cut, too.'

Paul looked at the shoulder. 'You'll probably need stitches for that one. Bastards! I'd better drive you to Casualty.'

'Is that necessary? They'll ask how it happened.'

'You can make something up. You had a fight with your girlfriend and she threw . . . a javelin at you. She's an Olympic contestant. Fiery temperament.'

'Ha ha.'

'They're used to unlikely stories at St Vincent's. Come on. Can you walk?'

Nathan sat where he was. His head drooped and he closed his eyes. The cigarette fell to the floor.

'Hey, little brother, don't pass out! What do they give people who've had a severe shock? Brandy, isn't it?' Paul rummaged in the cupboard, knocking over tins and bottles. 'Nothing.' He opened the small fridge and produced a tin can. 'Only beer.'

'Beer's fine,' said Nathan weakly.

Paul opened it and handed it to him. Nathan's hands were shaking. 'Where's Lanh?' he asked.

'University library. She'll be home at ten. I'll leave her a note.' He started scribbling one.

'Don't tell her what happened. Okay?'

'Okay. But I'd really like to dob Vinh in to the cops. He must have known what those thugs were going to do to you. He's the bloody gang leader.'

'Nothing he could have done. I broke the rules. I got bashed for it.'

'With a knife? That's monstrous, Nathan. Why in hell did you get mixed up with them in the first place?'

'Ssssh,' Nathan held his hand up. 'Head hurts. I'm lucky. Could've killed me. Or slashed my face.' His eyes closed and his head sank to his chin again.

Paul stared at him in alarm. 'Christ! You've probably got concussion. I should call an ambulance.'

Nathan held out one hand to silence him. 'I'm fine. We'll go in the V-Dub.'

Paul helped him to his feet, put one arm around his good shoulder and they set off slowly down the stairs. When they got to the car parked below in the street Paul saw that there were tears on his brother's cheek. 'Pain's getting worse? Look, I'll call an ambulance.'

'No, no, it's not that.' Nathan said faintly. 'It's just that I've got my audition for NIDA tomorrow and I don't think I'll be fit enough. If I don't make it this year, I don't know, Paul . . .'

'You'll make it. I'll phone them, go there myself if necessary, tell them you've had a bad accident. They'll give you another day to audition. I'll demand it!' said Paul arrogantly.

One thing you could say in Paul's favour, he was loyal to his family, thought Nathan. And he had inherited from their mother that sense of 'entitlement' that had embarrassed them on occasions, and at other times had filled them with admiration.

Nathan grinned. 'Thank you brother,' he said gratefully.

Sally has been trying to ring Nathan from the ship to wish him good luck for his NIDA audition but keeps getting his recorded message. As it costs about twenty US dollars a minute to call from out at sea she leaves only a brief message on his machine. She is disappointed that she can't get through to him and finds it odd that he is not at home rehearsing his pieces on the night before such an important event.

She comes back up on deck where the sun is sinking, the sails are full and a few people have already changed into evening clothes and are sitting by the bar listening to the bronzed, bleached-haired pianist playing 'Strangers in the Night'.

Another group are still in the pool learning to scuba dive. Their heads are deep underwater. Bubbles rise. They have been down a long while. The instructor is down there with them. People stand around the pool watching – anxious relatives and curious onlookers who wish they had the courage to stay under water for twenty minutes at a time. The men watching wear T-shirts saying Georgetown, Boston College, Maui 90 and Henley Competition. The women wear bikini tops and sarongs around their waists. They are all Americans. The Chileans lie in the shade, sleeping behind their sunglasses.

Richard is reading over by the Polaris Trio. He seems absorbed. 'Strangers in the Night' does not bother him. Sally goes across and sits opposite him, asks if he would like a drink and he says a fruit punch would be nice. She brings back two tall glasses the colour of sunset, each with a cherry and a slice of orange on top. 'Lethal,' she tells him, sipping hers. He smiles and drinks his to the bottom.

A middle-aged woman sitting beside the ship's doctor leans across to warn Sally about being stung by sea anemones. She introduces herself as the doctor's wife and says she has been on five of these cruises because it's lonely being left at home in Seattle when her husband is working. She doesn't bother going ashore at the islands much any more because she's seen it all before. Her husband treats more sea anemone stings than anything else on these cruises, she tells Sally.

Sally thanks her for the warning.

She wanders across to the railing to watch a sailboat racing by. The sea is changing, becoming shallower and paler green. There is a rim of white water breaking on a reef. Now they are coming close to the island of Raiatea. In the distance coconut palms line the beach. There are rows of thatched huts with pointy roofs and one white wooden church with a tall spire.

'Hi, Sally!' It is Fleur, the statuesque French-Canadian girl. 'Would you and Richard like to join us for dinner tonight? Us and the Partingtons.'

'Oh, thanks. We would. I'm sure we would,' Sally is pleased. For two nights she and Richard have dined alone. She glances across at him reading by himself. 'I'll just go and check with Richard.'

That morning she and Richard had started talking to the Canadian couple on the outrigger canoe trip to a tiny 'motu', or island. The Canadians had introduced them to another friendly couple, English travel agents named Jeremy and Alice. The six of them had snorkelled around the reef together and later shared a picnic lunch on the beach. Being un-American, neither of these couples had planned their trip with friends so, like Sally and Richard, they didn't have 'a group'. They had joked about this, and decided that as foreigners they should stick together.

Gavin and Fleur are honeymooners from Toronto – Gavin

is Jamaican, an orthopaedic surgeon in his forties with a dark skin and a droll wit. Fleur, in her twenties, is a dental hygienist. (Sally thinks that in the old days Fleur would have been called a dental nurse, but concedes that the idea of nurturing is unfashionable today.) The other couple, Jeremy and Alice, are in their late thirties and live in the Cotswolds when they are not in London managing their travel agency. They all have good senses of humour and have felt slightly left out by the organisation of set dinner tables on board the *Windsprite*, so their banding together is a mild form of protest.

At dinner that evening they order wine and tell jokes about travelling. Jeremy, who once worked as a purser on the grandest of ships, tells a true story about an elderly American couple who boarded the *Queen Elizabeth 2* for an extended cruise. At the end of the first week at sea the old gentleman died of a heart attack. It was Jeremy's task to inquire of the old lady, with great delicacy, whether she would prefer to leave the ship at the next port or to have the body placed in a coffin (the *QE2* always carries a number of coffins, he explained) in cold storage until the end of the cruise. The old lady said she would naturally prefer to put the body in the deep freeze. She had waited all her life for this cruise. She then went on eating her soup. At the end of six weeks, when the cruise came to an end, Jeremy again approached the old lady and asked gently how she would like things arranged for her husband's body. She said she had a special request. Jeremy listened attentively. Even though he was dead, she hoped her husband was still entitled to his duty-free alcohol. Jeremy assured the old lady that he was and that he would see that the alcohol accompanied her and the body when they disembarked.

After telling a few more ghoulish anecdotes they start talking about themselves. They exchange stories of the way they first met. It occurs to both Richard and Sally that their new friends will be hurt if they continue the pretence that they are a happily married couple just like them and do not reveal the truth of their odd relationship until later.

The three couples leave the deck at midnight after dancing to the Polaris Trio which they are beginning to find less insipid. They are, in fact, quite exhilarated, after doing the rhumba, the tango and the samba under the stars, and stumble a little tipsily down to their cabins. Alice and Jeremy wave a noisy goodnight and open the door to their cabin which happens to be diagonally opposite Sally's.

'Oh, you two are right beside us!' Alice exclaims. 'I didn't realise. We'll be able to pop across and borrow things.' They all laugh and Richard follows Sally into her cabin, waving his goodnights.

Inside, she sits on the bed and he in a chair facing her.

'Musn't disillusion them, must we?' Richard says ironically, then more sincerely, 'I really like those two. Fleur and Gavin, as well.'

'So do I. It was a great night,' Sally says happily.

'Yes.' He looks at the floor, then raises his eyes and gives her a wide, deep look. 'May I stay with you tonight?'

Sally feels a tightening in the chest. Her hands clench of their own accord. She shakes her head. 'We agreed about that,' she says gently.

'I know. But I thought perhaps you'd changed your mind.'

'Did I give you that impression? I'm sorry. I didn't mean to.'

'I thought tonight it felt just like it used to between us . . .' he begins emotionally.

'Tonight was fun, Rich, but everything's different between us now.'

'Why? Why does it have to be different? We were dancing together. I felt close to you. You felt it, too. Were you just acting, or what?' he demands angrily. 'Out of pity for me? It makes me ridiculous that you pity me.'

She carefully folds her wrap and places it on the bed beside her. 'I feel affection for you, not pity. I'm deeply fond of you. I don't want you to suffer. But I don't want to sleep with you, either,' she says quietly.

'I see.' He looks embarrassed. 'I made a mistake. I'm sorry.' He goes towards the door.

'I'm sorry, too,' she says gently.

'I'll say goodnight then.'

Sally wakes early next morning. The ship is slowing down. They are approaching the island of Moorea. She dresses quickly in shorts and a T-shirt and hurries up to the top deck, which is deserted. Everyone is still asleep. The ship glides in between two mountains towards the Bay of Opunohu. Ahead is an eerie peak. Described in one guidebook as 'shark's tooth', it is nothing so commonplace. It looks primitive, sacred, as if the gods could demand sacrifices from this rock.

As the ship glides closer to land it becomes colder. The mountains close in. There is a range of them, like jagged teeth. Awesome. The ship slowly turns and goes out towards Cook Bay. Apparently Cook found Opunohu eerie and beautiful, too.

As Sally pads barefoot along the salt-sprayed deck going back down to her cabin, she feels sure that Nathan is in trouble.

Nathan lies still in his immaculate hospital bed, tightly tucked in like a mummy. He has been told he will have to stay until the knife wounds begin to heal. They are deep and need more than a few stitches.

Vinh, too frightened to come and visit in person, has sent a bunch of carnations and a get well card with his very best wishes and deepest apologies but no forwarding address. He has moved away from the flat he shared with the 'undesirables', he writes and sends his 'loving thoughts' to Nathan's family. Nathan re-reads the carefully written card and pushes it aside. 'Wanker,' he says not unaffectionately.

Nathan, in his gregarious way, is already on friendly terms with the three other men in his room. They are all old and suffering from bad cuts and abrasions, one after being hit by a car on a pedestrian crossing near his home, one after falling off a ladder while mending his roof and the other after being mugged by some thugs in middle-class Mosman. Nathan, being young and the victim of an attack in cosmopolitan Chinatown where these three men have never been, is something of a novelty.

He has introduced the old men to a dice game called Pass the Pigs. Excited cries of 'Hey, I've got a double snouter!' and 'My turn to be swineherd!' float down the corridor causing some of the nursing staff to smile and others to threaten confiscation of the pigs. Nathan has also introduced his elderly companions to the latest music, and they take it in turns to borrow his Walkman headphones to listen to CDs of *Zooropa* by U2, *Equinox* by Jean-Michel Jarre and the soundtrack to *The Piano*. In between times he entertains them with anecdotes about the theatrical profession and impersonations of the hospital staff.

Due to Nathan's hospitalisation, NIDA has agreed to postpone his audition until December.

Sometimes he loses consciousness in the middle of telling the old men a story, which causes them to exchange looks and shake their heads. Nathan does not tell them about the brain scan he has had nor about the series of tests he is still undergoing. He does not like to think about the outcome of these himself.

Having no success at contacting Nathan by phone, Sally rings Paul and hears about the attack in Chinatown. Paul does not mention the knife wounds, telling his mother that Nathan got away with only a few scratches and is just in hospital for a day or two under observation. Nevertheless, Sally says she will get off the ship at Moorea and fly home immediately. Paul, sounding almost authoritarian, tells her not to be so foolish. Nathan is being well cared for and there is nothing more she can do. He is in fine spirits, cracking jokes and making all the young nurses fall in love with him. 'My father needs you much more than Nathan does right now, Mum,' says Paul, mildly reprimanding.

In the afternoon, Sally and Richard go ashore and hire a motor scooter to ride around Moorea. To Sally's relief, Richard behaves as if the conversation in her cabin the night before had never taken place. 'Helmets are compulsory now. Not like in Bali twenty-two years ago,' Richard remarks as he hands her one.

She jumps on behind, clasps him loosely round the waist and they are off, wobbling at first, but soon growing steadier, past the palm trees, hibiscus and bougainvillea, the shops selling *magasins*, over stone bridges with white French railings, away towards the mountains. They climb up Mt Belvedere to see the lookout and the marae where there are sacrificial grounds. Anchored far below in the Baie de Cook they see their beautiful four-masted ship.

Then back on the scooter and down the winding track to the coast where water laps the edge of the road and white fishing nets like bundles of cobwebs hang drying in the trees.

They stop at the Sofitel Hotel where they've been told there is good snorkelling. They park their little bike and, like a couple of hippies wearing nothing but sarongs, flowers and sandals, they lug their snorkelling gear and helmets through the luxurious gardens of the hotel, past the restaurants to the end of the pier. Pretending to be guests and not fooling anyone, they place their bulky possessions on a couple of the hotel's banana chairs, put on snorkels and flippers and nonchalantly climb down into the sea.

Richard strikes off towards the reef and Sally follows. Two suntanned fish-like creatures gliding over coral, they discover caves and forests, follow schools of shimmering silver fish, striped blue and black zebra fish, even an eel. Sally often signals to Richard at particularly interesting things she wants him to see, and he twists easily in the water to come and look.

When they have seen enough underwater life, they return to the pier, stretch out side by side on the hotel's comfortable chairs in the sun and gaze at the azure lagoon where they have just been. Waves crash on the reef and beyond that, hazy in the distance, is Papaeete in Tahiti. It looks like New York City. Decadent, Sally thinks, and expensive. But jobs beckon and many of the island people now live there in slums. Tomorrow the ship will return there. And then they must fly home. She does not want to go. It is too soon. She has not made her decision.

She watches a bronzed couple paddling an outrigger canoe very slowly across the lagoon as they stare down at the coral. A tiny seaplane buzzes off like a yellow gnat. Then the only sound is the roar of the surf on the reef, flags flapping at the end of the pier and a splash of water as someone dives into the sea.

'Nine days away is not enough,' Richard says.

'I know.'

He waves towards the restaurant halfway along the pier. 'On our last day in paradise, let's go and have a big French lunch.'

They eat a whole *langouste* each with French bread and glossy little limes, a salad of fresh pawpaw and coconut pudding. But they drink the house wine instead of champagne, and Richard drinks his very slowly.

In the carpark as they load their snorkelling gear and wet towels onto the scooter, Richard is quiet. Subdued.

'Rich. It's all right,' Sally says.

He gives her a questioning look.

'I've decided to stay with you.'

In rugged jungle country not far from the border of East Timor, Meg, James Parker, his director Geoffrey Byrnes and their driver, José Martinho, share a can of cold baked beans, two bananas and three Diet Pepsis for their lunch.

The trip to Dili is taking longer than they'd anticipated. Meg has a strong suspicion that José has lost his way.

Until this point everything has gone according to plan. None of the three 'tour advisers' has had any trouble convincing airport officials in either Darwin, Bali or Kupang that they were genuine. The computer search on James Parker at the airport in Bali had come up with nothing, which was a great relief, because although Parker had never been to Indonesia, his record as a critic of oppressive regimes in South East Asia was well known. If Parker had been turned back in Bali the others would have gone on without him, but if he had been revealed to be a journalist, then they, too, might have been suspect. Coming into West Timor from two different directions and meeting up at the car hire office in Kupang, as well as deciding to cut costs by sharing a vehicle and driver to travel to Dili, had worked well.

After booking the car for the next day, Meg, James and Geoffrey had strolled up Jalan Pahlawan together past the military headquarters, climbed the hill to the cemetery to take a few photos of the headstones inscribed in Dutch, Bahasa and Chinese, and then sat in a waterfront bar frequented by tourists. As in most cafes, shops and bars in Kupang there was a framed portrait of President Suharto on the wall. The people they'd met so far, they commented to each other, were friendly, open and polite. As they drank their *Bier Bintangs* a well-dressed young man, noticing Meg's EAT carry-bag, came across to their table and introduced himself as Fernando Lopez. He asked about the nature of their tourist ventures and then promptly offered himself as their guide.

'West Timor is a very historically interesting place for tourists. Joseph Conrad stopped here and so did Captain Bligh. You know Bligh of the *Bounty*?'

After chatting to him for a bit Meg asked, 'And what is Dili like these days? Interesting for tourists?'

'Ah, Dili is straight out of *Casablanca*!' enthused Fernando.

'You've been there?' James asked with sudden interest.

'Never. But so I believe. You know the movie *Casablanca*?'

They said that they did. Meg smiled a little, thinking of Peter, which encouraged Fernando to continue even more enthusiastically. 'East Timor is interesting but I think West is more friendly and more beautiful. For your tourists I recommend the island of Semau, a short boat ride from here. Your tourists like snorkelling?'

They nodded with false enthusiasm.

'Good! I will take you to fascinating place. Your tourists will snorkel over whole Japanese ship. Sunk by allied bombers fifty years ago. Many Japanese dead down there. Very fascinating for British and Australian tourists.'

'Very fascinating,' they agreed. They said that unfortunately they had to press on early tomorrow morning to drive to East Timor but they left their cards with Fernando and said they would be in touch if they ever needed a guide in West Timor.

Fernando was persistent. He assured them that he knew the mountain roads of West Timor better than anyone, the villages and the ruins from the time the Portuguese ruled. He would guide them to the border and then take a bus back to Kupang.

They looked at him thoughtfully but decided against it. He was smart. Perhaps he would be genuinely helpful; perhaps he was an informer. They told him they already had a driver who was familiar with the area.

Now, not sure where they are and wondering whether they have already crossed the border several times without realising it, Meg thinks that employing Fernando would not have been such a bad idea.

José is philosophical about being lost. He speaks Bahasa and Portuguese but little English. James and Geoffrey decide to use the lunchtime stop as an opportunity to film some 'stand-ups' in the jungle. They have agreed on a sign they will use, scratching the tips of their noses, to let Meg know when they want to disappear to do some voice-overs for the documentary. They tell José they want to take some pictures for their brochure of the lush vegetation and the root system of a giant tree. They start climbing up the track and Meg studies the map to try and work out which way they should go next. In fifteen minutes James and Geoffrey are back and they set off along the mountain road with Meg navigating. In less than half an hour they have reached the border.

Being a remote spot it is patrolled by only a handful of Indonesian military. They wear the distinctive red berets and carry automatic rifles. José reassures them that this is a party of British and Australian tour operators preparing brochures so their stills cameras are not confiscated. After checking their passports the soldiers search the Land Cruiser ineptly, not being sure what they are looking for. They discover none of the Sony High 8 movie cameras, the tiny audio tapes or the many cartridges of film.

When they are all safely back in the car and waving a friendly goodbye, they breathe audible sighs of relief. José lights up a 'kretek', overpoweringly sweet, and Geoffrey, who doesn't smoke, accepts one.

They approach the town of Balibo where on October 17, 1975, almost eighteen years ago, five Australian newsmen were killed by the Indonesian military. The Australian Government has still not demanded an explanation or an apology for the deaths of this news team sent to investigate rumours that the Indonesians were crossing the border and burning villages in East Timor. Ever since the Indonesian invasion, the issue of East Timor has been kept at a distance.

Meg glances at James to see if he is preparing to leap out and film a 'stand-up'. Having been here before, she knows the spot where the Australians died and can take him to it. She imagines he would like to intercut it with footage of the five young television journalists before they were lined up against the wall of a house on which one had painted an Australian flag. Recently, there has been evidence to suggest that they had been murdered, not with a clean short burst of fire from the Red Berets' automatic weapons as has been officially reported, but had been hung upside down, had their genitals cut off and stuffed into their mouths, and then been attacked with knives.

To their surprise, José, who is in his early twenties, knows the story of the five Australian newsmen and when James asks to stop near the spot where they died to take pictures of the 'beautiful scenery', José agrees with a puzzled expression. 'Australian tourists like to see where killing of your people happen?'

The tour advisers realise that although José is a poor navigator he is smart enough to catch on to the fact that their interest in East Timor is rather more political than most travel agents', and they should be careful.

As they approach Dili, Meg notices changes since she was there two years earlier. The road that was a dusty track is now sealed. There are powerlines, new bridges and signs attached to some of these developments which bear the names of Australian companies. The Indonesian military is very much in evidence.

The Hotel Turismo where she had stayed last time looks run down and seedy.

They book into a new hotel called the New Resende. The Timorese staff who carry their bags look frightened and will not make eye contact. The receptionists, smiling pleasantly, are from Bali and Java. The foyer has the usual large portrait of Suharto and the guests appear to be mainly Indonesian officers and businessmen.

They bid goodnight to José who will stay at a less salubrious hotel down the road. Already he has noticed the downcast eyes of the Timorese and the new Indonesian signs that cover the old Timorese ones on shopfronts. His countrymen, who once owned businesses, are now sweeping the streets for the new owners.

That evening at dinner, Meg, James and Geoffrey are careful to dress like people in the travel industry and even to display tokens of their trade – Meg's EAT bag, Geoffrey's folder from his London travel agency and James's small Timorese statue, supposedly given to him by the headman of a village in the mountains.

When they have finished eating they agree that the noise level in the dining room is loud enough for them to safely start planning the next day's excursion to the countryside where they have contacts to meet. They are suddenly approached by a rather sad-faced Indonesian who has been sitting alone at the next table, watching them with interest. 'I am Sapardi,' he says, eagerly shaking their hands, 'Tour operator from Java.' He nods at the travel bag and folder on their table as if these are an unspoken invitation to join them and sits down. They introduce themselves. Beaming, Sapardi tells them, 'The Indonesian Government is pleased to welcome foreign tourists to East Timor.' They thank him. James orders Sapardi a beer. He looks very pleased and says expansively, 'We plan to build many more hotels in Dili, first-class like this one, with Indonesian staff. Very friendly.' They say they are pleased to hear it, and they will perhaps bring their tours here.

'It is difficult to attract tourists to East Timor. The local people are not so friendly. Very lazy. And ungrateful. It is difficult for Indonesia to find money for roads and schools, hotels and tourism in East Timor, but we are trying.'

They nod sympathetically.

Sapardi offers them his assistance. Would they like him to take them to particularly beautiful places in the countryside tomorrow?

They thank him but explain they already have a driver who will guide them to the beauty spots. Sapardi slumps back into sadness. They offer him another beer and their business cards. He is immediately more cheerful. 'New Resende has very good entertainment. Karaoke!' he says enthusiastically. 'Later you see performance of officers and girlfriends singing "New York, New York", "Blue Suede Shoes", many western songs. You like to join us in singalong?'

Meg seems tempted to accept but the others hastily explain that as they only have a few days to see the whole country they must leave the hotel at dawn tomorrow and will need an early night.

'God, Meg,' says James as they make their way down the corridor to their rooms. 'We're trying to keep a low profile here. I didn't realise you were such an exhibitionist.'

She grins. 'Usually I'm not. But it was such a bizarre vision, belting out "New York, New York" alongside an Indonesian colonel and his girlfriend. Isn't that exactly the sort of thing a tour adviser far from home would do?'

'Not unless she wanted to attract a lot of curiosity.'

'I'm sure we've done that already.'

Before sunrise next morning, James and Geoffrey are on the waterfront filming the place where, eighteen years ago, Indonesian destroyers and frigates started shelling the town of Dili.

The sleepy town is just beginning to stir, cooking smells wafting across from the hotels, shops opening up, street-sweepers busy on the pavements.

Geoffrey decides to risk a stand-up. He stands on the wharf beside James and, holding the tiny camera in the palm of his hand a couple of feet in front of James's head, he begins rolling.

'This is the wharf on which Indonesian marines, paratroopers and infantry landed on December 7th, 1975, and moved out into the town of Dili with their guns blazing. They ordered the people out of their homes and offices. Some of the civilians were raped, some murdered and the rest evacuated to a camp in the countryside,' says Parker gravely. 'About a hundred and fifty people were brought here to this wharf where they were executed by Indonesian soldiers, their bodies weighted and dumped in the sea. One of those who died was an Australian freelance journalist named Roger East who'd come to East Timor to investigate the disappearance of the television news team . . .'

Suddenly there is a shout and a group of soldiers appear from inside a building opposite the wharf. They march purposefully towards the two men filming on the wharf. Geoffrey deftly drops his hand-held camera into his open backpack and he and James wait with frozen smiles for what is to come. Before the soldiers reach them, James has walked towards them with his hand out ready to shake theirs. '*Selamat pagi*,' he says grinning. But the soldiers are suspicious and not inclined to return the greeting. They demand passports and to search both men's bags. James's wallet is snatched from his hand and Geoffrey is shoved hard up against the sea wall and about to be body-searched when a voice hails him from along the wharf. Sapardi is running towards them.

Sapardi appears to know the soldiers. He explains things in Indonesian, patting both foreigners on the back from time to time as if to demonstrate their harmlessness. There is a good deal of nodding and some questions from the soldiers and eventually the one holding Geoffrey lets him go, the wallet is returned to James and the bags left unsearched. The soldiers smile, and with some muttered apologies and even a few friendly waves, they march off back to their building.

'The soldiers want to take you away for questioning but I explain to them you are colleagues of mine in tourist business, special operators like myself. Very important to economy of Indonesia. Soon you bring rich tourists to East Timor, maybe to Java also. They wish you good luck and are sorry they suspect you.'

'Sapardi, thank you,' says James with real gratitude.

'Now we friends, you call me Pardi,' beams the tour operator.

It had been decided by the group that if any risks were to be taken, such as filming under the noses of the military, it would be safer for James and Geoffrey to take them than Meg. They had never been to Indonesia before. Even though Meg had recently been issued with a new passport which showed no record of her having visited Indonesia or East Timor before, any government official checking up on her would have revealed her to be a journalist previously known to the authorities. All three had been issued with short-term visitors' visas which had lulled them into a false sense of security, but after the episode on the waterfront they decided to be more careful.

'I think we should abandon the idea of trying to film those mass graves twenty miles the other side of town,' said James to Meg. 'I'd like to get away from here as soon as possible. What do you think?'

'I agree. I saw the graves two years ago and they'd be good to have on film, but it's not worth the risk of having to hang around Dili any longer.'

'We should avoid the churches, too. They're all heavily guarded,' Geoffrey warned. 'I noticed yesterday that anyone going into the cathedral was being questioned.'

'A pity we can't call on your friend the Bishop, Meg,' said James. 'He sounds an interesting guy.'

'He is. He must still be befriending Fretilin supporters, because his house is constantly being watched.'

'It seems the bishops are the last line of defence for the Timorese people,' Geoffrey suggested.

James nodded. 'Let's cut our losses and get out of here this afternoon. We'll get José to drive us up into the countryside where we're going to meet the first of the interviewees.'

'How dangerous is it for them, agreeing to take part in all this?' Meg asked. 'Even though they'll be filmed against the light so their faces are dark, mightn't they be recognised?'

'We've arranged for a couple of them, survivors of the Santa Cruz massacre who probably would be recognised, to be taken over the border into West Timor as soon as we leave. But they're all being very brave about the filming and determined to tell their stories. Apparently there was another massacre that took place after Santa Cruz, which we've never even heard about.'

As they packed up and loaded their gear into the Land Cruiser, they talked in undertones about the other members of the team and hoped that they were safe.

Their cameraman, with his bird-watching equipment, would now be trekking into the mountains to look for Fretilin forces. He would discover that although the movement was not all that strong the civilian resistance in mountain villages was huge. The Indonesians had not succeeded in annexing the country. There was total hostility towards them. The Fretilin people were quite confident. They had supplies and a security backup in the villages. Their numbers had increased since the second massacre when a lot of young resistors left Dili for the mountains. A few days before, they had ambushed an Indonesian patrol and killed nine soldiers.

But the three tour advisers, stealthily loading their vehicle, knew nothing of this.

The other member of the team, the doctor, was at this very moment passing unchecked through the heavily guarded Dili airport, carrying the camera which would help him with his medical survey.

They had arranged that the doctor would stay at a different hotel from them and if they met each other by chance, in the main street of Dili, they would make no signs of recognition.

As they drove out of Dili that afternoon they passed the taxi which was bringing the doctor from the airport. James, sitting beside Meg in the back seat of the car, recognised him at once and nudged her excitedly. 'The fourth member is here,' he said very quietly. Geoffrey showed no sign of having seen him.

As they drove further away from Dili and into the countryside, James and Meg relaxed, while in the front seat Geoffrey navigated and smoked José's kreteks.

'Are you missing the family?' James asked her.

'I haven't had time to think much about Peter and Nick until now. But yes, I am.' She hadn't yet told him about Claudia. She should. He would be intrigued, perhaps offer some useful advice. He was a loyal and sympathetic friend. But travelling through rugged East Timor gathering unauthorised political information was probably not the time for such a personal confidence.

'I only met Peter once, at the wedding, but he seems a terrific bloke.'

'He is. I still can't quite believe we're together. I'd sort of resigned myself to being an ageing career woman, having left marriage far too late and then, there he was!' She smiled. 'I've been lucky.'

'So has he. Are you happy?'

'Absolutely.'

He clasped her arm affectionately. 'You deserve to be. If he ever gets less than perfect, let me know.'

Meg laughed. 'What about you? Are you going to marry Kate?'

He raised his eyebrows. 'I don't have a very good track record as a husband. Two divorces. She'd be mad to take me on. At present it seems to work well keeping our separate houses. But sometimes I think, yes, I'd like to be married. I miss her terribly. I'm meeting her in Bangkok when I leave here.'

'Ah! At the Oriental perchance?'

He grinned and nodded. It was an old joke they shared. He had once confessed to Meg that, in spite of his impeccable left-wing politics, whenever he emerged unscathed from some dangerous job, he liked to live it up at a luxury hotel.

'Just for a couple of nights. Then we'll spend a few days on an island. Unwind from all this.' He grinned. 'Provided we don't all end up in some Indonesian jail.'

'We might get to meet Gusmao.'

He sighed. 'We might indeed.'

'I found something interesting in my mother's files today,' said Claudia brightly.

Peter frowned. 'What were you doing going through her files?'

'It's okay. She said I could. It was the East Timor file. Huge.'

'I didn't know you were interested in East Timor.'

'Of course I am. It's where my mother is endangering her life, isn't it?' She pulled a dramatic face. 'No, I originally got the file out because I was researching an article on East Timor to help get me into Journalism, but now I've changed to Design I don't need it any more.'

'So why are you still going through it?' Peter asked suspiciously.

Claudia gave him her most innocent smile. 'Because, as I told you, it's interesting.' She opened the manila folder on her lap, took out a letter and read aloud, 'Darling M, In answer to your question about the possibility of joining the team of "tour advisers" in East Timor in September, I think it's a brilliant idea. Will call you on Thursday the 22nd at 8 p.m. when P. is away, as you suggested, to make the arrangements. Can't wait to be close to you. It's been far too long. All my love, J.'

Peter held out his hand calmly. 'Give me that,' he said, without expression.

Claudia handed it over. 'I thought you'd find it interesting.'

She watched him read the letter carefully, then fling it down on the sofa beside him and sit very still, staring straight ahead.

'The letter's dated August 20th. You were away on Thursday the 22nd at 8 p.m.' Claudia reminded him. 'You were away for nearly two hours, taking me to a photographic exhibition that Meg had insisted I go to instead of her.'

Peter turned to look at her, his face twisted with pain. 'Give me that file.'

She hesitated.

'I said, give it to me!' he shouted angrily.

At the end of ten days, Meg, James and Geoffrey, having covered the island from north to south, left East Timor by the same route they had come in.

By the end of the trip they were playing tour advisers to such perfection that Meg wondered whether tourism was her true vocation. They had been searched by soldiers at roadblocks only twice and both times James and Geoffrey had managed to conceal the six precious tapes inside their boots and underpants – 'the ultimate bromide' according to James. The tapes were small but had sharp edges.

At Kupang airport they parted – Meg to fly the old hippie trail on Miparti Airlines down to Darwin and Sydney, James and Geoffrey to Bali, Bangkok and London. The other two members of the team were still in East Timor so they knew they must not celebrate the success of their mission prematurely, but they felt elated, nevertheless. They embraced on the tarmac, promising to be in touch as soon as possible. Meg made a mock ceremony of flinging her EAT bag into a rubbish bin and then retrieved it quickly. She was not yet safely home.

As always, she felt sad to be saying goodbye to James. They saw each other once a year if they were lucky and the stimulation she felt in his company was something she missed when they parted.

But as the little plane climbed high above the Coral Sea she was already thinking of Peter. And Nicholas, of course. The wild and playfully lovable Nick. And Claudia, who would probably be fine by the time she got home. She must really try harder with her, be more relaxed, more affectionate. If Claudia wants to study fashion, then let her, Meg told herself. I'll support her. Be proud of her. Perhaps she's right, I am too 'driven'. I must slow down and enjoy her while I have her with me. Meg thought of Peter, of embracing him in the hallway when she got in late tonight, and felt a wave of tenderness.

For the whole ten days she had been away Meg had had no contact with Peter. It was safer, the group had decided. So now the need to see him was like an ache. He would not be expecting her so soon; she'd thought the trip would take two weeks, so she would be able to surprise him.

It is eleven at night when the taxi pulls up outside their cottage by the water. The moon is full and glimmers on Snails Bay. The house is in darkness except for their bedroom light. Nicholas will be asleep, and Claudia. Steven and Toby will have gone back home now that Sally is back from her cruise. Meg is glad Peter is still awake. She will creep into the house and in a minute be lying beside him.

Not until she is standing in the hallway does she begin to feel uneasy. Moonlight makes a pattern on the familiar old rugs but the house feels disturbed. Is somebody ill? She peeps anxiously in at Nicholas's room and sees him sleeping peacefully in his bottom bunk. She is tempted to kiss him but doesn't, for fear of waking him. The dog is not in his usual place on the floor of Nick's room. Perhaps he is in with Peter.

Meg tiptoes down the hall towards their bedroom. Her heart is beating wildly. She stops before she reaches the open door and almost gags. There is a perfume. Fruity, expensive. Calvin Klein's Eternity. And the familiar creaking of their bed. And soft groans and then a cry, like a bird. Little startled cries like yelps, but not of pain. Meg covers both ears with her hands and lets out a sound of her own though she is not conscious of doing it. And then her husband is standing there in the light at the open door, looking shocked, unfamiliar, gleaming with sweat, hiding himself with the first garment he could grab – a traditional Japanese kimono.

'Oh, Peter,' she whispers and her voice sounds broken and old.

He looks at her guiltily, regretfully and worst of all, with pity.

'What is it?' says the arrogant English voice behind him. 'That bloody dog got out of the laundry again?' Then comes a burst of playful laughter. 'Don't worry about it. Come back to bed, my darling. Ravish me!' She whimpers urgently, 'Pleeease, come back!'

He turns towards the figure out of sight in the bed behind him and half smiles. Meg sees on his face an expression that jolts her, makes her want to vomit or scream. Her husband feels love for this woman. He cannot help himself. He does not want to know what Meg feels any more. It is too late. He is in love with Claudia as he once was with her.

When he turns back to Meg his expression is one of grave detachment. 'I'm sorry,' he whispers.

Meg can scarcely breathe. 'Go! Please go. Take her and go,' she whispers and stumbles away, down the hallway, outside to the moonlight where she stands in the garden they planted together and weeps till she is blind with it.

Hours later, tossing sleeplessly on the top bunk in Nicholas's room, because she cannot bear to enter the room that the lovers must have treated as their own all the time she was away, she has a sudden realisation. While she wept in the garden, hearing them leave the house in a hurry, quietly flinging clothes into bags like burglars who have been disturbed and feel cheated, she had realised nothing. She had listened to the car doors slam and the engine rev in the silent night and heard the car drive off and still she had not realised. But now, as the sickly sunrise stains the banana-coloured bedcover, she sees that it is all her fault. She had kept him in the dark. Clasped her secret selfishly. Not let him see. Pretended she was open. Lied that Nicholas was her firstborn. Let him think that he was sharing in this special, only child. He had been duped. Felt betrayed. And so had Claudia. She had been abandoned at birth. Meg had betrayed them both. And now they had punished her.

She had been warned. For months Claudia had been signalling that she would be revenged, giving hints that Meg refused to see. The playful comments about the difference in Meg and Peter's ages. The criticism of Meg and the subtle flattery of Peter, the flirtation with other men when he was watching. The prolonged glance between them on the steps leading up the cliff to Tanglewood. The mosquito bite only Peter could attend to.

And then Meg had made the decision to go away and leave them alone together. Was she blind? Or just plain stupid? She had been so sure of her love for him that she had never doubted his for her.

She sees that she has been an imbecile.

# CHAPTER EIGHTEEN

Nathan had decided on the bastard speech from *King Lear* as one of his audition pieces for NIDA. He was practising in front of a full-length mirror he had just bought at the Bondi Market for three dollars (a bargain he thought, seeing it only had one long crack) when the phone rang.

'Blast!' said Nathan, still playing Edmund. The answering machine, like the mirror, was broken, but now that he was out of the drug business he didn't really need it any more.

He swept across the room, snatched up the receiver and said nothing.

'Nathan? It's Steven.'

'Lag of a brother? Why bastard? Wherefore base?

When my dimensions are as well compact,
My mind as generous and my shape as true,
as honest madam's issue? Why brand they us
With base? with baseness bastardry? base, base? . . .'

'Shut up Nathan. What are you rehearsing?' asked Steven, not really wanting to know.

'Edmund's bastard speech.'

'Should suit you.'

'Thanks.'

'Have you heard the news? Claudia's run off with Peter to Queensland. Meg came back early from East Timor and caught them in bed together and chucked them both out.'

'Uh huh.' Nathan sounded non-committal. 'Was it going on while you and Tobes were staying there?'

'Well, I had suspicions, but you know what she's like, she flirts with everyone. Even me! I didn't think she'd dare try anything with Peter. I mean, he's Meg's husband. Her stepfather. It's sick.'

'Well, Peter must have agreed to it. He's not a moron or a kid.'

There was silence. Nathan wondered whether he had hurt his younger brother's feelings. He knew Steven once had a crush on Claudia.

'You didn't, ah, ever get involved with her, did you?'

'She's twenty-four, Nathan,' Steven said gruffly.

'And you're sixteen. Stranger things have happened,' Nathan said.

'Give me a break.' There was a pause. 'What do you think of her?'

'She's a siren, Steve. You know what that means?'

'Sure, sure, I've read *The Odyssey*.'

'Of course. You're a classics scholar. What *does* it mean?'

'A woman who lures men onto the rocks, makes them fall in love with her, then breaks their hearts by abandoning them. You think she does that?'

'Yep.'

'You don't think it could be real love? With Peter, I mean.'

'Nup.'

'Why not? They're the right age for each other. She's beautiful. He couldn't keep his eyes off her all the time we were there.'

'Well, he's mad. She's a siren.'

Steven sighed, disillusioned. 'I feel pretty bad about it, then. I was in the house when it all started. Do you think I should've tried to stop them?'

'What, by throwing a tantrum? Don't even think about it. There's nothing you could have done.'

'I still feel bad. Meg's really cut by it. She looks awful. Gone all blotchy and thin. Mum said her hair's falling out.'

'Cancer?' said Nathan in alarm.

'No, stress. Grief. Mum's minding Nicholas and we're all trying to pack up the house. Dad's having this awful radiotherapy every day that zaps his groin . . .'

'Shit!'

'I know. It's fun and games at our place,' said Steven morosely.

'Cheer up, brother. At least we've got our parents back together again. You're glad about that, aren't you?'

'Yeah, I suppose.'

'What do you mean "suppose"? You're the one who was most cut up about Dad leaving. Paul's thrilled they're back together. Toby's running round inviting all the neighbours in, he's so happy. Even the arseholes. And I'm pretty pleased. Look, as soon as this audition's over I'll come across and finish the packing for you, cheer Mum up with a few bad jokes and give Dad a massage.'

'You just haven't got a clue how serious Dad's condition is, have you Nathan?' said Steven gloomily. 'I'll tell you one thing, it's going to be a rotten Christmas.'

Virginia and Marina had selected their Christmas tree from the depths of the rainforest that morning and now that the sun was going down they began to decorate it. First they raided the box of traditional things: silver bells, handmade angels and cloth reindeer, stars, fairy lights and crystal balls. Then they added the

Aboriginal decorations: tiny wooden boomerangs, woomeras, shields and some of the totems of the local people, a white cockatoo, a black snake and a crocodile.

Marina sat back on her heels to admire the tree.

'This Christmas is going to be a knockout! First Aboriginal Christmas on our own land for centuries.'

Virginia smiled at her. She looked radiant.

'What if we invite lots of people to this first black Christmas?' she asked Marina.

'Yes! Heaps. Not just the artists and the relations. Everyone! The Mundu Barangai people and the Ngakumai. The white people down south, too. Would Meg and Sally come?'

'They might.'

'We could invite my dad! Uncle Dusty and Aunty Tilly have never been down here. I reckon they'd come, you know. Fly in the plane and all. They can afford it. Be worth it to show them this land you've given us.'

'We'll invite them.'

Marina looked at Virginia thoughtfully. 'You're not sad about giving up the land? Now that it's all been decided.'

'No! I feel vast relief at not clinging on to it and excited about what you people will do with it. I'll still have my house and a few hectares. I've grown dull being in one place so long. Building up an empire. It's time to let go and move on.'

'Like old Les Anderson, eh?' She laughed.

Virginia joined in. 'What a shock that was! Growing dope for years and years and spreading rumours it was mine. No wonder some of the neighbours resented me. And selling the stuff for a fortune. Les Anderson the drug baron!'

'Well, the law got him in the end.'

'Certainly did. Ten years behind bars and no more cane farm.'

'At least he won't have to put up with his new black neighbours.'

'Old Les gets justice at last. Why don't you make a bid for his farm in a year or two when the Aboriginal tourist business really takes off?'

'Might just do that,' Marina said with a grin. 'Or the

government might buy it back for us. We'll apply for native title now that Mabo's changing history.' Then she turned to Virginia and asked gently, 'So where will you go?'

'First New York to see Guy. Then on to Europe. Then India. I've got enough saved up for that. Then I'll come back here and paint a bit, see how you're all getting on and when I run out of money I'll teach down south at an art school like I used to years ago. I like teaching.'

Marina came and put both arms around Virginia's neck. 'I'll miss you. I don't know how I'll stand it.'

Virginia held her at arm's length. 'Come with me then.'

'Really? You mean that? Yow!' Marina leapt in the air. Then she changed and looked serious. 'It might not be too bad, travelling the world with you.'

'I wouldn't want you to put yourself out.'

'Nah, I wouldn't be doing that,' she said cheekily.

'What do you think Hannie will say about me taking you so far away?'

'Probably want to come with us. And bring the whole extended Murri family. You and I will have our first major fight and all my relatives will say, "We told you so. Cultural differences too great in this relationship. Should've married a black brother and had six babies by now. Give up, sister!" And it'll be a bloody great disaster.' Marina grinned. 'Well, don't ask me stupid questions.'

Hannie had been made one of the elders in the tribe of Ananda's new owners and her plans were already underway. She had borrowed money from a bank and bought a four-wheel drive vehicle licensed to carry ten passengers and was starting Mundu Barangai Safari Tours. She planned to take tourists on a tour of what was once the hunting and fishing grounds of the Mundu Barangai tribe at the Gorge, then to their battlegrounds at various rivers along the way to Cape Tribulation. She would guide the tourists on walks through the rainforest, telling where Wurrumbuh the flesh-eating spirit lurked, where sacred eggs of the cassowary could be found, explaining about native foods and medicine. When she collected the tourists from their smart hotels she would explain that this one was built on sacred mangrove swamps, and that one was once a burial site where bodies were wrapped in paperbark and placed in the trees. When the juices dripped down, men drank them to become strong.

Hannie was delighted to hear that her ex-husband Dusty and her sister Tilly would be flying down from Cape York for Christmas. As yet she had not been told anything about Virginia and Marina's plans to go away together.

She had arranged special events for Christmas Eve. The Ngakumai people who lived inland in the mountainous rainforest were coming to stay. They were famous as dancers and musicians and would take some time off from entertaining tourists to relax as guests of Ananda. They would bring their instruments – didgeridoos, clapsticks and tape-recorders and their spears and body paint. So there would be a party. Being rainforest people, the Ngakumai were much smaller and more agile than the coastal people.

The hosts, some of whom were descended from the Mundu Barangai tribe, would prepare the main course for Christmas dinner. There would be bush turkey baked the traditional way in an earth oven with yams and native figs. (And some roast turkey with gravy, potatoes and cranberry sauce done in the invaders' way, just in case the bush turkey was inedible, Marina had insisted.) The second course would be the traditional British fare of plum pudding and brandy sauce made by one of the artists from down south. Virginia would contribute macadamia nut icecream and soursop cocktails and everyone else would bring the beer. It would be a very communal Christmas dinner.

'Why don't you and Nicholas come up here and have Christmas with us?' Virginia asked Meg on the phone. 'It'll be historic. The natives are entertaining the invaders and then the invaders are getting off the land, well most of it, forever.'

Meg tried to laugh and sound enthusiastic. 'I take it you're not inviting the press this time.'

'Certainly not. This is a private thing. You can come, but only if you leave your tape-recorder home.'

'I'd love to, but I'm not good company right now.'

'Oh Meg! It's horrible, I know. But try not to be too sad.'

'I'm angry with myself, not sad. I was a fool. She wanted to punish me for abandoning her and this was the perfect way to do it. And he was attracted to her. I could feel it. Why was I such a fool as to go away and leave them together?'

'You had a job to do. You trusted them,' Virginia said. 'You *wanted* to trust them. Maybe it was a test. And they failed it.'

'They didn't fail, they've got each other!' Meg began to sob.

'Don't cry, Meg. Ssshh,' Virginia soothed. 'It's awful. You gave her everything while she was with you. You trusted her. She behaved like a shit. They both did.'

'I can't believe it, Virginia. I've lost two people I love.' Meg fought hard to control her emotions. 'I feel as if I've gone crazy. I don't know what I believe any more. I've never felt so wretched in my life. I've thought of . . . ending it.'

'Don't. I forbid it!' said Virginia so furiously that Meg had to laugh. 'Where are you?'

'At home. In the cottage. Nick is with Sally. I should be over there helping her to pack, not burdening her with my child, but I've got no will left. I can hardly move. I wrote the East Timor pieces and then I just sort of collapsed. Went into this trance. I suppose it's depression.'

'Of course it's depression. You have a right to be depressed. But don't, for God's sake, think of anything rash. You're too good for that. You're a beautiful, strong, wise woman and I absolutely forbid you to think of such a thing. You have friends who love you. And a wonderful son. Are you listening?'

'Yes,' said Meg in such a small voice that Virginia said, 'Are you still there?'

'I'm here.'

'Well, stay there. Don't go anywhere. I'm going to ring Sally.'

'Don't, please. She's got enough to . . .'

'Shut up. I'm ringing her.'

Sally was there in half an hour and found Meg sitting on the floor. The living room was a mess and Meg's eyes were wide and distracted. Sally hugged her and then listened quietly while Meg blamed herself for the muck she had made of her life. When she cried, Sally held her. Meg apologised for being so pathetic and Sally reminded her of how she had comforted her when Richard first broke the news that he was leaving her for a younger woman. 'I felt desperate, like a madwoman, and so ugly and worthless. You were wonderful. You shrugged it off, told me he was just going through some mid-life crisis. You said it would pass and he'd probably come back. That really cheered me up, although I didn't quite believe it. I was still dreadfully hurt and angry but I think it stopped me doing anything self-destructive.'

'And it turned out to be true,' said Meg. 'He did come back.' She sniffed and mopped her eyes. 'And you were prepared to forgive him, take him back and nurse him during his illness. You're different from me, Sally. Noble. I'm not. Peter's noble, too. He tried to teach me how to be less serious, to relax and have fun, to be affectionate. I was learning, but not fast enough apparently. I'm still driven and a workaholic and completely unlovable. They both know that. That's probably why they fell in love . . .' She broke off and began to sob. 'Nicholas would probably be better off with them.'

'Meg, that is absolute rubbish,' said Sally gently. 'Nicholas needs you.'

Meg and Nicholas had bought their small Christmas tree at the Balmain Market and were trudging down the hill with it towards home when they saw a familiar figure sitting on the stone sea wall near the house.

'Claudia!' yelled Nicholas in excitement. 'She's back.' He ran towards her. 'Where's Daddy? Is Dad back, too? Where's Dad?'

Meg stood still, feeling suddenly queasy. She watched Claudia shake her head at Nick's questions, then stand up and walk towards her. She was suntanned and looked even prettier than Meg remembered.

'May I talk to you in private?' she asked Meg coolly.

Nicholas, standing behind her, looked as if he was about to cry. Meg scooped him up.

'You're alone?' Meg asked pointedly.

'Yes. Quite alone.' She half smiled, then glanced down at Nick. 'Your Dad's going to write to you.'

'When?'

'Soon.'

Nick turned his head away, clinging tightly to Meg.

'You'll have to wait a minute,' Meg told Claudia and walked away, carrying Nick and dragging the tree behind her. She disappeared into the boathouse next door, where Nick still liked to play at helping the boat builders, even though Peter was no longer there. In a few minutes Meg re-emerged. She did not invite Claudia into the house. They sat on the stone wall at a short distance from each other, facing the harbour. There was a light breeze that smelt of salt and the air was pleasantly warm.

'What is it you want to talk about?' Meg's voice was calm although she was shaking and still felt waves of nausea.

'It's some news I have for you,' said Claudia lightly.

Meg waited.

'About Peter. And me.' She turned to face Meg, smiling slightly. 'And your grandchild.'

Meg caught her breath. She stared at Claudia.

'I thought you might be pleased, Mother.'

Meg could not speak for a moment. 'Are you sure?' she murmured.

'About the pregnancy? Oh yes. Just like you, I fell in love. For a short time.'

Meg went pale. What sweet revenge. She looked beseechingly at Claudia. 'Where is Peter?'

'I really don't know. Somewhere up north. Mooching around in the rainforest.' She kicked her heels against the sea wall, sounding bored. 'He says he can't believe I no longer love him.' She turned to Meg, inviting her to share the joke. Meg turned away.

'Does he know about the . . . pregnancy?'

'Oh yes. Unlike you, I felt he had the right to know he's going to be a father. And the child has a right to know him, too.'

'You're going to have the child?' Meg looked appalled.

Claudia laughed a short brittle laugh. 'Coming from you, that's a bit rich. Of course I'm going to have the child. And I'm going to keep it.'

'What does Peter think about this?'

'I don't care what he thinks. It's over. The affair is over. He'll pay me something for the child, of course, and he can see it if he wants to. His conjugal rights will be respected, unlike my *own* father's rights.' Claudia tossed her head angrily.

'Claudia, are you sure this is what you want to do?' Meg pleaded.

'Yes! I bloody am. I've never been surer of anything in my life!' she said triumphantly. 'Seeing you begging for mercy from *me* is something I've looked forward to for a very long time.'

'We've made a decision. We're accepting your invitation to come up north for Christmas!' said Sally jubilantly.

There was a loud exclamation of shock and delight. 'Great! How many of you?' asked Virginia.

'Well, quite a few. So we're driving.'

'Driving? It'll take you a week and a half!'

'I know. We all feel like an adventure. We're coming to bid your Ananda farewell.'

'Wonderful. How many did you say were coming?'

Sally laughed. 'I hope you'll be able to fit us all in. I'll count. There's Meg and Nicholas, me, Toby, Steven, Nathan . . . listen, great news! He got into NIDA!'

'Nathan did? Fantastic! He'll be sane again.'

'For a little while. And talking of sanity, his brain scans came out clear. No more blackouts. He's quite recovered from that nasty bashing.'

'Thank God! So there'll be six of you coming for Christmas?'

'No, seven.'

'No problem. Who's the seventh?'

'Franca. I didn't think you'd mind.'

'My mother?' Virginia sounded shocked. 'But she's never

even been here. She'll think it's a wilderness. She'll hate the heat and the wet and the spiders and snakes . . .'

'She won't! She's been longing for you to invite her to Ananda for years. I thought you knew that.'

There was silence. 'Yes, I did know.'

'So. Why didn't you?'

Virginia sighed. 'Selfish motive. Purely selfish. Privacy. I didn't want her meddling with my things. My garden, my students, my . . . strange sort of life. I didn't want her expert opinion, her judgement, her thoughts, however subtle. I love her dearly, but from a distance.' There was a silence in which Virginia sensed Sally's disapproval. 'But you're right. She should come. Thanks for inviting her. I'd better read her book.'

'Yes, you had,' said Sally lightly.

'How's Meg?'

'Not great. Very low in fact. Claudia's parents have arrived from Switzerland to pay her debts and take her home. I gather they're not exactly thrilled at the news of her pregnancy. But they seem to be used to her appalling behaviour and forgive her anything.'

'And Claudia's agreed to go with them?' Virginia asked in disbelief.

'Apparently she doesn't mind going. She's done what she came here to do. Fuck Meg's life up. Break her heart.'

'Little wretch. I pity that baby. Any news of Peter?'

'He wrote Nick a postcard. No forwarding address.'

'No message for Meg?'

'Nothing,' Sally said. 'I'm so glad she's decided to come to you for Christmas. Try and lift her spirits, will you? Distract her with . . . something. I'm quite concerned about her.'

'Will Peter try to follow Claudia to Switzerland?' Virginia asked.

'Perhaps.'

'Poor fool. So she's broken two hearts. Three if you count young Nick.'

'I know. Meg says he spends every free minute next door at the boatshed polishing away at Peter's boat so as it'll be ready when his dad comes home.'

'So. Tell me some good news,' Virginia said.

'Okay.' There was silence and then Sally burst out, 'Richard's in remission!'

'Oh, Sally. That's marvellous!'

'Yes, isn't it? The disease has stopped spreading. He has a good chance of recovery.'

'Oh Sal!'

'Amazing, isn't it? So I can afford to leave him for a few weeks. He's insisted in fact. He wants me to take a break before we . . .'

'What? Before you what?' said Virginia sharply.

'Now listen, Virginia, it is *my* life you know,' Sally laughed. 'Before we move back together again.'

There was a long pause. 'Well, if that's what you really want . . .' said Virginia stiffly.

'It really is,' said Sally happily. 'I can assure you that it is.'

The postcard had a picture of a palm tree, a white beach, some blinding blue sea and a boat. Not much to go on. The postmark was partly obscured. It could have been Mooloolaba, Mullumbimby, Maroochydore or some other remote place starting with M.

All Meg knew was that Peter was somewhere in Queensland. The message on the postcard made no promises to Nick to see him, just told him about the boat in the picture. Meg read it aloud to him whenever he asked her, which was often. Nick had started to suck his thumb and carried a scrap of old blanket around with him, in which he'd wrapped the postcard.

The convoy was on its third day of driving up the highway towards far north Queensland when Meg announced that she and Nicholas would be leaving them.

Sally guessed at once it was the wretched postcard. 'What makes you think he's near Maroochydore? And if he is, how on earth will you find him?'

Meg was vague, said it was just a hunch; she'd look around for a day or two and catch them up later.

Sally sighed. 'Okay, but let me take Nick. If you do find Peter and he's in a bad way, you won't want Nick witnessing the misery.'

Meg agreed. Nick was content to stay with the others, particularly as Toby had promised to let him share his tent, and the convoy departed with much waving and tooting of horns.

Meg branched off the highway and headed for Maroochydore. It was a small place, but it had an airport. Peter had once confided to her that whenever he felt depressed he liked to go somewhere where there were two things – an airport and a wilderness. She had laughed at this. But he had told her seriously that it was logical. The wilderness was to walk in and try to solve his problems; the airport would provide the means of escape if the problems were too great. At Noosa Heads, not far from Maroochydore, there was a magnificent national park.

It was late afternoon when Meg booked into a motel on the beachfront at Noosa. The tide was high and surf pounded the tiny beach. No sign of boats or palm trees. The sea was not blinding blue, but grey and angry. The black rocks looked murderous. 'Why did I come here?' Meg wondered.

Next morning Meg walked the damp main street, peering into coffee bars and dawdling by real estate windows to see if there was a picture of the kind of place Peter might have rented. She prowled through photographic shops in the hope of finding him picking up processed film, idled past the post office, the Commonwealth Bank where he had an account and even the icecream shop which he haunted wherever he was. But there was no sign of him. In the afternoon she would call at every cheap motel, ask if he had been there. But first she must walk in the national park.

Taking a path out of town through the damp forest she smelt a wonderful warm flax smell, like drying rope, and felt comforted. The sun came out, glinting gold shards through the dank leaves. Soft rain fell on the forest roof and steam rose all around her making her feel safe, cocooned, as if in a hut thatched with yeast-smelling pandanus leaves. She began to hum. 'Today I feel hopeful,' she thought. 'For the first time in weeks, and I'm not sure why.'

She entered the national park and caught sight of the blue-black boulders, living stones like sculptured humpback whales or sleeping dolphins. Mighty creatures resting, all wet from the sea, on a white deserted beach.

Meg walked for several hours, past the Boiling Pot, where waves surged into a circle of rocks and smashed and foamed up over the top like milk, along a narrow trail to Tea Tree Bay where the paperbarks peeled, on through the creamy yellow bottle-brush trees where bees buzzed to Fairy Pools and Dolphin Point and, suddenly, there on the right, almost hidden by bush, was the sign. Tanglewood Track. Was this the reason she had left the convoy and come here? She had forgotten until now, but perhaps five years ago she had walked this same trail and discovered the sign and been surprised, not realising there were other Tanglewoods besides her house on the cliff. She had told Peter about the coincidence and he'd suggested that one day they should go to the Noosa Heads national park together and walk along Tanglewood Track. It was ages ago. He'd probably forgotten.

She walked on past beautiful sheltered bays, deep blue, with rocky beaches and sat on the cliff to watch a school of dolphins playing in the sea far below.

At last she reached Hell's Gates at the end of the peninsula. Here there was no human, no plane or ship, no bird or leaping fish, only wind. She leaned over the abyss, looking down at a mighty wave that curled like a wall of aquamarine, thick and translucent as glass, solid and still for an instant, like a frozen sculpture. Then another wave rose like a ship from the deep and together they rolled and rolled and hurled themselves at the cathedral walls, bursting with the basso sound of a giant heartbeat. Spray rose in slow motion and stung her eyes. The sky, so immense, roared down at her and she lifted her arms as if to fly.

From a long way off she heard a shout. Saw a figure running. Blurred. In the distance. Waving frantically.

She dropped her arms, feeling foolish, rubbing her eyes full of salt, edged back from the cliff, looked for her backpack safe up on the path and was bending to retrieve it when she was grabbed from behind. Tackled. Embraced. Gripped in a hug and covered in hot tears and kisses.

She pushed the man away finally, laughing, and held him at arm's length. 'You know, it's amazing, I just had this feeling . . .'

'Oh God. Promise you'll never, ever . . .' He was crying.

She looked aghast. 'Did you think I was going to jump?'

'Meg, I've been like a madman. Obsessed. Trying to punish you. But now I don't care about anything except getting you back. Forgive me. I went crazy.'

Meg laughed wildly. He did sound a little crazy. 'I wasn't going to jump,' she said. He hugged her. They clung together, buffeted by the wind. Suddenly she pushed him away and stared into his face. 'The baby. What about the baby?' she accused him.

There was silence. The wind ripped through the pandanus palm beside them. He looked at her, baffled. 'What baby?'

'Your baby. The one Claudia's expecting.'

'What? She told you that?' he said incredulously. He shook his head and said quietly, 'Did you believe her?'

Meg nodded.

'She can't have children. It's one of the few things she's told me about herself that I'm convinced is true.'

'How do you know that?'

'She's been having tests for years. In London, Tokyo, Sydney. She's infertile. She showed me the latest gynaecologist's report. It arrived in the post while you were away. She was quite upset by it.'

'But her parents are here. They believe she's pregnant.'

Peter shook his head and gave a wan smile. 'They've been deceived before.' He held Meg close and whispered, 'She's a liar. And I've been a fool. Such a fool. I love you. Can you forgive me?'

Meg did not answer. She was crying, too. 'Okay,' she whispered at last. 'But only because I've been a bloody fool myself.'

'I don't care about that. About Parker. As long as it's over with him, I don't care.'

'What's over with him? Who, James?' Meg looked aghast.

'I read his letter to you. Claudia found it in your file on East Timor.'

'Claudia found a letter from James to me? Peter, I have never had a letter from James in my life. He phones me. You know that.'

Peter put his hand into his jeans pocket and produced a crumpled page which he handed to Meg. She read the letter and then crushed it angrily. She turned away, closing her eyes against the tears. 'You believed that? I'm so sorry. You were right about her. She wanted to destroy us.' They held each other close. Then Meg uncrumpled the paper and looked at it again. Smiling through her tears she said, 'It's a damn clever forgery.'

As they walked back together, arms around each other, through the national park, she asked him gently, 'The affair with her. Was it just revenge because you thought I was with James? Or were you really attracted to her all the time?'

'At first I was just angry with you for going to East Timor and leaving me behind. I wished I was that guy with all the passports.'

'And Claudia knew it, didn't she?'

'Yes. And she knew I was angry with you about something else.'

'Not telling you about her birth. Letting you think Nick was the only one.'

'Why did you do it, Meg? Let me go through that charade of believing you'd never been pregnant before?'

'I'm sorry. Perhaps I wanted to pretend it was the first so that you'd stay with me, protect me and become the father. It was wrong. You had every right to be angry.'

'Yes, I was angry. Then she produced that letter. I wanted to fax you straight away, demand to know if it was genuine. But she persuaded me not to. Said it would jeopardise the whole trip. Told me not to be hysterical. What was a bit of a fling between old friends? She thought I must have known about it. The affair had been going on for years. She said you'd told her all about it. Then she started to seduce me. To be honest, it wasn't hard. I was furious. With you. With myself . . .'

'And she's very attractive.'

'Not any more,' he said bitterly. 'Not to me.'

They walked on in silence.

'How did you know I was here?' he asked.

'I didn't. But remember your cure for depression?'

He looked puzzled for an instant, then laughed. 'Walking.'

'And if that failed?'

'Flying away.'

'There must be dozens of places in Queensland with wilderness reserves and airports, but this was the first one I thought of,' Meg said. 'I was lucky.'

'So was I.' He hugged her. 'And guess what? I found Tanglewood Track.'

'Does it lead anywhere?'

'To a glorious beach called Alexandra Bay. Deserted. We can go there tomorrow. Watch the sunrise.'

When they got back to Meg's motel at Noosa, Peter brought his backpack round from the room he had been renting in a house near the national park and they rang Virginia to say they were sorry to cause her inconvenience but there would now be eight extra people for Christmas dinner at Ananda, not seven.

The three women sit together under a jacaranda tree in Meg's garden by the water having afternoon tea. It is a fine day in mid-November, 1994.

Music comes from the stone cottage behind them. Strings. Rather peaceful, reminiscent of rolling green hills in the country. They sit at a small round table covered with a white cloth. On it is a silver teapot, china cups and saucers and a plate of salmon and cucumber sandwiches.

The women wear long summer dresses and ribbons trail from their straw hats. They look old-fashioned and quite elegant, although one of them has bare feet. They are enjoying themselves. Sometimes they throw back their heads and laugh. A family of teal ducks glides by on the shimmering green water that laps at the low sandstone wall.

'You know,' says Meg, 'I'm rather glad the Tanglewood years are over.'

'Over, are they?' Virginia throws crumbs to the ducks. 'You mean our youth has gone? No more risk-taking, no frivolity, disastrous marriages, misguided ventures doomed to ruin, no debts, no excitement, no gambles, no wild fun?'

'Yes,' says Meg. 'I do mean that.'

'How dull! So what are the years we're living now?'

Sally looks up. A breeze catches the branches of the tree above them and a cloud of blossoms whirls down around their heads like purple snowflakes. 'The jacaranda years!' she says.

'The jacaranda years?' asks Meg.

'Yes. Graceful, delicate, late-blooming, sedate . . .'

'Sedate? Surely we're not that,' Virginia protests.

'Sitting here, sipping tea in Edwardian hats. Of course we are. Just a little.'

The blossoms, like tiny bonnets of crushed velvet, plummet into their teacups, fly across their faces, settle on their hats, their dresses, their bare toes and make a lavender carpet at their feet.

'Well, better to be sedate than in chaos,' Virginia concedes. 'I don't mourn the Tanglewood years. Crashing around in the wild bush searching for the meaning of life and only getting scratched.'

Sally suddenly looks sad. A silence falls between them. Sally turns away. Meg puts a comforting hand on her sleeve.

'How is he?' she asks quietly.

'He's not in remission any more. The cancer's definitely spreading. I wanted to keep him at home but he'll suffer less in hospital.' She looks at them both, eyes unusually bright, lips tight. 'In hospital he can have all the morphine he needs.'

'Oh, Sal,' Virginia sighs. 'I didn't realise . . .'

'I know. It happened suddenly. But it's okay. He's not suffering,' she says.

'But you are,' Meg says gently.

Sally nods. 'You know what's so awful about it? Richard and I are happier together now than we've ever been. More in love than when we were passionate young things of twenty. Can you believe that? All those years in between when we tormented each other, him having affairs and me playing the martyr, were wasted time. How stupid people are! How fucking wasteful! Crashing around in the bush is right . . .' She turns her head away to hide the tears, wipes them angrily and turns back with a grim smile. 'It's ironic, isn't it? We were actually looking forward to growing old together. We talked about it a few weeks ago. And now he's going to die!'

'Oh, Sal,' Virginia grasps her hand. 'What about the liquid nitrogen treatment? Cryotherapy?'

'Didn't work. We've tried everything.' She smiles wanly and squeezes them both by the hand. 'He doesn't want to keep on fighting. He's worn out. Soon . . . in the final stages, I'll need you both.' She fights back her tears.

'Of course,' says Virginia.

Meg holds her hands. 'We'll be there.'

They are silent.

'What is that piece?' Sally asks, helping them over the awkwardness. 'Is it Bach?'

They listen as the strings float out over the treetops and across the bay.

Meg nods. 'His *Christmas Oratorio*. "The Shepherd's Pastorale". Do you like it?'

'Mmmm.'

'I'll make you a tape of it.'

'Thanks. I'd like that. I could play it to Richard. He still enjoys music.' Then Sally abruptly and bravely changes the subject. 'You didn't go to the APEC conference in Jakarta, Meg?'

'No, I sent Jenny Douglas, one of my hot young investigators. She'll be more welcome there than I would,' says Meg, trying for Sally's sake to be cheerful. 'And she's keen to get into the East Timor debate. There have been riots in the streets of Dili today, deeply embarrassing the Indonesians on the eve of the

Asia-Pacific Economic Co-Operation Summit. When Clinton flew into Jakarta last night there were Timorese protesters all over the US Embassy compound.'

'Bet you wish you were there,' says Virginia.

'I do. And I don't,' Meg replies enigmatically.

'You've done a lot for human rights in East Timor, Meg, but I think you were wise to let Jenny go to APEC,' Sally says. 'You said you'd heard from Claudia?'

'She rang me reverse charges from Switzerland a few days ago. Actually in the middle of the night. She's trying to decide whether to do a course in hotel management or to become a ski instructor. She seems to have rather a lot of men in love with her and she's still living with her parents.'

'Poor old Jane and Michael,' Sally sighs.

'Better them than Meg. But don't let her get too friendly,' Virginia warns.

'I'm not. Peter thinks I'm mad to pay for her calls and Nick pulled the phone away last time she rang. But it's odd. I don't feel resentful of her now. We've both apologised for the damage we've done to each other's life and she seems to feel we're quits. She's put me at a distance that makes me feel safe, treats me a bit like an older sister and calls me Meg, never Mother.'

'You're very forgiving,' Sally says.

'I think I'm finally beginning to understand her. She is like an emotionally handicapped child who demands a mixture of guilt and sympathy from a parent. Her pain gets relief only by inflicting pain on others, particularly those close to her.'

'So you've given up being close?' asks Virginia.

'Yes, I feel detached. Perhaps it's cowardly but I feel it's better this way and so does she. She's still quite proud of me, you know. She read my pieces on East Timor reprinted in the *Guardian* and was boasting to her friends about the awards I'd won, so she says. And a few weeks ago she rang me in great excitement when she heard that there could be a United Nations referendum on East Timor's future.'

'Be careful, Meg,' says Sally.

'Oh, I am. I don't give in to impulses any more.'

'You really have changed in the past few years, you know.

Whoever would have thought that Meg, the wisest of us all, would have to guard against impulsiveness?' Virginia teases.

'Whoever would have thought that Virginia, so sex-obsessed and bossy, would turn into a celibate philanthropist?' Meg replies. 'I thought she'd end up an entrepreneur with a harem of toy boys.'

'Did you honestly?' Virginia looks hard at Meg, who nods, and then at Sally, who stares, and then gives an uncertain smile.

'You know what I'm talking about, don't you Sally?'

'I'm not sure. Tell us,' she says.

'I'm gay. I have been for almost a year.'

Meg looks astonished.

Sally laughs. 'What do you mean, gay for almost a year? You're either gay forever or you're not.'

'It's not always that simple. I told you before I went travelling. Don't you remember? I *thought* I told you, when you both came to Ananda last Christmas.'

'You didn't. I would've remembered,' Meg looks stunned.

'You just said you were going overseas . . . with Marina,' Sally says.

Virginia nods. 'With Marina.'

'Marina? But she's . . . like a daughter,' Meg says.

'No. A protégé in the beginning. And then much more.'

'But why did it take . . . so long for you to find out?' Sally asks. She and Meg look so bewildered that Virginia laughs.

'I always knew.'

'Even when you were going after all those boys up in Townsville, even when you were married to Lewis, when you lived with Heinrick?' Meg demands. 'I don't believe you.'

'I've always been bisexual. Extraordinary isn't it?' Virginia says calmly.

'I can hardly believe it,' says Sally. 'We've known you over thirty years.' There is a thoughtful pause. 'Did you ever feel interested in either of us?' she asks seriously.

'I didn't find you attractive enough,' Virginia says with a deadpan expression.

They look at her blankly.

She bursts out laughing. 'Suckers!'

They smile with relief.

'Of course I found you attractive. Both of you. But I thought you'd be too shocked. You're both pretty conventional when it comes to sex, you know. Anyway, I loved you as friends. That's quite, quite different.'

'And now it's too late. We've missed out.' Sally says, sounding oddly disappointed. She looks thoughtful. 'I remember an arrogant bloke who took you out a few times after you left Lewis, telling me that he wasn't bothering with you any more because you worshipped at the shrine of Sappho. I laughed at him and said that was just sour grapes because he wasn't getting what he was after.'

'He was right. Although I wasn't brave enough to admit it then. It wasn't exactly the thing to be a lesbian in Melbourne in 1972.'

They stare out at the water, each lost in her thoughts. 'There's a strange old man staring at us from the sea wall. Do you know him?' Virginia asks Meg.

She shakes her head. 'He's admiring the jacaranda tree.'

'This *is* quite a shock,' Sally says. 'Why didn't you tell us?'

'You didn't ask.'

There is silence for an instant and then they start, each one, almost silently, to laugh.

'Does your mother know?' Sally asks.

'Franca? Why do you think I never invited her to Ananda until you forced me to?' This causes a fresh burst of hilarity. 'Yes, of course. She's known for years. Only I didn't realise it.'

'Does she mind?' Meg asks.

'Of course she minds. She's Italian.' More gusts of laughter. Marina's mother, Hannie, was far more understanding. Disappointed, of course, that Marina won't be marrying a Murri man to help the survival of her race, but she said a rather wonderful thing to us: "As women we love everyone". It was her blessing.' Virginia sighs deeply. 'I think my mother's accepted us, too. And so should you.'

'We do!' says Sally.

'Of course we do,' says Meg.

'We're just a bit mad at you,' Sally says.

'For not telling us until we were all nearly fifty, ' says Meg.

'Decades in the dark . . . '

'We feel a bit cheated . . . '

'You always did like secrets . . . '

'You're a sneak . . . '

'Perhaps we should roll her on the grass and stuff her mouth with jacaranda petals.'

'No, it wouldn't be dignified.'

'That nice old man would be shocked. Ladies in hats don't behave like that.'

'Certainly not at tea time.'

'Well, thank goodness for that,' sighs Virginia. She waves at the old man, who waves back and then turns and goes slowly on his way.

## ALSO FROM McPHEE GRIBBLE

**TANGLEWOOD** Kristin Williamson

Meg, Sally and Virginia meet at Melbourne University in 1962. Talented, hopeful and full of the cheeky bravado that wards off fear they hitchike north to sleep on beaches and plan their futures. As predicted Meg will become a political activist and Virginia an artist. But Sally, who has a desire to nurture, devotes twenty five years to an ambitious husband while teaching other people's children and bringing up four of her own. When her husband leaves her she is devastated.

Kristin Williamson's first novel explores the intimate relationship between three women over a period of thirty years. A chronicle of our times it uses Australian political and social life as a background, examining themes like feminism, mental illness and the impact of childhood trauma. A procession of Australian characters blends convincingly into the narrative – an eccentric desert painter and his aboriginal companion, young Vietnamese refugees struggling to make a new life in Sydney, an unscrupulous banker turned film producer, an heroic, award-winning journalist who tries to resist introspection, a doctor who plays jazz piano and specialises in mending broken hearts and Sally's frank, affectionately demanding teenage sons.

With humor and courage three modern Australian women reveal their mistakes, their grand passions and their secrets.

**ALSO FROM McPHEE GRIBBLE**

**A FAIR EXCHANGE** Gillian Bouras

When Gillian Bouras, bestselling author of *A Foreign Wife*, went to live in a Greek village for a few months in 1980 she never imagined she would still be there ten years later. In *A Fair Exchange* she further explores the upheavals and pleasures of exchanging one home for another. Out of her experience has grown a love of words and the patterns they make in her life; and despite her nostalgia for Australia, she cannot resist the impact of foreign landscapes and the people that surround her.

**A FOREIGN WIFE** Gillian Bouras

Gillian Bouras is an Australian married to a Greek. From the ambiguous position of a foreign wife, she writes of life in a Greek village. Her fellow villagers regard her, the migrant in their midst, as something of a curiosity. They, in turn, are the source of both her admiration and her perplexity.

*In 1969 we bravely organised two weddings. An Orthodox ceremony was then a legal requirement of the Greek State, but I wanted some English spoken over me as well. The first service passed in a sort of blur . . . A short time later I walked down a familiar fleur-de-lis carpet towards a Presbyterian minister who welded familiar words and music into a brief service of blessing. It was George's turn to be confused.*

**ALSO FROM McPHEE GRIBBLE**

**MONKEY GRIP** Helen Garner

In her classic novel, Helen Garner charts the lives of a generation. People are exploring new ways of loving and living – and nothing is harder than learning to love lightly. Nora and Javo are trapped in a desperate relationship: the harder they pull away, the tighter the monkey grip.

*It was early summer. And everything, as it always does, began to heave and change.*

*It wasn't as if I didn't already have someone to love. There was Martin, teetering as many were that summer on the dizzy edge of smack, but who was as much a part of our household as any outsider could be . . . But I fell in love with our friend Javo, the bludger, just back from getting off dope in Hobart: I looked at his burnt skin and scarred nose and violently blue eyes.*

**POSTCARDS FROM SURFERS** Helen Garner

In stories that are piercingly honest, often very funny and always woven in ways that surprise, Helen Garner teases out life's dailiness to show the darkness underneath – but also the possibilities of joy.

*'Is it allowed?' he said.*
*'Who by?' I said. I was trying to be smart; but seriously, who says we can't? Isn't that why men and women make love? To bend the bars a little, just a little; to let the bars dissolve?*

'Everything she touches on rings true . . . '

*Sydney Morning Herald*

**ALSO FROM McPHEE GRIBBLE**

**WILD CARD** Dorothy Hewett

In this extraordinary autobiography, Dorothy Hewett traces the personal and political metamorphoses of her first thirty-five years. A woman who challenged sexual and political conventions, Hewett is also one of Australia's most famous playwrights and poets. In combining the passions of her life with her power as a writer she has created a classic of people, place and political history.

After university, several failed love affairs, an attempted suicide and a major poetry prize, Dorothy Hewett joined the Australian Communist Party in 1945. Four years later she left her first husband and moved to Redfern, Sydney, with her lover, a boilermaker. Hers is a life of extremes: the pleasures and purgatories of a woman who has tackled everything placed in her path with a searing honesty, energy and intellect.

'Hewett has lived out a soap opera of a life. If she were a man, her life would be described as Rabelaisian, and she, a hell-raiser.'

*Independent*

**ALSO FROM McPHEE GRIBBLE**

**SALT** Gabrielle Lord

Sando and Hedda are running for their lives. They break out of Sydney, the walled city of 2075, into an Australia decimated by civil strife, rising salt levels, ravaged ozone layer, and daily temperatures of fifty-seven degrees.

Their flight to this salt-encrusted otherworld forces them to face its unimaginable inhabitants, bred in a secret weapons laboratory, while they themselves struggle to hold on to their love for each other and for the truth in a gripping battle against ancient human evil with a terrifying future face.

A dazzling and haunting novel from the best-selling author of *Fortress.*

'A writer of power and passion.'

*Sydney Morning Herald*